The Blood Witch Saga (Books 5-8)

ISBN: 9781804679968
Perfect Bound

First published in 2023 by bookvault Publishing, Peterborough, United Kingdom

An Environmentally friendly book printed and bound in England by bookvault, powered by printondemand-worldwide

BOOKS 5-8

THE BLOOD WITCH SAGA

THEOPHILUS MONROE

THE BLOOD WITCH SAGA

THEOPHILUS MONROE

Cover Design by Deranged Doctor Design

Proofreading/Editing by Mel: https://getproofreader.co.uk/

For information:

www.theophilusmonroe.com

Chapter 1

I GRABBED A VIAL of blood from my shelf. It wasn't to drink. It was one of my regular donors—willing humans on call willing to meet my dietary needs. With my blood magic, all I had to do was dip my wand into the vial and cast a simple summoning spell. Jonathan would show up within the hour, craving my bite.

I called it my Grubhub spell. Ready to eat meals delivered to my door at a warm ninety-eight point six.

It wasn't for me. It was for my new progeny, Tommy. He planned to share with Mel—Mercy's progeny and Tommy's new girlfriend. He had the whole evening planned. A romantic candlelight feeding. The string quartet he'd booked was due to arrive at any minute. We didn't often welcome outside observers when we fed. The quartet hailed from Vilokan—members of the Voodoo Academy's orchestra. They were hougans and mambos. That's what voodoo folk call their priests and priestesses, respectively. They knew about vampires already. So long as the youngling lovers didn't leave a cold body behind, their presence wasn't a problem. The scene might traumatize them a bit, but I was paying them well. Besides, Vilokan offered great mental health services. The resurrected Sigmund Freud himself was the head psychiatrist at the Vilokan Asylum of the Magically and Mentally Deranged. He took Cain's place and was doing admirable work. I told Annabelle—the Voodoo Queen—to reserve a few sessions with the famed psychotherapist the next day. The quartet might need it.

Connor was relaxing on my bed in nothing but his boxers. A bit overdressed for my taste—but we'd already had our fun. Given my aversion to sunlight, when I wasn't owning the night, Connor and I owned the day—in bed. What better way to pass the time when the sun was up?

Given the hot yoga routine Connor and I just completed under my sheets, he'd sleep through the night like a baby.

With Jonathan summoned, I kissed Connor on the lips and tucked him into bed. By the time I got dressed and left my room, he was already snoring.

The string quartet was setting up downstairs. They were tuning their instruments. Mercy and Sarah were discussing *something* in her room. Their voices were raised. It didn't sound like an argument, but whatever they were discussing was serious.

Sarah had a unique gift. She could sense other vampires. For centuries, her gift was more like a curse. She felt it every time a vampire was killed. It made her something of a recluse. Before she joined us in New Orleans, she lived where Mercy grew up—back in her human life—in Exeter, Rhode Island.

They were surely discussing council business. Mercy was the leader of the council. Sarah and I were both members. The council's authority took a serious blow during the ordeal with Corbin. He'd sowed seeds of doubt among vampires in North America. Could a council truly govern vampires? Vampires understood powerful authority figures. The sire bond probably had something to do with that. We all had our mini-kings, our sires, who we had to obey. Well, most of us did. Annabelle killed mine seconds after he bit me. I was the exception rather than the norm. Most vampires grew up into the bloodsucking life following orders, obeying someone stronger and more powerful than they were. If a youngling survived, and didn't get staked the first few months when the cravings were at their worst, it was because they followed their sire's lead.

Now that Sarah could both sense the deaths of vampires and the emergence of *new* vampires, we could keep tabs on vampires all around the country. Any time more than two or three younglings appeared in an area, Sarah got anxious. She wanted to investigate. Mercy was more inclined to delegate those investigations to council loyalists. Noble and well-behaved vampires strategically stationed in every major city across the country.

If I were to guess, they were discussing something Sarah picked up with her abilities. I'd sat through my share of those arguments in the past and they always ended the same way.

In about five minutes, Sarah would emerge, her face contorted in disgust. She'd stomp past me. I'd ask what happened. She'd give me the "talk to the hand" gesture and retreat to her room to mope. Meanwhile, Mercy would make a call to the loyalist nearest to the situation and get the skinny on what was going on.

I wasn't about to wait around for that. I needed to get downstairs to chaperone Tommy's in-house date with Mel. I couldn't trust the two younglings to exercise restraint. When vampires fed together, it was a semi-erotic experience. Easy to lose control. If they bit each other after they were done, it was euphoric. It also allowed the vampires to accelerate their maturation. A helpful trick for a couple of younglings still working to master their cravings. I had to make sure that our human donor was safe.

When I got downstairs, someone knocked on the door. I welcomed Jonathan in. He was one of my favorites. He was a good-looking, clean cut man of twenty-two. He was sweet. I'm not talking about his personality. I'm talking about his flavor. He was like cheesecake. Sweet, rich, and filling. The perfect date meal.

Tommy was busy setting the table. He was dressed to the nines. He was a tall man with dark shaggy hair. Wee Willie Winker—the faerie refugee who'd helped me escape the Seelie forest and defeat Corbin once and for all—was flying around the dining room lighting candles with his magic. Tommy must've had a hundred of them scattered around the room.

It would be a lie if I said I wasn't a little jealous. Connor was sweet, but he wasn't the grand gesture type. Connor was a spur-of-the-moment romantic. Tommy had planned this meal for almost a week. If he hadn't won Mel's barely beating heart yet, he would by the end of the night.

He wasn't proposing or anything like that. Vampires rarely married. This wasn't a special occasion. That's part of what made it so sweet.

"Is Mel ready?" Tommy asked.

I shrugged. "She's still getting ready in her room. Need me to check?"

Tommy nodded. "How much time do we have if we fill the wine glasses with Jonathan's blood? You know, before the blood loses its potency."

I smiled. "It'll be good for a half-hour or more. You don't want to feed straight from the tap?"

Tommy shook his head. "I'd rather keep it intimate. Make it more about *us* than the meal."

I turned to Jonathan. I patted him twice on his chest. His pectoral muscle wiggled when I touched it. I chuckled. What a show-off. Meals like Jonathan were always eager to please. "Wait here."

I headed back upstairs. I passed Mercy's room. She and Sarah were still arguing. I knocked on Mel's door.

"Come in!"

Mel was from England. Mercy didn't turn a lot of people. I didn't either. I'd turned Tommy by accident. You could say he was a whoops baby. That didn't mean he wasn't mine. I was proud of him. He was the only vampire I'd ever sired.

Mel was wheelchair bound before Mercy turned her. Her fibromyalgia was crippling. Becoming a vampire took away the pain. It gave her back her legs. It allowed Mel to resume the passion of her youth. She was a dancer, and a damn good one. My dance skills were limited to shaking my butt and the macarena. Mel was an artist. She was graceful. Becoming a vampire was the best thing that ever happened to her—and that Mercy was her sire was like winning the lottery. I couldn't think of a better mentor for a young vampire taking her first literal steps into immortality. It almost made me feel bad for Tommy. I wasn't the best sire around. In vampire years, I was practically a toddler. Then again, my bloodwitchery allowed me to mature faster than most.

Mel was as pretty as a picture. Her long red hair was curled and pulled back. A few stray strands fell over her face. She was wearing a stunning black dress that showed a lot of leg and a feast of cleavage. I wasn't sure if Tommy could keep his eyes up where they belonged.

"You look beautiful."

"Thanks, love! You, too!"

I laughed. My hair was a mess. I was in sweats and a tank top. "You're lying. But thanks."

"You look like I'd expect after all the sounds that were coming from your bedroom all day. Nothing more beautiful than that!"

I smirked. "Yeah. Good thing vampires heal well. My hips are all out of joint."

"Maybe if I play my cards right, I'll get some of the same! Been too long since I had a good pounding."

I chuckled. "Play your cards right? Honey, you could drop deuces and threes and you'd do just as well as if you laid down a royal flush. That boy is pulling out all the stops."

Mel blushed a little. "I'm a lucky girl."

"Not half as lucky as he is. You're a prize. He's just about ready. What's your ETA?"

"Five minutes. I'm almost done."

"Come down as soon as you can. I'll let him know."

When I got back downstairs, the orchestra was playing. I took Jonathan's wrist in my hands and bit into it. I held his wrist over both wine glasses and massaged his arm, squeezing enough blood out to fill each glass half way.

It didn't take much blood to satiate a vampire's hunger. If a vampire drained someone, it was either because they went into a frenzy and couldn't control themselves or because they were greedy. This was enough blood to keep both Tommy and Mel satiated for the night.

No need for a bandage. The enzymes in my bite would do the trick. I pressed my hand over the wound and channeled a little healing magic to speed up the process even more. "You're free to go."

Jonathan nodded. "Thank you!"

I shook my head. "No, thank you! I'll call you again soon."

Jonathan headed out the door. Tommy waited anxiously by the table. Willie flew over to me and landed on my back. Faeries are small, about the size of a newborn baby, minus any of the baby fat. He held on to my shoulders as I stepped aside to watch from afar. With Jonathan gone, though, Tommy and Mel didn't need much supervision.

Mel came downstairs, her heels clicking against the hardwood steps.

Tommy's jaw fell so far I was afraid he might have to pick it up off the table.

Mel giggled. "Like what you see?"

Tommy gulped and shifted his feet. "Uh huh!"

Mel giggled. She moved to her side of the table. Tommy scurried around to Mel's side of the table. He almost tripped over his own feet. He pulled out her chair for her. I always found that form of chivalry a bit demeaning. What girl can't pull out her own damn chair? Still, it was the sentiment behind the gesture that counted.

I headed back upstairs to give the two love birds their privacy. I didn't want to hover. No one likes a helicopter sire.

When I got to the top of the stairs, Mercy's bedroom door swung open. I waited for Sarah's inevitable retreat. Instead, Mercy came out.

"Hailey, would you join us for a moment?"

I tilted my head. "Sure. What's up?"

Mercy cleared her throat. She gestured toward her open door. I stepped through and Mercy closed the door behind me.

"Tell Hailey what you told me."

Sarah sighed. "Someone has sired fifteen new younglings in Exeter."

I raised one eyebrow. "In Rhode Island? That's Prince Ladinas' territory."

Mercy shook her head. "Ladinas usually has his area locked down tight. I got off the phone with him a minute ago. He needs our help."

I snorted. "If he turned fifteen younglings, I hate to say it, but he's asking for it."

Sarah shook her head. "He isn't the one who did it. It's a young vampire in his domain."

"How could a youngling even pull that off? Turning that many people, what are the chances? He'd have to drain them and heal them somehow before they died."

Mercy nodded. "Ever hear of Mug Ruith?"

I shook my head. "Can't say that I have."

"He's a sorcerer. A blind, ancient, druid. He's appeared several times throughout history. Initially, the second century before the common era. Some legends put him in Jerusalem at the time of Christ. He also served in the court of High King Cormac mac Airt in the third century."

I tilted my head. "That's some lifespan."

Mercy nodded. "If he's still around today, that's not the half of it. His name appears in the records of nineteen Irish kings. He disappeared from the record for centuries and hasn't turned up again until now."

I bit my lip. "He either has some kind of immortality magic or he's a vampire. There's no other way to explain it."

Mercy nodded. "That he's creating a coven of vampires might lend credence to the latter theory. Though he isn't turning them himself, so perhaps it is his magic that sustains him. Either way, he has to be stopped. Whatever he's planning can't be good."

Sarah nodded. "No one makes so many younglings in such a short amount of time unless they're up to something nefarious."

"You said he's blind?" I asked.

Mercy nodded. "He relies entirely on his spirit gaze. It's a power most druids possess that allows them to see through the power of the mind. It allows him to see shadows in the physical world. When it comes to magic, he can see everything. If you have so much as a tingle on the tip of you wand, he'll spot it from a mile away."

Sarah grabbed a book off of Mercy's desk and pointed to a passage she'd highlighted. "That's not the worst of it. There's a prophecy here, attributed to Saint Columba. Mug Ruith possessed some kind of flying machine. The saint's prophecy indicates that he'd return in his *Roth rámach*, a flying wheel of some kind, and lay waste to Europe before the last judgment."

I scratched my head. "A flying machine? He had this thing thousands of years ago?"

Mercy nodded. "According to the legends, he did. I'm not sure how much of what's written is true to history, but it was said it blinded anyone who looked at it, deafened anyone who heard it, and killed anyone struck by its weapons. Chances are the stories are embellished. They usually are."

I sighed. "Perhaps another theory is at work. If Mug Ruith is a druid, and he could travel between the gates, he could also move through time. What if he has some kind of modern fighter jet, maybe a military grade helicopter, and he used it to kill people in the past?"

"I had that thought as well," Mercy said. "Whatever the case, I'm not especially keen to allow Saint Columba's prophecy to come true."

I shuddered. "This guy sounds like a genuine piece of work. It's certainly more than what Ladinas can handle alone."

Mercy nodded. "I've already put a call in to Pauli. He'll teleport us there within the hour so we can meet with Prince Ladinas and come up with a plan."

I scratched the back of my head. "I'll go get changed."

"Don't forget your wand," Sarah said. "Our best chance is to fight magic with magic."

I grinned. "Please. You know what they say about a witch and her wand? Don't leave home without it."

Sarah rolled her eyes. "That's American Express."

I shrugged. "Same principle applies. Besides, it's not like anyone would ever give me a credit card. Are you kidding?"

Mercy shook her head. "I certainly won't be giving you mine again soon."

I shrugged. "You've got Nico's money. You can afford it."

"That's not the point. There's no reason you needed twelve pairs of shoes, Hailey. You can only wear one at a time."

I snickered. "You sound like someone who grew up during the Great Depression."

Mercy stared at me blankly. "Hello. I sort of did. I was still a relatively young vampire in those days."

I rolled my eyes. "It's not like blood supply was affected by the economy."

Mercy shook her head. "Stalking unemployment lines for a meal isn't quite as thrilling as the clubs. Then again, it's funny. Even though not a lot of people had much in those days, there were just as many drunks then as now. Talk about pissing away whatever money you had. Still, have you ever fed on someone down and out? The blood tastes like oatmeal."

"Gross! Oatmeal sucks!"

"It's edible. Fills the hole. More boring than anything else. Especially for a young vampire who craved a spicy feed. To quote Dickens, it was the worst of times, it was the shittiest of times."

I tilted my head. "I don't think that's the right quote."

"I know. It wasn't the best of times, no matter how you look at it. Things are much better these days."

"Even with the council in disarray and one bad guy after another threatening our existence?"

Mercy shrugged. "At least it keeps things interesting. Gather your things. Make sure you're wearing something suitable for a fight if it comes to that."

"I'll come along." Willie hopped off my shoulder and fluttered his wings. "I know a few tricks myself, you know."

"Are you okay with that, Mercy?" I had to ask. Willie was cute as a button but, well, you know Mercy. She's not exactly a sucker for the adorable. To say that Willie grated on her nerves would be an understatement. He could be a bit much. His high-pitched, ear-piercing voice didn't strike the vampire's ear well at first. He was also like an Energizer battery. Once he started talking, he kept going, and going, and going. He'd kept me up late into the day on several occasions. Ironic for a faerie known for his ability to put people to sleep—hence the name Wee Willie *Winker.*

Mercy sighed. "I suppose his unique *abilities* could come in handy."

I smiled widely. "The more the merrier!"

Chapter 2

PRINCE LADINAS WAS A real prince. His royalty didn't come by way of self-proclamation, like when Corbin declared himself the Vampire King. Ladinas was a prince in his *human* life. I didn't know the exact situation, but there were a lot of princes-turned-vampires in the sixteenth century, when the Ottoman empire took over the Romanian principalities. It was one reason Transylvania became the vampire capital of the world. To help the Romanians resist Ottoman control, an underground sect of the nobility banded together and accepted the bite—courtesy of the late Count Dracula.

Yeah, Dracula was dead. Thanks to yours truly. I'm not usually one to brag, but come on. I killed *freaking Dracula.* If that didn't earn me some badass cred, what would?

There were vampires who lamented Dracula's death, but few in North America. It didn't put me at odds with Ladinas. Dracula and the other Romanian vampiric nobles parted ways long before my time. Then again, I'd never met the prince in person. He came to the states after Nico died and Mercy went to Europe to secure the support of the old world vampires. He was among the few who accepted the authority of what they called the "American Council." He fled Romania when Corbin claimed control over the vampires in the region. He helped secure the council's authority in New England. Now, though, with seeds of doubt sown across vampire communities around the country, many vampires were clamoring for stronger leadership.

Vampires didn't respect the popular vote. There was only one way for vampires like Mercy—older than most, but hardly the oldest vampire in the country—to gain respect. Eventually, she'd have to prove her merit through strength. If that meant staking her opposition, that's what she'd have to do. We'd hoped to avoid that, but with an ancient druid who might have been a vampire on the scene, we had little choice.

Mug Ruith wasn't only a threat to Mercy's authority. His emergence also presented an opportunity. If we could stop him, any vampire who wanted to challenge Mercy would think twice about it.

A flash of rainbow-colored light signaled Pauli's arrival. He was one of the most powerful voodoo hougans I knew. He had the aspect of Aida-Wedo, the Loa of rainbows and snakes. In his boa constrictor form, he had impressive, multi-colored bioluminescent scales. He could also teleport over vast distances. When he wrapped himself around us, he could take us with him.

"Pauli's here, bitches!"

I laughed. Pauli was known for his entrances—and his flamboyance. He was a gay man and an equal-opportunity flirt. If you were a man, he'd come on to you. A lot of gay men reciprocated his flirtations. Pauli saw straight men as a challenge. If he couldn't seduce them, he got his kicks out of making them squirm.

Mercy showed Pauli her phone. "Can you take us here?"

Pauli huffed. "Is this an all-girl trip?"

Mercy nodded. "Sarah's staying here to keep tabs on Tommy and Mel. It's just Hailey and me."

"Don't forget Wee Willie!" Willie piped up.

Pauli grinned. "Wee Willie Winker wants a ride on Big Willie Pauli! More than happy to oblige."

I glared at Pauli. Perhaps the most unsettling thing about working with him was that when he shifted between his snake and human forms, he was naked. He used his shape-shifting abilities to elongate his "big willie" beyond what was natural.

"Please return to your snake form." I rolled my eyes.

"This *is* my snake form, honey!" Pauli did a little dance, his legs wide, as his oversized member smacked between his knees.

Mercy snickered. "Just take us to Exeter, Pauli."

Pauli stuck out his tongue and blew a raspberry. "You're no fun."

With Willie on my back, Mercy and I hugged. Not to display our affection—Mercy never showed affection. It allowed Pauli to wrap himself around us in his *actual* snake form.

With a flash of colorful light, we appeared on a small street in Exeter. Since it was an hour later there, it was already dark.

"Call me when you're ready to go home," Pauli said.

Mercy nodded. "Thanks, Pauli."

I cleared my throat. "Where do we go from here?"

Mercy pointed at a manhole cover on the ground under my feet.

"You can't be serious. Ladinas lives in a *sewer*?"

Mercy grinned. "Don't judge a vampire's domain by its manhole cover."

Pauli giggled. "I can find innumerable pleasures inside a man-hole!"

I took a deep breath. Pauli disappeared in a flash of light as he returned to New Orleans.

Mercy chuckled as she reached down and pulled the cover off the hole. "Follow me. We have a bit of a hike ahead of us."

Chapter 3

IT'S A COMMON MISCONCEPTION that New Orleans doesn't have a sewer system. There is one—but because of the city's altitude below sea level, it wasn't much of a haven for vampires. It was much more limited than what they had in Rhode Island.

Mercy and I both pulled out our wands. Almost any magic could double as a flash-light. While Mercy wasn't a blood witch like me, she was talented. It was in Exeter, as a young girl, where she first met Moll and learned the craft.

Willie flew beside me with a bubble of gold and green faerie magic surrounding his form. Our combined magics gave us more than enough light to see where we were going.

The floor was damp and littered with puddles. I was glad I was wearing my boots. Our voices echoed through the sewers. Given how well vampires can hear, I realized how setting up a lair in the sewers could be advantageous. The acoustics amplified every sound, including our footsteps. Ladinas would know we were coming well before we arrived in whatever chamber he called home.

This wasn't Mercy's first trip through the sewers. She visited Ladinas once or twice before. I didn't join her those times. The sewers were a maze. All the tunnels looked the same. Somehow, Mercy knew where to turn.

We were in the sewers about half an hour before we arrived at a large, sealed door. Ladinas had a small security camera mounted above it. Mercy knocked three times. The lock clicked, and the door swung open.

A young blond-haired boy greeted us. He was young for a vampire—couldn't be over fifteen.

"Hello, Demeter."

The boy nodded. "Good to see you, Mercy."

"Demeter is older than he looks," Mercy said.

"Just celebrated my two-hundredth vampire birthday last week."

I chuckled. "Never would have suspected."

Demeter grinned. "I get that a lot. This way. Ladinas is expecting you."

We stepped into the chamber. My eyes surveyed the place. Who would have thought a place so luxurious could exist in the middle of the sewers? The walls were lined in polished mahogany. The floors were a brilliant white marble. Several glass oil lamps mounted to the walls illuminated the room. The furniture was built of mahogany which matched the walls. Red velvet padding covered the seats and backs of the half-dozen couches and chairs. There were several rooms off the perimeter of the primary chamber. A hint of frankincense with notes of rose swirled through the air. The fragrance called to mind the St. Louis Cathedral back in New Orleans.

The room was more like a high-roller lounge than a throne room. Still, there was a single tall-backed chair at the front of the room where Prince Ladinas sat.

He stood when he saw us.He approached Mercy with a wide smile and open arms. Mercy wasn't a hugger. She smiled and extended her hand before he could wrap his arms around her.

"Hello, Ladinas."

"Mercy Brown. Why is it that every time we meet, you're more beautiful than the last?"

Mercy shrugged. "I don't know. Maybe because your pickup lines each time we meet are more desperate than the last."

Ladinas chuckled, then he looked at me. "You must be the delectable Hailey Bradbury."

I snorted. "I prefer the badass Hailey Bradbury, but you know, to each his own."

Mercy snickered. "You'd do well to keep your flirtations to yourself. After Corbin's advances, Hailey's understandably cynical when old world vampires take an interest in her."

I huffed. "Besides, I got a man."

Ladinas shrugged. "What's your man gotta do with me?"

I laughed. "I don't wanna hear that, see."

Ladinas winked at me, then he turned to Mercy. "This one's a firecracker. I can see why you like her."

"Don't underestimate Hailey," Mercy said. "She's only been a vampire for seven years, but she's the strongest witch I've ever met. Moll included."

Ladinas nodded. "Then you may be exactly what we need. Mug Ruith's abilities are unlike anything I've seen in five hundred years."

I bowed my head slightly. "We also have a faerie here to help."

"I noticed! What's your name, little guy?"

Willie flew a circle around Ladinas. "Wee Willie Winker. The one and only!"

Ladinas laughed. "I've heard of you. Is it Winkie or Winker?"

"I've been called both. Why do you ask?"

Ladins chuckled. "There was a Scottish woman in my court back in Moldavia. A blood maid. She sang a little rhyme about you to her child."

I snorted. "A blood maid?"

Mercy nudged me. "It's like a milkmaid. But she provides blood."

I shuddered. "That's some kind of life."

"We revere our blood maids," Ladinas said. "They live lives of luxury. They also allow our kind to live in relative peace without the need to feed on the general human population."

"What was this nursery rhyme?" I asked.

"I don't recall it word-for-word. It speaks about how Willie here visited children at night to help them sleep."

Willie nodded. "That's right! Haven't done that job for a while. But those who revere the fae often summoned me to perform such a task."

I raised an eyebrow. "So, you're like melatonin?"

"With more personality! In other parts of the world, I'm known as the sandman."

I raised an eyebrow. "Is the tooth faerie real, too?"

Willie shuddered. "She is. But she joined the unseelie court about three hundred years ago. Summon her now, and she'll yank every tooth out of your mouth and stuff a roll of quarters down your throat. If you wake up the next morning, consider yourself lucky."

I winced. "I've had that dream when all my teeth fell out. I hate that nightmare. My parents played the role of tooth fairies when I was a kid. I'm grateful they didn't invoke the real thing."

Ladinas shook his head. "Faeries are no joke. I'm certainly glad you're on our team."

"One question," Mercy said. "If the tooth faerie belongs to the Unseelie court, and you've been exiled from the Seelie kingdom, does that make you an Unseelie faerie?"

"Faeries are the guardians of otherworldly magic. The difference between the Seelie and the Unseelie is less a divide between good and evil and more about philosophy. The Seelies believe that magic from the otherworld should only be granted to those who prove themselves worthy. The Unseelies bestow power on those who pay the price."

I raised an eyebrow. "What is that price?"

Willie shrugged. "It depends on what the Unseelie court desires or demands. Sometimes it's the completion of a particular task. The court is also known to accept human souls as payment."

"So you can sell your soul to the unseelie faeries and get power in exchange?"

Willie shook his head. "That's demons, not faeries. The Unseelie court collects souls offered in sacrifice."

Mercy tilted her head. "Human sacrifice?"

"That's right. It's given some of the ancient druids a bad name. Most of the druids were a peaceable people, they honored and revered nature. They were granted power on that account. There were some, however, who sought power from the Unseelie realm. Most of them paid for that power with souls."

"Is that how Mug Ruith gained his power?" I asked.

"I don't know. I'm not privy to the Unseelie court's dealings."

I bit my lip. "What does the Unseelie court do with human souls? Do souls give them power or something?"

"Not at all. They eat them. Human souls are a delicacy for our kind. Quite scrumptious, I'm told, but it's not a part of the Seelie diet."

I bit my lip. "I know a couple of druids in Missouri. Elijah and Emilie Wadsworth. Do they get their power from the Seelie king?"

Willie shook his head. "Good friends of mine, they are! They're different. Elijah's mother is a dryad, a protector of the Tree of Life. Their power comes directly from the source. That's why they're more powerful than common druids."

I pinched my chin. "Exeter is the location of one of several mystical convergences on earth. When I was in the in-between and met Merrick, I learned that something was changing. The era of the gatekeepers was over. We've entered an era when the gatekeepers could no longer protect the world from the gates to the otherworlds. He told me in the absence of the gatekeepers, the responsibility to protect the world from forces that emerge from other realms would fall to several appointed guardians. I'm one of them. So is Mercy. I wonder if that has something to do with Mug Ruith's arrival."

"It's possible," Ladinas said. "I knew Merrick well in life. No vampire I've ever known knew the druids better. If he was worried about such things, we should be as well."

Mercy tilted her head. "Where exactly is Mug Ruith gathering the younglings?"

"In the forest just east of town."

Mercy sighed. "That's what I was afraid of. Those are the forests where Moll gathered her coven when I was still just a girl. It's where she taught me the craft. If there's a place here where there's a mystical convergence, I'd bet dollars to dog nuts, that's it."

I chuckled. "It's dollars to doughnuts."

Mercy raised an eyebrow. "It is?"

I smiled. "That's the saying. Who would want dog nuts? Gross!"

Mercy furrowed her brow. Clearly, my revelation had rattled her world.

"Do you think we can stop them?" Ladinas asked. "My thought was Mercy could use her compulsion ability to chase off the younglings. Then we could take on Mug Ruith three-to-one."

Mercy winced. "About that. Dracula stole my compulsion ability right before Hailey killed him."

Ladinas grunted. "That certainly complicates things."

"No worries," I said. "I can exsanguinate the vampires. It'll turn them feral, but it should free them of any sire bonds that might compel them against us. I don't know how powerful this Mug Ruith is, but I haven't met a sorcerer that I couldn't take."

Ladinas smiled. "If you bested Dracula, far be it from me to underestimate your skill. The sooner we take him out, the better. At the rate he's gathering young vampires, there's no telling how many he might have in his company if we wait even another day to attack."

I twirled my wand between my fingers. "Let's go kick some ass."

Chapter 4

LADINAS LED US THROUGH a door off his chamber. Demeter was with us. The door opened to a long hallway that ended with an elevator.

"Seriously? There's an elevator that leads down here?"

Ladinas chuckled. "It's not common knowledge and will only work for me."

Ladinas pressed his palm on a small screen on the wall next to the elevator. The screen flashed a green light and the elevator doors parted. We stepped inside.

Ladinas pressed his face to a retinal scanner inside the elevator and pressed a button with his thumb.

"High tech!" Mercy laughed. "I like it."

Ladinas nodded. "It's important that we old world vamps keep up with the times. Especially with our security measures. It sure beats a trek through the sewers every time I come and go."

I chuckled and did a quick sniff-check of my pits. So far, I was tolerable. "Tell me about it."

The elevator opened up into an armory. I'd never seen so many guns in my life. Not a lot of vampires used guns. Why would we? There were also several swords and daggers. One wall featured bows, crossbows, and a table that had what looked like grenades. There was a room filled with lockers. Presumably, the vampires who worked with Ladinas had personal armor and weapons that weren't available for common use.

"Holy crap," Mercy said. "I didn't know you were so stacked!"

Demeter reached into a cabinet and pulled out a few vests. "Put these on. They're bullet proof. More importantly: stake proof."

I grinned. "Nice! Why don't we have these?"

Mercy shrugged. "That's a good question. Mind if we keep a couple?"

Ladinas nodded. "Help us stop Mug Ruith, and you can have whatever you like. I can always get more. I have a military connection."

Demeter grabbed a large rifle and slung it over his shoulder.

"Guns against vampires?" I raised an eyebrow.

Demeter laughed. He grabbed a small metal box from one of the cabinets and showed it to me. "Wood-tipped bullets. As good as a stake."

I tilted my head. "Sure, if it doesn't go straight through the heart. Unless the bullet stays in there, the vampire will revive fast."

"Not necessarily. These rounds shatter on contact. It throws a dozen splinters into the chest. They aren't a hundred percent, but given my aim, there's a better-than-average chance it'll stake the vamp and, short of performing open heart surgery, there's no way to remove the splinters."

"Damn." Mercy shook her head. "I'm impressed."

"Without a lot of practice," Demeter said. "You're better off fighting the way you know. I'll have your back. I should be able to drop quite a few younglings."

I nodded. "I'll exsanguinate them as well. Even so, ferals are unpredictable. Keep them off of me so Willie and I can engage Mug Ruith."

Demeter grabbed a crossbow and tossed it to Ladinas.

"No rifle for you?" I asked.

Ladinas shrugged. "I'm a better shot with this."

Mercy and I each took a couple of stakes for good measure. We weren't about to use any of the other weapons that the Exeter vamps had in the armory. Demeter is right. Without training, this wasn't the time to experiment. Besides, Mercy and I were there more for our skill as witches than warriors.

We left the armory. We had to pass through a series of doors, also protected by retinal scanners. When we got to the last door, two vampires stood guard holding rifles that matched the one Demeter had over his shoulder.

"Impressive security," Mercy remarked. "We're not half this stacked at Casa do Diabo."

I smiled. "That's because no one there is dumb enough to screw with us."

Ladinas nodded. "You have magical protections. Not to mention, who is going to walk into the home of a couple of badass vampire witches? We don't have the aid of magic here, so we have to rely on more conventional methods."

I raised my eyebrow. "I'd say this is beyond conventional."

Ladinas laughed. "Perhaps. We do what we can."

The building housing all that badassery was unremarkable. It looked like an abandoned warehouse. Three military-grade 'Humvees' were parked outside.

"No need to drive," Ladinas said. "It's not a long walk from here."

"I know the way," Mercy said. "Even after all these years, some things you never forget."

Willie flew beside me as Mercy and Ladinas led us down a street, through an alley, and into an old neighborhood.

"This is where I grew up," Mercy said. "Most of the houses are gone, of course. All new constructions."

Ladinas nodded. "Most of this area has been rebuilt a couple of times since then. I have copies of almost all the historical records back at my base."

Mercy pointed down a street as we passed it. "That's where the cemetery is where they buried me."

"You were buried?" Demeter asked.

Mercy nodded. "It's a long story. People thought I'd died of consumption. After Nico turned me, I rested in my grave awhile. My own father exhumed my resting body after I'd fed on my brother and cut out my heart."

"That didn't kill you?" Demeter asked. "How can a vampire live without a heart?"

Mercy smirked. "Moll performed a spell. Fed the ashes of my heart to my brother. It kept me alive while it damned him to hell. For years I lived without a heart at all."

"The infamous heartless vampire," Ladinas chuckled. "Kept alive by magic."

"Technically, not having a heart gave me a few advantages. But having my heart back again also has its perks."

"How so?" Ladinas asked.

Mercy shrugged. "I can *feel* more than I did back then. When you're a heartless vampire, you don't have a lot of remorse. You don't feel much at all."

"Not even love?" Ladinas asked.

Mercy chuckled. "Especially not love."

"Not true," I added. "You loved Ramon."

Mercy sighed. "I'd rather not talk about that."

"His family isn't far from here," Ladinas said. "They're doing well."

"You've been keeping tabs on Ramon?" Mercy asked.

Ladinas shook his head. "He reached out to me a few months back. He was concerned about the vampire presence in the city. I assuaged his worries. His family, along with the rest of the humans in the area, are under my protection. I haven't heard from him since. He was told how to reach me if he needed help. I presume he's well."

Mercy would never admit it, but she still had feelings for Ramon. She'd never interfere in his new life. He became human again—thanks to the workings of the Morrigan and the Cauldron of Rebirth. He had another chance at a normal life. The last thing Mercy wanted was to pull him back into the world of vampires. She certainly didn't want to turn him again. Ramon never made a great vampire. Even after a couple hundred years, he'd never got total control over his bloodlust. Still, Mercy felt responsible for him. I could tell from the look on her face she was relieved that he was well, and that Ladinas intended to protect him. Still, concern accompanied her relief. Her narrowed eyes and curled lip gave it away. Not that she didn't trust Ladinas. It was the looming larger threat that concerned her. If we didn't stop Mug Ruith and eliminate his newly turned younglings that night, she wouldn't leave town until we did. She didn't say it outright, but I knew Mercy. Even if we killed Mug Ruith and his vampires, Exeter was still home to a mystical convergence. There was no telling what might emerge from there in the coming months if the gates to the otherworlds were truly shattered and unguarded.

We reached the edge of the forest. There was magic in the air. Most people couldn't sense it, but I wasn't most people. It was potent stuff. Almost as strong as the magic I could wield by drawing on the mystical properties latent in blood.

A flame from what was probably a campfire flickered in the distance.

Mercy sighed. "That's exactly where Moll used to gather her coven. Let's try to get a good look at what we're facing before we charge in."

"You know a good place to look over the clearing where we can't be seen?" Ladinas asked.

Mercy nodded. "I think so. Follow me."

Mercy took us up a steep hill. "Stay low. There aren't as many trees up there to hide behind."

Mercy was right. The hill she led us up gave us a view of the clearing below from over the treetops, but there wasn't much we could hide behind. If we could see them, they could see us. Since vampires can see as well in the dark as in light, we had to be especially careful.

The clearing below included the campfire we spotted before. Several large boulders surrounded it. It resembled a druidic circle.

"That's new," Mercy remarked. "Mug Ruith must've constructed the circle himself."

I counted the surrounding vampires. "There are only five inside the circle with him. Where do you think the others are?"

"There's no way to know," Ladinas said. "They're probably off feeding. That's another problem altogether. One thing at a time. We should take advantage of the situation while Mug Ruith's numerical advantage isn't as great as it could be."

We commando crawled on our bellies down the hill until we were back under the forest's cover. Willie didn't have to crawl. He just walked on foot. At his stature, he was as low as the rest of us already.

"I'll open fire first," Ladinas said. "The crossbow isn't as loud as a rifle. I can probably drop one or two before they know what's happening."

"I'll open fire on the rest. It's up to you ladies, and Willie, to deal with Mug Ruith."

We got into position. Mug Ruith was facing the opposite direction. That gave us an advantage. If he didn't see us coming, I could exsanguinate him before he struck us.

Ladinas shot his crossbow. One youngling dropped. I aimed my wand and released my exsanguination spell at Mug Ruith. Another vampire dropped beside him. My spell hit some kind of barrier surrounding the sorcerer. It radiated with red magic before fading again from view. He turned and looked at me. His face was like leather and wrinkled. He was bald. He had a long crooked staff in his hand.

Demeter opened fire. One shot after the next, the other vampires fell. Mercy pointed her wand at Mug Ruith and blasted him with fire magic. The flames poured over his forcefield but didn't penetrate it.

"I can take it down," Willie said. "It's magic from the Unseelie. Take your shot when his shield falls."

Willie flew circles around the sorcerer, lobbing balls of golden light at him. His forcefield weakened with each strike. Mug Ruith slammed the butt of his staff against the ground.

Several arms blasted out of the ground from within the circle. Vampires crawled out of the ground, their bodies caked in mud.

Demeter fired again. Ladinas continued shooting bolts at the vampires. It worked, but they weren't fast enough. Three of the younglings charged after me. I raised my wand and cast an exsanguination spell. The blood exploded from their bodies.

I tightened my grip on my wand. I inhaled and drew in the power from the blood. Willie's magic was working, but it was taking time. I had to do something before Mug Ruith launched a counter.

I gathered the blood and formed a shell. I allowed my magic to connect to the blood in the air and formed a prism around the sorcerer.

A stream of blood flowed between the prism and my wand. Mug Ruith touched his staff to the prism. A red magic sparkled around the tip of his staff and it spread through the prism. It flowed from the prism through the stream that connected it to my wand. When it struck me, I flew back with an incredible force. My body struck a tree, and I went into convulsions. It was all I could do to maintain my grip on my wand.

"Hailey's down!" Mercy cried. "Retreat!"

The sound of Demeter's gunshots echoed around me. The world was spinning all around. Something grabbed me from behind and lifted me from the ground.

It was Willie. I didn't realize he was so strong, but he took off, pulling me through the trees.

I gasped for air. My vision faded to a blur. Everything went dark.

Chapter 5

I WOKE UP ON one of Ladinas's red-velvet couches. Willie was sitting on my chest, his bony faerie feet on either side of my face. He had his hands on my head. He was channeling some kind of magic into me.

"What's going on?" I groaned.

"She's awake!" Willie shouted.

The sound of footsteps was followed by Mercy's concerned face looking over mine. "Is she better?"

"For now," Willie said. "She's been infected by an Unseelie curse. I can hold off the effects for a time, but I can't cure it."

I snorted. "A curse?"

"I've slowed down its progress. It's dormant for now. Eventually, it will adapt to my magic and I won't be able to stop it."

"What happens if it spreads?" Mercy asked.

Willie sighed. "She'll die. I think."

"You think?" I groaned. "That makes for a shitty day."

"Let's assume the worst. How much time does she have?" Mercy asked.

"A day. Two at most."

"You said you can't cure it here," Ladinas said. I couldn't see him but I recognized his voice. "Where *can* you cure her?"

"I need several ingredients. They're only found in the Seelie Forest."

I shook my head. "You're a wanted faerie. I can't ask you to take me there. If the Faerie King catches you--"

"Let me worry about that," Willie said. "I will not let you die."

"Is there any other way to stop it?" Mercy asked.

Willie sighed. "Only if we kill the sorcerer and use his staff to withdraw the curse."

I grabbed the back of the couch and pulled myself up. Willie hopped off my chest and fluttered his wings. He hovered in front of me. "Then that's what we'll do. We're going to kill the sorcerer."

Mercy took a deep breath. "I don't know that we can."

"I just need a clean shot. I can do it."

"The curse weakens your magic," Willie said. "It won't work."

"Then I'll use my telekinesis. I can throw something at him and knock him out."

"It's too risky," Mercy said. "We threw everything we could think of at Mug Ruith and nothing phased him."

"The faerie is right," Ladinas said. "We managed to eliminate the younglings, but it's just a matter of time before he either revives them, pulling the splinters from their hearts, or makes more to replace them."

"Then this is our chance! We take him out now!"

I stood up. My knees buckled under me. Mercy caught me by the arm. "You're in no shape to fight."

"We're going to the Seelie Forest," Willie said. "It's the only chance we have. Besides, there might be a few things we can pick up while we're there to help defeat Mug Ruith."

"A few things?" I asked.

"Once we heal you in the Seelie Forest, we need to bust into the Unseelie Realm. Somehow, Mug Ruith has a staff vested with their power. We can find something just as strong, if not stronger, that can neutralize his power. We can fight his faerie fire with some of our own."

"What if you get captured, Willie? What will we do then? You know as well as I do that the Faerie King thinks vampires are an abomination. Helping us is forbidden."

"Then I'll come with you," Mercy said. "I'll help protect Willie and you both."

I grunted. "Fine. We'll go. Can you make a portal here?"

Willie shook his head. "We need a mystical convergence. One we know that's already connected to the faerie realm."

I shook my head. "If the sorcerer is still there, how the hell are we going to pull that off?"

"We fight," Ladinas said. "I'll mobilize every vampire in the area. We'll come after him with everything we've got."

"Do you think you can take him?" I asked.

Ladinas shook his head. "Not without magic that works against his power. We don't need to take him. We just have to draw him away from the convergence and buy you enough time to go through."

"What if he catches you? A lot of vampires could die."

Ladinas shook his head. "He's one sorcerer. There are openings to the sewers everywhere. He might be powerful, but he doesn't know the way. We can lose him. How much time do you need, Willie?"

"Just a few seconds. It's simple enough, but we can't pull it off while he's guarding the convergence."

Ladinas nodded. "Then it won't be a problem. We can buy you the time you need. Just get back here as soon as you can. Come back with a way to kill him and we'll end this once and for all."

I gulped. "Blood. I need some blood. I'm weak."

Ladinas snapped his fingers. A few seconds later, Demeter appeared with a young man in tow. He looked like a young professional—from the neck up. Below that, he was wearing nothing but Speedo shorts.

I raised an eyebrow. "Is this your preference?"

Ladinas smiled widely. "I enjoy variety in my meals. Mercy chose him for you while you were asleep. We have several willing blood maids at our disposal."

I chuckled. "Mercy certainly knows my preferences. Good thing he's clean shaven."

"I'm with you," Ladinas said. "No one likes a mouth-full of beard."

"Amen, brother!"

The man approached me, his face devoid of any emotion. What was the "male" equivalent of "maid"? Manservant? That seemed awfully archaic. The word "maid" was a bit off-putting in its own right. Blood bitch? Men could be bitches. Blood *person* might be the most politically correct term, but isn't everyone who isn't dead a blood person? Whatever. He was a ready and willing meal.

The man tilted his head back, exposing his neck.

"You're seriously cool with this?" I asked.

The man looked at me and bowed his head. "It is an honor to be of service."

I bit my lip. "Do you also do foot rubs?"

Mercy cleared her throat. "Just take your fill, Hailey. You heard Willie. You're short on time."

"Look, if I'm going to die, there are worse ways to go than having an almost-naked adonis at your feet."

"You will not die!" Mercy stomped her foot.

I sighed and rolled my eyes. "Fine. Chill. I'll bite him!"

I sank my teeth into the man's neck. Ladinas curated his stock well. This guy was delicious. More savory than sweet. The meat and potatoes of blood bitches.

I knew when to stop. After a few years, it's an instinct. When feeding, a vampire can hear her meal's pulse. The rate of blood flow into my waiting mouth was another sign. I pulled away. Ladinas handed me a handkerchief. I took it and wiped my mouth.

"Would you like another?" Ladinas asked.

I smiled. "I'd love another, but I shouldn't. That will keep me satiated long enough. After all, I only have a couple of days before I kick the bucket."

"Stop it!" Mercy huffed. "I told you. We're going to save you."

I shrugged. "I hope you do. If not, well, I guess it's off to hell. Corbin will be thrilled to see me."

"How can you be so cavalier about this?" Mercy asked. "Do you realize how many people's lives depend on you pulling through and stopping this sorcerer? Do you know how much you mean to your progeny?"

I shrugged. "He'd get by. If I die, I'm sure you'll pull something out of your ass and beat the sorcerer. Mercy always wins."

"I have nothing in my ass at the moment that can thwart faerie magic."

I smirked. "Then call Pauli. You never know what he has up there!"

"This isn't a joke, Hailey. I can't lose you!"

I tilted my head. "Excuse me?"

Mercy took a deep breath, held it in for a moment, then released it in a long, drawn-out exhale. "You heard me. *I* can't lose you. You're like a daughter to me. You've never seen me at my worst."

I bit my lip. "What are you saying, Mercy?"

"Damn it. Are you really going to make me say it?"

I smiled widely. "Yes, I am."

"I fucking love you, Hailey. If you die, it'll destroy me. I'd be a terror without you."

I smirked. "Fucking love you too, momma!"

Ladinas tilted his head. "Mercy is your sire?"

I shook my head. "My sire was killed just seconds after he bit me. I don't think of him as a sire. Just a bite donor. In all the ways that matter, Mercy is my sire. Even though I am technically Mercy's step-sire now."

"Say what?" Ladinas asked.

Mercy shook her head. "Long story. She had to claim Nico's status on the vampire family tree in order to defeat Corbin in hell. That means, if she wanted to, she could exercise Nico's sire bond over me."

"Merrick's spell?" Ladinas asked.

I nodded. "That's the one. I don't really use it. It seems wrong to force my will on someone. I wouldn't do that to Mercy. She *is* like a mother to me."

"Not to mention, if you ever tried, you'd have to add a qualifier to any command you issued. 'And when you're done doing what I said, don't shove your boot up my ass'"

I laughed. "Fair enough."

"And if you don't fight for your own damn life, I'll shove my boot up the ass of your corpse."

I shuddered. "Well, that's graphic."

"Not to mention," Willie piped up. "What about that wolf-shifter boy waiting for you back in New Orleans?"

I took a deep breath. He had a point. Connor had lost a lot of people as of late. He lost his old girlfriend. His father was also killed during our conflict with Corbin. Sure, Connor's father got involved with the Order of the Morning Dawn. Join up with those anti-vampire, anti-witch bigots and you deserve whatever you get. Even so, he was Connor's father. Connor and his dad might not have seen eye-to-eye on a lot of things, but when someone is gone, a lot of those issues that seemed to be so important before suddenly don't seem like big deals at all.

I wasn't eager to die. Don't get me wrong. Allowing some kind of unseelie curse to eat away at my insides didn't sound like a pleasant experience. At the same time, I'd never had to fight for my own life before. Not really.

I'd always risen to the occasion when I had to fight for someone else. I wanted to woman-up and go kick that sorcerer's ass. That's the way I wanted to save my life. Giving Mug's ugly mug a swift punch to the face, followed by an exsanguination spell targeted directly at his skull. That was one of several visions of the sorcerer's demise I had in mind.

I had quite the imagination. Bind him in chains. Use my telekinesis to send him flying. I'd drop and impale him on a flagpole. I could bind him in blood chains and sink him into the ocean. Preferably into a school of tiger sharks. The blood chains would whip them into a frenzy. There was always the wood chipper option. They say vampires can only die when you burn out their hearts, or lop off their heads. Werewolves were supposedly only vulnerable to silver. Wood chippers trumped all. There wasn't a creature on earth—supernatural or not—who could survive *that* gruesome fate.

If I had to kill the sorcerer, I'd find a way. Going to the faerie realm? It might be the best chance we had to save me, but it also meant risking Willie's life. The plan to distract Mug Ruith involved luring the sorcerer away from the convergence with an army of Ladinas's vampires. How many vampires might the sorcerer kill before they got away? Why was my life more valuable than theirs?

Then again, if I died trying to kill Mug Ruith in my condition, which was likely, Mercy would have to fight him alone. Mercy was a great witch. Don't get me wrong. She was an even better vampire. A much better vampire than I was. This was more a witch-battle than a vampire-battle. That meant I was the best shot anyone had to defeat Mug Ruith—and I had to be at full strength to do it. If we could steal a weapon, a power of some kind, from the Unseelie faeries that would level the mystical battlefield, we had to try.

This plan might put some people's lives at risk. Failure would put the lives of everyone—not just in Exeter, but throughout the world—at risk. After all, some dead saint once predicted that Mug Ruith would destroy all of Europe with some sort of mystical flying machine. Just because the prophecy was about Europe didn't mean he wouldn't destroy North America first. We didn't see any evidence of the sorcerer's flying machine but, if the legends about Mug Ruith and the saint's prophecy held any water at all, he had *something* that could fly and destroy civilizations. Maybe it was a modern aircraft. Maybe it was something more supernatural. Despite my curiosity, it was better if we never found out. The only way to ensure that his murder machine didn't launch was to kill Mug Ruith before he got that far.

I popped my knuckles. "Alright, Ladinas. Assemble the vampires. We're going to the faerie realm."

Chapter 6

LADINAS SENT A GROUP-TEXT to the local vampires. There's a stereotype about older vampires that they're clueless when it comes to technology. It was definitely true with Corbin. Mercy wasn't entirely helpless, but she still tended to fall back into old habits. She was as likely to forget her phone at home, leave it sitting on the charger, as she was to have it with her. Half the time she had her phone, the battery was dead. She made some of the funniest autocorrect errors I'd ever seen.

Some of her typos were classic. She once attempted to text me to say that she was going to kick my ass when she got home. Well, the "k" and the "l" are next to each other on the keyboard.

Ladinas was the exception to the technologically inept ancient vampire stereotype. He'd not only used technology to make his underground lair a secure fortress, but he used it to communicate with loyal vampires in the region.

Ladinas pocketed his phone. "We'll be ready to move within the hour."

Mercy raised an eyebrow. "You can coordinate an attack in an *hour*?"

Ladinas nodded. "We run drills. I operate a well-oiled machine."

Mercy grinned. "Talk about leadership."

Ladinas shook his head. "Leadership isn't my forte. I'm a strategist. These vampires don't follow me because they believe in *me*, Mercy. They still believe in you and your cause. They follow me for your sake."

Mercy bit her lip. "Seriously?"

Ladinas nodded. "You're a hometown girl, the progeny of Niccolo the Damned, and you've defeated Moll, twice, as well as Corbin."

Mercy shook her head. "Hailey played a larger role in our defeat of Corbin."

"Under your leadership, she did. There are some who doubt the efficiency of a democratic council. Most of the vampires around here would rather see a centralized leader, something closer to a monarchy. Still, they're more loyal to you than they are to any theory of vampire governance."

Mercy took a deep breath. "I had no idea."

I rolled my eyes. "You're pretty oblivious sometimes. Sure, Mercy, there are powerful vampires who oppose you. That's because you're a threat. You're a threat because so many more vampires *want* to follow you."

Ladinas pointed at me. "What she said. When I sent out my group text indicating *you* needed our help, you wouldn't believe the eager responses I received. They're still coming in. I had to turn off my notifications."

"Hailey needs their help as much as I do."

I shook my head. "Witches follow me. When it comes to leading vampires, Mercy, you're the bloody queen!"

Mercy bit her thumbnail. "Thank you Ladinas. Make sure everyone knows I'm grateful. I don't know how long this venture into faerie land will take. I'll thank them myself when we return."

"Come back with everything we need to defeat Mug Ruith, and you'll have every loyal vampire in the region ready and waiting to fight at your side."

Ladinas and Demeter took us back up to the armory. This time, the place was buzzing with vampires. When we stepped into the armory, every head in the place turned to look at us.

I nudged Mercy. "I think they're star-struck."

Mercy grunted. "Shut up."

I snickered. They say the best leaders are the ones who don't want to be leaders. The ones who come to power out of necessity, out of the sheer force of their virtue rather than the lust for power, are the leaders that people *want* to follow. Not because they are afraid of their leader, but because they *believe* in their leader. That was Mercy—even if she didn't realize it. The fact that she didn't see it was exactly why she was a strong leader.

"Everyone clear on the plan?" Ladinas asked. "The goal is not to engage the sorcerer. I don't want to lose any of you and, trust me, we won't stand a chance if we have to fight him head-on. Our mission is to buy Mercy and Hailey time so they can escape to the faerie realms. They'll return with a weapon we can use to stop him."

One of the vampires—an older gentleman I'd never met—raised his hand. "What of the younglings?"

"We eliminated most of them," Ladinas said. "That also only bought us a little time. We don't know if Mug Ruith is a vampire himself, or if he's using a vampire to turn his younglings. Either way, we have to assume that a vampire allied with him is still out there. That means he'll replenish his youngling army sooner rather than later."

Mercy stepped forward. "Thank you, everyone, for your willingness to help. I promise, we'll come back with what we need. In the meantime, while we're gone, make sure any younglings that Mug Ruith revives or makes, remain in check. We can't have dozens of new vampires terrorizing Exeter."

The vampires nodded in agreement. The same older vampire who spoke before stepped forward and bowed his head in Mercy's direction. "It's an honor to fight for you, my liege."

Mercy released a nervous laugh. She wasn't used to this kind of treatment. She certainly hadn't ever been anyone's "liege." "The real honor is to have each of you fighting at my side, having my back."

"We're both grateful!" I piped up.

My words didn't carry the same authority with the vampires as Mercy's, but they weren't rude about it. Several vampires made eye contact with me, grinned, and nodded.

The vampires suited up in stake-proof vests. Many of them took rifles and side-arms from the armory. Demeter distributed the firearms. A few vampires took bows and quivers. Some of them took crossbows, like Ladinas. Almost all of them carried swords, sheathed, and strapped to their backs. They also had daggers in smaller sheaths on their belts and strapped to their legs. Some of the daggers were made from oak rather than metal. Fancy stakes, shaped like knives, but more effective against vampires.

Demeter led the vampires out of the armory. Ladinas pulled up the rear with us. Willie hovered behind me. He fluttered his wings like a hummingbird. They were a constant blur. He could move like one, too. Impressive given his size. He was a *wee* Willie, but compared to any other creature that could move like that, he was large.

Ladinas had a headset on that he was using to communicate with Demeter.

"Once the convergence is clear, Demeter will let me know. They're going to haul ass out of there and draw the sorcerer as far away as possible."

"We'll move fast," I confirmed.

Mercy put her hand on my shoulder. "*Can* you move fast? You were pretty weak when you woke up."

"I feel a lot better since I fed. My natural abilities are sustaining me well enough. There is something off, though. I can feel the curse lurking under whatever magic Willie used to restrain it. It's like a pressure-cooker of nastiness, ready to explode."

"That sounds right," Willie said. "We should be prepared. I cannot say for certain *where* in the faerie realm we'll emerge once we pass through my portal. Since Mug Ruith is using power from the Unseelie faeries, there's a good chance we'll start in that realm. The ingredients we need to heal you, however, are in the Seelie Forest."

I nodded. "We'll do what we must. If we hit the Unseelie Forest first, perhaps we can gain what we need there before we get the ingredients we need to dispel the curse."

Mercy shook her head. "Saving you comes first."

I snorted. "Saving the fucking world comes first, Mercy."

"And how much good will any magical weapon do if we don't have you to wield it? I might be a witch, but I'm not on your level. You are the top priority, and that's that."

I grunted. "Don't make me use Nico's sire bond."

Mercy smirked. "You wouldn't dare."

We took the same route we did before to the forest. We waited behind the trees. Several gunshots fired in the distance. The vampires shouted war cries. It wasn't the tactic one would use if they intended to take the sorcerer by surprise, but that was the opposite of the mission. They were trying to lure him away from the stone circle.

Ladinas touched his earpiece. "It's working. Mug Ruith is in pursuit. Time to move in."

Ladinas and Mercy led the way. We reached the convergence. Gunshots still sounded in the distance. No screams, so at least there was that. Given that we didn't know the full extent of the sorcerer's power, I was anxious about what he might do.

We didn't have time to worry about it. As soon as Willie cast his magic, there was a good chance Mug Ruith would sense it and return to the convergence.

Willie flew around the circle. He lobbed orbs of magic at each of the stones and carried it with him until something like a large green and gold tornado swirled over the site.

"That's it!" I shouted. "That's the portal."

"Looks just like a druid portal," Mercy said. "See you on the other side."

Ladinas looked at both of us. "Good luck."

I nodded back at him. Mercy and I dove into the portal. Willie jumped in with us. The magic swirled around us and the next thing I knew, a force I couldn't explain pulled us through what looked like some kind of wormhole, a channel, or a thread of mystic energies connecting the realms.

We landed on our feet in a dark forest. I looked around. Gigantic mushrooms surrounded us. The trees were tall and their branches full.

"Where are we?" I asked.

"Just as I suspected, we arrived in the Unseelie Forest. We must move fast before anyone notices our presence."

"How far from here is the Seelie Forest?" Mercy asked.

"Not far. But don't think we'll be safe when we arrive. Remember, my king isn't any more welcoming than the Unseelie King. "

I nodded. "Lead the way, Willie."

Chapter 7

I CLUTCHED AT MY chest and fell to one knee.

"What's wrong?" Mercy asked.

I shook my head. "That damned curse. It's like coming here awakened it."

Willie nodded. "It's to be expected. We're in the Unseelie Forest, the place where the curse originated. Once we get back to the Seelie Forest, my magic will be stronger. It will help restrain the curse longer."

Mercy nodded. "Like I said, Hailey. We can't get what we need from here until you're well."

I sighed. I hated to admit it but I couldn't deny what I was feeling. It was as if the curse was sucking the air out of my lungs every time I took a breath. As a vampire, I didn't have to breathe, strictly speaking. I could survive under water if I had to. That didn't mean struggling to breathe wasn't uncomfortable and painful. It was like I'd inhaled metal shavings.

The skies above us were illuminated with a dark violet magic. It gave the illusion of night. In these realms, there wasn't a sun. Whether it was light or dark depended on the magic in the air.

The air was sweet, but the scent didn't hit my nostrils right. I sneezed. The pain spread across my chest.

"Damn it!" I screamed. "It's like I'm allergic to these damned mushrooms and trees."

Mercy shook her head. "Magic mushrooms are no joke."

I chuckled. "Like you'd know."

Mercy shrugged. "I was around in the sixties and seventies. Shrooms never did much for me, but I enjoyed the residual effects when I fed on hippies."

I bit my lip. "I didn't know it worked like that."

"Our bites filter out alcohol. Other hallucinogens get through."

Willie huffed. "Unseelie magic fills everything in this forest. Don't touch the mushrooms."

I grunted. "The spores are in the air. I'm not sure touching them is the problem."

"Then don't breathe," Mercy said. "You don't have to. It might be less painful not to breathe than to inhale this stuff."

I winced. "This stuff doesn't affect you at all?"

Mercy shrugged. "I feel nothing unusual. It must be on account of the curse."

"Keep up the pace!" Willie said. "Less talking, more walking."

"He's right," Mercy said. "We don't have to breathe to live. We have to breathe to talk."

I scratched the back of my head. She had a point. The more we talked about it, the more air I inhaled. The more air I inhaled, the more my lungs burned.

Several red lights floated in the distance. They looked like fireflies but a different color.

"What are those?" Mercy asked.

"Unseelie faeries," Willie said. "They're watching us."

"Are they going to come after us?" Mercy asked.

"So long as we're fleeing the forest, I think they'll leave us be. There's a treaty between the Seelie and Unseelie that allows for safe passage so long as we don't take anything."

I huffed. "Well, that will not hold when we return to get what we need."

"Stop talking!" Willie and Mercy said in concert.

"Sorry."

Mercy glared at me. Even saying "sorry" violated the no-talking rule.

The glow of the Unseelie appeared to get closer as we followed Willie down a long and winding trail.

"Are you sure they'll leave us be?" Mercy asked.

"They should. Unless—"

"Unless what?" Mercy asked.

"Hailey's curse. It's Unseelie magic. They think we stole something."

I stomped my foot on the ground. Willie and Mercy turned to me. I pointed straight ahead and grunted.

"Grunting takes breathing," Mercy said.

I pointed more forcefully ahead. How much clearer could I be without using words?

"She's right," Mercy said. "We should pick up the pace."

We took off running straight ahead. Until a woman appeared out of nowhere in the middle of the trail. Her eyes were dark. Red magic glowed from her eye-sockets, down her cheek. It resembled the look of a drunk girl with too much makeup who'd spent the night crying at a bar.

"Hello, ladies."

Mercy tilted her head. "Who are you?"

The woman looked at Willie. "Care to introduce me to your friends, Wee Willie?"

"Leave us be," Willie said. "I'm trying to save one of them from an Unseelie curse."

"Since your faerie guide is so rude, I'm the Leanhuam-Shee. You are vampires, are you not?"

Mercy nodded. "What is it to you?"

"Don't talk to her," Willie said. "We don't have time for this."

"You can call me Leann if it's easier."

"What do you want, Leann?" Mercy asked.

Leann stepped past Mercy and approached me. She placed her hands on my forehead. A tingle passed through her fingertips. The pain in my chest subsided. "That should help for a time."

I grunted. "Thanks. I think."

"Don't thank her! We must keep moving!"

Leann raised her hand. "Quiet, Willie."

"I know your curse," Leann said. "Let me guess. Mug Ruith is responsible."

I nodded. "How did you know?"

Leann smiled. "He's the one who got away."

"You two were lovers?" I asked.

"Leann!" Willie piped up. "We don't have time for this."

"I've given her time. You should thank me, Willie. If you don't like what I have to propose, you can go with Willie. Try to find your cure. Has he told you the ingredients required?"

"Not specifically."

"We have everything we need in the Seelie Forest!" Willie shouted. "That's all that matters."

Leann laughed. "Most of the ingredients are common. The spores of a mushroom connected to a faerie ring. Water drawn from a Seelie spring. A scrape of moss from the north side of a fae-wood oak. It's the last ingredient that will be a challenge."

"What is the final ingredient, Willie?" I asked.

"Are you going to tell them, or should I?" Leann asked.

Willie grunted. "The blood of the Faerie King."

I gulped. "The same king who wants you dead or exiled?"

Willie folded his arms around his chest. "What other king is there?"

"Willie!" I shouted. "I told you, I won't put you at risk to do this!"

"It's not a risk! You can draw on his blood. That's what you do!"

I bit my lip. "Maybe. I can access the power in blood, but I've never dabbled in faerie blood before."

Leann raised her finger. "That's what I'm here to offer you."

"Do you know what she is?" Willie asked. "Don't trust her!"

I tilted my head. "What are you?"

"I'm a faerie, of course. I don't have wings. Faeries come in many sizes and shapes."

"You're not telling them the truth," Willie said. "She's a vampire faerie!"

Mercy smirked. "I wasn't aware there was such a thing! Were you made by Baron Samedi?"

Leann laughed. "I was the *inspiration* and pattern of the Baron's creation. Like you, I consume human blood. I feast on their souls. You're not so different from our kind. You are to humans what the Unseelie Faeries are to our kind. I am invisible to women. On earth, at least. I seduce men, I make love to them, and feed on their souls through intercourse. I only consume their blood when I've taken all I can *recreationally.*"

"She kills everyone she feeds upon," Willie said. "She's not like you two."

Leann shrugged. "There are differences between our kinds, I grant you that. When Baron Samedi created the first vampire, he fused Niccolo Freeman with *my* essence. I was the prototype. Fascinating history, of course, but that's not why I'm here."

"Why are you here?" I asked. "What do you want from us?"

"I want what you want. I want the one who got away back in my thrall. I want to finish what I started with the one called Mug Ruith."

I shrugged. "Fine with me. We just want him gone."

"And you should! Let me guess. He's rallying vampires to his cause."

I nodded. "He's been turning younglings. Probably not himself. We think he's using another vampire to do it."

"Why do you suppose he'd do that?" Leann asked.

"We don't know," Mercy said. "I suspect you're about to tell us."

"Because my magic, my essence, is a part of your kind. He's not making an army of vampires to fight. He's using vampires as a source of power."

"Like batteries?" I asked. "If you know what batteries are."

"I visit earth from time to time," Leann said. "I know what batteries are and the analogy is accurate. He's creating vampires, but using a bit of the power he stole from me to prevent the Baron from claiming their souls. He's using their souls, combined by their nature, to gain faerie magic for himself."

"Why is he using a convergence to connect to this realm?" I asked. "If he's getting the power he needs from vampires, why bother?"

"Like attracts like. The more power he gains from the vampires, the more he can draw from our realm. He won't rest until he's drained all the power he can from our realm. He'll use that power to terraform the world. Then create an Unseelie Forest of his own where he's the Faerie King."

I glanced at Mercy. "The prophecy."

Mercy nodded. "There's a saint of old who said that Mug Ruith intended to use some kind of flying machine to destroy Europe."

Leann nodded. "A vessel forged from the trees of our realm, granted flight by our magic. When all is said and done, he'll leave the Unseelie Forest little more than a shade of what it is now."

"Where has he been all these years?" I asked. "It's been centuries since he showed his face on earth."

"That's because he was *my* prisoner. I made the mistake ages ago of seducing him. I underestimated the power he'd already gained from our realm through human sacrifice. He warped that power, corrupted it through a magic I do not know. When I took some of his power, he infected me in turn. The magic he used has spread slowly through the centuries through my form. I held him prisoner, I tortured him, I begged him to tell me how he did it. How to cure the curse he cast upon me. He never broke. Over time, the infection weakened me. He escaped my prison and returned to earth."

"So Mug Ruith isn't a vampire?" I asked.

Leann shook her head. "He is not. But he could be."

"You want me to turn him?" I asked.

Leann nodded. "If you can do that, he'll be beholden to your sire bond. You can compel him to return to me, where I can bind him forever."

"Don't listen to her!" Willie pleaded. "There's another way."

Leann raised her finger. "I believe Mug Ruith infected you with a curse like mine. However, I cannot approach the Faerie King. If you can acquire the cure, I only ask that you secure a dose for me as well. Curses like that are like viruses. Once you're cured, the same curse cannot afflict you twice."

"That might be true. I still can't get to him. We tried. He's powerful."

"I can give you what you need. Consider it a simple trade. The cure for the power to resist any spell Mug Ruith might cast against you."

"What happens after you're cured?" I asked. "You come back to earth and start feeding on people again?"

"Dearest witch, I've never stopped feeding on men. I will do nothing more than I've always done. Trust me, those I choose are men who deserve it. You've never heard of me until now. I can promise you, unless you come upon me by chance, you'll never hear from me again."

"Can we trust that you'll stick to your word?" Mercy asked.

"Ask Willie."

"Willie? What's the truth?"

"Faeries cannot lie. They can deceive. What she says is true, but it is likely she has other plans and schemes she's yet to reveal."

I tilted my head. "That applies to both the Seelie and the Unseelie faeries?"

Willis pinched his chin. "I think so! I'm not really sure now that you mention it. It's not a topic we think much about. It's sort of like your digestion system. It's just the way it is. Not suitable for civilized conversation."

Leann waved her hand through the air. "This realm courses with dark magic, but it *is* faerie magic. There are legends of Unseelie faeries who gained the power to speak untruths. I am not one of them. My schemes do not concern the earth."

I rolled my eyes. "Which is exactly what an Unseelie faerie who could lie would say."

Leann snickered. "That's true. You'll have to decide for yourself. You can trust that I'm speaking the truth and take this opportunity to both save yourself and defeat Mug Ruith. Or you can go about your business and fend for yourselves."

I pressed my lips together. "Suppose we do this. We still have a problem. How can we get the Faerie King's blood without putting Willie at risk?"

"Or being taken prisoner by the Seelie Faerie King ourselves," Mercy added.

Leann pinched her chin. "You wield the power of blood, do you not?"

I nodded. "In a way."

"What kind of power can you gain from blood?" Leann asked.

"There are powers in all blood I can wield, like any witch who dabbles in blood magic might. As a blood witch *and* a vampire, I can access other powers latent in the soul."

"You can gain vampiric abilities, new skills, by cycling the blood through your soul."

I narrowed my eyes. "That's exactly correct."

"Bite me," Leann said. "Use my power to seduce the Faerie King. He'll give you whatever you desire. Including his blood."

"Are you sure that's safe?" Mercy asked. "I've never fed on a faerie before. What will it do to her?"

Leann laughed. "It will not harm you at all. We are more alike than different. The only side-effect I can imagine is that with my blood, you'll be more like me. Your soul will once again be your own. The Baron will have no leverage over you and if you ever die, your eternal destiny will depend on you alone."

"I won't be damned to vampire hell?" I asked.

Leann shook her head. "You'll join me here if you like. It's not paradise, I grant, but it certainly beats hell."

"You're telling me that if I ever die I'll be an Unseelie Faerie like you?"

"I suspect so," Leann said. "Of course, it's never been done before. And it may never happen if your earthly form never perishes."

"And before I die?" I asked. "How will I be different after I do this?"

"Again, there's no way to say for sure. You will live. I can promise you that. Given your current predicament, I'd say that's a step up."

I took a deep breath. My lungs didn't hurt. Whatever power she'd used to restrain the curse, albeit temporarily, was working. "What are your thoughts, Willie?"

Willie shook his head. "I cannot make this decision for you. It could work. There is still another option."

"Your original plan. We take the king's blood by force. If by some miracle we escape the Seelie Forest, we still have to come here and steal a power or a weapon that we can use against Mug Ruith."

"Attempt that," Leann said, "and every faerie in the Unseelie Forest will rise up to stop you. You'll never make it back to earth."

"Is this true, Willie?"

Willie sighed. "It was always a long-shot. She's right. Our chances of escape are slim."

I grunted. "Alright, Leann. I'll do it."

Leann tilted her head to the side. "Take and drink."

I bit the faerie. Her blood tingled in my mouth. The power penetrated my body. It didn't cure the curse, of course, but it was like I'd fed on a thousand men at once and cycled the power latent in their blood.

After releasing Leann, I took a step back. "I can feel it. I'm changing."

"You're cycling my power. You have everything you need to secure our cure."

"One question," Mercy said. "If he cursed you the same way he cursed Hailey, why aren't you dead?"

Leann shook her head. "That's where vampires and I differ. It is not easy to kill me within the confines of the Unseelie Forest. The power here sustains me. So long as I am here, the curse is dormant. I can only make brief trips to earth where I must go to feed. My trips to the Seelie Forest are even more dubious. You are my only hope. Complete this task and I will give you what you need to stand against Mug Ruith."

Chapter 8

LEANN WAS KIND ENOUGH to escort us to the border of the Seelie Forest. Then again, I suspected kindness had little to do with it. She couldn't get what she needed without me.

Now came the less-than-delightful part. Find the Faerie King and seduce him. If he was anything like Willie by appearance, it was going to take an Oscar-worthy performance to pull it off.

This wasn't the first time I'd had a seduce-and-betray mission. The first time I met Corbin, the plan was to seduce and assassinate him. Things didn't go quite according to plan post-seduction. At least Corbin was attractive. We were the same species. Of course, I didn't have to sleep with the king. I just had to get close enough to bite him and collect his blood.

We crossed the border into the Seelie Forest. The green and pink magic that filled the skies made it brighter than the Unseelie Forest.

Mercy nudged me in the ribs. "Ready to go represent the lollipop guild?"

I huffed. "Shut up."

"Nothing wrong with screwing a faerie!" Willie piped up. "Size isn't important."

Mercy and I exchanged glances and laughed. I bit my tongue. I wasn't trying to offend Willie but, you know, that's the sort of thing one would expect a wee little man to say.

"I'm not going to screw him. I just have to seduce him and convince him to trust me so I can get his blood."

Mercy snickered. "What? Doing a faerie isn't on your fuck-it list?"

"What the hell is a fuck-it list?"

Mercy grinned. "Everyone you want to fuck before you die."

"I don't have a list like that. Besides, I'm with Connor! Do you have a list like that?"

Mercy shrugged. "Maybe. None of your business."

"I know you're a fan of *Interview with the Vampire.* You realize, Brad Pitt isn't an actual vampire, right?"

Mercy sighed. "One of my few regrets. I should have turned him while he was still young."

"He's still young enough. Who are you to complain? You're old enough to be his great-great grandmother."

"I look good for my age, don't I?"

I chuckled. "One of the many perks of being a vampire. You're a regular g-gilf."

Mercy raised an eyebrow? "G-gilf?"

"A gilf with a stutter. What do you think it means?"

Mercy chuckled. "I suppose we'd better gather all the simpler ingredients first."

Willie flew around me and grabbed onto my back. "There's a field of mushrooms not far from here. We'll be there soon."

We continued hiking straight ahead. Willie flew off my back to lead the way down a small trail between two large trees.

"Don't touch the trees."

"Why not?" I asked.

"Faeries live within the trees. Touch one and you'll be sucked into someone's home."

"Don't touch *any* tree?"

"There's no telling which ones are occupied."

"How many faeries live inside a tree?" Mercy asked.

"Depends. Some of them house hundreds."

I scratched the back of my head. "How do so many fit inside a tree?"

Willie smiled from ear to ear. "Magic! Duh!"

We continued down a path. I'd call it a trail, but since the faeries didn't walk a lot, there wasn't much of a beaten path. The grasses were full and green. Flower blossoms of every color imaginable were scattered throughout.

A green orb appeared ahead from behind one of the trees. It moved in our direction.

Willie ducked behind me. "I'm not here!"

"What's the deal?" I asked.

The green glow materialized into the shape of a faerie about Willie's size. She had pink hair and a cute button nose.

"What are you doing here Willie?"

Willie peeked over my shoulder. "Wanda! Fancy seeing you here."

"I live here. I thought you were in hiding. Are you mental? If the king finds you--"

I cleared my throat. "I'm Hailey. Nice to meet you."

Wanda grunted. "Look at me when I'm talking to you, Willie!"

Willie took a deep breath and flew around me, his head hung low. "I had to come."

Mercy tucked a strand of her dark brown hair behind her ears. "I take it you two know each other?"

"You could say that."

"Could say that?" Wanda huffed. "I'm his wife!"

I almost choked on my tongue. "You're *married*?"

"Have you been poking humans? Have you poked these vampires, Willie? Tell me the truth."

I shook my head. "He's never poked me."

"Me neither!" Mercy said. "Haven't seen him do any poking at all."

Wanda folded her arms in front of her chest. "I don't believe you. Like you could resist Wee Willie."

I bit my lip. "He's a stallion, but no. I swear. He's been faithful."

"That better be true, Willie. If I find out you've been poking around, Wee Willie will become No Willie."

"Damn," I chuckled under my breath. "She's not playing, Willie."

"She never does. I promise, baby! You're my one and only."

Wanda smiled. "Better be. Now, what are you doing here? It's not safe, Willie!"

"Hailey was cursed by Mug Ruith. We're here to gather the ingredients for the antidote."

"I knew you weren't the smartest faerie in the forest, Willie, but that's suicide. You can't possibly get the last ingredient. Not when the king wants your head on a pike."

I wasn't sure if it was wise to tell Wanda our plan. Even Willie wasn't a fan of it and given that Wanda hadn't exactly presented herself as an open-minded faerie, telling her about Leann wasn't likely to go over well.

"We're going to keep Willie out of it. We don't want to put him at risk. I'm going to approach the king myself."

Wanda stared at me blankly. "Good luck with that. You're a vampire. The king thinks your kind is an abomination."

I shrugged. "If he knows what's at stake, how Mug Ruith is using faerie magic, and intends to create a new Unseelie Forest on earth, I'm hoping he'll be empathetic to our cause."

Wanda pinched her chin. "Good luck with that. I suppose you need a few more ingredients."

I nodded. "We do."

"Follow me!"

We didn't need Wanda to show us where to get what we needed. Willie already knew. Still, she was there and wasn't going anywhere. She was less interested in helping me than she was in making sure that we got in and out of the forest as quickly as possible. She was worried about Willie. I couldn't blame her. I was worried about him, too. It was the primary reason I was reluctant to come to the faerie realms to begin with.

Willie joined Wanda and flew ahead of us. They were bickering about something. Probably Willie's foolishness. He helped me to begin with, which was why he was exiled from the forest. Now, he was helping me again and put himself at risk to do it.

We stopped at a tree. Wanda flew right into it.

"What's going on?" I asked.

"This is our home," Willie said. "She's getting a few supplies."

"Does she know we need two doses?"

"I told her we want to make more than one. Just in case Mug Ruith curses someone else."

"Smart," Mercy said. "Probably shouldn't tell her the full truth."

Willie sighed. "I know. If she finds out, though, she won't like it."

Chapter 9

WANDA EMERGED FROM THE tree. It was sort of strange. A knot on the trunk twisted open and closed as she came and went. Wanda was roughly the size of Willie. The tree wasn't large. Its girth could barely accommodate one, much less a family of faeries. Magic must've shrunk them down to the size of ants when they went inside for a tree of such diminutive proportions.

Wanda's arms barely fit around two beakers

They were nearly half her size, but when she handed them to me, they fit easily into my palms.

"I can ask my neighbors if you need more."

I shook my head. "Thank you, Wanda. Two should be sufficient. I don't need to drink an entire beaker for this to work, do I?"

Wanda shrugged. "Hard to know? Not sure the proper dosage for giants."

I chuckled. "I'm not a giant. I'm human."

"What's the difference?"

"I haven't met a lot of giants. I assume it's mostly a difference in size. Giants are bigger than humans."

Wanda shook her head as she flew past me and grabbed Willie's hand. "Big folk all look the same to me."

Mercy and I looked at each other and laughed. We followed Willie and Wanda through the trees until we reached a field of faerie shrooms. Several small creatures buzzed around. They glowed with a white light and had human-like bodies. They were five or six inches tall.

"What are those?" I asked.

Willie turned back. "Pixies. Another kind of faerie."

"Faeries and pixies aren't the same thing?" Mercy asked.

Wanda huffed. "Why do they always think we're all the same?"

I cleared my throat. "You *just* said big people all look alike."

"That's true, though! We're clearly different from pixies!"

I snickered. "Clearly? I see the difference. I'm guessing their magic is different?"

Willie nodded. "Pixies are like your honeybees, but way smarter. They're as intelligent as any faerie. However, their purpose is to nurture the forest. Our purpose is to protect it and to ensure that our magics aren't exploited by outsiders."

Mercy smiled. "Outsiders like us?"

Willie nodded. "Pretty much."

Willie and Wanda darted around the mushrooms. A pixie buzzed around me, sniffing at me as if confused about what I was. I handed Mercy the beakers. I held out my hand and the pixie hovered over it. She waved something like a wand at my face. I sneezed.

She flew off, giggling.

"What was that about?" Mercy asked.

"Just how they say hello," Willie said. "Don't mind them. Pixies don't bite. Just watch your eyes."

"Watch our eyes?" I raised an eyebrow.

"I said they don't bite. They poke people in the eyes instead. You'll be fine so long as you stay calm and don't make any sudden movements."

Wanda flew around the mushrooms, gathering spores. Willie darted in and out of the trees on the perimeter. They each flew back and dropped various ingredients into each of the two beakers in Mercy's hands. The pixies flew around both of us, examining us, speaking to each other in such a high pitch that I couldn't make out their words. Then again, they were probably speaking Pixish. If that's a thing.

I watched as the two faeries navigated between the mushrooms and trees, playing with the pixies as they went about gathering the ingredients. The beakers were about half full by the time they were done.

"All that's left is the Faerie King's blood," Wanda said. "You sure he'll agree to help?"

I shrugged. "What choice do I have? It's that or I die."

"And if she dies," Mercy added, "I don't know if I'm strong enough to take on Mug Ruith alone."

Wanda sighed. "Well, we certainly don't want that sorcerer making a new Unseelie Forest. That would be dreadful."

Willie was turning purple holding his breath. Apparently he was afraid if he opened his mouth he'd give away our *real* plan.

"Where do we go next?" Mercy asked.

"Willie can't come with you," Wanda said. "And I'm not leaving his side. You'll have to go looking for the king alone."

I tilted my head. "Could one of these pixies lead the way?"

"Sure," Wanda said. "But they're known for taking the scenic route. Follow a pixie's lead and she'll give you a tour of every tree between here and your destination."

I cleared my throat. "Alright. Well, you're right. It's probably best if Willie keeps his distance. How do we find the Faerie King?"

Wanda shook her head. "You don't find him. He finds you. It's a wonder he hasn't yet. Get as far from here as possible and we'll go in the opposite direction. Don't leave the forest. Not if you *want* the king to find you. If you want to speed things up a bit, whistle a tune."

"Whistle, what kind of tune?" Mercy asked.

"Doesn't matter! Just purse your lips and blow. The Faerie King can't resist a good whistle!"

I sighed. "Yeah, well, I can't whistle for shit."

Wanda giggled. "You're not whistling for shit, silly. You're whistling for the king!"

Mercy snickered. "She means she doesn't know how to whistle. I suppose I'll have to do it."

"You don't know how to whistle, Hailey? It's easy peasy! I'd show you, but then the king might show."

I bit my lip. "Yeah, well, I've tried to whistle more times than I can count. My lips just don't work that way."

"It's more about breath control than your lips," Wanda said. "You're probably blowing too hard."

Mercy raised an eyebrow. "That's what he said."

I stifled a laugh. "We don't do that! He's afraid of my fangs."

"He thinks you're going to bite it right off or something?"

I grinned. "Probably. No skin off my back. I'd rather not do it, anyway. Yuck."

"Do what?" Wanda asked. "I'm not following."

I sighed. "You don't want to know."

Willie flew over to me and wrapped his arms around my neck. "You be careful. Come find me when you're done."

"How are we going to find you?" I asked.

"Easy! We passed our tree before. That's where I'll be."

"And how do I find that tree? The trees all look similar."

"Don't worry," Wanda said. "I'll be on the lookout. Can't be too careful when your hubby's a wanted faerie. Just head back this way and I'll find you."

I nodded. "Alright. Well, thanks for the ingredients. Is there anything I need to do once I collect the blood to make this elixir work?"

"Not much," Willie said. "Just make sure it's well mixed and it should do the trick."

Chapter 10

Mercy and I headed off through the forest while Willie and Wanda left in the opposite direction. We barely left the mushroom and pixie clearing when I heard a lot of high-pitched screaming and shouting. It was coming from the direction Willie and Wanda took when we parted ways.

"Damn it! We have to go back."

Mercy grabbed my hand. "It sounds like a lot of faeries out there. If we go after Willie and Wanda our presence will only confirm that he's helping us."

I yanked my hand out of Mercy's grip. "Once we reveal ourselves to the king do you really think he'll assume it's a coincidence that Willie returned at the same time we came to the forest? They'll know he was the one who brought us here."

"Do you really think the king is there? He wouldn't be out on patrol looking for Willie. They're probably lackeys. Soldiers, if the faeries have soldiers. If they see us, they will not be concerned with taking us as prisoners. They'll either kick us out of the realm or kill us."

I huffed. "I'd like to see them try."

"You don't understand how powerful faeries are. If Mug Ruith got his power *from* faeries, how powerful do you think actual faeries are? Besides, even if we could fight them and get away, we're not really sure how to kill them. If it's *possible* to kill them at all."

I grabbed my wand from the pocket I'd sewn into the thigh of my pants. "I'll take my chances. Willie came back here to help us. I won't allow them to arrest him."

Mercy grabbed my wrist and wrested my wand out of my grip. "I know you can use Nico's sire bond to make me give this back. Listen to me for one second before you rush in there and compromise this entire mission."

I clenched my fists. "Fine."

"It's too late. They have Willie. Our best chance to save him is to stick to the plan. We go to the king. You use Leann's seduction ability to convince him to *both* give you his blood *and* free Willie."

I snickered. "Free Willie."

Mercy shook her head. "That movie was lame."

"Was not. It's a classic. Whatever. I guess you have a point."

Mercy nodded and placed my wand back in my hand. "We'll save him. You will, anyway. Who knows what they'll do to me?"

I took a deep breath. "Go back to Wanda. She's not the outlaw. If my plan fails, it will fall to you two to save Willie and me."

Mercy pressed her lips together. "If the plan fails, there won't be *any* saving you. The curse will take you if the faeries don't."

I shook my head. "There's more than one way to take someone's blood. If he won't give it to us, if Leann's abilities don't work, there's no one who I'd trust to do what has to be done more than you."

"I already told you. We don't know how to kill faeries."

"Maybe not. I bet Wanda does. And even if you can't, you don't have to kill one to take his blood."

Mercy sighed. "Hopefully it won't come to that."

Mercy turned to leave.

"Mercy."

"Yes, Hailey?"

"Be careful."

Mercy nodded and handed me the beakers. I ripped off the bottom of my shirt and tore the piece in two. I tied the cloth around the tops of the beakers to keep the ingredients contained."You too. You've got this."

The shrill faerie screams stopped. That meant they probably had Willie. Hopefully, we were right that they wouldn't arrest Wanda. Aiding and abetting, or whatever. Faerie laws weren't human laws. There was no way to know for sure.

All I could do was run as far away as possible. One problem I didn't think of when I sent Mercy away—I didn't know how to whistle.

It's always the minor but crucial details that I overlook in the heat of the moment. All I was thinking about was Willie—and keeping Mercy safe. She was right. We didn't know how to fight the faeries. I thought if I sent her to Wanda I could carry out the plan, seduce the king, save Willie, and be done with it. Mercy would be fine. No risk of something bad happening to her while I was attempting to seduce the king. I'd take the elixir, bring Leann her share, and we'd leave together to stop Mug Ruith.

If only I could whistle.

I pursed my lips and blew. Nothing but the sound of air escaping my lips. I tried that thing that some people do where they put their thumb and forefinger in their mouths to whistle. I ended up with spit on my fingers, but that was it. I wiped my fingers off on my shirt.

I tried to mimic the sound of a whistle by throwing my voice into falsetto. Nothing happened.

I sat down in the grass. There had to be a way to get the king's attention. If I couldn't whistle with my lips, maybe I could use something else to make a similar sound. When I was a girl, I used to use blades of grass to make a high-pitched squeak. I'd put the blade between my thumbs and blow on it. I plucked a blade from the ground and made the sound. It wasn't close enough to a whistle.

I set the beakers beside me. I looked at them for a moment.

That might just work.

I pulled the remnants of my shirt off one beaker. I emptied the contents into one hand. I was careful not to drop any. I didn't know how precise the quantities were for the elixir and didn't want to risk screwing it up.

I placed the rim of the beaker on my bottom lip and blew. It produced a sound a lot lower than a whistle, but it was a whistle of a sort. I repeated the sound a few times before I put the ingredients back into the beaker and tied the cloth from my shirt over it again.

I looked around and waited. It was a long shot, but unless I could train myself to whistle the usual way—something I'd failed to do after years of trying—it was the best shot I had.

Three glowing green orbs appeared in the distance. They emerged from a tree straight ahead. If that was the king, that tree was his castle.

The orbs didn't take shape. I had no way of knowing if one of them was the king or not. But if the king sent them, if they were more of his soldiers, I knew where to find him.

I'd encountered the Faerie King once before. When I entered the faerie realm on my quest to recover Merrick's grimoire. If the faeries showed their true forms, I'd know if the king was with them. I didn't know how to force them to do that. I didn't know if any spells I had would do a darn thing to slow them down. What I knew how to do was run. As a vampire, there was a chance I could outrun them.

I took off toward the tree they had emerged from. They came after me. I juked my body like an NFL running back. I wasn't much of an athlete, but when you have adrenaline on your side, there's no telling what's possible.

Two of the three faerie orbs collided. They shrieked. The other orb shot at me. I ran so hard that if the ground had feelings, it would scream in pain.

I held the beakers tight with one hand and gripped my wand with the other. I aimed my wand at the ground. My magic might not hurt the faeries, but I could still use it. The force sent me flying fast toward the tree.

All I had to do was touch it. That's what Wanda said. My body slammed into the trunk—but it didn't hurt. It didn't stop me. Instead, golden magic surrounded me. It flowed around me like sap.

My feet landed on a wooden floor. I looked up and saw the Faerie King sitting on a throne grown from vines. Green and pink blossoms sprouted from it.

The king stood from his throne. Now that I was in his domain—inside his tree—we were of a similar size and stature. "The blood witch returns. I'd say it's a pleasant surprise, but it's neither under pleasant circumstances that you're here, nor is it a surprise."

"What are you talking about?"

The Faerie King smiled at me. "I've been expecting you, Hailey."

Chapter 11

"WHAT DO YOU MEAN you've been expecting me? I thought this was going to be a surprise."

The Faerie King stood from his throne as he laughed. "For centuries the security of our realm was secured by the gatekeepers. Merlin and Lilith traversed the fabric of time and ensured no one could enter our forests, or pass between any realms, without their permission. There were rare exceptions, of course. There were always ways to bypass the gatekeepers, but such incursions were rare enough that we could deal with it. Such is no longer the case."

"You're talking about the mystical convergences."

The Faerie King nodded. "That's one word for it, I suppose. Despite the gatekeepers' ability to move through time, there was always a point in the future in every realm they couldn't move beyond. Naturally, we assumed it was the end of time."

"Well, we're still living and breathing."

The Faerie King nodded. "The time the gatekeepers could not move beyond came and went. I have a theory if you'd like to hear it."

I shrugged. "I'm all ears."

"The gatekeepers were mortal. Descended from dryads, yes. Their power came from the Tree of Life. But they were mortal, no less. Given enough time, they could only do so much. They could only keep the gates for so long. Every mortal is finite. The realms are infinite. Inevitably, a time would come when they'd done all they could do."

I tilted my head. "I've met Merlin. He's just a boy. He lives with his father in Missouri. He's supposed to go back in time later, go to Camelot, go to Annwn to guard the gates."

"And he will go *back.* He cannot go forward. While he exists in many times, past and future, his life still has a beginning and an end. Nonetheless, the gatekeepers themselves knew this was true. They allowed the gates to open, they strategically granted power to a few who were worthy, so that when their time ended, when the era of the gatekeepers passed, the era of the guardians could begin."

I pressed my lips together. "Merrick told me I was a guardian. So was Mercy."

"Merlin's father, Elijah Wadsworth, is numbered among them as well. So is your old friend, Nicky or Nyx, in Kansas City. There are more who you do not know and still more who must become guardians. Vampires are especially well-suited for this role."

"Because we can live forever?"

The Faerie King nodded. "I believed your kind to be an abomination. Now, I believe your creation was planned all along by the gatekeepers."

"You're telling me that Merlin and Lilith schemed to create vampires? I thought we were made by Baron Samedi. Made from the essence of the Leanhuam-Shee."

The Faerie King tilted his head. "Perhaps Baron Samedi was simply doing what the gatekeepers told him he must. To create a formidable race that might protect the gates in the future. However, I must ask, how do you know of the Leanhuam-Shee?"

I took a deep breath. I hadn't expected this conversation. Leann said I'd have to seduce the Faerie King. I had to make a choice. Tell the Faerie King the truth or stick to the plan. Was this conversation just a way to distract me until the Faerie King's legions could return and bind me? Or was it Leann who deceived me? She was among the Unseelie, after all, a murderess who fed on human souls. I had to find out more. That meant telling the Faerie King as much as I could—except that I'd cycled Leann's power. I had to keep that ace in my back pocket, just in case.

"Mug Ruith escaped the Unseelie Forest. He came to earth through the convergence in Exeter. He started making vampires. That's what got our attention."

The Faerie King narrowed his eyes. "What do you mean he escaped?"

"He was a prisoner in the Unseelie Forest, wasn't he?"

The Faerie King huffed. "Hardly. He *ruled* the Unseelie Forest. There isn't a creature there who doesn't do his bidding."

I gulped. "Including Leann?"

"Especially Leann. She is his queen, bound to him by a curse."

I grunted. "Well, isn't that dandy?"

"What is it you're not telling me, Hailey?"

I took a deep breath. "Mug Ruith hit me with a curse. That's why I came here. I needed a cure."

"My blood."

I nodded. "Right. Leann found us when we passed through the convergence. She asked me to bite her. She said her power could be used to seduce you into giving me your blood. All she wanted in return was a dose of the cure herself and she said she had something she could give us that would allow us to overpower Mug Ruith's magic."

The Faerie King shook his head. "You've been deceived."

I snorted. "Yeah, I was picking up on that."

"Mug Ruith's curse afflicts all of the Unseelie. It's a part of what makes them Unseelie. It's one reason why our forests are divided. They don't serve him willingly. They do so because they have no choice."

"Like a sire bond with vampires?"

"Similar, yes, but it's more than that. The Unseelie are irrevocably corrupted. Even if the curse was removed, their nature would remain warped, tainted, and power-hungry."

I tilted my head. "If Mug Ruith's curse corrupted them, what about Leann? She said she'd attempted to seduce and feed upon Mug Ruith. That's when he cursed her."

"A half-truth. Leann is a faerie, but she is also a demon. A succubus."

I gulped. "Some kind of nasty hybrid?"

"You could say that."

"Well, that tracks. Succubi drain people's souls through intercourse, right?"

"Precisely. Faerie magic isn't passed through blood that way. If you cycled her power, she infected you not with faerie power, but with demon blood."

"Is there anything we can do to fix that?"

The Faerie King shook his head. "The power will transform you if you use it. Until you do, it will have no power over you."

"So she wanted me to seduce you so I'd transform?"

"That's a part of it. She wanted my blood for the cure, just as you assumed. She also knew if you used her power against me, it would kill me. Her goal is not merely to spread the Unseelie Forest to earth. She wants to corrupt all the faeries, to claim my forest as her own, and from there, all the otherworld."

"So if I don't use her power, we stop her, right?"

"She intended to help you kill Mug Ruith both so that she might have her revenge on him, but also so that you, the protector, might become like her. Her counterpart on earth. You must never use her power."

"Wait. Does that mean no sex?"

"No intercourse at all. If you do, you'll both kill your lover and begin the transformation into a succubus yourself."

"Well, isn't that fantastic? Connor is going to be thrilled."

"Who is Connor?"

I sighed. "My wolf-shifter boyfriend. Are you certain there's no way to fix this?"

"There is one way, but it won't be easy."

"I'm up for the challenge."

"You must kill Leann before your power takes hold. It will not cycle through you completely until you use the power. If she dies, her essence within you will fade."

"Let me put these pieces together. Mug Ruith's curse can only be cured with an elixir brewed from your blood. Leann knew that, which is why she tricked me into all of this. Mug Ruith knew it as well, but he also knew she could never come to the Seelie Forest herself to secure your blood for herself."

The Faerie King nodded. "She is not at all averse to spreading the Unseelie Forest to earth. She simply wishes you, as her progeny, to be the one who spreads it. Not Mug Ruith, who still controls her through the curse."

"If I'm like her progeny, does that mean she can manipulate me, too?"

"Only if you cycle her power and become a succubus yourself."

"How do I kill a succubus?"

"Leann was not wrong. Vampires were made in part from the blood of a succubus but you are also very different. You only consume souls through feeding. You need not kill everyone you bite. That is to say, you are a weaker version of what she is. The same principle applies to how you might be killed. A stake through the heart will kill you, though only temporarily. Your heart must be burned. A succubus can be killed if staked once. There is no need to burn her heart."

"Alright. Well, that makes this a lot easier."

The Faerie King extended his finger. "Except the stake must be forged from the Tree of Life."

I bit my lip. "Alright. Well, the Seelie Forest is connected to the garden groves, correct? We can get to the Tree of Life from here."

"Herein lies the problem. Leann's power has not matured within you, but it's still a part of you. The Tree of Life will not yield the weapon you require to you so long as you're corrupted."

I pressed my lips together. "I brought a friend with me. She's a vampire and a witch as well. Can she get the stake?"

"Perhaps. If she's worthy. Still, to remove Leann's infection, you will have to be the one to drive the stake through her heart."

I nodded. "Alright. So, Mercy gets the stake. She gives it to me. I do the deed. Badda bing. Badda boom. I can screw my boyfriend again."

"Again, this presents us with another complication."

I sighed. "Of course there's another complication. Should have seen that coming."

"In your hand, a living branch or, in this case, a stake from the Tree of Life will burn. The pain you'll have to endure to use the stake will be unlike anything you could imagine. If you do not finish the deed quickly, it may even kill you."

I scratched the back of my head. "Alright. If that's what it takes. I can handle the pain."

"There's still one more matter that must be addressed."

"My cure?" I asked.

The Faerie King laughed. "Yes. I'll give you what you need. However, with Leann dead, you'll still have to deal with Mug Ruith."

"If I'm cured of his curse, he can't use that against me again, though, right?"

The Faerie King nodded. "That is correct. You will be immune to the curse. There are many other ways, however, that he might kill you. He will not be easy to defeat."

I shook my head. "I'll find a way to handle him. Immunity won't hurt. How about that cure?"

The Faerie King glanced down at my hand. "Give me the beaker. I trust the other necessary ingredients are ready?"

"Willie and Wanda took care of that."

The Faerie King smiled. "Yes, Wee Willie Winker. He's been a thorn in my side for years. I hope his exile, however, has proven useful to you."

I tilted my head. "He's been invaluable."

The Faerie King nodded. "Just as I'd hoped. Willie is not our prisoner. We took him before for his protection. When you leave, should he wish to go, he may still serve as your guide. He may even be able to help you defeat Mug Ruith."

"What about Wanda?" I asked. "Surely he'll want to go back to his family."

"Do this, Hailey. Defeat Leann, and I'll lift Willie's exile. I will grant him free passage in the Seelie Forest. He can come and go between earth, to accompany you as a guardian, and here where he may live his life with Wanda."

I smiled. "Sounds like a deal."

"Give me the beaker. I only need one. The other can be discarded."

I handed him both. "You can get rid of the second one yourself."

The Faerie King tossed one beaker aside. He removed the cloth from the top, bit his hand, and his golden blood flowed into the beaker. "Well, how about that? Not everyone bleeds red."

The Faerie King swirled his blood with the ingredients in the beaker and handed it to me. "My blood is different, even from the other faeries. Drink this, and Mug Ruith's curse will fade."

I took the beaker. I raised it toward the Faerie King. "Bottoms up!"

I drank the elixir. A tingle swelled through my body. My vision blurred. The Faerie King took my hand and helped me down to the ground. "This will take some time. You must rest."

Chapter 12

I WOKE UP IN an egg-shaped chamber. The grains of the oak and the glowing golden sap that seeped through suggested I was still inside the Faerie King's tree. I knocked on the wood.

"Hello! Your Highness?"

No one responded. Why was I trapped in a tree? Why would the Faerie King heal me if he intended to put me into some kind of faerie prison the moment I lost consciousness?

There must've been a reason. Willie said faeries couldn't lie. Leann was a succubus, a demon, and a faerie at the same time. Not even Willie knew that about her. She'd been among the Unseelie for so long we have assumed her demonic nature to be a quirk of her particular "brand" of faerie. The Faerie King knew better. I didn't know how old he was, but I had the distinct impression he'd been around a lot longer than faeries like Willie and Wanda.

"Hello!" I shouted again. Still no answer.

At least the elixir worked. The curse was gone. I wasn't going to die. At least not because of the curse.

One side of my egg-shaped prison glowed green. I was about to touch it, to see if I could push myself through, when another body passed through and struck me in the chest.

I fell back, and Mercy was on top of me.

"Damn faeries!"

"What happened?" I asked.

Mercy shook her head. "Wanda sold me out. Tried to make a deal with some of the Faerie King's lackeys. Let Willie go free and they could have me."

I sighed. "Well, I'm cured at least."

Mercy tilted her head. "Are you serious?"

I told Mercy about my conversation with the Faerie King. How I was damned to abstinence until we killed Leann. How she'd have to be the one to secure a stake from the Tree of Life.

"If that's the case, why are we stuck in this... whatever it is... like prisoners?"

I shrugged. "Beats me. The Faerie King added his blood to the beaker. I drank it. He told me I needed to rest. It would take time for the elixir to work. The next thing I knew, I woke up in here."

"Any sign of Willie?"

I shook my head. "He wasn't in the Faerie King's throne room. They must've taken him elsewhere. The Faerie King said he'd be free. Once all this was done, he could come and go at will between earth and the Seelie Forest."

Mercy huffed. "Would have been nice if the faeries explained what was going on before they grabbed me and threw me in here."

"Did you fight back?" I asked.

"I didn't have a chance. Those little buggers are fast. I didn't even see them coming."

I shook my head. "There must be a good reason."

Mercy shrugged. "Maybe he doesn't trust us. Just because faeries can't lie doesn't mean they can't be deceived. And like you pointed out before, we don't know that she can't lie. If she's a demon, well, that's sort of what they do."

"If I was trying to trick him, why would I tell him *everything* Leann wanted us to do?"

Mercy shrugged. "Maybe he wasn't sure that was the truth. One's fiercest enemy will always present himself first as your friend."

I nodded. "Like Leann."

"Right. But perhaps the Faerie King needed to do a little digging to see if your story checks out. You might have told him the truth, but he doesn't know that. It would be irresponsible for him to simply take you at your word. There's too much at stake."

I took a deep breath. "Maybe you're right. I wonder if I could blast us out of here with a spell."

Mercy chuckled. "It might work, but trying to escape wouldn't do much to convince the Faerie King that we're on his side."

I bit my lip. "Yeah, you're right. I suppose a little patience won't hurt. Especially now that I don't have to worry about the curse."

Mercy and I sat down beside one another. I was still tired. Being cursed and cured took a lot out of me. The Faerie King's blood in the elixir didn't satiate my vampiric needs like human blood might. What I would have given for a nice, young, clean-shaven man like Johnathan, ready and willing to open his veins. Usually I could go awhile between feedings. A few days to a week. I could go longer than that if I had to. Doing magic, especially blood magic, made me hungry a lot sooner. Drinking from a succubus, having a sorcerer's curse tear me apart from the inside, and getting cured again, all stoked my appetite.

I rested my head on Mercy's shoulder. She grunted at first—she didn't like to be touched. Then she relaxed and wrapped an arm around me. She ran her fingers through my long, blond hair.

"Hang in there, Hailey. We'll get through this."

I closed my eyes and drifted off. I'm not sure if I totally fell asleep. My body jerked a little. That happens sometimes when I'm falling asleep. Vampires don't *have* to sleep, but as a witch, I slumbered more than most. My magic was stronger when I was well-rested. A little sleep also helped with my cravings.

Mercy shook me awake. When I opened my eyes, I saw another green patch appear on the side of the shell of our cage. Willie flew through and landed on my lap.

"Hailey-boo, and Mercy, too!"

I laughed. "You're well! We were worried about you."

"Understandable! The Faerie King told me everything, but it's all hush-hush. He wanted me to tell you that all was going according to plan, but he couldn't have you two running free. It was best if everyone thought he'd taken you two as prisoners. Can't let anyone know what's happening. There are faeries who engage with the unseelie. Can't risk word of what's going on reaching Leann."

I took a deep breath and released it. "Well, that's a relief. I thought he'd turned on me. Tricked me into drinking that elixir so he could imprison me."

"No worries, Hailey-boo! Glad to hear you're cured!"

I smiled. "You had the right recipe."

"Of course I did!"

The egg-prison started to shake and shift. The change sent Mercy rolling over onto me. She quickly rolled back. "What is happening?"

"We're moving!" Willie said. "Carried by faeries out of the Seelie Forest and into the garden groves!"

Mercy tilted her head. "What are the chances I'll be able to get the weapon we need from the Tree of Life?"

"No clue!" Willie said. "I imagine there will be a test."

Mercy grunted. "I hate tests. I'm guessing it isn't multiple choice."

I shrugged. "Could be worse. Short essays suck, too."

Mercy bit her lip. "Been a long time since I went to school. I'd think essays would be better. At least then I could bullshit my way through it. I suspect it's more like a trial than a test. Something to examine my worthiness or some shit."

"That's exactly what it is!" Willie said. "At least, I assume, that's what will happen. The Tree of Life doesn't bless just anyone. I recommend against bullshitting. The dryads will see through it."

I smiled. We were joking about the test format, of course, but only because Mercy and I were both skeptical we'd pass. I already knew I couldn't do it. Mercy had a lot of virtues, but she also had a lot of skeletons in her closet. There are times in her past when they were *literal* skeletons.

If this was the only way we could kill Leann, and the only way to get rid of this power she tricked me into taking, we had to try.

Chapter 13

Faeries don't fly straight. I'd seen it in the forest before. Even those faerie soldiers, when they were coming for me, didn't fly in straight lines. Mercy and I were like jelly beans in an Easter egg. When the faeries bounced, we bounced.

Willie didn't hang around with us. I couldn't blame him. He was probably one of the faeries carrying us through the forest on our way to the garden groves and the Tree of Life. When he flew out through the oaken shell that formed our little prison he told us to hold on tight.

Hold on to *what* exactly? Our asses?

I don't think I'd ever heard Mercy drop so many f-bombs in such rapid succession. I let a few fly myself. When you're being jostled around and thrown into walls and each other, gosh darn it, and gee whiz don't cut it.

As vampires we could take a beating. We heal fast. When Mercy and I bonked heads, I'm pretty sure it gave me a concussion. I saw stars. Nothing I couldn't overcome in a minute or two.

In the words of the King—not the Faerie King, the King of Rock 'n' Roll—we were all shook up.

The shaking stopped suddenly.

"About damn time," Mercy rubbed the back of her head.

"At least now we know what it feels like to be a scrambled egg."

"That's not funny."

I smirked. "It's a little funny."

Mercy held out her arm and rubbed away a bruise. I had a few, too, but they were fading. Vampire healing rocks.

The light coursing through the surrounding sap turned from gold to an emerald green. The dome over us parted at the apex of the egg and split open. The light of the garden groves hit my face.

I gasped. On earth, sunlight was a problem. Here, it didn't hurt us at all. Then again, there wasn't a sun there at all. The light emanated from the sky itself. This realm *was* light—pure and warm. I could have stood there staring into the light for hours. I hadn't stood in the sun since I was sixteen. That was going on eight years ago. Since then, the few times I'd ventured out into daylight, I was running to take shelter as it burned my flesh. More than a minute or so would leave scars that wouldn't heal as fast as other wounds. This light was healing. My entire body tingled.

When the egg fell away, Willie flew around us. Five other faeries, including the Faerie King, hovered in the air straight ahead. A giant tree, full of green foliage and adorned with a red, bulbous fruit, stood behind them.

I gulped. "The Tree of life."

Mercy nodded. "It's beautiful."

"Follow me," the Faerie King said. "We must appeal to the dryad within and hope he'll sympathize with our situation."

I cleared my throat. "By the way, King whatever your name is, if you have the need to transport me in one of those things again, mind adding a little padding?"

The Faerie King laughed. "My name is Oberon. I apologize for the rough ride. It was the only way to bring you here with no one knowing I was helping you."

I nodded. "Right. We wouldn't want Leann to find out. I get it."

"More than that!" Oberon rested his bony hand on my shoulder. "I have a reputation to uphold. Aiding vampires violates my own laws. Those laws haven't changed. You two are a necessary exception."

"What about these other faeries who helped carry us out?"

"They are my most loyal and trusted subjects. They understand what's at stake. Come, let us summon the dryad."

Oberon approached the Tree of Life. Mercy and I followed him and Willie flew up close behind us.

Oberon tugged on his beard. It was only about six inches long, but nearly reached his waist. He took a deep breath and with green magic in each of his palms, he placed them on the trunk of the Tree of Life.

He squeezed his eyes shut. Was he concentrating or *communicating* with the dryad-protector of the great tree?

The bark on the tree was moving. Almost like it wiggled. A shape that matched the tree's bark stepped out of it. Then a hand. Soon, an entire tree-like creature was standing in front of us. It's strange to see something that looks like it would *move* like an animal. It was human-shaped mostly, but the limbs were long and gangly, and the creature's head was boxy and had a face nearly twice as long as the average human's.

Oberon fluttered his wings and backed away from the dryad.

"Lugh!" Oberon giggled. "You're looking fantastic!"

Mercy nudged me. "I wonder if he barks."

I snickered. "Was that a *tree* joke?"

"Thank you, Oberon," Lugh said. "I see you've brought two of the chosen guardians."

I waved my right hand through the air. "Hey there!"

Lugh tilted his head and narrowed his eyes--which looked almost like knots in the trunk of a tree. "Hello. Oberon, may I have a word?"

"Yes, you may!" Oberon exclaimed.

Lugh walked off in the grass, and Oberon followed. The dryad must've known we could have heard what he was saying on account of our enhanced vampiric hearing, so he spoke a tongue I'd never heard. Mercy's furrowed brow suggested the language was foreign to her as well.

I sighed. "My parents used to speak Pig Latin around me when they were trying to keep secrets. It didn't take me long to figure it out."

Mercy grinned. "This language is distinct. I've picked up a few languages through the years. It's not like anything I've ever heard."

I snorted. "Sort of sounds like Klingon. Do you think they're speaking Klingon?"

Mercy laughed. "It's not Klingon, Hailey."

"Do you know Klingon?"

"No. But I seriously doubt that the Tree of Life's protector-dryad and the Faerie King speak a made-up language attributed to a war-hungry fictional race."

I shrugged. "Maybe the otherworld is infested with trekkies. You don't know."

"Do you see a television set *anywhere?*"

I shrugged. "Maybe he has one inside the tree. You'd be surprised what you can fit inside a tree with a little magic. Besides, if I lived inside a tree, I'd be bored, constantly."

"Don't you mean you'd be a board?"

I shook my head. "The tree jokes keep coming."

"I think Lugh has wood for you, Hailey."

I rolled my eyes. "He has wood for everyone."

"He's covered in bark but isn't wearing clothes. Is that a twig between his legs, or is he just happy to see you?"

I laughed. "You're horrible. You really think you're going to pass this test of virtue?"

Mercy sighed. "I can hear him telling me already. Yeah, we'll overlook all those people you killed back in the day, but you told penis jokes. That's unforgivable."

I tilted my head. "How many people *have* you killed?"

Mercy sighed. "There was a brief period where I gave in to my urges and accompanied Ramon on one of his dismemberment binges. We only killed people who deserved it, though. Heroin dealers. Politicians. People like that."

"You put drug dealers and politicians in the same category?"

"Depends on the politician. This one was running the heroin dealers and using the cartel to fund his campaigns. Plus, he was harassing his intern. Couldn't have that."

"So you were acting as an angel of wrath."

Mercy chuckled. "I did it to feed and indulge in my darker urges. Ramon and I targeted scoundrels just so we could justify it to ourselves."

"Well, it's your past. It's not like you still do that kind of thing."

"Then, there was that time I castrated a priest. He deserved it, too."

"I'm not going to ask why. I can connect the dots."

"When I was first turned, I fed on my younger brother."

"This isn't confession time, and I'm not a priest. Even if I was, I don't have anything you could lob off."

Mercy snickered. "I'm just saying, if this test involves a catalogue of my past indiscretions, there's no way I'll pass."

I shrugged. "He just said we're both guardians."

"Right. Because we kick a lot of ass. That doesn't mean he's going to give us a stake to kill Leann."

"Doesn't mean he won't."

"Think about it, Hailey. This is the Tree of *Life*. Killing shit isn't exactly its modus operandi."

"By that reasoning, why would it give a stake to *anyone*, no matter one's resume of virtue or record of vice?"

I shrugged. "I don't know. Maybe to *save* me from becoming a fucking succubus."

Mercy smirked. "That's redundant, Hailey. You realize that's what succubi do, right?"

I snorted. "Right. They literally screw people to death. Not exactly my idea of the best way to cap off a romantic evening."

"Then take the purity pledge. Lots of people do it, you know."

I rolled my eyes. "Yeah, right. Religious tweens take the purity pledge. Most of them break it. What you're talking about is like a nun's lifetime celibacy vow. I'm not built for that!"

Mercy snickered. "Well, hopefully, the dryad values your sex life as much as you do."

"It's more than that. Oberon explained it all to me. If I ever give in, even once, that's the only way I'll be able to feed. Every time I do it, my victims will die."

"Then don't give in. Even once."

"Whose side are you on, anyway?"

"I'm on your side. I'm just telling you, I'm not exactly optimistic that the dryad is going to be as quick to help as you're hoping."

I shook my head. "Oberon wouldn't have brought us here if there wasn't a chance this would work."

"Oberon wants Leann dead as much as you do. She's a threat to the Seelie Forest."

I scratched the back of my head. "I know. Hopefully Lugh sees it the same way."

Oberon was raising his voice. Lugh was shaking his head. I didn't know what they were saying, but it didn't look good. When Oberon threw his hands into the air and Lugh returned to the tree, the news he brought would not be good.

Oberon flew over to us. He was shaking his head.

"What's the verdict?" I asked.

"The Tree of Life will not provide a weapon meant to kill."

Mercy nodded. "Could have seen that coming."

"So we're screwed?" I asked. "Is there nothing we can do?"

"There is one option, but I don't like it."

I shrugged. "I'm listening."

"The Tree of Life will not provide a weapon. This is not the only tree that might give us something that can be used against the succubus."

Mercy shook her head. "The Tree of the Knowledge of Good and Evil?"

Oberon nodded. "Also known as the Wayward Tree. You'll have to venture into the land of darkness, into Samhuinn. The Wayward Tree is protected by thorny vines. If you can retrieve a thorn from the Wayward Tree, it can kill the succubus."

I bit my lip. "I'm guessing there's a catch."

Oberon nodded. "You'll be able to wield it without pain. That's the good news."

"And the bad news?"

"The Wayward Tree is also vested with powerful magic that will invigorate the darkness within you. It may awaken Leann's essence and transform you the moment you touch it."

"What if I use it?" Mercy asked.

"Hailey still needs to use it to kill Leann. It's the only way to purge Leann's essence. You might kill Leann if you strike her with it, but it won't cure Hailey."

"What will it do to Mercy if she holds it?" I asked.

"Temptation. Beyond what you could imagine. There is no reason to corrupt the both of you. Hailey must take and wield the thorn."

Mercy shook her head. "But you said it will change her, maybe the second she takes it. What will happen to her if she uses it and stakes the succubus?"

"That is why this must be done quickly. When Hailey strikes Leann, it will be as if she plunged the thorn into her own heart at the same time."

I bit my lip. "What if I don't touch it at all?'

"How can you possibly strike the succubus if you don't?" Oberon asked.

I smiled. "Telekinesis. It's one of my abilities."

Mercy cleared her throat. "We'd still have to bring the thorn to Leann. How are we going to get it to her in the Unseelie Forest if we don't touch it."

I pinched my chin. My shirt was already torn. I'd needed it for the beakers. There wasn't much left. "What if we wrap it in material? I could rip my pants. Maybe Mercy could tear off a piece of her dress."

"I cannot say. Take extreme care to ensure it doesn't come into contact with your skin. Not until it strikes Leann. Then, however, you must touch it if you wish to be cured. If you can wait to touch it until the moment before it strikes her heart, you might purge her essence from you before it transforms you."

"How much time are we talking?" Mercy asked.

Oberon shook his head. "I cannot say. The transformation won't take more than a few moments. It must be simultaneous."

"And if I hold the thorn too long before I strike her?"

"It may kill you when it kills her. Once your essence transforms, and nothing of what you are remains, destroying the succubus will destroy you."

I nodded. "Alright. We'll have to be careful. I still think we can pull this off. We just have to make sure that the thorn is in position, that I call when I'm ready to strike, and I make sure it's my hand rather than my telekinetic ability that plunges it into Leann's heart."

Mercy nodded. "It could work, but only if Leann doesn't see it coming. Demons are fast and formidable. So are faeries. She's a bit of both. It's essential she suspects nothing."

"That will be difficult to ensure," Oberon said. "The trees of the Seelie Forest are connected to the Tree of Life. The root system extends deep into the soil of the garden groves. The Unseelie Forest is connected in the same way to the Wayward Tree."

"What does that mean, exactly?" I asked.

"Faeries can travel through the root system," Willie piped up. "If the Wayward Tree is wounded, if someone takes a thorn from the vine that protects it, the effects will radiate throughout the Unseelie Forest."

Oberon nodded. "That's why I didn't suggest we use the Wayward Tree from the start. If you acquired a stake from the Tree of Life, Leann would never know. There is a risk. She'll know what's happening before you even leave Samhuinn. Any faerie in the Unseelie Forest will see what's coming."

I bit my lip. "Fair enough. Maybe she'll know we're coming for her. That makes this harder, but not impossible. She still won't expect me to use my telekinetic abilities."

Oberon crossed his arms in front of his chest. "If I were her, and I found out you'd taken a thorn from the Wayward Tree, I'd do whatever I could to ensure that you touch it. If you're changed before you use it against her, and if you staked her with it after you're changed, you could die."

Mercy nodded. "It's a fair point. Just by forcing you to change, Leann could ensure her own safety. She'd both eliminate you as a threat and turn you into the creature she wants to use as her progeny on earth."

I took a deep breath. "You're absolutely certain that I will die if the thorn transforms me before I can use it?"

"If it happens too soon, Leann will control you. It may not matter if you live or die."

"It's like a sire bond, right? And since I have Nico's bond, if I'm turned into a succubus will that still be active?"

"It is likely," Oberon said. "I cannot say for certain."

Mercy's eyes widened. "That means Leann might not only be able to control you, but she could use you to control me as well."

"How many vampires are still alive who Nico turned?" I asked.

Mercy shook her head. "Not many. Corbin is gone, for instance. His lineage would not be affected. Still, probably half the vampires across the world can trace their lineage to one of Nico's living progeny."

I clenched my fist. "If I touch that thorn and don't kill her fast enough, Leann will not only have me. She'll have a vampire army. All she'd have to do is manipulate the chain of command via sire bonds."

Mercy shook her head. "This might not be worth the risk. Celibacy is still an option, Hailey."

Oberon shook his head. "It's not much of one. You're not the only one who could take a thorn from the Wayward Tree. If Hailey does not give in and become a succubus, all Leann would need to do is capture Hailey. Since your portal home goes through the Unseelie Forest, and the trees there are all connected to the Wayward Tree, I suspect Leann won't allow you to return to earth until Hailey's transformation is complete."

Chapter 14

THIS WAS AN AWFUL plan. The problem was that it was our *only* plan. We had little choice. I couldn't stay in the Seelie Forest or the Garden Groves forever. I was still the best chance anyone had to stop Mug Ruith back on earth. I had to stake Leann with a thorn from the Wayward Tree. I couldn't touch the thorn and I had to go into the Unseelie Forest to do that. If they captured me, Leann could take me into a tree. Since the Unseelie forest was connected to the Wayward Tree, if I so much as touched a tree in that forest, the influence of the Wayward Tree could catalyze my transformation into a succubus.

I was a fly, Leann was a spider, and the Unseelie Forest was her web.

Willie, Mercy, and I headed out from the Tree of Life toward the blighted Samhuinn. I wasn't looking forward to it. I'd been to hell—and this place was just as bad. Annabelle had gone there several times. Mercy once or twice. Their stories about the place weren't exactly inspirational. The place was pure nastiness. The weather there was bad enough—hot as hell, dry as a desert.

There were also monsters. Dragons were a problem. Especially when traveling on foot with no comparable beasts of our own to fight against them. If we saw any, there was only one thing to do—run. The place was also home to a few vile demigods. Snakes were a problem. The most famous of them all was Nachash. Cain dealt with him before. It was the same snake that tempted his parents and earned humanity a permanent exile from the garden groves. I wasn't sure how much of that story was true. Suffice it to say, though, that if a creature holds a part of the blame for the worst of all human inclinations, it's not the sort of creepy crawlie you want to engage. I didn't know what else we might encounter but it was a pretty sure bet that anything we met wasn't going to be cute and cuddly.

The plan was to get in and out of there as soon as possible. The longer we lingered in the realm, the more likely it was we'd encounter *something* dangerous. As if we hadn't already had a terrible, horrible, no good, very bad day.

Crossing the border from the garden groves into Samhuinn was jarring. Sort of like hopping out of a hot tub and directly into a pile of snow—except in this scenario what we were jumping into wasn't freezing cold but unimaginably hot. It was like when the timer goes off, and you bend over to take a pan of cookies out of the oven, and are greeted by a blast of hot air. One degree more and I'd be a vampire roast—all the better for the creatures of this God forsaken realm to serve up for dinner.

Pity the monster who ever tried to make a meal out of Mercy. She was saucy, but also tough. If a dragon tried to swallow her whole, she'd kick out his incisors from the inside. Provided he didn't burn her to death with his breath first. The moral to the story—no matter how much a bad ass you might be, don't get eaten by a monster.

Willie said he knew the way. Some kind of faerie rite of passage. When faeries came of age, they made pilgrimage to both the Tree of Life and the Wayward Tree. Since each tree was connected by its roots to the Seelie and Unseelie forests, respectively, Willie said visiting each tree helped young faerie's natural magic mature. It's how they could discern the difference between Seelie and Unseelie magic.

Willie wasn't phased at all by the heat. The ground was so scalding that I smelled the rubber of my shoes melting.

Vampires don't usually sweat much. Even when I was still human, I perspired less than most. From both the heat of the place and my exertion, my clothes were soaked. The air was so arid that my eyes were dry. They also burned from the sweat.

I could barely see Willie as he flew ahead of us. Mercy wasn't fairing much better.

When you're in hostile lands, home to innumerable deadly creatures, the last thing you want to lose is your eyesight.

My hearing was still intact. I wondered how long it would take before it was also compromised. There were a few times back when I was human that I worked out so hard my ears felt like they were pressurized, like when you go up in an airplane. That hadn't happened to me as a vampire, but this was uncharted territory. I was supposed to be extremely strong *and* fast, but in this place, I felt mortal.

There was something tall and shadowy in the distance. My vision was still too blurred to make it out. Since we were heading straight for it, I hoped it was the Wayward Tree.

As we got closer, the shape crystalized. It was definitely a tree and, so far as I knew, it was the only thing that grew in Samhuinn's arid soil.

As we approached the tree and slowed down, my vision returned to normal. The Wayward Tree was *flourishing,* as if it hogged every last nutrient the soil in this place could offer. It was almost like the tree made the land desolate. If the Tree of Life fed the garden groves and made those lands flourish, this tree did the opposite.

We approached the tree. The vine encircling the trunk was covered in black blossoms. The thorns were almost two feet long.

"How are we going to break one off without touching it?" Mercy asked.

I grunted. My pants were too hot in this place as it was. I dug my nails into the material and ripped it across my thigh, just under the pocket where I kept my wand. I did the same with the other leg.

"We only need one, Hailey."

I nodded. "Yeah, well, if I'm going to wear cut-offs, both legs need to match."

I slipped my legs out of the torn portions of my pants. "Are you sure we can even break these thorns off?"

Mercy nodded and pointed at the vine. "Looks like one was broken off already. You can do it."

"Who would break off a thorn?" I asked.

Mercy shrugged. "Willie?"

Willie was flying around, keeping watch. He looked at the vine. "Could be anything. There's a reason the Wayward Tree is protected. Any number of creatures could have attempted to steal one of the tree's fruits and broke a thorn by mistake."

I sighed. "It doesn't matter. Let's get this thorn and get the hell out of here."

Mercy yanked the pant leg out of my hand. "Let me do it. If I touch it by accident, it might awaken some of my primal vampiric urges, but it won't change what I am. It's safer this way."

I nodded and watched as Mercy placed my pant leg around one of the thorns and snapped it off. She tied each end of the pant leg shut. "Got it. Now let's go kill a succubus."

Chapter 15

We didn't run so hard leaving Samhuinn. We hadn't encountered anything on our way to the Wayward Tree so we weren't as anxious about the return trip.

We were about halfway back to the garden groves when the ground under our feet shook.

"What the hell is that?" Mercy asked.

Willie gulped. "Earthworms."

I chuckled. "Worms? Why would earthworms make that happen?"

"These aren't worms like you know from earth," Willie said. "These are big. Enormous."

I tilted my head. "How big *exactly*?"

The ground under our feet cracked.

"Run!" Willie screamed.

We took off as fast as we could. I looked back over my shoulder just in time to see a giant worm-like creature, with massive jaws and pointed teeth, break through the ground where we stood before, chomping at the air."

I grimaced. "Nasty!"

"They can't see or hear. They sense their prey by vibration."

"So we stand still?" Mercy asked.

Willie shook his head. "It will sense the last place you stepped. It's coming here next. The only way to get away from an earthworm is to run faster than it can burrow. And it's best if you keep some space between you. Multiple vibrations might confuse it."

Mercy and I looked at each other and nodded. We took off at opposite angles, both heading toward the garden groves. An earthworm broke through the ground just behind me. Another one blasted through the ground near Mercy.

"There are two!" I screamed.

"Probably more!" Willie shouted back. "Keep running!"

I didn't stop to ask questions. I ran as fast as I could. More earthworms were shooting out of the ground. I counted six at once and two more a half-second later. There were probably even more.

Another one blasted out of the ground about twenty feet ahead of me. Were these bastards anticipating the direction we were moving? I changed my angle and ran harder. The more I changed my path, the more confusion. That was the theory anyway. I didn't have a chance to stop and ask Willie questions. Willie flew ahead and took chunks of ground and rock and threw them around. The vibrations distracted the earthworms. The little guy was downright brilliant sometimes. The worms were taking the bait and emerged wherever he directed them.

Willie was making bigger vibrations than the pitter-patter of our vampire feet. It was working. He was luring them away from us.

When we reached the edge of the garden groves, I collapsed in the grass. I laid there a moment, staring at the bright sky and took several deep breaths.

Willie landed beside me, giggling. "Well, that was fun!"

I turned and saw Mercy strolling through the green grass, heading toward me. I looked back at Willie and tilted my head. "You have a strange idea of fun."

I stood back up. What clothes I had left were still soaked. I smelled like a gym bag. Mercy wasn't half as wet as me. Maybe I was sweating out Leann's essence. How lucky would that be? It couldn't be that simple. It never was.

Mercy looked me up and down. "You look like shit."

I laughed. "Gee, thanks. That's what I was going for. I hear the shit look is in this season."

"We have one more problem."

I rolled my eyes. "There's always one more problem."

"We have to go through the Seelie Forest to get to the Unseelie Forest."

I shrugged. "Why is that a problem?"

"Because Oberon doesn't want anyone knowing we're running free."

Willie giggled. "Don't you worry about that! I have that covered."

"Please tell me that doesn't mean another ride in a wooden egg."

Willie pressed his lips together and grunted. "Okay."

"Okay, what?"

"You told me not to *tell* you it means another wooden egg. So I will not tell you!"

Chapter 16

THE FIRST TIME WAS bad enough. This time, I was sweaty and stinky. I felt bad for Mercy. No one wants to be stuck in a confined space with someone who smells like a foot. As many times as we bounced off of each other on our trip back through the Seelie Forest, my stench was all over Mercy as well. At least we matched. We were odor twinsies.

It was a good thing Mercy had that thorn double wrapped in my two torn-off legs. I thought it was overkill, but given our rough ride, and how sharp those thorns were, it was likely to bust through like a single-bagged milk jug.

The egg shell opened as before when we arrived at the border of the Seelie and Unseelie forests. The Faerie King wasn't there but his lackeys were—they'd helped Willie carry us through the forest.

I had a small egg on the top of my head that matched the one we rode in. I didn't have a mirror to check, but I took the heel of Mercy's foot in my eye on the ride and probably had a black eye.

I also broke a nail. That would take time to grow back. The faerie realm's public transit system sucked pixie balls.

We stepped out of the egg and onto the dark and damp ground of the Unseelie Forest.

"How are we going to do this?" Mercy asked. "Until we know where Leann is, it's hard to make any definitive plans."

I nodded. "I'll approach her once we find her. She's expecting me to return with the elixir. Get the thorn into position. Untie one end so I can pull it my way with my mind."

"The easiest way to stake her would be to make sure she's between us. You might not get credit for the kill, though, if you aren't touching the thorn when it kills her."

I nodded. "Right. Which is why you need to position yourself somewhere to the side. Make sure there's a straight path to my hand that won't hit Leann or anything else. Once I have it in my grip, I'll stake her. Hopefully, I'll be cured, she'll be out of the picture, and we can turn our worries back to Mug Ruith."

Mercy tilted her head. "Didn't she say before that she'd find us when you came back with the elixir?"

I nodded. "I believe so. We'd best put a little distance between us if we're going to pull this off."

"I'll stay with you." Willie hopped on my back. "She'll expect that I'll be with you."

"She'll expect I'll be here, too," Mercy said. "But if she asks, I guess you could tell her we split up looking for her. You know, to cover more ground."

"Sounds reasonable enough to me. I don't see why she'd question that."

"Hopefully, the other Unseelie faeries won't bother us." Mercy turned past one of the trees to find another path. She had to be far enough away that it looked like we'd split up, but not so far I couldn't call the thorn. There had to be a clear flight path between Mercy and me, so the thorn would arrive when I needed it.

We hiked through the Unseelie Forest for nearly half an hour and hadn't seen a single faerie, much less Leann. Willie hopped off my back and with his wings aflutter, he stretched out his arms and legs. "Maybe we should look closer to the portal where you first arrived."

I took a deep breath and glanced through the trees at Mercy, who looked back at me. She shrugged. "It's worth a shot. Do you know how to get there? I'm lost. Everything here looks the same."

Willie giggled. "Every tree is very different! No two trees are alike, Hailey. You just have to have the eyes to see and appreciate the differences."

I scratched my head. "I get it. No two trees have exactly the same branch pattern. They don't have the same number of leaves. The bark is like a fingerprint. Those aren't the kinds of differences I can easily commit to memory. Maybe if we had something to mark the trees with so I could identify them and make sure we weren't going in circles."

"We're not going in a circle. The gate back to earth isn't too far from here."

I rubbed my brow. The one positive development since arriving in the Unseelie Forest was that it was cool. My sweat dried up, but my clothes were still damp. The breeze chilled the material against my skin. "Lead the way."

Willie flew a few paces ahead of me. He didn't move too fast. He was a lot faster than most bi-pedal mammals. As vampires, we could keep up fairly well, even if he flew ahead at full speed. If reaching the destination was our goal, moving faster would have made sense. We were surveying our surroundings, keeping an eye open for Leann or any other faeries who might be in the area.

Mercy maintained her distance. When Willie and I arrived at the clearing where we'd first appeared when we arrived in the Unseelie Forest, I examined the area. Still, no Leann. I turned and looked for Mercy. She was staring at the ground with one hand over her mouth.

"Did you find something?" I shouted my question through the trees.

Mercy looked up and her eyes met mine. Even from a distance, I could tell she was troubled. I ran over to her and Willie flew behind me.

When I saw what she was looking at, I gasped. There was blood—more violet than red—smeared all over her body. A large thorn was stuck in her chest. Her mouth was agape, as if she'd been taken by surprise.

I opened my mouth but couldn't find the words.

Mercy shook her head. "Someone killed Leann before we could."

My heart thumped hard in my chest. "Who the hell killed her?"

"Who do you think?" Willie asked. "There's only one person who had something to gain by murdering Leann."

Mercy nodded. "Mug Ruith. He must've learned of her plan."

I fell to my knees and rested my face in my palms. "I can't be cured. I can't be with Connor. I can't be with anyone."

Mercy rested her hand on my shoulder. "We'll find a way to fix this. There has to be another way."

"If there was, don't you think the Faerie King would know it?"

Mercy shook her head. "Not necessarily. Leann wasn't only a faerie, Hailey. She was a demon. Oberon doesn't know everything."

"Who the hell might know? Demons aren't exactly open about their weaknesses and secrets."

"You're still a vampire, Hailey. We both are. That means you have a connection to Baron Samedi. he can see everything we can see. We are his eyes and ears in the world. Perhaps he will help."

I huffed. "You expect Baron Samedi to come to my rescue?"

Mercy sighed. "He's the one who first made vampires by using the essence of a succubus to forge our kind out of Niccolo's spirit. He managed to turn Nico into a vampire, a hybrid between a human and a succubus demon. If there's a way to isolate Leann's essence and purge it from your body, he knows how to do it."

I bit my lip. "We'll need Annabelle or another powerful mambo to summon him. We might be his eyes and ears, but he can't materialize out of nothing."

"What do we do now?" Willie asked.

I stood back up and took Mercy's hand. "There's only one thing we can do. We have to go back and try to stop Mug Ruith. We know what he's planning now. We'll deal with my *problem* later."

"Are you sure?" Willie asked. "We could always go back and ask Oberon if he knows another way."

I shook my head. "If he knew another way, he wouldn't have sent us to the Wayward Tree to recover the thorn. Mercy is right. Baron Samedi is the only one who might have the answer. With Leann off the map, though, Mug Ruith still has control over the Unseelie Forest."

"Do you think he's still here?" Mercy asked. "If he's the one who killed Leann, he must've been here recently."

Willie grunted. "If he was here, he'd use the faeries in the Unseelie Forest against us. It's reasonable to assume he's already returned to Exeter."

Mercy kicked a rock at Leann's staked body. "We still don't know how to kill him."

I stared up at the sky, clenched my fists, and screamed.

Mercy put her hand on my shoulder. "Calm down, Hailey."

I shrugged off her hand and stomped away from her. "Don't tell me to calm down! We're just as screwed as we were when we came here. The only plan we had is fucked. I'm fucked because, well, I'll never get fucked again. Chances are that ass hat sorcerer is already growing shrooms in Exeter and he's getting more powerful with every vampire he turns."

"That's not true," Mercy said. "You're immune to his curse now. Plus, you aren't dying."

I huffed. "Might as well be."

"Stop whining. So you can't make love to your boyfriend for a while. Boo fucking hoo. You can resist the urge until we find an answer."

I shook my head. "You heard what Oberon said before. It's only a matter of time before someone finds a way to turn me. If Mug Ruith stole a thorn from the Wayward Tree before us, who is to say he won't use one on me and complete my transformation? He'll use me the same way we feared Leann might. He'll force me to use the sire bond to control other vampires."

Mercy shook her head. "The only reason he could manipulate Leann was because of the curse. He doesn't have that kind of control over you."

I grunted. "You're right. This might be pointless, but we might as well give him our best shot."

Mercy stepped up next to me and put her arm around my shoulder. "Back to Exter?"

I nodded. "I don't know what else to try."

We started to move back to the portal when something grabbed my ankle. I looked down, and a root had wrapped itself around me.

"What the hell?"

Mercy bent over to pull at it, but when she did, another root shot out of the ground and wrapped itself around her body. It pulled her down into the ground. The soil enveloped her. Then the root on my ankle tugged hard. The ground under me cracked.

"Willie! What is happening?"

"It must be the Unseelie Court! I'll try to free you!"

Willie lobbed a green ball of magic at the root around my ankle. The root loosened just in time for another one to shoot out of the ground. It wrapped itself around my waist, my chest, then my neck.

"Let go of me!" I screamed.

The roots yanked me down into the ground. A violet magic enveloped me as it pulled me deeper.

With a thud, I fell onto a hard surface. Mercy was there as well, her body still wrapped in roots. I tried to move, only to discover the roots remained firmly wrapped around my body as well.

A faerie woman approached us. She was like Willie, but her skin was a deep shade of purple, her hair long and black, and her eyes glowed with violet energy. She was as tall as we were—just as Oberon was when I entered his tree.

"Who the hell are you?" I asked.

"My name is Malvessa. I'm the Empress of the Unseelie Court."

I snorted. "I thought Leann was in charge here."

"She is not one of us. She has never been one of us."

"But didn't she rule this place?"

Malvessa narrowed her eyes. "She exploited us for power. That hardly makes her a queen."

"What do you want with us?" Mercy asked.

"I want what you want. Mug Ruith is a threat to all of us. He did us a favor, I suppose, by killing Leann. We are free, now, to operate in our own flesh however we wish. Still, he draws power from our realm and seeks to enslave many of our kind to serve him in his new forest on earth. We'd very much prefer that not to happen."

I struggled against the roots that constricted my body. "you and me both, sister. If you want our help, choking me out isn't the best way to get on my good side."

Malvessa laughed. She raised one hand, and the roots loosened and fell from my body. They returned to the domed black ceiling above. "I simply needed to be sure you'd listen. I've been observing you since you returned to the Unseelie Forest. When I heard you intended to go after Mug Ruith I intervened."

"I thought you *wanted* us to kill him."

"I do! But if you're going to attempt it, I'd prefer to see you succeed."

Mercy glanced at me and shrugged. "She has a point. A few tips wouldn't hurt."

I took a deep breath. "What do we need to do? Do you have a weapon we can use against him? A spell, perhaps?"

Malvessa laughed. "You already have the weapon you need."

Mercy held up the thorn, still wrapped in my pants. "The thorn from the Wayward Tree?"

Malvessa nodded. "Mug Ruith is powerful in his own right, but the greater dose of power he's accumulating is coming through the sacrifice of your kind. He's creating vampires that he might draw power from what your kind has in common with the succubus. Now that he's eliminated Leann—a necessary move since she was scheming to betray him—he requires another vampire whom he might bind and turn into her replacement."

I shook my head. "I'm already cured. That won't work."

"Not you," Malvessa said. "The older and stronger the vampire he corrupts, the better. Your power as a witch must've been a draw for him before. However, this one will do just as well."

Mercy grunted. "The name's Mercy. Not this one."

Malvessa smiled. "Pardon me for failing to ask. Time is of the essence here. The longer this takes, the more power he'll accumulate.

He's already taken more than he needs to complete his mission and create a new Unseelie Forest."

"Are you saying that Mercy is who he is after?"

"I'm suggesting that she might make fine bait."

Mercy raised an eyebrow. "Bait? You can't be serious."

"Since much of his power has been extracted through vampires, and through the succubus, he can be weakened in much the same way that he killed the Leanhuan-Shee. The thorn you hold will not kill him. He is not a succubus, himself. It will give you a chance to beat him."

"Why is he planting his forest, then? Why does he need it if he can curse vampires and make succubi for himself?"

"An Unseelie Forest of his own will give him access to immense power. The larger his forest, the stronger he might become. That is why you must act fast."

I furrowed my brow. "One question. Once he's gone, that convergence will still be open, connecting our realms. What are *your* plans once Mug Ruith is gone?"

Malvessa grinned widely. "My interest is in my own realm. I cannot close the gate between worlds. I can dislodge it from the Unseelie Forest. What realm it might connect to after that will be your problem."

Mercy sighed. "You're saying that there's no telling what monsters might come through the convergence next?"

"Monsters? Angels? Gods? How could I possibly know what will happen. I simply intend to ensure that no other sorcerers from earth take an interest in my domain."

I glanced at Mercy. "That means Willie won't be able to move freely between the Seelie Forest and earth. He'll have to choose where he goes."

Mercy nodded. "It would be best if he remains with Wanda. You're right, though. It's his choice."

I interlaced my fingers and popped my knuckles. "Alright, Malvessa. Send us back. It's time to take the fight to Mug Ruith."

"One question before we go," Mercy piped up. "Do you happen to know how to purge the succubus essence from Hailey?"

Malvessa shook her head. "If I knew how to do that, the Unseelie Faeries would not have endured the Leanhaun-Shee for so long. I know even less about your kind. I am sorry that I cannot help."

I bit my lip. "No problem. You've helped enough. Thank you for the assist."

Malvessa laughed. "I'm hardly the virtuous King Oberon. My interests are my own. Still, if it so happens that saving my realm and our faeries from Mug Ruith also protects the people of the earth, then so be it. Do not mistake this assist, as you called it, for an alliance. Should we cross paths again, under circumstances that are not suited to our mutual benefit, we may very well be enemies."

"Noted." Mercy nodded. "The same goes for you. Don't get any funny ideas about taking over and making an Unseelie Forest on earth after we get rid of Mug Ruith."

"Please." Malvessa rolled her eyes. "Earth is a lesser realm. My ambitions remain here."

I smiled and bowed my head. "Let's keep it that way."

Chapter 17

MALVESSA CHANNELED MORE ROOTS to carry us back to the surface. I wasn't sure if we were inside a tree or some kind of cave when we were speaking to her. Magic was involved. Whatever the case, her roots dropped us back on the ground next to Leann's bloodied body.

Willie was sitting on a large rock with his elbow on his knee and his chin on his fist. When he saw us, he flapped his wings and flew circles around us.

"You're back! Willie was so worried!"

I smiled. "We're fine. It was Malvessa."

Willie shuddered. "You're lucky to be alive at all!"

"Our interests align for now," Mercy said. "She told us how to stop Mug Ruith. We just have to get back to earth and use the thorn against him."

"Right-o!" Willie exclaimed. "Let's go!"

"One thing." I raised my hand to get Willie's attention. "Malvessa said she's going to try to separate the convergence from the Unseelie Forest after we stop him. If you come with us, Willie, you might not be able to get back here."

"You should probably go be with Wanda," Mercy added.

Willie waved his hand through the air. "Nah. She's a nag! Besides, the veil between the worlds is like swiss cheese. If this convergence won't get me back, there are many others that might. What's important now is to stop that sorcerer!"

I grinned widely. "Alright. Glad to have you on the team."

"Are you sure you don't want to tell Wanda goodbye?" Mercy asked. "It might be a while before you get back to see her again."

Willie shook his head. "Wanda will be fine. Earth will not. She will understand."

I bit my lip. "Are you sure about that? She didn't seem to be especially understanding, before."

"Don't worry about her. I've made my choice. Willie wants to fight!"

I smirked. "You really should choose between the first and third person and stick with it."

Willie tilted his head. "Who are these persons you speak of? I see two of you. I am the third. That means we are three persons together!"

Mercy snickered. "Mercy thinks he has a point, you know. It's not exactly a shocker that Wee Willie Winker never attended human grammar school."

I narrowed my eyes. "Hailey finds Mercy annoying sometimes."

We returned to the convergence. It wasn't visible to the vampire eye, but we knew it was there. Willie activated it before when we were back in the forests outside Exter. Would any magic do? It didn't take much. All Willie did was lob one of his magic balls at the clearing.

Magic balls. Not the best name for what he did, I suppose. I wasn't sure what else to call it. Referring to them as faerie balls was ripe for confusion.

No one wants to get blasted with faerie balls. That's the sort of thing that will really ruin your afternoon.

Green and golden magic swirled around the clearing.

"Cannon ball!" I jumped in and tucked my knees. It didn't make a splash, but it worked well enough. Mercy probably belly-flopped in behind me. Willie might have performed a swan dive. He wasn't anything like a swan, but he was the only one who had wings, so he was the best candidate.

We landed in a forest of gigantic mushrooms.

"What the hell?" I asked. "Is this Earth or did it take us back to the Seelie Forest?"

Willie sighed "It's Earth, alright.

Mercy pointed at the sky. "Look at that."

I followed Mercy's finger with my eyes to what looked like a massive wheel of oak floating through the sky. Something like gigantic oars swept through the sky as if the wheel was floating down a river. "Is that what I think it is?"

Mercy sighed. "It's Mug Ruith's flying machine. *Roth rámach.* The one from Saint Columba's prophecy. He's terraforming the forest."

"This looks more like the Seelie than the Unseelie forest."

Willie nodded. "You're right. It makes little difference. It's still a great source of power. It's not the trees or mushrooms that make the Seelie Forest seelie, or the Unseelie Forest unseelie. It's the connection of each to the Tree of Life or the Wayward Tree, respectively. It's the decisions made by the faeries who inhabit and rule it."

"Which tree is this place connected to?"

"Neither," Willie said. "There is no master tree to norm the magic of this place. Everything here is connected, but it operates according to the sorcerer's will."

Mercy sighed. "How are we going to get to him? I'm betting he's up in that giant wheel."

"I can fly up there!" Willie fluttered his wings.

I shook my head. "We aren't sending you up there alone. We have to do what Malvessa suggested. He wants more power. That means more vampires and a succubus. All we need is a hook and a worm."

Mercy shuddered. "I have seen enough worms today to last my immortal existence."

"You realize I'm not talking about literal worms."

Mercy rolled her eyes. "I know. I'm the bait. The oldest vampire with the most influence who he might use in his quest to expand his power. If I'm the worm, though, and the thorn is the hook, how are we going to reel him in?"

I narrowed my eyes. "Not by going after him like this. We need to know more about what's happened since we left. We should go back to Ladinas and find out what he knows."

Chapter 18

THERE WAS NO WAY to get past Ladinas's security measures to go through the armory. He had cameras around there, but he didn't tell us they were monitored. Unless they triggered an alarm, or he or one of his vampires was watching the monitors, they wouldn't see us anyway. The only way to get back to his lair was to reprise our journey through the sewers. Yes, I called it his lair. Birds have nests. Dogs have dens. Men have caves. Vampires have lairs. At least some of them do. Why didn't I have a lair? I wanted a lair!

Casa do Diabo was cool and all, but you can't have an above-ground lair. At least, if you do, it has to be hidden from view. You might get away with a lair at the top of a skyscraper, for instance, if it was hidden behind the façade of a Fortune 500 executive office. The key to a lair was that no one knew it was there. With Casa do Diabo we took the opposite approach—we were hiding in plain sight. There was even lore about the vampires who lived there. Most people laughed it off, but the stories were well-enough known that people steered clear. It worked but, damn it, it just wasn't as cool as a lair!

So, we went all Teenage Mutant Ninja Turtle and headed for the sewers. Why couldn't Ladinas's lair be behind something more sanitary? The basement of a deodorant or pot-pourri factory, perhaps.

Add the sewage smell to my body odor and killing Mug Ruith might not take any effort at all. I'd just show up and raise my arms and say, "take a whiff, buddy!" He'd gag. Death by asphyxiation. Victory: mine.

If Ladinas wasn't home, we were wasting time. If he wasn't home, chances were Mug Ruith had him. Could a dude become a succubus? I'd heard of an incubus before. They were a nineties rock band. Also, a demon who can bone the soul right out of someone. I had to wonder, if I became a succubus, could I do an incubus? Would we kill each other or would our soul-killing sex cancel each other's out?

I had to chase those thoughts out of my mind. This wasn't about me. Not right now. Still, you try having demon blood in you that wants to transform you into a homicidal horn ball and see if you can focus on anything else.

Saving the world was old hat. Been there, done that, killed the bad guy and got the t-shirt.

What I was going through was *existential.* It was like when I became a vampire. It felt like the world I knew before was being yanked away from me and a new life was being thrust upon me. That word "thrust" was going to take on a whole new gruesome meaning if Leann's essence took over.

I still didn't know how Mercy found the way, but we arrived back at Ladinas's door. She knocked. The camera focused on us. I could hear the little mechanisms in the camera moving as it turned and zoomed in on us. The door clicked and opened.

Willie was on my back. He hadn't said much since we got back, which wasn't normal for him. Something was bothering him but I didn't know what it was.

Ladinas welcomed us in himself this time. Demeter was somewhere across the room, most likely, but there were too many vampires in the room to know for sure. If it wasn't for the unusual quiet, I'd have thought a party was going on. You don't get that many vampires in one room without a lot of chatter and noise. The air was thick with stress. It was almost like a funeral and when I walked in, it was like I was the widow everyone felt bad for. Everyone wanted to say something to me but no one could think of the right words to use without resorting to trite cliches.

Then again, maybe they were responding to Mercy, who walked in behind me. She was the famous one, after all.

Either way, these vampires weren't here because they delighted in Ladinas's hospitality. They were hiding.

I guess when a giant wooden wheel is rowing through the skies, younglings are being bred faster than rabbits, and a nasty sorcerer was out there extracting power from vampires, taking cover was a rational response.

"Are you well?" Ladinas asked.

I nodded. "I'm cured. The sorcerer made a lot of progress while we were gone."

"How long ago did he go Proud Mary?" Mercy asked.

Ladinas tilted his head. "Proud Mary?"

"You know. Big wheel keep on turning."

I chuckled. "Right. Tina Turner."

Mercy huffed. "Try Creedence Clearwater Revival. I was living *in* New Orleans when the song came out. Fogerty's version, the original version, is more my style."

I shrugged. "I don't know who that is."

"Seriously? Kids these days." Mercy shook her head.

I furrowed my brow and looked at Ladinas. "More to the point, what do you know about this flying machine? What can Mug Ruith do with it? Does it ever land? We know he's planting a faerie forest. How much land has he covered so far?"

Ladinas narrowed his eyes. "We know little. So far, all he's done is fly around and blast the land with a green beam of magic. The trees change shape. Giant mushrooms sprout up everywhere. It's like he's engaged in some kind of high-level botany project."

"Has he spread into Exeter at all?"

Ladinas shook his head. "So far, he's stuck to the surrounding forests. That doesn't mean Exeter is fine. All the vampires he's been making mean a lot of missing persons. I suspect he isn't transforming the city because he's treating the place like a farm. Raising up humans until he can harvest them as vampires."

Mercy nodded. "He can draw power from the vampires. It connects him to the Unseelie Forest. At least it did. Now that he's gained enough power to grow a forest of his own, I suspect he'll be able to draw as much power as he needs from his new forest. Especially if he enslaves faeries from the otherworld to tend to the forest."

"What is his end game?" Ladinas asked.

I huffed. "He's a bad guy. He wants to take over the world like most bad guys do. Seems kind of dumb, if you ask me. Way too much responsibility."

Mercy chuckled. "It does get a little old. The whole power-trip thing, right? You'd think, eventually, the bad guys would learn that it just isn't worth it."

I snorted. "If I was a villain, and I might be one sometime soon, I wouldn't take over the world. If anything, I'd take over an Island in the Caribbean. Use my powers to fill my island with naked men—preferably a few who have massage skills, cooking skills. You know, things that are useful."

"You're a vampire, Hailey. The islands aren't nearly so enjoyable at night."

"I'm just saying, maybe there's more to it that world domination. Corbin only wanted to take over the world because he thought it was the only way to ensure a secure future for vampires. It wasn't just because he got off on power. There has to be more to it than that for Mug Ruith."

Ladinas shrugged. "Well, good luck finding out. We've tried to reach out to him several times. The man isn't much for conversation."

Mercy stared at me. "What are you getting at, Hailey? Are you second-guessing our plan?"

I shook my head. "Not really. I mean, we learned most of what we know about his plans from a succubus and from a self-proclaimed empress of the Unseelie Forest. It would be nice to know what he's *really* up to and why before we drive a thorn through his heart and I exsanguinate his ass to hell."

Mercy rolled her eyes. "He cursed you before. You were going to die. He turned dozens of people against their will just so he could use the vampires like batteries to charge up his power. Whatever his end game, we can't let him realize it."

I nodded. "I know. You're right. We still have to get his attention. We need him to make a move. Ladinas, where can we bring Mercy so that he'll see her? We think he won't be able to resist coming after her. She's the most powerful vampire around."

Ladinas tilted his head. "I'm older."

"But Mercy is also a witch. She's like a poor man's me."

Mercy raised an eyebrow. "Excuse me?"

"Only when it comes to witchcraft! You're the queen when it comes to bloodsucking."

Mercy smiled and nodded. "Damn straight."

Ladinas pinched his chin. "I don't have any way to fly you up to his ship. We might be able to go back on the hill where we were before. We could shoot up some flares to get his attention."

I scratched the back of my head. "What if Mug Ruith only takes Mercy and leaves me behind?"

"Then I try to stake him by myself. I have the thorn."

I sighed. "He's strong. I don't know if you can get close enough."

"I'm a determined bitch. I'll find a way. But if he tries to take me, you come along if you can. Same plan that we had for Leann except, this time, you can't touch the stake. Killing him won't purge her essence from you, but you can still use your ability to pull the stake through the air. He doesn't know you're telekinetic. We might be able to take him by surprise."

I nodded. "We'll only get one shot at this."

"We'll have to act fast. The first chance you have, you have to take it."

"The stake won't kill him. Malvessa made it clear it will only weaken him. He might still wreak a lot of havoc with his ship if we don't kill him as soon as we stake him."

Ladinas turned to the rest of the vampires in the room. "Alright, everyone! Time to arm up!"

Mercy grinned. "If he gets away from us, take him down."

Ladinas smirked. "This is what we do. All we need is an opening, and that sorcerer is going down."

Chapter 19

WILLIE PULLED ME ASIDE as Mercy followed Ladinas, Demeter, and the other vampires through the security door to the armory.

"What's up, buddy?"

"Something about all of this doesn't feel right. That forest he was making, it was like the Seelie Forest."

"Right. He's still in charge of it. He's using the power himself."

"I understand that. I said it before. It's the character of the one wielding the power that matters. That forest isn't evil. There's good magic there. If there's a way to use it, to save it, we should try. Especially since it's over a convergence."

"Do we know what will happen to the forest if we kill him?"

Willie shook his head. "Someone will have to take charge of it. Someone who can handle magic."

"Ladinas doesn't have anyone here who can do that."

"I can," Willie said. "What I'm trying to say is this. If you stop Mug Ruith, I'm not going back to New Orleans. We can't let that forest fall into the hands of someone unseelie."

I chuckled. "Wee Willie Winker as a Faerie King. I like it! You might even bring Wanda back as your queen."

Willie winced. "Yeah. I'll have to think about that."

I chuckled. "Well, your marriage is your business, Willie. Whatever the case, I think it's a splendid plan."

"I am sorry I cannot come back to help you get rid of Leann's essence."

I shook my head. "Don't worry about that. If I need your help, I'll know where to find you."

"But first we have to stop Mug Ruith!"

I gave Willie a thumbs up. "That's right. We've got this."

Willie thumbs upped me back. "Right-o Hailey-boo!"

Willie and I pulled up the rear and followed the rest of the Exeter vampires through the security door, up the elevator in groups of six or seven at a time, and to the armory. Ladinas had to stay in the elevator to activate the palm and retina scanners. The vampires knew what to do. Some of them had their own lockers with stake-proof armor. Demeter fitted Mercy and me into a set of our own again. Since my shirt was shredded, mine wasn't covered. It didn't matter. It would stop a stake if Mug Ruith or any vampires with him knew I was wearing it or not.

I touched my leg. My wand was in my pocket, ready for action. I didn't need rifles or crossbows. My magic was my weapon.

We headed out through a few more security doors and went outside. We were fortunate when we returned from the faerie realm that it was night. It was still dark. We had plenty of time before sunrise. We didn't know how many vampires Mug Ruith had with him. He might have been more vulnerable during the day. He wouldn't have any vampires to protect him. Provided they would protect him. He was sacrificing them for his cause. Still, we couldn't fight him during the day any more than the vampires at his side could fight alongside him.

Mug Ruith had created most of this new faerie forest during the day while Mercy and I were gone. If we didn't end this at night, now, there was no telling how much more he might do the next day. We didn't know how much more powerful he might be the next night if we missed this chance.

The vampires marched through Exeter to the edge of town. We had to go straight through Mug Ruith's faerie forest to reach the hill. It was risky. We were in his domain. He had control of the magic that flowed through the trees and mushrooms.

I expected vampires to jump out at us from behind the trees. Maybe more would blast up from under the ground like before. If not vampires, maybe more roots like Malvessa used to pull us into her chamber.

The magic radiated off of everything. As a witch, I could feel it. It wasn't a magic I knew how to harness, but I knew if I could, there would be very little I *couldn't* do. That scared me—because at the moment, Mug Ruith controlled all of it. He knew how to use it. Why, then, didn't he stop us then and there? Perhaps he didn't know we were coming. He was still in his flying wheel soaring above, blasting the ground around the perimeter of the forest, planting more trees and sowing more seeds and mushroom spores. Every second that passed made him stronger.

We made our way to the top of the hill without any interference. We didn't crawl on our bellies this time. We were trying to get the sorcerer's attention. Mercy and I stood at the apex of the hill. Demeter launched a series of flares toward Mug Ruith's flying machine as it flew overhead.

The giant wheel violated every principle of aerodynamic science. There was nothing about its shape or structure that suggested it could fly. Faerie magic powered it—a lot of it.

The wheel turned slowly in the sky. The oars on the side continued to row. It crept its way back toward us and hovered over where we stood.

A green beam of magic blasted from the bottom of the wheel and enveloped Mercy and me. It didn't hurt. It tickled a little. It tugged at us until we found ourselves floating over the ground. Like a tractor beam on the Starship Enterprise, it drew us into the hull of the wheel.

When the magic faded, Mercy and I were standing alone in a closed room. It wasn't egg-shaped at least.

Mercy huffed. "Well, great. We're in a prison."

"I'm not so sure. I guess he left Willie behind. He was on my shoulders when the beam struck."

"He doesn't want a faerie interfering with his faerie magic."

I nodded. "Probably not. Stand on the opposite side of the room. If he shows up, we need to be ready."

The ceiling above us turned green—just like the egg shell did when Willie passed through it.

"I think he's coming." Mercy untied the top of the pant leg that was still holding the thorn from the Wayward Tree. "Be ready to do this. Don't hesitate."

I nodded and watched the green glow get brighter. Mug Ruith passed through it and floated down to the ground.

"Welcome, guardians. It's high time we had this conversation."

"No conversation!" Mercy shouted.

I tilted my head. "What are you doing here? What is your purpose?"

"I'm doing my part to save the world!"

I snorted. "Save the world?"

"Hailey!" Mercy shouted.

I furrowed my brow. "No, I want to hear this."

Mug Ruith looked my direction. His eyes were blank, his irises faded. I almost forgot he was blind. He was looking at us in spirit gaze. Maybe he sensed my magic as a witch. Still, it was as if he was looking through me rather than at me. "I was imprisoned in the Unseelie Forest for centuries. When the gates failed, I escaped."

"Yup," Mercy said. "Knew that already."

Mercy stared daggers at me across the room. I couldn't do it. I had to hear him out.

"You've been sacrificing people's lives. You really expect us to believe you're saving the world?"

"I am a druid! The earth is and always has been my home. Do you know what the Leanhuan-Shee intended to do? I knew this gateway was the key to her plan. I had to gather power by any means necessary to protect and seal the portal."

I shook my head. "You still took people's lives. You turned dozens of humans into vampires. How did you do it?"

"There are some of your kind who understand what I'm doing."

"I need a name!" Mercy demanded. "What vampire is helping you?"

Mug Ruith shook his head. "It doesn't matter. You don't know him. He's not among those who were with you when I brought you here."

"You cursed me!" I shouted. "I was going to die."

"You attacked me first. The curse never would have killed you. You're a guardian. I can only protect this portal. There are others elsewhere and you're needed. Still, I had to do what I had to do."

"Leann is dead," Mercy said. "She's no longer a threat. You can stop this. We can guard the convergence."

Mug Ruith tilted his head. "She's dead?"

"You killed her!" Mercy shouted.

Mug Ruith shook his head. "It wasn't me. Though I would have done it if I had the chance."

"How many more people have to die?" Mercy asked.

"This is just the beginning. I must maintain my power. I must get stronger. The powers from the other side are infinite."

I tilted my head. "You won't stop sacrificing people so you can gain power? This is how you intend to protect the world?"

"You don't understand what's at stake. You don't know the Unseelie Faeries like I do."

"I've heard enough," Mercy said. "This has to stop."

"I am sorry. I cannot stop. The sacrifice is necessary for the sake of the world."

I raised my hand. I wasn't sure I could do it. Mug Ruith furrowed his brow. He raised one hand and clenched his fist. A blast of magic hit me and threw me back.

As I hit the wall, I saw Mercy take the thorn in her hand. Her eyes were always red, but when she touched the thorn, they glowed. She charged Mug Ruith and plunged the thorn into his chest. "This ends today!"

I struggled to my feet. The whole airship shook. The surrounding wood cracked.

"What have you done?" Mug Ruith cried.

"What I had to do."

"My power is the only thing stopping the Unseelie Faeries from invading."

"Malvessa told us she had no interest in this world," I grunted.

"She lied!"

"Faeries can't lie!" Mercy screamed.

Mug Ruith shook his head. "The Wayward Tree invigorates the Unseelie! That's the seat of the original deceit. Most faeries cannot lie. That's not true of Malvessa. She's already coming. I can feel it!"

"How do we stop her?" I asked.

"This thorn purged me of my power. I can't wield it. My vessel is failing. If she gets control of the forest, all will be lost. There will be no stopping her!"

The floor beneath us cracked. The crack widened. I could see the forest below. It was a long drop.

When the vessel fell apart, we fell with it. This was going to hurt. Mercy and I could survive. Could Mug Ruith? He wasn't a threat. He knew things we didn't.

As we fell, gunshots fired. Demeter was a crack shot. I didn't realize he was such a great sniper. Blood spurted out of Mug Ruith's chest as his body hurtled to the ground.

Something grabbed me by my stake-proof vest. I craned my head back. It was Willie. He cast some magic around me. It formed a bubble and slowed my descent. Willie left me and darted through the air and grabbed Mercy. He gave her a bubble like mine.

"Willie!" I screamed. "You have to take the forest!"

He didn't respond. He was too far away. I looked down. We were floating down over the stone circle. Red magic swirled over the ground. Mug Ruith's body crashed to the ground just outside of the circle.

A host of dark figures blasted out of the portal. They had wings. As they emerged the trees all around turned black. The mushrooms burst, filling the air with spores. I didn't know if Malvessa was one of the faeries. From a distance, I couldn't tell.

Willie flew down and found the biggest tree that hadn't yet turned. He flew into it. The foliage glowed green. Somehow, he was using its power. The dark power continued to spread but it didn't encroach on Willie's tree. It was a single Seelie stronghold in an expanding Unseelie Forest.

My bubble landed next to Mug Ruith. It popped when it hit the ground. I ran over to the sorcerer. His chest was covered in blood—both from the thorn and from Demeter's shot.

He was barely breathing. Somehow he survived the thorn, the gunshot, and the fall. He wouldn't live for long. I grabbed his feet and dragged him toward Willie's tree.

Mercy was running ahead. She saw everything that happened. She touched Willie's tree and disappeared. I picked up the pace. With my vampiric strength, it wasn't as hard as one would think to drag the sorcerer's dying body behind me. More Unseelie faeries were flying out of the portal. How long could Willie hold the tree? Would it stand against an entire Unseelie Forest?

Still holding on to Mug Ruith's ankle, I touched the trunk of the tree. It pulled both of us in.

We found ourselves standing in a hollowed-out room, not unlike Oberon's throne room. This room, though, was bare. No fancy furniture or decorations.

"Why did you bring him in here?" Mercy asked.

"Because he's still alive. Just barely. If he knows anything that might help, we need answers."

Mercy sighed. "Fuck it. I already touched it once."

Mercy yanked the stake out of Mug Ruith's chest. She bit him on the neck and sucked the blood out of his body.

"What are you doing?"

"I'm saving his ass. At least this way he'll be bound to me as his sire. Grab your wand. Get a healing spell ready."

I bit my lip. "Just when shit couldn't get any crazier."

Mercy bit him again. She continued draining him of whatever blood he had left. I aimed my wand at the sorcerer and cast a healing spell over him. It took a lot of power. He wasn't just drained of blood; he had some serious injuries.

Mug Ruith gasped for air. His eyes shot open. His irises were dark now. The only light we had in the room was from the magic that Willie was using to maintain control of the tree. I leaned over and looked Mug Ruith in the eye. His eyes *were* red. By the way he looked past me, though, he was still blind. My spell hadn't healed everything. It did make him a vampire.

Mercy grabbed the sorcerer by his neck and pulled him to his feet. Not the gentlest approach, but certainly effective. He was weak. His knees wobbled under him, but Mercy maintained her grip on his jugular. "Tell us how we can stop them."

Mug Ruith grimaced. He gestured to the thorn that was lying on the floor. The thorn was coursing with magic. He might not see everything, but his spirit gaze allowed him to see magic clearly. "Use it on Malvessa."

"I can kill her with it?" Mercy asked.

Mug Ruith shook his head. "Not you."

I gulped. "I have to do it? If I touch that thing, I'll become a succubus."

"And it was a succubus, the Leanhuan-Shee, who dominated the Unseelie Empress before. She won't be able to hurt you if you change."

Mercy gulped. "Hailey. You don't have to do this."

I took a deep breath. "Yes, I do. If it stops this from happening, well, I'll just have to deal with it."

"It will turn you into a demon! We don't know if there's any way back from that if you do it."

"If I don't do this, Malvessa will rule an Unseelie Forest on earth."

"There is a way you can come back from this," Mug Ruith said. "It's not common. It may only be a myth, a legend."

"Spit it out!" Mercy demanded.

"The thorn will affect your transformation, but it will not be permanent until you embrace your power as a succubus. You can resist it and purge the demonic essence from your spirit, but only through repeated acts of valor, through the sheer force of your will."

"Acts of valor? What does that mean?"

Mug Ruith shook his head. "I cannot say. The Wayward Tree corrupts, but only when you allow its corruption to claim you. Your will is paramount. You must resume your role as a guardian. Fight what's evil.

Only you mustn't kill a human—not by your abilities as a succubus, and not by any other means. You must remain pure of heart."

"But I can kill Malvessa with the thorn, right?"

Mug Ruith nodded. "You can. Kill her if you can catch her. If not, the next best thing is to chase her back through the portal. If your faerie here can reclaim the forest, he can hold her off as I did before."

Mercy cleared her throat. "One last question. Who the hell is the vampire who helped you before? I can make you speak now that I'm your sire."

Mug Ruith took a deep breath. "His name is Ramon De Leonne."

Mercy gasped. She took two steps back. She shook her head. "No. It can't be. Ramon became human again."

"When he learned of the convergences, and my plan to stop it, he found a young vampire to turn him again. He wanted to help. To save his family."

"Who turned him!" Mercy screamed.

Mug Ruith shook his head. "It doesn't matter. He approached Ladinas first. Ladinas turned him down and offered him protection instead. Ramon was dissatisfied with that arrangement. No matter, Ramon's sire is dead. He was among those you killed when you came after me in the forest the first time."

"They weren't killed," Mercy said. "Those bullets leave wood splinters in the heart. They can still be revived. It's not easy."

Mug Ruith pressed his lips together. "It's not possible. Ramon burned out his sire's heart himself. Then he ripped him to shreds. He's out of control. He's a monster. It took all my effort when I still had my power to restrain him. Now, he has an entire army of equally brutal and vicious vampires that he turned for me. They were meant to be sacrifices. That's not going to happen anymore. Thanks to you."

Mercy slammed her fist into the side of the wall. The entire tree echoed with thunder when she struck it. "Fuck!"

"I know you love Ramon, still. I'm sorry this happened."

Mercy clenched her fists. "Go kill that damned faerie. Make it painful. I'll deal with Mug Ruith."

"Don't hurt him!" I grabbed Mercy's hands and stared her straight in the eyes. "I know you blame him for what happened to Ramon, but he's under your control now. He still knows strong druidic magic. We might need him."

Mercy huffed. "Fine. I won't kill him. That doesn't mean I can't kick his ass until I feel better."

Mug Ruith gulped. His eye sockets widened and his eyes wandered. Mercy delivered a swift kick to his face, and he fell to the ground. "I'll deal with him later."

I took a deep breath. I picked up the thorn. A pain spread through my body. My blood boiled. I started to sweat. I had the sudden urge to screw every male in sight—Mug Ruith, even Willie.

"What's happening?" Mercy asked.

I shook my head. "Don't worry about it. It's done. I'm a succubus. Good fucking times."

"No good fucking times for you, missy."

I glared at Mercy. "Not funny."

Mercy smirked. "Let's end this."

"Wait!" Willie said. "I need you here. It's not safe for you out there."

"I'm not staying in here while Hailey goes to battle alone."

"She's not alone," Willie said. "Ladinas and the others are coming down to fight. I need your help to hold this tree as long as possible. If we lose this tree, even after Hailey kills Malvessa, I won't be able to reclaim the rest of the forest. You can wield magic. I need your help."

"I'm a witch," Mercy said. "I don't know faerie magic."

"You don't need faerie magic. Any power you can lend me, I can repurpose."

Mercy huffed. "Fine. I'll try."

I nodded. "Willie. How, do I get out of here?"

"This tree can't hold you. You're a demon now. Walk through it."

I huffed. "I'm not a demon. I just have a demon's body. Sort of."

"All the same," Mercy said. "Go kick some faerie ass."

Chapter 20

I PUSHED MYSELF THROUGH the tree. Walking through wood is weird. I wasn't thrilled about becoming a succubus, but if immunity to faerie magic and the ability to move through faerie trees was a perk of my new nature, I intended to make the most of it.

No sooner did my feet hit the grass and dozens of red faerie balls came flying at me. One of them struck me in the chin. Don't hit me in the chin with your balls. I'll bite you down to size.

I tightened my hand on the thorn. I charged every faerie I saw. When I struck them, they exploded in a shower of red magic. I dropped five or six of them before they got the message and fled.

The boulders surrounding the portal shook. One of them flew out of the ground. I looked past it and saw Malvessa. She used her power to throw it at me.

I braced myself. When the boulder hit me, it shattered around my shoulder. It also hurt like hell. She threw more at me. One after the other. I lost my balance and fell back.

"You think you're so clever, vampire!" Malvessa shrieked.

She grabbed a branch from one of her dark trees and snapped it off. She had a stake. She charged at me as I got to my feet. The stake hit my chest. My vest stopped it.

"Yup. More clever than you, bitch!"

Malvessa's eyes widened. I took off after her. She darted through the trees. She was fast. So was I. She had wings. I didn't.

She flew over me. She placed her hands on either side of her face, pushed her thumbs to her temples and wagged her fingers as she stuck out her tongue. "Na na na boo boo!

I flipped her off. Never flipped off a faerie before. It was oddly satisfying.

"I can do this all night! Can you do it once the sun comes up? Don't think so!"

I grunted. She had a point. All she had to do to avoid the thorn was stay beyond my reach.

I was going to have to get creative. I had my wand. Most of my magic didn't work well on faeries or anyone wielding faerie power. I learned that lesson the hard way when I tried to capture Mug Ruith in a blood prism. It didn't matter that his curse wasn't meant to kill me. I thought I was going to die, and that wasn't a feeling I wanted to experience again. I didn't know what Malvessa could do if I tried to throw a spell at her. I didn't know much about the extent of her abilities. All I knew was that her magic couldn't hurt me. That might not be true if she reflected my own magic back at me.

My telekinesis might work if I could throw something at her. I couldn't throw the thorn at her. I couldn't move objects at will. All I could do was pull objects through the air toward me. Given that Malvessa could fly, she could easily soar up over the trees, and there wouldn't be anything I could use to knock her down.

Gunshots sounded from a distance. Demeter was one hell of a shot, but hitting a faerie was more than I could expect.

I was at a loss. Malvessa was right. All she had to do was evade me until morning. I'd have to hide back in Willie's tree or retreat to Ladinas's lair. There was no telling how many faeries she might bring to earth while I was out of commission.

The sound of several sets of footsteps approached. I turned to see Ladinas, Demeter, and the rest of the vampires heading my way. I was glad it was them. I didn't know where Ramon was with his vampires. With Mug Ruith down, he was probably off wreaking havoc on the town or hiding somewhere to regroup with his army of younglings. I had no reason to suspect he'd take sides with Malvessa. He had his own agenda. Knowing Ramon's history, that agenda included a lot of dismemberment. Taking over the world or wielding faerie power wasn't his priority.

"How can we help?" Ladinas asked.

I pointed at Malvessa as she flew around the top of the trees. "We have to bring her down. I need to stake her with this thorn, or at least chase her back into the portal. I can't get to her."

Ladinas chuckled. "We've got this. Demeter?"

Demeter smiled widely. He extended his hand. One of the other vampires handed him what looked like some kind of bazooka.

Demeter took a knee and lifted the bazooka to his shoulder. "Check this shit out."

I watched as Demeter fired something at Malvessa. It wasn't a rocket, which is what I expected, but a giant net.

It expanded over her and fell around her. I didn't know if it would hold her but it gave me a shot.

I took off toward the net as it pulled the Unseelie Empress down. She fluttered in a panic in the net.

I plunged my thorn into the net and hit her between the wings. She shrieked and exploded in a puff of red magic. Screams sounded from all around the forest. The Unseelie Faeries blasted past us. They avoided me—for good reason. They poured through the portal. As the faeries retreated, the surrounding forest changed.

The trees turned green again. The mushrooms swelled. A palpable magical tingle spread through the air.

I chuckled. "Willie is taking the forest back."

Ladinas grinned. "I think it's high time we call him Big Willie."

I snickered. "I'm not sure that comes out the way you mean it."

Ladinas laughed. "Fair enough. Good work. What's next? Any thoughts?"

I took a deep breath. "You don't want to know what I'm thinking."

Ladinas tilted his head. "What's that?"

"I want to rip off your clothes and have my way with you."

Ladinas's eyes widened. "Far be it from me to say no to a good time."

I shook my head. "Trust me. It wouldn't be a good time for you. I'm a succubus now. My desires aren't exactly savory."

Ladinas took two steps back. "Alright, Glenn Close."

I tilted my head. "Huh?"

"*Fatal Attraction*. Don't tell me you don't know that movie."

I snorted. "Heard of it. Never seen it."

"The point is, I appreciate your desire for me. Given what you've shared, I'll have to pass. I prefer my love making not be accompanied by death. Nothing personal."

I snickered. "No offense taken."

Chapter 21

WE SETTLED ON THE title King Willie over Big Willie. This was his Seelie Forest, now. If he chose to share his rule with Wanda, that was his business. His primary goal, though, was to guard the convergence. So long as he ruled the forest, we had a good chance of keeping the bad faeries away. That didn't mean the convergence wasn't still a problem. The convergence could connect to another realm. Maybe even Samhuinn. If those earthworms came through, there'd be a problem. Still, the Seelie Forest was a first line of defense against whatever might attempt to break through.

We went back to Ladinas's lair to shelter for the day. Mercy pulled me aside.

"I have to talk to you about something."

I took a deep breath. "You're staying."

"I've been in New Orleans for more than a century. It's time I returned home. These vampires could use someone who can handle magic."

I raised one eyebrow. "That's not the reason. You and I both know why you're staying."

Mercy took a deep breath. "Ramon."

"If anyone can get him under control, it's you."

Mercy shook her head. "I had to use my compulsion abilities before to keep him in check. Now that those abilities are gone, this will not be easy."

I hugged Mercy. It was the closest thing to any sort of intimacy I'd get with anyone in the near future. "You've got this."

Mercy hugged back, then put her hands on each of my shoulders. "*You've* got this. Remember, you can overcome this through the force of your will."

I shook my head. "I don't know what I'm going to tell Connor."

"If he loves you, he'll wait. You're worth it."

For some reason, tears welled up in my eyes. Was it because Mercy was staying here and I had to go back to New Orleans without her? Or was it because it scared me that Connor and I wouldn't make it? Probably some of both. He would want to wait for me, but I didn't know how long it would take to overcome this succubus problem. It could take years, maybe decades. I couldn't expect him to wait that long. I didn't know if I could trust myself around him. My urges were strong. I wasn't even particular about it. I couldn't look at anyone with a Y chromosome without having unsavory urges.

I was even attracted to Mug Ruith. How gross is that? He looked like someone had dipped his entire body into a wood chipper. Still, he had the working parts my succubus nature required. I had to wonder what would happen if I screwed a vampire. Technically, a succubus fed on souls. Baron Samedi held the souls of every vampire. Would I rob the Baron of the vampire's soul if I laid with a vamp? Would it hurt the vampire at all? I didn't know and I couldn't afford to experiment. If I fed the succubus once, the change would be permanent.

Mug Ruith was sitting by himself in the corner. Imagine that. He wasn't making friends. "What are you going to do with him?"

Mercy shook her head. "I don't know."

"What about Mel?" I asked.

Mercy sighed. "She should be with me."

"Tommy is still my progeny."

"He has to stay with you."

I grunted. "They will not like that. They'll want to be together."

Mercy shrugged. "Distance makes the heart grow fonder."

I snorted. "That's the kind of crap that people in long-distance relationships say to make themselves feel better."

"If Pauli will help, perhaps they can visit each other periodically. Until they both have their cravings totally mastered, that's how it is going to have to be."

I laughed. "I can handle Tommy. You really think Mel is going to play ball with this plan?"

Mercy shrugged. "She doesn't have a choice. It's not forever. None of this is forever. Don't forget that. We're all going to get through this."

"I'll have to take your word on that. Right now, it's pretty overwhelming."

Mercy rolled her eyes. "I get it. But you killed freaking Dracula. You defeated Corbin. You just killed the Unseelie Empress. This isn't the biggest challenge you've faced."

I shook my head. "It's one thing when your enemy is someone else. It's another thing entirely when my enemy is a part of me."

"You didn't have to deal with cravings as a youngling like a lot of vampires do. Annabelle helped with that. So did your magic. What you're enduring is unique, but at its basic level, it's a craving you have to resist. It's not anything other vampires haven't overcome before."

"Most younglings slip up once or twice. I can't slip up even once."

"You know what's at stake. Bad vampire pun not intended. It's not just your future and who you'll become. Other people's lives are at stake. When a youngling slips up, they might tell themselves they can get away with a reckless feed without a body left behind. You're guaranteed that anyone you screw is as good as dead. You're not a killer. Never have been. Stay true to yourself and you'll be fine."

A wide grin split my face. "I might need a distraction. Maybe I'll redecorate Casa do Diabo."

"Don't go crazy. It's still *my* house."

Chapter 22

MERCY CALLED PAULI TO come pick me up. He couldn't find Ladinas' lair so we had to wait until nightfall.

You know what's really crazy? I had desires for Pauli when he showed up. That he was naked when he shifted out of his snake form didn't help. Thankfully, he didn't reciprocate my desires. He was like me—he exclusively desired anyone and everyone with a Y chromosome.

Maybe I'd join a convent. I'd have to convert to Catholicism. I wasn't sure if they accepted vampires. They probably didn't accept succubus demons. I don't know why not. Go figure. Still, it was a way to avoid temptation.

Monastic living probably wasn't the test of character and virtue I'd need to overcome this. I was a guardian. New Orleans was riddled with mystical convergences. If the city wasn't already swarming with otherworldly monsters, it was only a matter of time. Hiding away and avoiding men at all costs would not cut it.

Pauli teleported me back to Casa do Diabo. Connor wasn't there. I wasn't looking forward to that conversation. I had to have the talk with Tommy and Mel first. Pauli was waiting to take Mel to Mercy.

Mel wasn't especially thrilled with the arrangement. I knew she wouldn't be. Tommy took it better. He was a glass-half-full type. Still, I could tell it broke his baby vamp heart when Pauli took Mel away. Young love was crazy like that. An old married couple, like Willie and

Wanda, might look forward to time apart. That didn't mean they didn't love each other. Love evolves and matures over time. Sometimes it's strained and fades.

When you're in a new relationship and infatuated with each other, even a few days apart feels crushing. Emotions like that could be especially volatile for a young vampire. I was going to have to keep a close eye on Tommy for a while. I'd have to accompany him on his feeds.

I wasn't looking forward to that at all. I wasn't even sure if I could feed directly from someone without indulging my demonic side. I was going to have to drink from a glass for a while. It was the safest option. Taking Tommy out for a feed and chaperoning his meals was going to be like taking a sober alcoholic to a bar. Come to think of it, maybe I could benefit from a twelve-step program. Hello. My name is Hailey, and I'm a murderous succubus.

There probably weren't a lot of groups out there for folks in my situation.

I decided to have the conversation with Connor over the phone. It was tacky. It wasn't a break-up, but it felt like it. I didn't know how I'd react if I was alone with him in person. I mean, good lord. I was attracted to Mug Ruith, Pauli, and even Wee Willie Winker. I knew it wasn't a real attraction. It was more like a hunger that manifested as sexual desire. I didn't trust that I could control myself around someone I genuinely wanted to be with. Maybe my love for him would give me the strength to resist. Maybe my succubus nature would take over.

Connor understood the reasons. He wasn't any more thrilled with the arrangement than Mel and Tommy were with their situation.

Usually, Connor and I talked for hours. If we weren't together in person, we could sit on the phone all day long and talk about nothing at all. This was possibly the shortest phone call we'd had in months. Once the truth was out there, once he knew we couldn't be together for a while, there wasn't much to say. He needed time to process it all.

I finally got my shower. I'm not sure I'd ever seen the shade of brownish-yellow that colored the water as it ran off my body. Once I sufficiently purged myself of the combined odor of sewage and sweat, I curled up in my bed.

Sarah agreed to keep an eye on Tommy. She wasn't his sire, but she was better suited to watch him at the moment. I was exhausted and, damn it, he was a dude. I needed some time away from someone who awakened my desires.

I turned off my phone. I didn't want any distractions. I wasn't sure if I could sleep. I didn't have to sleep, and it's difficult for vampires to get to sleep.

I was just dozing off when the doorbell rang. I pulled the covers over my head. Sarah could handle it.

A few minutes later, there was a knock on the door.

I groaned. "What do you want?"

The door squeaked when it opened. I felt someone's fingers run through my hair. I turned to see Annabelle looking at me.

"How are you doing?"

I sighed. "How much do you know?"

"Pretty much everything. Mercy called to explain what had happened. I told her I'd keep an eye on you."

I sat up in bed and tucked my knees into my chest. "I don't know if I can do this."

"Of course you can. I hate to do this to you right now, but I have something to show you."

I rolled my eyes. "What is it?"

Annabelle showed me her phone. "Ever see anything like this before?"

I rubbed my eyes. The picture was just a shadow, but it was something large. "Some kind of swamp monster?"

Annabelle shrugged. "Maybe. These things have been seen all over the city. They cast shadows, like this, but otherwise they're totally invisible."

"Have they done anything bad?"

"Not yet. But whenever there's something like this that pops up in the city, it's my job to look into it. Given that the gates to the otherworlds are shattered, and you're supposed to be the guardian, I thought you should see it."

I took a deep breath. "It might be harmless. Not everything that looks scary really is."

"Whatever these things are, they're not supposed to be here. In my experience, creatures out of their element turn violent sooner rather than later."

I rubbed my brow. "Where was this taken?"

"In the alley, just outside of Vilokan. They're all around the French Quarter. Social media is lighting up with supposed sightings."

I grunted. "No rest for the wicked, I suppose."

Annabelle grinned. "You're not a full demon. You're definitely not wicked."

I shrugged. "I have wicked thoughts. You wouldn't believe the shit running through my head."

"Thoughts are just thoughts. It's the choices you make that matter."

I swung my feet off the edge of the bed. "You're right. Let's go check it out."

The Blood Witch Saga Continues in...

Monsters and Mambos

Mercy's story continues in *The Fury of a Vampire Witch*, Book 1, ***Bloody Queen.***

Notes on the universe: the character of Wee Willie Winker first appeared in Ovate's Call in The Druid Legacy!

THE BLOOD WITCH SAGA

MONSTERS & MAMBOS

THEOPHILUS MONROE

Cover Design by Deranged Doctor Design

Proofreading/Editing by Mel: https://getproofreader.co.uk/

For information:

www.theophilusmonroe.com

Chapter 1

If there's a shadow, there had to be something between it and the nearest light source. Shadows didn't just jump off people in a fit of rebellion, jealous that their owner was stealing all the limelight. That kind of thing only happened in Peter Pan.

Peter Pan wasn't real. Last I checked, I *was* real. You'd have to have a real deranged mind to make *this* shit up.

These weren't normal shadows. They weren't all the same. The size could have been deceiving. Shadows were like that. This was the third one Annabelle and I chased. The first looked like a giant stick man, its legs twice as long as they should have been relative to its body. Its hands fell to its knees, and it moved slowly down a wall as we pursued it.

The second one appeared to be some kind of swamp monster. Maybe a yeti. Its frame was broad and droopy. Was it fur or ooze that was hanging from its arms? Hard to tell with a shadow. It first appeared in an alley, on the side of a restaurant off Bourbon Street. Mercy and I swung around in the space between the nearest light, casting shadows of our own in an attempt to battle the thing. It ignored us completely. Eventually, it marched off the side of the wall. Maybe we annoyed the damned thing, or perhaps he was bored and would have left regardless of our presence.

The shadow we were chasing now? It appeared on the side of St. Louis Cathedral in Pere Antoine Alley. It was about twenty feet removed from the magical doorway which opened up for a select few leading into the underworld voodoo city of Vilokan.

And it looked like a freaking clown. bushy hair, like Ronald McFucking Donald. Large oversized-feet. I had to wonder, given what they say about men with large feet, if clowns were also ridiculously well-hung. No one knew because no one ever slept with a clown. If someone did, no one mentioned it. It wasn't the sort of score anyone bragged about to their friends.

I was convinced that clowns were universally virgins. Probably wasn't right, but visualizing anything else was too troubling. I know, I know. People who play clowns don't live that way all the time. Still, anyone who could assume such a nightmarish form and haunt children's birthday parties wasn't the kind of person I wanted to call a friend.

The best way to stop a clown epidemic? Don't let them reproduce! Natural selection isn't always a bad thing.

"I don't understand," Annabelle huffed.

"A trauma from early in life."

Annabelle looked at me and raised one eyebrow. "What are you talking about?"

"You said you don't understand. It's the most likely explanation why *anyone* might ever become a serial killer *or* a clown."

Annabelle rolled her eyes. "Clowns aren't as evil as serial killers."

"Look, if you want to get into *levels* of evil. I mean, there's Lucifer, of course. After that? Clowns and serial killers."

Annabelle shook her head. "You're forgetting demons. They're definitely more evil than clowns."

I stared at Annabelle blankly. "That's not funny."

Annabelle narrowed her eyes. "You're not a demon, Hailey."

I shrugged. "Not yet."

"Just because you bit a succubus, and its blood started to transform you when you touched the thorn from the Wayward Tree, doesn't make you a demon."

"Right. It just means I'm becoming one. A fucking succubus. Screw me and die!"

The shadow clown faded away. It didn't walk off the wall like the stick man or swamp monster shadows before. As we talked, it was like it blended into the other shadows on the cathedral wall.

Annabelle put her hand on my back. "You aren't without hope, Hailey. It's possible to beat this."

"Right. No sex for me. Purge the succubus demon blood from my body by drowning it in virtue. Did you forget that I'm a freaking vampire?"

"You're also a witch."

I cackled. "Yes, my pretty."

Annabelle rolled her eyes. "Stop it. You know better than anyone that being a witch doesn't make you wicked. I'm a witch of a sort too, you know."

"You're a mambo. There's a difference."

"Perhaps. As a vodouisant, as a mambo, I can wield the power of the Loa. As a witch ,you harness the power of nature. As a blood witch, you harness the power of the soul, the power of life itself. Some witches, though, call upon the gods and goddesses much like I might appeal to a Loa."

I shook my head. "It's still different. You have the aspect of a Loa."

"So do you."

I sighed. "Right. I have the aspect of Erzulie. The Loa of love. A lot of help that's been."

"It helped you stop Corbin."

"Yeah, once. I made him think he loved me. Erzulie's aspect helped me beat him once. Until he decided to carry out all his plans of world domination for my sake. So I could rule the world as his vampire queen. What a freaking wedding gift."

"It doesn't matter, Hailey. Corbin was literally the devil for a while. You stood up to him. You never considered his temptations for even a second. Why do you suppose that is?"

"Maybe because Corbin was a sociopath? He wasn't really my type. I prefer men who don't have aspirations involving murder and world domination. Call me picky, but I have my standards."

Annabelle pressed her hand to the wall, and the mystical door to Vilokan appeared beneath her touch. "You're missing the point, Hailey. You're worried about becoming a succubus. Perhaps there's something in Erzulie's aspect you haven't yet considered that might help."

I tilted my head and tugged on my earlobe. "How could the aspect of a Loa of love possibly help suppress the lusts of a succubus? That seems a little counterproductive. I need to stay away from love as much as possible. If I thought I could love, right now, I'd still be with Connor."

"I thought you two didn't break up."

"We're taking a break. Until I get better. When I'm around him, I can barely keep my hands off him as it is."

"Even when he's shifted into wolf form?" Annabelle smirked.

"No. That's freaky. Why would you ask something like that?"

"Do you still love him when he's shifted?"

"Of course I do!"

"But you don't desire him like that."

"Right. Because I'm not a freak, homie!"

Annabelle smiled and nodded. "So there is a difference between love and lust. One doesn't necessarily lead to the other."

"Do you think I could see Connor if he's shifted?"

Annabelle shrugged. "Possibly. That's up to you. Almost everyone has lusts. Even married people often experience lust for others. That doesn't mean that every husband who notices an attractive woman, or any woman who fantasizes about Magic Mike, is going to cheat."

I nodded. "Right. Because their love for their spouse is stronger."

"Which is why you should see Connor. Even if only in wolf form."

"Because my love for him can help suppress my succubus urges?"

Annabelle nodded. "Exactly. And besides that, a little training with other mambos who share Erzulie's aspects can't hurt. It may ultimately be the key to purging the succubus essence from your body once and for all."

I shook my head. "We don't have time for that. I'm supposed to be a guardian. Appointed by the gatekeepers of Guinee to stand between the otherworlds and earth. New Orleans has so many mystical convergences that it's like paranormal swiss cheese. There are strange monsters casting creepy shadows all over the city. Maybe they're harmless, but whatever's responsible for those shadows is probably from a different realm."

"We're going to get to the bottom of this. I wouldn't rule out anything, but we don't know for sure that these shadows are due to something coming through a convergence. Think about it. What other realm has clowns?"

I stared at Annabelle blankly. "Hell. Clowns come from hell."

Annabelle rolled her eyes. "Why do you hate clowns so much? Sounds more like they come from your nightmares than hell."

I shifted my feet. "Many people get the creeps from clowns. I'm not alone in this!"

"I can assure you, Hailey. Clowns aren't from hell. They're from earth."

"That doesn't mean these shadow-casting monsters are from earth. Maybe they're invisible shapeshifters."

"Why shapeshift if you're invisible? What's the point?"

"I don't know! I'm thinking out loud, here."

Annabelle gestured toward the door. "What do you say we go inside for a bit?"

I shrugged. "If we aren't going to chase these monsters, I should go home. Tommy is at Casa do Diabo. I'm his sire. He's my responsibility."

"Sarah is there. She'll monitor him."

"Why does it feel like you're trying to bait me into an intervention?"

"You're not an addict, Hailey. This isn't an intervention. That doesn't mean our voodoo mambos can't help."

"Right. You want me to learn more about Erzulie's aspect."

"That's one option. There are also vodouisants with the aspect of Baron Samedi. If vampires were originally made from mingling the essence of a succubus with humans, and you've been given extra succubus juice, perhaps there are mambos who wield the Baron's aspect who can help."

I bit my lip and twirled one of my blonde curls in my finger. "Are you sure that's a good idea? What if they try to help and it makes things worse?"

Annabelle rested her hand on my shoulder. "how long have we known each other? The better part of a decade now?"

I nodded. "Ever since I became a vampire. When you healed me and took me in."

"I'm also the Voodoo Queen. I wouldn't ask you to try this, Hailey, if I thought it could make things worse."

I took a deep breath and held it a moment before I released it slowly through pursed lips. "We still need to deal with these monsters."

"You're not in any condition to do that, Hailey. You're distracted. If not by your worries, then by every man with a beating heart who walks by."

"I don't stare at every man!"

Annabelle raised an eyebrow. "Yeah. You sort of do."

"I can't help it! I know most of them aren't attractive. It's those damned succubus urges. It's like everyone who walks past is a juicy steak."

"Isn't it like that, anyway? You're a vampire."

"Sort of. But this is way more intense. I can't control it. All I can do is resist the urges as best I can."

"You have to resist the urges completely. If you don't, you'll complete your transformation into a succubus demon. That's why we need to find a solution to this problem as soon as possible."

I huffed. "You don't trust me."

"You just told me you can't control this. Tell me, Hailey, what happens if you're in the middle of combatting some monster from the otherworld, and some dude walks by in tight jeans?"

I rolled my eyes. "If some asshole is walking past me while I'm fighting a monster, he's an idiot."

"You're missing the point. You're distracted right now. You aren't in any condition to guard any convergence, much less fight a monster. Not until you get past this."

"You make it sound like I'm sick or something."

Annabelle smirked. "Well, I'd say you have the fever. For everyone."

I shrugged. "Not you. You don't have a–"

"Right, I'm well aware of what I don't have. But is there a single man you've seen as of late who you don't have an urge to seduce?"

I snorted. "Not really. Freaking embarrassing. Did I tell you I found Pauli attractive before?"

Annabelle laughed. "Well, he is a good looking man. I hate to be the one to tell you this, though. You're not his type. For the same reason that I'm not yours."

I chuckled. "Yes, like Pauli, my checklist for men is pretty short at the moment. Have a penis? You're Hailey material."

Annabelle shook her head and laughed. "You don't mean that. That's just the succubus talking. It isn't you."

I grunted. "It's not like I'm possessed, Annabelle. The succubus isn't some entity inside of me trying to take control of my body and mind. It's a part of me. It's trying to become my body and mind."

"But it can't do that. Not so long as you keep to your purity pledge."

I snorted. "I was ten years old when I took that pledge. I was a student at a private Christian school. They gave us cheap little rings and everything. I gave up on all of that later."

"When you became a witch and, later, a vampire?"

I snorted. "In the back of the bus with Evan Schneider. We were on our way home from a mission trip to the reservation."

Annabelle laughed. "Sounds familiar. I went to Catholic school as a girl. Whatever the nuns didn't find out never happened."

I followed Annabelle down the stairs into Vilokan. "Look at us now. You're a Voodoo Queen and I'm a witch, a vampire, and in the process of turning into a demon. The mentors of our youth would be proud."

Annabelle turned back and winked at me. "You realize my predecessor, Marie Laveau, was also a devout Catholic. Many mambos are quite devout."

"But you haven't been to mass in ages."

"That's not true. From time to time, I go. I live under a cathedral, after all. I try to maintain a cordial relationship with the bishop."

I raised my eyebrows. "The bishop knows about Vilokan?"

Annabelle nodded. "It's been a part of the church's legacy for going on two centuries. It's not exactly public knowledge, but if the bishop wanted to, he could make things a lot more difficult for us."

"How so?"

"He could close our doors. Our entrance is on the side of his cathedral. So long as we're fighting against evil, protecting the city and the church, the bishop turns a blind eye to most of what we do. They're more concerned with demons than mambos and hougans. So long as he knows in advance when demonic activity is afoot, and I alert him of the risk, he cooperates with us."

I snorted. "Demonic activity is afoot. What are you going to tell him about me?"

"Hopefully nothing. If we can take care of this little problem and remove the succubus energies from your body, he doesn't need to know."

I sighed. "What if you can't?"

"I don't know. It wouldn't hurt to let him know. They do have rites effective at exorcising demons."

"If I was possessed, I'd be all for it. That's not what we're dealing with."

"Which is why I haven't told him what's happening. Since you're *becoming* a succubus, I don't know for sure what an exorcism would do to you, but I have an idea."

"An exorcism binds a demon and sends it back to hell, right?"

Annabelle stopped on the stairs and turned back to me. "That's right."

"An exorcism would send *me* to hell."

"That's my fear."

I shook my head. "Been there. Done that. Would have got the t-shirt, but it wasn't exactly a vacation."

"Willing to give the mambos a chance?"

I nodded. "I'm not optimistic it will work, but you're right. It might be the best shot I've got."

Chapter 2

I WAITED IN ANNABELLE'S office while she left to find the mambos she thought could help. When the elevator dinged, and Annabelle walked through, two young mambos followed her into the room.

The two girls couldn't be any more different.

I knew Ellie. She was one of Annabelle's classmates when she was just a student at the Voodoo Academy. She was a few years older than me, of course, but by mambo standards she was young. She had the aspect of Erzulie and an affinity for the color pink. The only thing she wore that wasn't pink was a pair of white yoga pants—albeit with a pink floral pattern. She wore a pink tube top. I wasn't sure if tube tops ever went out of style, but they certainly weren't as popular as they were back in the early noughties. She was wearing pink converse sneakers and her bleached blonde hair had pink highlights. She was probably the whitest girl in Vilokan. Her skin was so pasty she could have been a spokeswoman for Elmer's.

The other girl was younger, probably in her late-teens. What pink was to Ellie, black was to her. She looked a lot like Wednesday Addams. Pretty, but that wasn't an adjective she'd probably take as a compliment. She had fine features and a complexion that suggested she might have been part Hispanic, part Black. She wore tight, strappy black pants and a lacy black top. Her necklace was made of bone—not uncommon among mambos. Were they animal bones or human? Didn't know. Wasn't about to ask. Her hair was as black as night, with bangs that fell nearly to her brows and two braided pigtails that reached her mid back.

"You already know Ellie," Annabelle said. "This is Holland."

I smiled at Holland. "College Samedi, I presume?"

Holland nodded. "How did you ever guess?"

Annabelle had her hand on Holland's back. "Holland graduated from the school last year. One of College Samedi's most promising and talented mambos in decades. She's young, but don't underestimate her."

"People who underestimate me have an odd habit of ending up dead."

"Not her fault," Annabelle said. "It was an unfortunate coincidence that the two professors at the academy who didn't recommend her early graduation fell ill last year."

"Was it?" Holland raised one eyebrow. "I don't believe in coincidences. I prefer to think of it as just desserts."

Ellie rolled her eyes. "So dramatic! I'm stoked to work with you, Hailey!"

I bit the inside of my cheek. Ellie was always a bit much. To hear Annabelle tell it, though, she'd come a long way from her My Little Pony and unicorns obsession back when they were students. Somewhere along the way, she adopted a valley girl cadence. Not common to the deep south, certainly not in New Orleans. It was mostly an act. She was a talented mambo, though, and her heart was generally in the right place.

I scratched the back of my head and turned to Annabelle. "So what's the plan? Ellie helps me master Erzulie's aspect like some kind of private tutor, and Holland uses her aspect to torture the succubus out of me?"

"Sounds about right," Holland said. "I've never played with a vampire before. Not to mention a demon in the making. It should be fun."

I gulped. Holland's almost monotone voice and lack of expression didn't do much to convince me that this process was going to be so enjoyable. "I'm also a witch. Don't forget that."

Holland steepled her hands in front of her face. "A delectable trifecta."

Annabelle chuckled a little. "Don't mind Holland, Hailey. Her bark is worse than her bite."

I smiled and exposed my fangs. "Can't say that about me."

A slight smile cracked at the corner of Holland's blood-red lips. "Don't worry. If there's anyone who can help you, it's me. I'll have you back to feeding and fucking in no time."

I almost choked on my tongue. "Alright. Well, sounds like a plan to me. What do we do? Light a few candles, make a few offerings, chant a few prayers?"

"That's not how this is going to work." Annabelle stepped back behind her desk. "This is an unprecedented situation. I've yet to explore all our records and volumes in our library, but so far as anyone is aware, no vampire has ever been turned into a demon."

I bit the tip of my thumb. "I'd like to keep it that way."

Holland sat on the edge of Annabelle's desk. "There is a rite I'd like to perform. It won't cure you. It will give us a better idea of how the demon's essence is interacting with your vampirism."

"And how Erzulie's aspect might affect it," Ellie piped up.

Annabelle sat down on her desk chair and kicked her feet up on top of her desk. "As you know, Hailey, Baron Samedi is a Ghede Loa."

I nodded. "Right. Death is sort of his thing."

"It's about more than that," Holland said. "The Ghede are guardians between modes of being. The boundary between life and death is just one of them. The most common, of course, but not the only change that can occur. Humans can become vampires. The Ghede are a part of that."

Annabelle cleared her throat. "Since we know that Baron Samedi first turned Nico into a vampire by drawing on the succubus demon's essence, at the very least, copying some of its properties, we think the transition you're experiencing is similar. The ritual Holland is going to perform will help us figure out exactly *how* similar it is. If we know that, we might be able to figure out a way to isolate it."

"And get rid of it?" I asked.

"Possibly," Holland added. "We might isolate it. Make the power from the demon cycling within you stop cycling."

I narrowed my eyes. "Make it go dormant?"

Annabelle nodded. "I can't say it would stop your transformation if you did the dirty with someone, but it might quell some of your urges."

I nodded. "So I can focus. I can fight whatever these monsters are that are casting shadows all over the city without distraction."

Annabelle gave me a thumbs-up. "That's the plan. For now, anyway. At a minimum."

"I still think there might be a way to remove it from you," Holland stated. "That's where Pepto Bismol over here comes into play."

Ellie sighed. "Don't call me that. I'm not diarrhea medicine."

I tilted my head. "Pepto is good for a lot more than that. Don't you know the jingle? Nausea, heartburn, indigestion, upset stomach, diarreeeeeha!"

Ellie batted her eyes. "I still don't like it as a nickname."

"Sorry, Pepto." Holland smirked.

I pressed my lips together to suppress my urge to laugh. "How might Erzulie's aspect help?"

"Demons don't love," Ellie said. "They're not capable of it. Depending on what we find out, working with the aspect of Erzulie might work against it like a kind of antibiotic."

Annabelle uncrossed her legs and lowered them from her desk to her floor. "There's no way to know how well it will work. At best, it helps stall the spread of the succubus contagion and eventually overtakes it completely. At worst, you gain a little mastery of an untapped ability."

I cracked my knuckles. "Alright, well, let's get this ritual over with. I have things to do, monsters to kill."

Chapter 3

VOODOO IS WIDELY MISUNDERSTOOD. It's a lot like witchcraft that way. Vampires, too, aren't usually like those you've seen in the movies.

Mambos, witches, and vampires, are common villains in Hollywood. On the whole, though, vodouisants are incredible people who do far more good than evil. The same is true of witches--they revere nature, the spirits, and are more likely to bless you than curse you. Vampires still drink blood. No way around that. Still, vampires rarely kill. Not because they value human life so much as because they value their own existence. It's self-preservation. Start dropping bodies and it's just a matter of time before you're struck through with pine. If not at the hand of a hunter, by an older vampire who doesn't want a youngling's extra curricular murders drawing attention to the rest of our kind.

On the scale of "evil," in fact, humans are the worst. More lives have been lost at the hands of other humans, through violence and war, than all the other supernaturals combined. It's not even close.

People fear us. Mambos, witches, and vampires. Mostly because they don't understand us. It's easier to fear a caricature of a villain than it is to confront the villainy within. The tendency toward evil, toward violence, that hides in the darkness of a human soul is the most terrifying monster in the world. Want to fight something evil? Start with yourself. Confront your darkness before you fuck with mine.

Annabelle led the way to what was a "training room" in the old Voodoo Academy. She had told a few stories about her first sessions there with the Loa of War, Ogoun, and a hougan named Mikah. She and Ogoun—she called him Oggie—were "involved." I suppose you could say Annabelle was hot for teacher. As well as I knew Annabelle, though, I knew very little about her relationship with the Loa. He had a host—a human body—that allowed them to have a relatively normal relationship from an outsider's perspective. Still, Ogoun rarely got involved in Annabelle's affairs. Mikah, meanwhile, became a crossroads guardian and was in a relationship with Isabelle—the spirit that sometimes possessed Annabelle and gave her otherworldly powers, including a soul-blade vested with the essence of a dragon named Beli.

It wasn't a surprise at all that Annabelle's relationship status was "It's complicated."

If I had a Facebook account, I'd update mine to the same. The only reason I didn't have one was because there were too many people out there who knew me in my human life, and presumed that I was dead, to get away with it. My parents knew what I was. Ever since I revealed myself to them, and told them in as vague terms as possible what I'd become, they stopped hiring private investigators to find me. I dropped by once a month just to let them know I was well. I didn't give them my number. If they knew the shit I was getting involved in, the battles I'd fought, the risks I had to take daily to save the world, they'd be more frightened for my well-being than proud. I didn't tell them much. I certainly would not find them now, and risk exposing them to the demonic nature growing within me. Besides, my succubus side gave me an unnatural attraction to every man I saw. If it gave me feelings like that for my dad, I'd be so creeped out they'd need to commit me to the Vilokan Asylum of the Magically and Mentally Deranged, toss me in the padded room, and throw away the key.

Seeing my parents from time to time was more than a way to pacify their worries about me. It also kept me grounded, reminded me of the human being I used to be. Vampires who forget that, who lose sight of their humanity, are the ones who become monsters.

Ironic, I suppose, since there's more than enough monster in humans to spare. There's also a lot within humanity that's beautiful, that motivates people to pursue virtue rather than vice. Vampire, witch, mambo, human, whatever. There's a little good in the worst of us and a little bad in the best of us. The key isn't so much about choosing one path or the other, but having the wisdom to discern the difference.

After all, even the world's worst villains believed they were heroes. Bad guys usually think they're the good guys.

The gymnasium at the Voodoo Academy wasn't a basketball court like the gym at most schools. It was a place designed to shelter the rest of the voodoo underworld from magical mishaps. When you're training mambos and hougans who can access impressive powers, safeguards are necessary. I knew from experience. My spell on Mug Ruith that reflected back and cursed me was one example. A magical "whoops" could have devastating unintended consequences.

When it came to the craft, I was more free-wheeling than most witches. I had a natural gift. As a witch, and a vampire, I could access the power in blood that few witches were brave enough to tap into. For me, it was second nature. It was a wonder I hadn't had more accidents than I did. After the incident with Mug Ruith, my X-number of days without an accident sign had to come down. I'd say I learned my lesson but, well, sometimes when people's lives are at stake, you have to take personal risks. This succubus problem directly resulted from that accident.

We didn't need the whole gymnasium. The only reason we were doing it there was because no one knew exactly what to expect. Holland and Annabelle both assured me I'd be fine. Why, then, conduct the rite in a super-warded place like the gymnasium? It begged the question—if no one knew what to expect, how could anyone be confident I'd be fine? It certainly wouldn't be the first time relying on the power of the Ghede blew up in someone's face.

There weren't any candles to light. No creepy little dolls. No human skeletons or shrunken heads. There was nothing about what Holland was going to try that screamed voodoo.

Annabelle and Ellie stepped aside, and Holland approached me. She placed her fingers to the side of my head. Her fingertips were like ice cubes. Most of my magic was warm. The power of the Ghede was chilly.

I took a deep breath.

"Try to relax," Holland said. "I'm going to create an astral reflection of your spirit."

"I'm going to be out of my body?"

Holland shook her head. "That's astral projection. You're not leaving your body. I'm using the power of my aspect to duplicate your astral form."

"So you're making another me?"

"Not at all. This is only a reflection. It has no personality of its own any more than your reflection does when you look in a mirror."

I chuckled. One of the most common misconceptions out there about vampires was that we didn't have a reflection. It was a carry-over from the days when mirrors were made of silver. Silver doesn't poison vampires like it does werewolves, but for some reason, whatever light reflects off our bodies isn't picked up in a reflection from silver. Silver mirrors were rare. Most common mirrors showed my reflection just fine, as did chrome plated items, or the still water of a pond or lake. Seeing a reflection of one's *spirit* was an entirely different thing. Would it look like me at all? I worked with spirits, especially when I drew on the power of the soul through blood witchery. I'd never *seen* one—certainly not my own.

"Will it hurt?" I asked.

Holland shrugged. "Do you want it to?"

I furrowed my brow. "No! Pain sucks."

Holland smirked. "To each her own, I suppose."

"It shouldn't hurt," Annabelle said. "You might feel a bit disoriented. That's completely normal. Don't worry about examining your spirit's reflection. We'll handle that. We need you to try to stay awake. This sort of thing has been known to send some into a slumber."

"What if I fall asleep?"

Annabelle grinned. "Then I'll have to catch you. You should wake again when we're done."

I gulped. "Alright. I'm ready. I think."

The chill from Holland's fingertips was like ten icicles driven through my skull, straight into my brain. It wasn't so much painful as it was numbing. No wonder this procedure knocked some people out cold. I was determined to stay awake. I was a blood witch! I defeated vampires over ten times my age. I even bested Dracula. Like a boss! I was confident I could stand strong while this Wednesday Addams wannabe channeled her Ghede magic into my cranium.

A dark figure passed across the back wall behind Holland.

"I see something!"

Holland narrowed her eyes. "That's normal. The brain can react in strange ways to this process. Keep your eyes locked on mine."

"It's not that. It's one of those shadow monsters we saw before. Holy shit! Annabelle! It's that freaking clown!"

"It's just a part of your spirit," Holland said. "Your mind is playing tricks on you. It's a reaction to my magic."

"It's not a trick! I swear!"

Holland sighed. "Calm down. I've almost got it. Just a couple more seconds."

"I don't see a shadow," Annabelle said. "Deep breaths."

"I don't see her spirit either," Ellie said.

"I can see it," Holland said. "It's remarkable. Also quite unusual. The succubus' power is there, but it's more subtle than I expected. There's something else. It's not a part of Hailey. It's something else."

"Not a succubus?" Annabelle asked.

"Some kind of parasite. I'm not sure what to make of it. It's something ethereal, probably picked up in the faerie realm, or maybe it came from a convergence and hitched a ride on Hailey at some other time."

"What is it doing?" Annabelle asked.

Holland shook her head. "I don't know."

"There's a freaking bug in my head!" I shrieked. "Get it out!"

"It's not that easy!" Holland shouted.

"The shadow is separating from the wall. It's moving toward us!"

"It's just a hallucination," Annabelle said.

"I'm not so sure it is," Holland added. "I'm not only reflecting Hailey's spirit, but my magic is interfacing with this parasite at the same time. Hailey might be seeing *its* reflection."

The shadowy figure materialized behind Holland. As I envisioned it, the clown had red, curly hair, a round red nose, and the most ridiculously colorful outfit imaginable. It had an enormous axe that it gripped with both white-gloved hands and raised it overhead.

I grabbed Holland and tossed her aside.

"Holy shit!" Ellie shrieked. "What is that?"

"More than a fucking reflection!" I grabbed my wand and blasted it with red magic. It was a one-size-kills-all sort of spell. It worked on most things. It basically harnessed a little power from blood, usually from my most recent feed, and converted it into a destructive blast.

My spell passed straight through the clown.

The bastard was laughing. It was that stupid chortle that clowns usually made. It was supposed to be funny. I found it unsettling. Certainly when the clown was wielding an axe and tried to take a swipe at my head.

I ducked just in time. I blasted the clown again, but it wasn't any more effective than my first shot.

The clown raised its axe over its head and prepared to chop me into bits. A green glowing blade pierced the clown from behind. Evil Boso screeched and disappeared in a dark cloud. Annabelle stood there with her soul blade in hand.

"Thank God, that worked!"

"My blade can send creatures from the otherworlds to Guinee."

"What the hell was that?" I asked.

"Mind if I take another look?" Holland asked.

"In my head?"

Holland nodded. "I want to see if that parasite is gone."

I winced. "Alright. Do what you have to do."

More icicles to the brain. This time it only lasted a couple of seconds.

Holland lowered her hands. "The parasite is gone. It must've sensed my magic as a threat and manifested as, whatever the hell that was, to stop us."

"Why the hell did it have to be a clown? I'm terrified of clowns!"

"That's why," Annabelle said. "Whatever these creatures are, they feed on people's spirits. It manifested in a form it knew would frighten you."

"You're talking about a monster that basically becomes your worst nightmare?"

Annabelle shrugged. "Looks that way. Whatever it is, it draws on something within the host and uses it to attack them."

"Why would a parasite like that want to kill a host?" I asked.

Annabelle shook her head. "Who knows? If it feeds on spirit, perhaps it can't get its fill unless it kills its host. Once it does, it moves on."

"And since I'm a vampire, killing me wasn't exactly easy."

Holland shrugged. "We know nothing. I've never heard of anything like this before."

"Neither have I," Annabelle said. "At least we learned *something* today."

"I'd call it a success," Holland added. "I got a good look at Hailey's spirit. Our theory might be effective. I could see a concentration of energy that represented the succubus. It was isolated, separate from the rest. Hailey's own spirit was mingled with several energies. It was quite brilliant, in fact. A lot more color than I'd ever hope decorated my spirit."

"Vampiric powers," I said. "I have a couple of those."

"Plus, your natural ability as a witch, your vampirism, and a subtle remnant of your soul."

I raised an eyebrow. "My human soul? I thought Baron Samedi claimed a person's soul when they became a vampire."

"He does," Holland said. "But for whatever reason, perhaps it's your power as a witch, he didn't get it all. In fact, while it was hard to tell, I'm not sure he got any of it. Your human soul is intact. With Erzulie's aspect combined with everything else, you stand a chance to stop the succubus' infection from spreading."

"How do we do that, exactly?" I asked.

"The same way you said the druid told you before. You overwhelm that part of you by expanding your spirit. By straining your spirit in a display of virtue."

"That sounds so damn corny." I huffed.

Holland smirked. "It really does."

"It's not corny!" Ellie piped up. "It's poetic!"

"It is what it is," Annabelle added. "I say we stick to the plan. You three will stick together for the time being. At least until we're sure Hailey is back to herself. I'll join you as well. If these parasites are using people's spirits, their minds, to manifest monsters that reflect people's nightmares, and if we're right that they will ultimately kill their hosts, it's just a matter of time before people start dying."

Holland nodded. "When that happens, the parasite will move on to someone else."

I huffed. "They're like ticks."

"Not like ticks," Holland said. "Ticks are like you. They drink blood."

I winced. "You're not the first person to suggest that ticks were the vampires of the insect world. You realize that's the only thing we share in common with ticks. We don't swell up fat when we feed. Most of us don't, anyway. We don't pass diseases. Except for the contagion that can turn someone into a vampire, but that's rare and the process is more complex than that. We only have two legs, are a lot prettier than ticks, and most of all, we're intelligent!"

Holland smirked. "DIdn't realize you were so sensitive to bug jokes."

I sighed. "I'm not. Not usually. That dumb parasite, whatever it was, left me a little out of sorts."

Annabelle nodded "It's to be expected. The thing was feeding on your spirit. That's bound to leave you a little bitchy."

I clenched my fists. "Did you just call me a bitch?"

Annabelle stared at me blankly. "No, I didn't. Relax, Hailey."

I huffed. "Whatever."

"How many sightings of these shadows have there been?" Holland asked.

Annabelle shook her head. "They haven't been reported to me directly. Not many of them, at least. A lot of hysteria on social media. There could be dozens of these things out there, if not more."

I took a deep breath. I knew I wasn't acting like myself. "This parasite didn't come from the faerie realm. Not if there are that many sightings. They must've come through a convergence."

"Have any of you ever heard of anything like this from any other realm?" Ellie asked.

Annabelle scratched her head. "No, but that's not a surprise. There are realms and dimensions I've never even heard of, much less visited. Some are large and expansive, others like the void, don't follow the rules of time and space at all. There's literally an infinite number of possibilities in terms of *where* these parasites came from. Even more, these things aren't visible. Even if I'd been to their realm, which I doubt, there's no guarantee I would have encountered them."

I nodded. "At least we know your blade can get rid of them."

Annabelle bit her lip. "It sends them to Guinee. Isabelle tells me they're not from there. A part of being a guardian, Hailey, isn't just to protect the earth but to respect the integrity of all the realms. We can't just send nasty creatures off to whichever realm is convenient."

I scratched the back of my head. "We could reach out to the Wyrmriders again. They can cast portals into the void."

Annabelle pressed her lips together. "Giant dragons flying through the city attacking shadows isn't ideal. Shadow monsters posted all over the internet is one thing. Can you imagine if people start posting pictures of dragons?"

"Not to mention," Holland added, "Annabelle couldn't stab that thing until it materialized."

I brushed a stray curl out of my face. "We need something we can use to fight these things that we can have ready at any time. A spell of some kind might work. I'm just not sure what kind of spell might be effective on these things."

"My soul blade worked to send the parasite away. What if we don't kill them, but trap them?"

I rubbed my brow. "I could use a blood prison. The last time I tried one of those, though, it didn't turn out so well. That's the spell that backfired when I used it on Mug Ruith."

Annabelle touched me on the shoulder. "Have you ever had issues with that spell in the past?"

I shook my head. "Not really."

"Then there's no reason to believe it won't work. If we can trap one, we can experiment on it. We can find a way to kill these things."

Ellie coughed in her hand. "Apologies for adding my thoughts, here. You two know a lot more about this kind of thing than I do. Holland made a good point, before. Unless we're there when one of those things manifests, when it's more than a shadow, we can't do much."

Holland spun one of the bones on her necklace between her fingers. "If we can find the host, I can do what I did to Hailey. I can force it out."

Annabelle nodded. "Alright, we are going to do this together. All four of us. First things first. We have to find a shadow monster. The host will be nearby."

"If we're on Bourbon street, that will be like finding a needle in a haystack." I twirled my wand in my hand. "I doubt these things are limited to the French Quarter. It's a tourist area. If people are getting infected there, they aren't staying there."

Annabelle headed toward the door. "Follow me. Let's dig a little deeper into the sightings people are posting online. There's a good chance that the same people capturing images of these shadows are the ones infected. We might be able to track some of them down."

Chapter 4

I DIDN'T HAVE PHONE service in Vilokan. No one did. Annabelle had a line hard-wired directly to her office, which must've been quite a project given the fact that we were underground and Vilokan was protected from the water table above by a magical barrier.

Ellie, Holland and I pulled up chairs behind Annabelle's desk. She opened her laptop. She brought up the sign-in screen and hit a connect button. Her computer started dialing a phone number. Then, the most god awful sound I'd ever heard. High-pitched ringing sounds followed by static.

"What the hell is that?" I asked.

Annabelle laughed. "It's called dial up Internet."

I snorted. "I thought that shit went extinct ages ago."

Annabelle looked at me and smirked. "You've seriously *never* experienced dial up?"

I shook my head. "Nope. What about you, Ellie?"

"We had it when I was young. I remember it."

"Holland?"

"I've never used a computer."

"Seriously? Not once?"

"I grew up in Vilokan. Had little need for it. Besides, I'm pretty sure it just makes people dumber."

Annabelle chuckled. "It also turns kind people into trolls."

"Seriously?" Holland raised an eyebrow.

I rolled my eyes. "Not literal trolls. Keyboard warriors who go around trying to start fights. They get their jollies out of infuriating people."

Annabelle opened her browser. The website loaded in sections. "What the hell is wrong with your computer?"

"Dial up is slow," Annabelle said. "Be patient."

I shifted in my chair. "I can feel myself growing old while we wait."

Annabelle looked at me with one eyebrow already raised. "You're a vampire. You don't grow old."

"Right. It's taking *that* long. Entire species are going extinct while we wait for this page to load."

"It's not *that* slow, Hailey."

"What is this page, anyway?"

"My home page is set to an aggregate of local news feeds, different articles and blog posts that other mambos and hougans in the city refer to me, and an array of local social media posts that pick up on certain keywords. It takes a minute or two to load, but it's a good way to keep tabs on what's going on in the world above."

I tapped my fingernails on the armrests of my chair. "Maybe we should just go to the surface. I can use my phone. This is going to take all night. I need to be home before the sun rises."

Annabelle waved her hand through the air. "Hold on. The page loaded."

"Yeah, well, now you have to go to Twitter or TikTok or wherever the hell people are posting these things. I don't think TikTok is going to work well on dial up."

"You're right." Annabelle narrowed her eyes as she scrolled down the page. "I might have something."

"From the news?" I titled my head.

"Look at some of these stories. Strange deaths all over the city."

"How strange?" Holland asked.

Annabelle pointed at her screen. "They found a body a couple blocks from the French Quarter. A leg missing and a giant bite-shaped wound in the abdomen. The weird thing is that they found a shark tooth buried in his skin."

I scratched my head. "Last I checked, shark attacks aren't exactly common in the *city*."

Holland laughed.

"You think this is funny?" Ellie grunted.

"Think about it," Holland said. "Hailey is afraid of clowns. That's the form the parasite took. A lot of people are afraid of sharks."

I snorted. "Yeah. In water situations. Why would someone be afraid of a shark if they were in the city?"

Holland glared at me. "Fear is irrational. There aren't clowns in Vilokan, either."

Annabelle scrolled down a little further. "This one is interesting. Three high school boys ripped to shreds. The suspect is one of their classmates, another boy that witnesses say the three victims were bullying. The cops who came to arrest him met a similar fate. Their bodies mangled, their chests ripped open and their hearts removed from their bodies."

I gulped. "I don't think a single high school kid could pull something like that off."

"It doesn't fit the M.O. If this kid is manifesting one of these monsters, why is it fighting *for* him rather than trying to kill him?"

Holland shook her head. "Maybe we were wrong. Fear might not be the only thing these monsters use to manifest."

Ellie snapped her fingers. "Adolescent angst. Trust me, I'd know. If you're being picked on, you want your bullies to get what's coming to them."

"You were bullied?" Annabelle asked.

Ellie nodded. "I was an awkward girl. The popular girls gave me a hard time."

I narrowed my eyes. "It's one thing to be angry, even think for a moment you want someone dead. It's another thing to actually do it."

Holland nudged me. "It's one thing to be afraid of clowns. It's another thing to actually be attacked by one."

"You're suggesting that these parasites latch on to any negative emotion? Fear, angst, anger, maybe even envy, and these monsters manifest to realize their host's darkest thoughts?"

Holland shrugged. "It's a theory."

"It tracks," Annabelle said. "If Holland is right, we might have a bigger issue on our hands than we thought."

"Why would this kid's parasite go after the police?"

"Maybe because he knew he was innocent. The cops came to arrest him and, to that boy, they weren't that different from his bullies."

Annabelle continued surfing through the news feed. "There's a man who was suspected of cheating on his wife. Someone attacked him in his car and ripped off his genitals."

"His wife, maybe?"

Annabelle shook her head. "The husband said she was inside the house."

"All of that detail is in the news report?" I asked.

"Not in so many words. My news feed gathers data from a variety of sources and collects it on one page. This is from a blog post. The victim here was a local minister. He was having an affair with his secretary and one of his parishioners found out about it. She posted evidence on the church's blog. The comments on the article are from other members of the church, including the victim's wife, who is accusing the author of the post of getting involved in a personal matter and attacking her husband."

I pursed my lips. "That could be what this was. We don't know if it was one of these shadow monsters manifesting to castrate the man. Not saying he didn't have it coming, but damn."

Annabelle took a deep breath. "More stories are aggregating from other sites, all originating around New Orleans, with a number of murders and mutilations."

I bit my thumb. "M and Ms. Melt in your mouth, not in your hand."

Annabelle and Ellie stared at me, devoid of expression. Holland wasn't as bothered by the comment.

"What?" I asked.

Ellie stared at me with wide eyes. "Did you seriously compare murder and mutilation to nuts covered in chocolate with a hard candy shell?"

I shrugged. "You realize what I eat on the regular, right?"

Ellie shuddered.

Annabelle patted Ellie on the shoulder. "Try not to think about it. It makes it easier."

I stood up and straightened my shirt. "Speaking of all that, I could really go a for a nice, warm, O-negative before the sun rises. What do you say we go get a few drinks? Not necessarily at the same place, for obvious reasons, and look up some of these suspects mentioned in your feed. Once we return to the surface, and the twenty-first century, it should only take a few minutes to track these people down."

Annabelle cleared her throat. "Are you sure you're good to feed right now? From an actual human?"

"I don't know. But a girl's gotta eat, right?"

"We could pick up some blood before we leave. They have a supply on hand at the Vilokan Asylum."

I rolled my eyes. "Mercy would never suggest that."

"I'm not Mercy. Obviously."

I sighed. "Old blood is sort of like drinking diet soda. The taste is there, sort of, but it never totally satisfies. I need my calories. I need fresh blood, where a bit of the person's soul still lingers within. That's what sustains us, you know."

"I know," Annabelle said. "But I'm not sure I can trust you to feed on a man right now without ripping off his clothes and succubusing him to an early grave."

I twirled my wand in my hand. "Did you seriously just say succubusing? I don't think that's a word."

"I can't think of anything else. You knew what I meant."

"Just drink girls," Ellie said. "You're only attracted to men right now, right?"

I sighed. "I am. I generally prefer the musky taste of a man, but I suppose I can set aside some of my preferences for the sake of not killing people. A small sacrifice in the end."

Chapter 5

WE DECIDED TO SEARCH for the bullied kid first. From what we'd found on Annabelle's news feed, he was clearly the one leaving the most bodies in his wake. The challenge was that we had to compete with law enforcement to find him first. That was another reason we made him a priority. The cops wouldn't know what to do with him. They didn't realize exactly *how* dangerous the boy was.

The police might think they had him locked up, but if this parasite manifested as some kind of vengeance monster every time someone threatened him, putting that boy in a cell could be the most dangerous thing anyone could do. I imagined the boy didn't even realize *what* he was doing. He was probably terrified. It's one thing to hold a grudge, to have angst directed at someone, it's another thing for a monster to materialize out of thin air and murder anyone who stokes your anger.

Have you ever seen how baseball players warm up before they go to the plate? They add weights to their bats and take a few practice swings. That way, when they get to the plate, their bat feels lighter. That was similar to the way it felt once we reached the alley outside of Vilokan and I turned on my phone. I never realized how *fast* my phone was until I had to sit there and watch Annabelle's stone-age Internet connection at work.

"What information do we have on the boy?" I asked.

Annabelle was scrolling through her phone beside me. Holland and Ellie were looking up and down the alley, probably expecting an ominous shadow monster to appear at any moment.

"Hold on," Annabelle said. "I'll text you a link to my aggregate feed. There are a few rabbit holes attached to the article we can follow. Maybe we can split them up and see what we can do. Locating a teenage boy who is frightened, probably running from the police, will not be easy."

I nodded. "We don't have to find him. If we get his address, I just need to find some of the boy's DNA. I can use that to cast a targeting spell. It'll basically turn my wand into a compass. Rather than pointing true-north, it will glow brighter whenever I point it in the boy's direction."

Annabelle bit the inside of her cheek as she scanned the article. "Funny thing is that the article doesn't mention the kid's name. Just his basic demographic info."

"Makes sense. When it comes to minors, they're extra careful about maintaining confidentiality until they make an arrest or formal charges are issued. Once you get a reputation for being a gruesome serial killer, and it goes on the Internet, that information will follow you around for life. Even if he is acquitted, what happens on the Internet, stays on the Internet."

Annabelle took a deep breath. "I think the fact that this boy is probably a timid young man, the idea that he single-handedly bested a bunch of cops is enough to establish reasonable doubt."

"Maybe, maybe not. It's one thing to say a young boy isn't capable of something like that, but in the absence of any evidence pointing to anyone else, a jury might assume he's far more capable than he appears."

Annabelle sighed. "Poor kid. I don't know how he's ever going to get through this."

"We have to find him first. We have the names of some of his victims. We can talk to their families and try to get the boy's name."

Annabelle narrowed her eyes and pressed her lips together. "I'm not sure if I just lost a child I'd be all that eager to talk with someone who isn't law enforcement about anything. We could go to the cops and ask."

I chuckled. "Yeah, right."

"I'm serious, Hailey. WWMD?"

"What the hell is WWMD?"

Annabelle smirked. "What would Mercy do?"

I tilted my head and stared up into the night sky above for a moment. "She'd use her vampiric allure to seduce an officer involved. She'd coax the information out of him."

"Then that's what you can do."

I grunted. "Probably not a good idea. Not given my current condition. Besides, I'm not as good at that whole allure thing. Not like Mercy is. I struggle to use it when I'm not hungry and on the prowl for a meal."

Ellie took my hand. "You can do it!"

"Yeah. Maybe if it's a woman cop. I won't want to have my way with her, at least. Then again, using my allure on a woman isn't something I have a lot of experiment with."

"Maybe it will be a woman," Annabelle said. "Even if it isn't, allow Ellie to help you through it. Use Erzulie's aspect to suppress your succubus urges."

"How do I even do that?" I asked. "It's something inside of me, a part of my spirit. It's not like moving an arm or a leg."

"It's actually a lot like that," Ellie said. "How do you know how to produce a specific spell when you cast it?"

"It depends. Sometimes I rely on an incantation that draws the magic through and forms it into the desired spell because my wand is incanted with it already. Some of my incantations are verbal, others are non-verbal."

"How do the non-verbal incantations work?" Ellie asked.

"It's more of a gut thing. All my spells began with some kind of verbal incantation. Over time, those I used frequently, became more second nature. Sort of like how when you first start learning to drive, you have to think about all the traffic laws, remind yourself to signal, keep a proper distance between the cars in front of you. Eventually, you drive and follow all those rules without even thinking about it."

Ellie nodded. "Like riding a bike!"

I licked my lips. They got a little chapped when I had the need to feed. "Right. I can't explain to someone how to do it. I just *do* it."

"That's how it is with a mambo's aspect. What begins with particular rites and rituals, intentional forms of intensive meditation, becomes as natural as breathing over time."

"Alright. Well, if we had *time* to master Erzulie's aspect within me, I'd say let's do it. We don't have that luxury."

Annabelle shook her head. "Since we're feasting on a buffet of metaphors, let me add one that might help. How does a parent teach a child to walk?"

I shrugged. "I don't know. Never had kids. Now that I'm a vampire, never will. I mean, I have a youngling who is like a baby vamp, but that's not the same."

"I haven't had kids either," Annabelle said. "Still, I know how it works. A mother might hold the child under the arms, or by the hands, while his little feet feel their way across the floor. The toddler doesn't have the muscle tone yet, or the balance, to pull it off. Until he can walk alone, the parent helps the child along. The mother lends her strength to her child. That's what Ellie can do for you."

I narrowed my eyes and turned to Ellie. "I'm not calling you Mommy."

Ellie chuckled. "That's fine. You can call me Daddy instead. Who's your Daddy, Hailey?"

I stared at Ellie blankly and parted my lips just enough to expose my fangs. "We're not doing this."

Ellie gulped. "Whatever you say!"

Annabelle backhanded me on the shoulder. "You're going to scare the piss out of her doing that. If one of those parasites attaches itself to her, another version of you might appear out of thin air."

I shuddered. "Yeah, let's avoid that."

Annabelle tilted her head. "Though, two Haileys at once. I can't say Connor would complain."

I huffed. "Well, Connor isn't saying much at all. When I told him what was happening, that we couldn't see each other for a while, he didn't say much. After about twenty seconds of silence on the phone, he said he had a lot to think about and hung up."

Annabelle rolled her eyes. "You're trying to protect him from yourself. I know what you're doing. Think about it from his perspective, though."

"I have. If I were him, I wouldn't want to get screwed to death."

"That's not what I mean. You're going through something traumatic and difficult, and the first thing you do is cut him out of the picture. That boy loves you, Hailey. I don't think he cares about the risk. He just wants to help you get through this. It's the sort of thing that people who love each other work through together, no matter the risks involved."

"We're talking about me becoming a succubus and murdering the man I'm in love with. That's not really a risk worth taking."

"What is love without risks?" Ellie asked. "Trust me. I'm the expert in all things love. Comes with the territory."

"I couldn't live with myself if I hurt him."

Ellie took my hand—which was a little weird. I barely knew the girl. She looked me straight in the eye. "Relationships are all about risk. That's the point. We make ourselves vulnerable to another person. We trust them no matter what. They become our refuge, our safe space. You're basically telling him he's not allowed to be vulnerable with you."

I cleared my throat. "This isn't some stupid psycho-emotional thing. We're talking about life and death."

Ellie nodded. "Of course we are. Love is serious business."

"You two are going to make me puke," Holland said. "Love this, love that. Smoochie smoochie."

I smirked. "If love is a life and death kind of thing, then maybe it's not so foreign to your Ghede death magic after all. Different sides of the same coin."

Holland narrowed her eyes. "Pepto and I have *nothing* in common. Besides, you might want to turn around and look on the side of the cathedral."

Holland pointed behind me. All of us turned and followed her finger to a giant shadow on the wall. It was like the stick-figured shadow we saw before.

"Do you think it's coming from one of us?" I asked.

"No way to know," Annabelle said. "We don't know how far these things can wander from their hosts. Maybe they have to be closer to manifest but have more range in their shadow form."

"So it could be anybody." I sighed. "Still, let's follow it. It looks like it's heading around to the front of the cathedral."

All four of us jogged down the alley and followed the shadow as it made its way toward the entrance. It shrunk down as a shadow might when someone moved further from the light source. It passed through the front doors of the cathedral.

"We need to follow it inside," Annabelle said. "We don't know what this thing will do, who its host is, or if it might do something horrible to someone."

"Sounds like fun," Holland smirked.

I snorted. "You really have a thing for the macabre, don't you?"

"I've devoted my life to the study of death. What do *you* think?"

I readied my wand, just in case. We headed through the large double-doors in the front of the cathedral. It wasn't the first time I'd been there. The shadow figure wasn't confined to any walls. It moved through the narthex, past a few statuettes, a staggered collection of votive candles, and into the sanctuary. The familiar and pleasing aroma of frankincense filled the air. I wasn't Catholic, like Annabelle. I'd only been to a few masses in my life. Despite my parents and the way they brought me up, I was never much for religion myself. Even as a witch, I didn't work with the gods and goddesses as closely as a lot of other witches did. Mercy was more attuned to that sort of thing than I was. She came from a bygone era. I thrived more on my natural talents than a dependency on deities. Some witches would say it was a weakness. I wasn't so sure. I'd yet to meet a witch who could best me in a duel if it came to that.

All that said, there was something about the cathedral I respected. Perhaps it was the artwork. I liked the smell. More than that, though, it was a keen awareness by the folks who gathered there that they were engaging something transcendent, something larger than themselves. The whole place reflected an awareness that when folks gathered there, they were approaching the Divine.

It's probably mildly scandalous to put it this way, but the devout who worshipped there had both a keen appreciation for a gracious and loving deity, but an equally keen awareness that God could really fuck you up.

Just ask Lot's wife. She second-guessed God once and he turned that bitch to salt.

I respected that about the Catholics. In the school where I grew up, the ministers and teachers had a very sentimental way of talking about God. Almost like God had the personality of a Precious Moments figurine. I'm not saying they were wrong. People can believe whatever they want to believe. I just wasn't a sucker for that kind of thing. The sentimental, wave-your-hands in the air, break down in tears, kind of religion never did much for me. It felt a little fake. On the other side of the spectrum, whether they be Catholics or witches, or mambos, or whatever, there were those who had no emotion at all, who performed rites and rituals as if going through the motions satisfied the Divine.

I say all that to say this. I always believed in powers greater than myself. I never questioned the existence of the Divine. Some form of the Divine, anyway. I just never found a way of relating to a God, or gods, or goddesses, that made sense. Most human religions were too sentimental or too dull and ritualistic for my taste. Either extreme, I suspected, had something right, but was also missing something crucial. What was it they were missing? Hell if I know. If I knew it, I'd embrace it. I suppose I just wanted to believe in something *real.*

Even if the religion itself did little for me, there was something *real* about the way the cathedral took the divine seriously. There were times in the past when I came into the cathedral for a while just to sit and think. I didn't genuflect when I entered the pews. I didn't cross myself or do anything like that. I just sat and allowed the Feng Shui of the place to calm my mind and sharpen my focus. Yeah, I know Feng Shui is Buddhist, but a witch, who might be demon soon, and three mambos, were walking into a Catholic cathedral. Mixing religions was already on the table.

The shadow figure moved through the sanctuary, gazing over the tops of the pews. The thing moved slowly, as if stalking its prey.

"I don't see anyone here."

Annabelle shook her head. "There's someone in the confessional."

I nodded. "Alright. I've seen that in the movies. That means there's a priest and someone else here."

"Probably the bishop," Annabelle said. "This is the night each week he takes confession."

I snorted. "You go to confession?"

"What if I do?"

I shrugged. "Just didn't know. Isn't it a little weird? I mean, the shit you get into—"

Annabelle winced. "Look, I'm as foul-mouthed as anyone, but could you at least try to watch your mouth in here? It's disrespectful."

"Fuck. My bad."

Annabelle rolled her eyes. She didn't scold me a second time. I think she knew I was a lost cause. At least when it came to things like that.

"Have your wand ready. If this thing materializes, we need to trap it."

I squeezed my wand and aimed it at the shadow monster. "Locked and loaded."

The creature's form expanded. He arched himself over the confessional. My wand shook in my hand.

"I'm not sure what to do. If he doesn't materialize, I'm not sure I can do anything to hold it."

"Wait," Annabelle said. "If this thing is going to attack, it might wait until the last second before it takes solid form."

Holland huffed. "Screw that. The thing could thrust its arm straight through someone's chest and materialize in that very moment."

"It's either the bishop or the parishioner. One of them is infected."

Annabelle called Beli's name. The soul-blade formed in her hand. "I don't want to do this, but we might not have a choice."

Holland cracked her knuckles. "I've got this."

"You've got what?" I asked.

Holland nodded at me. "Be ready, witch."

Holland slid open the confessional door.

"What's the meaning of this!" the bishop screamed. "This is a private confession!"

Holland jumped on the bishop's lap and pressed her hands to his skull.

A middle-aged woman in a long dress and short curly hair jumped out of the other side of the confessional. Her eyes widened when she saw the shadow beast. She screamed and took off down the aisle.

"It's him!" Holland shouted. "Do it now!"

No sooner did Holland say it and the monster changed. He was still tall and lanky, but now he resembled something like a walking tree. Like those tree-ents from the *Lord of the Rings.*

The monster turned to chase the parishioner. I didn't need an incantation. It was one of those spells I could cast by feel. The power of blood, the last feed I had which was some time ago, swelled up within me. After this, I was going to need to feed. I was already hungry, but I had to pull this off.

A red prism formed around the monster. The beast released a screech so high-pitched my ears ached. It blasted its shape against my prison but it couldn't get out.

"You did it!" Annabelle shouted.

She was about to wrap her arms around me. She was a hugger. Not at all like Mercy. When she grabbed me, my head spun. A warm hand grabbed mine.

"Hang in there," Ellie said. "Draw strength from Erzulie."

If I knew how to do it, I would have. Unless Erzulie could deliver a stream of fresh blood to my lips, I didn't know what good it would do. I was short on blood. If I didn't feed soon, I'd turn feral—and coming back from that isn't easy. If that didn't happen, I was afraid the succubus would take over. I'd be too weak to fight it off.

My knees buckled. "I need... to feed..."

My body went limp. The last thing I remembered was Annabelle's arms catching me as my vision went black.

Chapter 6

I WOKE UP ON my back. Blood was flowing into my mouth. I grabbed someone's wrist and pressed it into my hungry mouth as I bit into it and gulped down as much as I could take.

My vision returned.

A gray-haired older man, probably seventy, in a black shirt and a white-tabbed collar was looking down at me. Annabelle's smiling face appeared over his shoulder.

I kept drinking. You never know what you're going to get when you feed from the clergy. If they're genuine, if they practice what they preach, they're sweet. If they're hypocrites, if they have some kind of dirty little secret on the side, there's nothing fouler. The bishop's blood tasted like honey.

He wasn't exactly smiling down on me. Feeding vampires wasn't a part of his usual job description. His wide eyes suggested curiosity more than disgust. When I had my fill, I released my bite from the bishop's wrist.

"Thank you." I took a deep breath.

The bishop shook his head. "I'm the one who should thank you."

I sat up and looked around. My blood prison was gone. So was the monster. "What happened to it?"

"The prison did more than we expected," Annabelle said. "I think when it was cut off from whatever energy it needed, probably coming from a convergence somewhere, it withered away until all that was left was a pile of dust."

"Where are Holland and Ellie?" I asked.

"Ellie swept up the monster's cremains. She took it out to the dumpster. Holland went to pick up a bite to eat. She should be back soon."

"Are you alright, Father?" I asked.

The bishop nodded. "I'm more concerned about you, child."

"I'm sorry," Annabelle interjected. "This is Bishop Alexander Carvallo."

I nodded. "Hailey Bradbury."

The bishop nodded. "Annabelle introduced us when you were out. Are you aware, child, that there's a demonic presence within you?"

I gulped. "You can sense it?"

The bishop smiled at me. "Those in tune with the Spirit can discern many things."

I tilted my head. "Holy crap. I don't want to screw you."

The bishop furrowed his brow. "Excuse me?"

Annabelle laughed so hard she snorted. "It's a good thing, Father."

The bishop tugged at his collar. "It's a succubus demon, isn't it?"

I sighed. "Damn, Father. I mean, Darn, Father. You really do have the gift of discernment."

The bishop took a deep breath and turned to Annabelle. "Why is this the first I've heard of this? We had an agreement."

Annabelle bit her lip. "I understand that. She hasn't been taken over. I wanted to try to help heal her before I looped you in on it."

"And what of this other devil? The one the girl in black pulled out of my head."

"It's not a demon," Annabelle said. "All we know is that it's some kind of parasite from another realm. It manifests in response to whatever negative emotions the host might harbor."

The bishop narrowed his eyes. "I see."

"What do you think it was trying to do?" I asked.

The bishop shook his head. "I don't have a clue."

"You must know something," Annabelle said. "It was drawing on your spirit. It manifests in response to some kind of angst, perhaps envy, rage, or something else unsavory."

The bishop's face went pale. "A temptation, perhaps."

Annabelle shrugged. "I suppose that's possible."

The bishop unbuttoned the back of his collar and loosened his shirt. "Lust."

I narrowed my eyes. "Lust? Aren't you priestly types celibate?"

The bishop nodded. "We take a vow of chastity. That doesn't mean we don't face temptation. I cannot reveal what's said under the seal of the confessional. Needless to say, though, the woman who was here stirred something up within me. I would not act on it, but I cannot deny the thoughts, the desires."

I snickered. "I guess that explains why this monster appeared as a giant wood!"

Annabelle pressed her lips together hard. She was trying her best not to laugh. "That's not funny, Hailey."

I shrugged. "It sort of is. What do you think that thing was going to do with that woman? I don't know that killing her was all it had on its mind."

Annabelle shuddered. "Thankfully, we won't have to find out."

I stood up from the pew and paced around the front of the sanctuary. "Let's look at what we know. A boy being picked on at school manifested a monster that murdered his bullies. I was always afraid of axe-murdering clowns. So, that's what the parasite attached to me became. A woman with an unfaithful husband manifested a monster that castrated her husband. A priest with secret lusts manifested as a horny wood. It makes sense."

Annabelle nodded. "These things realize people's secret desires. They're manifesting to fulfill things that people wouldn't normally experience or realize."

I rubbed my forehead. "Why am I not feeling the urges produced by the succubus anymore?"

"Maybe it's just me," the bishop said. "I'm a consecrated priest. It grants me some resilience against demonic attack."

I nodded. "Maybe that's it."

"It might be more than that," Annabelle said. "You also helped defend a holy man. You said that something virtuous, a valorous act that the demonic presence couldn't tolerate, might cure you."

I shrugged. "There's only one way to know."

"Take you outside and parade you around a few drunk men in the French Quarter?"

I grinned. "That might work. I was thinking, to be sure, I might allow Holland to get in my head again. She could see the succubus nature within me before. If it's gone, she'll know."

"You also just drank my blood," the bishop said. "Perhaps that has something to do with it."

I bit my lip. "I wonder if I can cycle the power in his blood. Maybe it will give me a vampiric ability to resist the temptation of the succubus."

Annabelle shrugged. "Worth a shot. Let's see what Holland says first."

Ellie came back first. Her pink top and floral yoga pants were coated in black dust. She didn't look too happy about it. I chose not to mention it. No one wants to be the clean-up girl. Sweeping up the remains of a monster couldn't have been a pleasant experience.

Holland came back a few minutes later with several bags of food. I could smell it the second she walked in—even over the strong fragrance of frankincense. Spicy gumbo. I was already full. Not that human food did me much good, but I could enjoy it if I wanted to. The only downside was that what goes in must go out.

The bishop grunted a little and cleared his throat. He was obviously perturbed.

"Sorry," Annabelle said. "We can eat outside. No food in the sanctuary."

The bishop bowed his head slightly and nodded.

Holland furrowed her brow. "An otherworldly monster just exploded in here, and you're worried about a little food?"

Arguing with a bishop about his policies didn't seem especially wise. Holland didn't have much of a filter. She was the sort of person who said what she was thinking and didn't give a rat's ass what anyone thought. It was an admirable quality, to a point. You didn't have to wonder what she was really thinking. It also created moments of awkward tension and I imagined it could lead to conflict that was otherwise avoidable. There's a reason why the *restraint* of pen and tongue is often lauded as a virtue.

"Perhaps there's a more comfortable place to eat. A hall, perhaps, or a room with a table?"

The bishop nodded. "Certainly. Follow me."

We followed the bishop out of the sanctuary, through the narthex, and down a narrow hallway. A man in coveralls was mopping the floor.

I leaned over to Annabelle and whispered. "Guess what?"

"What, Hailey?"

"I don't want to do that guy either!"

Annabelle grinned. "Maybe it's because he smells of tuna and beer."

I tilted my head. "*That's* what the smell is? I assumed it was just really bad body odor."

"That might be it as well. Still, that's progress. Unless he's also a priest who pushes a mop on the side, it helps us narrow down the cause."

"I'm going to pull Holland aside so she can give me another read."

Annabelle nodded. "You aren't seeing any shadows, are you?"

"Not at the moment. Are you seeing any?"

Annabelle shook her head. "Just want to be ready in case another one of those parasites gets into you. The last time Holland did that, it left you barely conscious, and we just saw how much it took out of you to cast a blood prison."

"That's just because I was famished. I feel like a new girl. Consecrated blood is killer stuff!"

"Interesting way to put it. We'll keep Ellie close by as well."

I shrugged. "Alright. You really think she can help, too?"

"We don't know how much of what happened is because of the bishop's blood. Given the risks involved with demon blood inside of you, and its essence trying to change what you are, our best chance is to hit this thing from as many angles as possible. Not to mention, say it is the consecrated blood that's subduing the succubus. What happens the next time we have to fight one of these things and you use some of the power of that blood for another blood prison?"

I shrugged. "I don't know. My guess is that if the succubus' essence is still alive within me, perhaps dormant or hiding, while the bishop's blood is circulating within me, it will get strong again. That's why I need to know for sure."

"We can't exactly expect the bishop to tag along as a ready-to-eat meal."

"Maybe another priest, then? Those vamps up in Exeter had blood maids. People devoted to vampires. Lived in luxury in exchange for opening their wrists when needed."

"You can't turn a priest into a blood maid, Hailey. They are devoted to the service of God, not a vampire who's fighting off her lesser demons."

I shrugged. "What's the difference? It's still fighting demons. You'd think they'd be all over that."

"They fight demons through exorcisms. Not all the clergy know about vampires, and most of of those who do, think vampires are demons already."

"I get it. Still, if it comes down to borrowing a priest, biting him a few times so we can stop murderous monsters from hell, or wherever these parasites came from, and allowing them to run rampage on the city while I also become a succubus demon, I'll go with the priest feast. It's the lesser of two evils. Plus, it rhymes."

Annabelle huffed. "Despite what some have said, might doesn't make right."

I smirked. "Bite makes right?"

"I don't think he ever said it, but Machiavelli might agree with you. I do not."

"What's Machiavelli? A dish at the Olive Garden?"

"I prefer Lincoln's reformulation of the maxim. Right makes might. The path of virtue nearly always prevails in the end. Those who follow the good find strength in their cause. Evildoers are limited by their ambitions."

"Cool. Bite makes right still has a nice ring to it. Thanks, Annabelle! I think I'll use it!"

Annabelle sighed. I knew I was irking her along. At the same time, I was only half-joking. So far, we only knew one way to defeat these monsters. I'd need a fresh supply of fresh, consecrated blood to keep it up. Blood prisons aren't hard to cast, not for me anyway, but they have a literal draining effect. The way I saw it, we could either keep experimenting on these things and hope that between the four of us we'd find a more efficient way to get rid of them, or drag along a man of the cloth.

Preaching to rooms of sleeping people once a week was hardly a better service to God than preventing someone from becoming a demon. At least that's how I saw it. Not a Catholic, but it just seemed like common sense. It's not every day that a priest has a chance to be a warrior—or a blood maid—in a battle against the diabolical.

All the theorizing would be for nought if the succubus nature was *already* dead. The only way to know was to allow Holland to finger my spirit again.

The bishop led us to a small room with a table in the middle. About ten folding chairs were arranged around it. I grabbed Holland by the arm. She snapped her head around so fast it took me off guard.

"Why are you touching me?"

"I wanted to ask you to check my spirit again. See if the succubus is still there."

"You didn't have to touch me."

I cleared my throat. This Holland girl was a tough nut to crack. Eccentric would be putting it mildly. She was so damn pretty, though, that her oddities were easy to overlook. We're so conditioned to think that pretty people are the standard, that loners and outcasts are also homely and less-than attractive, that when someone is beautiful *and* weird, it's a little confusing. Holland wasn't so much socially anxious as she was socially awkward. She had that "I'm me, deal with it" attitude that a part of me admired.

On the surface, she and Ellie were total opposites. One had the aspect of a Loa of love. The other, the aspect of a Ghede Loa of death. Ellie wore pink. Holland wore just as much black. While Ellie hid behind a facade of glitter and glamor, Holland let it all hang out. At their core, though, I suspected they were both misfits who felt like they didn't fit in. Ellie did her damnedest to embrace what she thought was pretty and popular—when she was a quirky geek at heart. Holland went out of the way to push people away, to embrace the bad girl image. They both acted like the other represented everything they abhorred the most. They were more similar than either girl would admit. They just dealt with their common insecurities in polar opposite ways.

After Holland shrugged off my touch, I followed her back out of the room while Annabelle served up the food. Annabelle knew what we were doing. She moved around the table so she could see us through the door—just in case I was infected by another parasite, and she had to spring into action.

The coldness of Holland's mind probe wasn't pleasant, but this time I was prepared for it. I crossed my fingers. I hoped the succubus was gone, that we could turn the page on that issue. It wasn't beyond the realm of possibility that the bishop's blood purified my spirit.

The chill spread throughout my body. Holland sighed when she removed her hands from my head.

"What did you see?" I asked.

"I always give the bad news first."

I smirked. "Of course you do."

"The essence of the succubus is still there."

My shoulders fell in disappointment. "What's the good news?"

"It's still isolated, and it appears dormant. Before, it was isolated, but active. I don't know if there's any kind of independent intelligence to it, but it's almost as if it realized you were fighting against it, took the opportunity to put itself to slumber when you ingested the Bishop's blood, hoping that you'd shack up with someone and complete the transformation on your own."

"You don't think the blood did anything at all?"

"I can't say. Possibly. Either way, the risks are the same, even if you don't have the same urges."

Annabelle cleared her throat. I turned and saw her looking on from the doorway, with the gumbo takeout in the bowls behind her. Ellie and the bishop were already digging in.

"I think it's time you gave Connor a call."

I sighed. "I don't know, Annabelle."

"You can manage your urges now. You know what's at stake. So does he. We know that Erzulie's aspect was fighting the succubus off before. Your best chance now is to lean into that. There's no better way to do that than to have the man you love at your side."

Chapter 7

CONNOR ANSWERED ON THE first ring. I chuckled a little. Was he *waiting* by the phone? He had a cell phone. I guess he was always by it. But it usually takes more than one ring to pick it up if it's in your pocket. It warmed my heart a little to think he was so eager to hear from me.

"Hailey?"

"You picked up quick!"

"I'm on the toilet. I was on my phone. You know, because that's what you do in the twenty-first century when you have to take a dump."

The warm and cozy feeling I had before disappeared fast. "Do you want me to call you back?"

"I'm fine. I'm not in any rush."

I sighed. "You didn't have to tell me you were shitting, Connor."

"Honesty is always the best policy. Especially in a relationship."

"Yeah, about our relationship–"

"You're not going to dump me while I'm... you know... dumping. Are you?"

I laughed. "God no! I just wanted to say I'm sorry."

There was silence for a few seconds.

"Connor?"

"Sorry. I was squeezing one out."

I sighed. "Nevermind. I'll just call you back."

"No! I'm fine! Why are you sorry?"

"I told you we couldn't see each other because I was worried about you. I was trying to protect you. I didn't even give you a chance to decide if it was a risk worth taking. Annabelle says that if a relationship is going to work, we have to get through the tough shit together."

Connor giggled a little. "Poor word choice at this particular moment in time. But you are helping me through a tough shit."

"Damn it, Connor!" I laughed. "We aren't supposed to be at this stage in our relationship yet where we casually talk about our poops with each other."

"When does a relationship cross that line, exactly?"

"I don't know! But I'm not calling you when I'm doing that. I won't answer if you call me, either. So freaking weird, Connor!"

"It's not weird. It's a bodily function. How much more *natural* could it be?"

"I'm trying to have a moment with you. This really isn't the best time."

"No, no. Look, I appreciate you saying it. You're right. I trust you. I don't think that any demon, or any temptation, could lead you to do something that would harm me. I want to help you."

"Well, good news on that front. I think the urges are suppressed for the moment. No hanky panky, though. It'll still kill you."

"Of all the ways to go, I could think of worse alternatives."

"Well, it will not happen today."

"Since shifters age no more than vampires, hopefully, it won't ever happen. Though if I had to choose one way to die..."

"Right, I get it. Doing me is better than burning in a fire or being buried alive."

"Don't sell yourself short. It's also way better than drowning, or acquiring a flesh-eating disease."

I laughed. "Yes. Sleeping with me really rates."

"To be fair, death by snakebite isn't even in your league."

"I'm honored!" I chuckled. "Real quick, though. Have you seen any strange shadows?"

"Like those monster things people are posting on the Internet?"

I nodded. "Yeah. I think I know what they are."

"Can't say I've seen any myself. Since you called last, I've been holed up in my apartment, drinking beer, and listening to Sarah McLachlan."

I snorted. "No, you haven't."

"You're right. I've been sitting in my living room, drinking beer, and playing video games. It's only marginally less depressing than listening to Sarah McLachlan's music."

"It could be worse. You could be listening to country."

"Nah. If my dog died, my tractor broke down, and I couldn't see my gal, I would have considered it. Things aren't quite that grim, though. Mostly because I don't own a dog or a tractor."

"Everything coming out okay?"

"Yeah. I'm good. Need to wipe my ass, but have you ever tried to do that while talking on the phone at the same time?"

I snorted. "No comment."

"It's not easy. I know these new phones are supposed to be water resistant, but if I drop mine in, I'm not reaching in for it."

I chuckled. "Funny you mentioned it. I saw an article on it the other day. Nearly one in five Americans have dropped their phone into the loo at one point. Not only do they lose their contacts but also their pride."

"Exactly why I'm waiting until we get off the phone before I finish up. I was going to shower and go to bed, but my clock isn't totally back to normal yet. I'm still mostly functioning on vampire time. Can I come see you?"

"Yeah. Sure. I'm not at home, though."

"Where are you?"

"I'm standing in St. Louis Cathedral at the moment."

"Seriously? Did you go to get exorcised or something?"

I chuckled. "Thought about it, but Annabelle thinks an all-out exorcism is too risky. I'm not possessed. The demon within me isn't an invading entity. It's more like a contagion trying to change me. Exorcise *it* and you exorcise me to hell with it."

"Given that you've done more than your share to piss off Lucifer, and that Corbin is there, too, I doubt a return trip to the hot place is something you'd like to experience anytime soon."

"Not soon. Not ever. Hell sucks. I guess that's why it's hell."

"So why *are* you at the cathedral?"

"Chased a shadow monster in here. Long story, but these things are parasites that latch onto people and manifest in ways that accord with someone's darker thoughts or sentiments."

"Someone went to church with naughty thoughts on the mind?"

I grinned. I wasn't going to give the bishop up. It took a lot of courage for him to tell us what he did, anyway. "Something like that. Anyway, I figured out how to kill it. Annabelle things I'm stronger with you. That Erzulie's power can protect me, maybe heal me completely, but since I love you, I can't really tap into it very effectively in a state of heart-break. Certainly not if you're not there with me. Killing these monsters also takes a lot out of me. I need you with me so that I can be stronger, so Erzulie's aspect can protect me, and I can keep fighting these monsters without becoming a succubus demon."

Connor snickered. "Did you make that up just now, or were you reading it from a Hallmark card?"

"I know. It's not the most romantic thing I've ever said to you. I'm a monster without you."

"That really could go on the inside of a card! I'd buy it."

I snickered. "Honey, I'm a monster, with or without you. And I bite."

Connor made a purring sound. "I like it. But no friskiness for you, young lady."

"If the temptation comes back, shift into wolf form. I don't think the urges will be as strong that way."

"I'm offended. You don't find my furrier, four-legged form as attractive as my human shape? I didn't realize you were so shallow. It's what's on the inside that counts."

"Yes. It does. Which is why I still love you, no matter what. Puppy love just isn't my style."

"Alright, Hailey. I need to get up. My legs are falling asleep. This will not be easy."

I chuckled. "Been there, done that. Good luck wiping."

"Thanks! I appreciate that. It means a lot."

"See you soon, ya goof!"

Chapter 8

It only took Connor about fifteen minutes to show. It must've been a quick wipe. Everyone else was cleaning up the mess from the meal when he arrived.

"Nice to see you, Connor," Annabelle said. "Good to see you back on your feet."

Connor glared at me. "Did you tell them I was on the toilet?"

I shrugged. "Nothing to be ashamed about. Everyone does it."

Connor rolled his eyes. He hugged me and kissed me on the cheek. He took a step back. "Was that okay?"

I grinned. "It was fine. I won't say I didn't have any urges to rip your clothes off and have my way with you, but we are in a church. And it wasn't any more than usual."

"Nothing succubus related, anyway?"

I shook my head. "Not in the least!"

The bishop was wiping off the table, pretending he didn't hear our conversation. I really wasn't very good about minding my company. I had a bigger case of foot-in-mouth than Rex Ryan. At least my issue was metaphorical.

"Back on track," Annabelle said. "When we saw the shadow that led us here, we were following up on a story about a kid who was bullied. One of these monsters, we think, manifested and tore his antagonizers to pieces."

"Damn," Connor said. "In most instances, I'd say a bully gets what's coming to him, but that's taking it too far."

"They certainly didn't deserve to die," I added. "I had my share of bullies back in the day. It wasn't real bad for me. Not nearly as bad as it was for others. Still, a death wish is extreme."

Ellie sniffed. "You might think different when you have a foot on the back of your head and you're gargling toilet water."

"That happened to you?" I asked.

"I didn't say that! I'm just saying, in the moment, wishing a bully dead makes sense."

I pressed my lips together. There was no reason to press Ellie on whether she'd experienced that kind of degradation in high school. The point was sound. The priest had only cursory, almost subconscious, lustful thoughts that he wanted to suppress and the parasite latched onto them. "None of that matters right now. We need a name for this kid. We also need to try to find him. All I need is a little DNA and I can cast the spell."

Connor cleared his throat. "All I need is the boy's scent."

I smiled and wrapped my arm around Connor's waist. "Always good to have a wolf in your pack."

Connor tilted his head. "I'm the wolf. If there's a pack here, I'm the alpha."

I chuckled and patted Connor on the butt. "Keep telling yourself that, buddy."

Annabelle scrolled through her phone. "Finding the victims isn't a problem. One of them has a visitation at the Greenwood Funeral Home tomorrow evening."

I pressed my lips together. "I'd rather not wait a whole day to go poking around and asking questions. There's no guarantee that anyone there will even know anything. I doubt anyone would be particularly responsive to questions pertaining to the deceased's bullying targets."

Connor pinched his chin. "Also, if it's a monster doing the killing, I don't know if I'll be able to pick up the host's scent from the body. If they've already embalmed the body, I won't smell much of anything other than toxic chemicals and the mortician."

Holland stepped up with her hands folded in front of her. "Toxic chemicals and the mortician. Killer name for a band."

I snickered. "Good one. We're just sort of at a loss for the best way to find the host for the monster responsible for killing all these kids."

"What do you suppose the chances are that the body of the victim is at the funeral home already?"

"Better than average," the bishop piped up. "Most bodies are kept at the funeral home for several days between death and the funeral. If the funeral is tomorrow, there's a good chance the body is already there."

Holland smiled widely. "That's fantastic."

"What are you thinking, Holland?" Annabelle asked.

"Why don't we pay the dead a visit? From what I understand, Hailey, your progeny has the ability to see dead people."

I nodded. "He does. I can speak to them as well. I gained that ability from Tommy when I turned him."

"Good," Holland said. "Then let's go."

"It's not that easy. A deceased person's spirit has to be nearby. The only other option would be to attempt a seance with Alexandra and the local coven. Most spirits don't linger around their bodies."

Holland waved her hand through the air. "I don't need a stupid seance. Those rituals aren't always reliable. Especially if a spirit has moved on. Get me to the body. I can bring the boy's spirit back to talk, no matter where he's gone."

"What if he's in heaven or at peace?" I asked.

"Then he can go back to that when we're done with him. The way I see it, this boy might have gotten more than what he deserved. He still was a bully. The least he can do is give us the name of the boy he was hassling."

I nodded. "Alright. So we break into the funeral home. Where is it exactly?"

"It's on Canal Street," the bishop piped up. "And you don't need to break in. We clergy have a pretty close relationship with the funeral directors and morticians in town. Let me make a call."

"What are you going to tell him?" I asked.

The bishop smiled and bowed his head slightly. "The truth."

"Seriously?" I raised one eyebrow.

"As many strange things that occur in New Orleans, child, there are few people who are more aware of what really goes on in the shadows than a mortician."

Chapter 9

THE BISHOP MADE THE call. I was marginally surprised that the funeral director on the other end of the line answered. It was approaching midnight. We still had enough night left that we could get some things done. On the bright side, so far, there had been no shadow monster sightings during the day. Did that mean they weren't active during the day, or just that no one could see them since everything was bright? Not sure. Didn't want to risk it. Even so, the most we could reasonably hope to accomplish in one night was to stop this particularly cantankerous parasite that was using some poor kid's angst to go on a homicidal spree. I didn't even know the kid's name, or what he looked like, but I already felt for him. Dead cops were already on his record--and he probably didn't have a clue he was doing it.

Still, it was something that we knew we could do. The more troubling question lingering in the back of my mind was how many parasites were out there? Equally troubling was the thought that if they were coming through a convergence, more could be on their way. For all I knew, they were migrating to our world by the thousands. What would we do, then?

If there's the potential in every human being to destroy the world, a hundred times over, if the worst part of him is brought out, what would happen if these parasites attached themselves to everyone on the planet and realized everyone's worst inclinations? The world wouldn't last longer than a day.

What began as a few shadows, a minor problem to investigate, had the potential to be the most challenging threat I'd ever faced. Fighting one bad guy who wants to end the world, or take over governments, or rule hell, is one thing. When you have thousands of ethereal creatures latching themselves to thousands—no, make that millions or billions—of human beings and making their darker side a reality, there was no way to stop it. I could spend the rest of my existence—which probably wouldn't be all that long if these parasites spread across the globe—fighting them one-by-one and I'd barely make a dent in the problem. I certainly couldn't cast a blood prison over the entire planet. As strong as I was, I didn't have anything close to that kind of juice. Even if I partnered up with every witch on the planet, I wasn't sure we could pool enough energy to pull something like that off.

The bottom line was that while we know how I could kill one of these monsters at a time, I didn't have a clue how bad the problem was or how long it would take before the parasites spread so far and wide that it was too late to fix. For the first time ever, I didn't have a villain I could target. There wasn't one bad guy responsible who had to pay. Even if I made someone pay, if there was someone who could shoulder the blame, it wouldn't solve the problem.

Maybe a little love, spread around the world, would help. Erzulie's aspect was what was keeping the succubus at bay, but what if we could fill the world with so much lovey dovey-ness that they didn't have any nasty thoughts the parasites could manifest? Holland could get the attention of the spirit of Michael Jackson. From what I understood, his spirit used to possess someone at the Vilokan Asylum. They figured it out when an ogre couldn't stop grabbing his crotch and breaking out into choruses of the late King of Pop's greatest hits. I also knew a necromancer. A couple of them, technically. One of them happened to be a werewolf. We could resurrect Michael Jackson, convince him to do a reprise of *We Are the World* and stop the parasites in their tracks.

This is the sort of nonsense that runs through my mind when I'm trying to solve a problem. It was probably the dumbest idea I'd ever had, but it was an idea. Sometimes I'd start with a dumb idea and it would help spark another idea that wasn't so ridiculous.

The bishop gave us the go-ahead. We piled into Connor's Escalade. How did he get such a fancy vehicle? He and his former pack of wolf shifters used to do jobs for old vampires, like Corbin, and covens of witches. They paid him handsomely. His money dried up, but he'd paid cash for the Cadillac SUV. He said he had enough in the bank that he'd be alright for a while. I didn't question it. I was his girlfriend, not his wife. His money was his business. I had to admit, though, that I always enjoyed riding in the Escalade. The road noise was barely audible. The ride was as smooth as rhythm and blues. The only thing I didn't appreciate about it was all the stares we got when we drove through the French Quarter. People were either thinking, "damn, they rich!" or "let's wait and see where they park so we can break in and steal stuff."

As a vampire, stares from anyone weren't exactly coveted. The first lesson most vampires have to learn—even the divas of our population—is that it's best to blend in rather than stand out. No matter how well you behave, there are always hunters out there waiting for a chance to stake you in the chest and burn out your heart.

The Greenwood Funeral Home was on the property of a cemetery by the same name. The building had pale bricks. The doors were unlocked. The bishop didn't come with us. Connor decided to wait in the car. I couldn't say I blamed him. It wasn't like we were going to Disneyland. This wasn't the happiest place on earth. It was a freaking funeral home. The rest of us hopped out of the Escalade and headed through the funeral home's glass-paned double-doors. The director was waiting for us just inside.

I don't know why. I assumed the funeral director was a man. The stereotypical image of a clean cut gentleman, in a black suit with a white shirt and black tie, wasn't at all like the *woman* who met us at the door.

"You must be Annabelle Mulledy," the woman said before she noticed my red eyes. "Sorry, not you. You're Hailey, right?"

I nodded and gestured to Annabelle as she stepped through the doors behind me. Ellie and Holland followed next. "That's Annabelle. The Voodoo Queen of New Orleans."

"I'm Jeanne," the funeral director said. "You come with the bishop's compliments."

Annabelle bowed her head slightly. "I'm honored. Thank you for meeting us at this late hour."

"I knew your predecessor. My predecessor, and his predecessor before him, knew her as well."

Annabelle grinned. "Yes, Marie Laveau was a fixture here for centuries. I can only pray that I might fill her shoes for half as long as she did."

Jeannie shook all of our hands. She was a pretty woman with long, dark hair. She wore a white blouse and a black overcoat. I suppose a lot of flashy colors that drew attention wouldn't serve a funeral director's role especially well. I hadn't been to a lot of funerals, but I imagined a calming presence was essential. A good funeral director was someone who didn't stand out in the crowd but ensured all things went smoothly. The last thing a grieving person would want to worry about were practical details. Funerals weren't weddings. Most people didn't grow up with lifelong dreams about their perfect funeral. What mattered was that events progressed as scheduled and people had the space to mourn as they saw fit.

"I realize this might be an unconventional request," Annabelle said. "We don't have a lot of options."

Jeanne nodded. "If there is something supernatural responsible for Trevor's untimely passing, I'm sure it's in the family's interest and everyone else involved that we cooperate with your request. I must insist, however, that you pay appropriate respect to the deceased and exercise discretion regarding these matters. If this request hadn't come from the bishop himself, I'd never consider anything of this nature."

I folded my hands in front of my waist. "I can assure you, we wouldn't be here if it wasn't necessary."

"I hope you'll understand if I must observe. For the family's sake. I must ensure their son's body is properly cared for."

Annabelle nodded. "Of course. I must warn you, though. We will be respectful, but what you see might be unsettling."

Jeanne laughed. "I'm a funeral director in New Orleans. Unsettling comes with the job description. Trust me, there's very little you could do that I haven't seen before."

I raised my eyebrows. "Are you sure about that?"

"You're a vampire, are you not?"

I nodded. "And a witch."

"You aren't the first of either class who has paid me a visit with an unconventional interest in the deceased."

"Perhaps another time we can exchange stories," Annabelle said. "May we see the body?"

Jeanne led us down a hallway to a room in the back of the building. Trevor's body was already in his coffin. I'd seen a lot of dead bodies through my years as a vampire. I didn't see a lot of embalmed bodies. The poor boy looked more like plastic than flesh.

"He looks well enough," Annabelle said. "Apart from being dead, of course. We read that his attacker mangled his body."

Jeanne nodded. "His face was untouched. The rest of his body isn't entirely presentable. I've pieced him together well enough for an open casket, but it wasn't easy."

Annabelle turned to Holland. "What are you doing?"

Holland was examining one of Jeanne's embalming appliances. It looked a little bit like a blender. It had a gauge on the front, a couple knobs, and a large clear canister on the top. "Jeanne, is this the Porti-Boy Mark IV?"

Jeanne shook her head. "It's the Mark V. This baby has an injection pressure range of eighty to a hundred psi."

Holland traced her hand along the tank. "Three gallons? Quarter horse power motor? Mag-Drive Pump?"

Jeanne nodded. "You know it!"

I cleared my throat. "You embalm people with a blender called a Porti-Boy?"

Holland turned to me with a blank stare, as if to say "duh."

"The best embalming machine on the market." Holland picked up a couple of metal rods. "Nice post aspirators!"

"Thanks!" Jeanne replied.

"Holland!" Annabelle coughed in her hand. "You can talk mortuary shop later. We need you to do your thing."

Holland stepped up beside me as I hovered over Trevor's body. "I'll need you to step aside. I can pull his spirit back here, using his body like a kind of homing beacon to draw it here. You're certain you'll be able to see him?"

I nodded. "It worked before. I can still see spirits wandering the graveyards from time to time. Not as many as you'd think. It's enough that I'm sure my abilities are still intact."

"Do vampiric abilities fade?" Annabelle asked.

I shook my head. "They don't. Once a vampire gains a new ability, we have it forever. We can turn them off though. With an ability like this, it can be unsettling. I keep the ability suppressed most of the time. I'm ready now, though."

Holland placed her hands on Trevor's body, one on his forehead, the other on his chest. "Ghede Nibo, I bid you to come. In the name of Baron Samedi and Maman Brigitte, I summon you. You who guide the spirits of the dead, Ghede Nibo, bring us the one who once inhabited this flesh. Loosen his lips and tongue that he might speak."

I watched a few moments. I was about to speak, to ask what was going to happen, when Annabelle grabbed my arm. "Give it a moment.

The Loa like to take their time, just so we know they come not by our command, but in honor of a request."

Holland repeated her prayer twice more. She waited a minute or two between each recitation.

"Is it working?" I whispered to Annabelle.

Annabelle nodded. "Don't let him mount you."

I raised an eyebrow. "Trevor?"

Annabelle shook her head. "Ghede Nibo. He has a reputation."

"What kind of reputation?"

"Let's just say he has a taste for sensuality. Those he mounts tend to act out in lascivious ways. Given your condition, that could be bad."

I glanced at Connor, who still stood by the door. He was the only male in the room. If Ghede Nibo mounted me—if he possessed me—and acted out on his desires through me, Connor was the only option. Other than the dead body. I couldn't even think that way. Succubi consume souls. They usually prefer their lovemakers warm at the start, cold at the finish.

Whatever the case, if the Loa mounted me and used me to entertain his desires, it wouldn't only turn me into a succubus once and for all, it would also kill my boyfriend. "Can I stop him from mounting me?"

Annabelle nodded. "Avoid eye contact. When Erzulie mounted you, when she gave you her aspect, it was subtle, wasn't it?"

I nodded. "I didn't even know she'd done it. It happened so fast."

"If you don't look him in the eye, he can't mount you. I'm not saying he intends to mount anyone, but I wouldn't put it past him. Especially since he knows we need his help."

Holland raised her hand. "Hush! He's coming. Don't sell me short, Annabelle. I can handle Ghede Nibo."

Annabelle shrugged and nodded at me. "She probably can. There's a reason I chose Holland to accompany us. She is the most powerful mambo with Samedi's aspect I've ever met. Still, remember what I said."

"No eye contact. It won't be a problem."

I heard the doors of the funeral home open and close. I wasn't sure if anyone else noticed, except for Connor. Wolf shifters and vampires alike could hear better than most. Footsteps tapped through the hallway until a slender figure entered the room.

The Loa was in black, wearing a long overcoat. I kept my head down, using only my peripheral vision to examine our guest. His skin was black as night. His hands were small and his fingernails were well manicured. From what I could see from the corner of my eye, he was what they might have called a "dandy" in the old days. His features were fine. He could have passed for a woman if dressed differently.

Holland held one hand on Trevor's body and turned around. Her eyes were glowing like red rubies. "Hello, love."

"My sweet!" Ghede Nibo exclaimed. "It's been too long. Why have you deprived me the pleasure of your company?"

"It's been three months since we last spoke," Holland said. "Since I allowed you to indulge in your desires through my body. I told you the time would come when I would need the favor you owed me in return."

I snorted. "What did she say?"

"Shh." Annabelle hushed me. I didn't need her to answer. Had Holland really pimped out her body to a Loa to store up owed favors? I had to admit, it was a pro move. Having a Loa or two owe you one could come in handy. Apparently, Holland had been currying favor with the Ghede, leaving them in her debt for whenever she might call upon them in the future.

Ghede Nibo laughed. "I shan't forget it! I know what you want. I heard your prayer. If you wish it so, I'll retrieve his spirit, but I must remain here that I can take him back where he belongs. I will not allow a spirit at rest to languish in the realm of the living."

"Agreed," Holland said. "Bring me the dead boy."

"I can bring his spirit, but he cannot speak with you. Not unless I mount you again. The blondes, either of them, would do as well."

Holland smirked. "No mounting allowed. Our vampire here can speak to the dead."

Ghede Nibo chuckled. "I knew I liked you, Holland. You're a clever one, I'll give you that. Very well. My word is my bond."

Ghede Nibo snapped his fingers. I looked back toward the coffin. A young male appeared out of thin air. He vaguely resembled the embalmed corpse, but dead bodies never really look quite like they did in life. He stood over his own body. He wasn't translucent, like some spirits, but appeared to me as corporeal as any of us. His hands were shaking. "No. That's me. That's my—"

"Hello, Trevor," I said. "You're right. That is your body."

"What is happening? It felt like a dream."

"You were murdered," I said. "We need to know who did it."

"I'm dead?"

I nodded. "Sorry to be the bearer of bad news."

Trevor squinted hard and grimaced. "It happened so fast. It wasn't a person. The thing came after me..."

"There's a boy that I hear you were picking on. No judgment here. There's no need to dwell on your mistakes."

"My mistakes? I wasn't bullying him."

"Do you know who I'm talking about?"

Trevor nodded. "Yes, but I wasn't picking on him. I was trying to stop him."

"Stop him from doing what? What is his name?"

"Daniel Branham. He was a loner. He didn't have a lot of friends. A lot of people gave him a hard time, made fun of him. He was weird, sure. But I wasn't a bully."

"You said you were trying to *stop* Daniel? Stop him from doing what, exactly?"

Trevor took a deep breath. "He sat beside me in algebra. I didn't talk to him much. No one really did. He always wore a long coat, even when it was hot outside. He got up from class and threw on his coat. A note fell from his pocket. I shouldn't have read it, but I was curious."

"What did it say?" I asked.

"It was a suicide note. It was also like some kind of manifesto. He said that everyone would remember him. Everyone would know his name. People would notice him. Every time they remembered everyone he wanted to kill, they'd have to remember his name."

"Was he going to shoot up the school?" I asked.

Trevor shook his head. "His note said something about his angel. His angel of vengeance would wipe out everyone who never talked to him, who turned away and made fun of him when they didn't think he could hear."

"Did you tell anyone about it?" I asked.

Trevor sighed. "I intended to. I confronted him about it, first. I thought if I talked to him, confronted him about it, maybe he'd reconsider. It was dumb. I should have gone straight to the principal."

"You probably should have. What happened next?"

"It got a little heated. He started screaming at me. He pushed me. I pushed him back into the lockers. A crowd of people gathered around, expecting a fight. Daniel didn't swing at me. He grabbed his note out of my hand and told me to mind my own business before he took off running down the hall. I headed straight for the principal's office, but I never made it."

"What happened?"

"Something grabbed me. It was black, it had wings, just like an angel. But it wasn't holy. It was evil. More like a demon. It pulled me into a janitor's closet. That's the last thing I remember."

"You weren't the only one. There was another boy who was killed."

"Who was it?" Trevor asked.

I turned to Annabelle. "Who was the other boy who died at the school?"

Annabelle checked her phone. "Wallace Jordon."

Trevor nodded. "That makes sense. Wallace was a bully. He gave Daniel all kinds of shit. Was there anyone else?"

I shook my head. "Not at the school. He killed the police who came after him."

"He didn't do it. That monster, that devil, whatever it was, did it for him."

"You're sure it was a suicide note?" I asked.

"It read like one. He didn't say he was going to kill himself, but it sure sounded like he didn't expect to be able to deliver the message himself."

"Is there anyone else he might have had a vendetta against? Anyone who he might have wanted dead?"

Trevor squinted. "No one hassled him as much as Wallace. Still, there was a girl. Very pretty. Way out of his league. He'd recently asked her to the homecoming dance, and she turned him down. It became something of a joke. She laughed right in his face. It happened at her locker, just a few lockers down from mine. I was there when it happened. He turned three shades red when she turned him down. He pulled his coat over his face and took off into the restroom."

"When did that happen?"

"The day before I—"

"The day before you died?"

Trevor nodded.

"What is the girl's name?"

"Savanna Higbee. She's on the volleyball team."

"Do you know where she lives?" I asked.

Trevor shook his head. "I knew her, but we weren't close friends or anything."

"Was there anyone else you can think of that Daniel might have held a grudge against?"

Trevor scratched the back of his head. "A lot of people were laughing about what happened. I think he intended to kill everyone. The note made it pretty clear."

"For whatever reason, he didn't finish his plans that day. Maybe he freaked out after two people died and he was afraid to carry out his plans."

"I don't know. I was dead at that point."

"Right. Thank you, Trevor. And I'm sorry this happened to you."

Trevor nodded. A tear fell down his ghostly face. "Me too."

I turned to Holland. "We're good. We have what we need."

Holland waved her hand. Trevor and Ghede Nibo disappeared.

"What did you learn?" Annabelle asked. "Do you know who did it?"

I nodded. "His name is Daniel. He's definitely infected, but it sounds like his parasite is carrying out murders on his behalf."

"It won't end there. It will kill Daniel when it's done."

"Most likely. There's a girl that I think might be his next target. Her name is Savanna Higbee."

"Did you say Savanna Higbee?" Jeanne asked.

"That's right. Do you know her?"

"She's friends with my daughter."

"We'll protect her," I said. "Do you have an address?"

"I can get it for you. It's in my phone, back in my office."

"Thank you," Annabelle said. "We'll head straight there. We won't let anything happen to the girl."

Chapter 10

I RODE SHOTGUN IN Connor's Escalade. Because I was *his* woman. Them other bitches? They were riding in the back. I had a feeling he enjoyed driving around all these beautiful women—as if he was fantasizing he was some kind of star and we were his entourage of admirers.

It was more like we were his owners and he was our dog—literally—with me being his primary owner, of course. Not that I'd tell him that. One secret I learned to dealing with men was that they all had fantasies. Some of them unspeakable. Many of then involving prestige, fame, and control. The key to keeping a man's metaphorical leash tight wasn't to yank on it, but to allow him to think he was in charge, to allow him to indulge in his fantasy world from time to time. He and I both knew, though, that all it would take was a little tug, maybe a few treats (back when I could give him the kind of "treat" I'm talking about), and there wasn't much he wouldn't do. He could enjoy his pimp-daddy fantasy for the moment. If I took charge, and snapped my fingers the right way, he'd be begging and barking like a dog—in his case, maybe literally. The real key, though, to maintaining that kind of control in a relationship, since he didn't really embrace a beta role, was never to mention it. Allow him to "play alpha" as much as he liked.

We were equals in our relationship. It wasn't anything weird. Still, in every relationship there's a subtle understanding of who is actually running the show. In our case, it was the vampire, not the wolf. It was one reason why I could laugh a little at the swagger he carried himself with as he accompanied us. It wasn't about him taking an interest in Annabelle, Holland, or Ellie. It was about an image he was living out more in his mind at the moment than according to anyone else's perception. I only realized it because I knew Connor well enough I could see through it.

It was adorable.

Sort of like when a little kid tries to tell his parents that *he's* the boss. It's not real mutiny. The parents aren't threatened by it. So long as the kid doesn't push it to the point of insubordination, it's cute.

I say all of that to confess this—a part of me felt a little guilty about how I'd treated him. I headed off to Exeter with Mercy to potentially save the world, yet again, and I left him sleeping in my bed without so much as a goodbye. I came back only to give him a phone call—didn't even tell him face-to-face—to say that I was becoming a succubus and we couldn't see each other. All it took was one call, and he came running back.

Connor never did shit like that to me. He didn't run off with other wolf shifters to go on life-threatening adventures without me. He included me in pretty much everything. He gave me the choice. If he had something to do, I could go with him or stay home. Most of the time, sunlight dictated my choice. Still, he communicated.

I took advantage of the fact that I knew I had him wrapped around my little finger, that he'd pretty much do anything if I asked. It wasn't just because I was more of an alpha in the relationship. It was because he loved me and while he liked to play like he was the man in charge, he put up with a lot of my shit just because he thought I was worth it. Maybe the little "treats" I gave him had less to do with it than his heart. Why else would he be there at my side knowing full-well I couldn't give him my cookie anytime soon?

Damn it. Introspection sucks sometimes. I'd been a pretty shitty girlfriend, and he was a good sport about it. I wanted to do better. He *deserved* better.

Connor's in-dash GPS told us where to turn. Jeanne wrote Savanna's address on the back of one of her business cards. It struck me as a little funny for a funeral director to have a business card. Where did they go to hand it out? Here you go. Have you ever considered death as an option for your future? I imagined sales in the funeral biz wasn't like it was in other industries. It had to be awkward if people were planning their own funerals. If you were dealing with the bereaved, it had to be awkward as hell. They must've been good at it. How else could you up-sell someone to buy a more expensive coffin when everyone knew that no one would ever see it again after the funeral? Was comfort really a concern? People didn't want to think about their loved ones being eaten by worms, I guess. The more air-tight, the better?

The funeral industry. The only line of work you could be in where, if business was dead, it was a good thing.

I'd put the address into Connor's GPS as soon as we left. It wasn't far from the funeral home. Just a few miles. Were we going to find anything? There was no reason to believe that Daniel was sending his parasite—who he thought was his personal angel of death—to kill Savanna at all, much less at that moment. Maybe he'd do it during the day. In that case, well, I wouldn't be there to help. Sure, for my benefit, Connor had a dark window-tint on his Escalade. I still couldn't leave the vehicle. Casting spells through windows wasn't ideal.

It was strange to hope that Daniel was going to send his monster after that poor girl. Not that I wanted her to die or anything. Quite the opposite. We just didn't know any other way to track him down. If we didn't kill his monster, he'd keep killing. When he was done, the monster would kill him. We didn't know how long that would be.

Connor parked outside of Savanna's house. Technically, her parents' house. It was a relatively new construction. Not like the older mansions, like Casa do Diabo, that were common in New Orleans. It was a nice house, two stories, with a fenced-in backyard. The fence was tall with the pickets nailed close together. We couldn't see into the backyard, which probably meant there was a pool behind the house.

Annabelle and Ellie were each sitting on bucket seats in the middle row behind Connor and me. Holland unbuckled her seat belt and laid down across the bench seat in the back.

"What are you doing?" Ellie craned her neck around.

"I'm sleeping. What does it look like I'm doing?"

"This is a stake out!" Ellie protested. "We're supposed to be watching and waiting!"

"You watch and wait. I can't see shit from back here. Might as well get a little shuteye."

"She has a point, Ellie," Annabelle said. "We don't know if anything's going to happen. You might as well get a little rest as well. Those of us who require sleep can go in shifts."

I cleared my throat. "You mean everyone except me?"

"I'll stay up with you," Connor said. "Besides, I can always sleep during the day."

"That's right," Annabelle said. "If this Daniel Branham and his monster don't show up tonight, we'll have to take you home."

"I can take my shift sleeping on the back seat if necessary. The windows will protect me from the light. Even so, if the monster shows after sunrise, I won't be able to do much to help."

"I don't think it will come to that," Connor said. "This kid has cops looking for him. If he has a half-wits' worth of intelligence, he'll only move under the cover of the night. He'll look for a place to hide during the day where no one will recognize him."

I chuckled. "Serial killers and vampires. Who would have thought we had so much in common?"

Annabelle grinned. "Many people think vampires *are* serial killers, Hailey."

"Yeah, you're right. Stupid bigots."

Connor grabbed my hand. "Let them be stupid. If people knew how many times you'd saved them from total destruction, how many times you averted a potential apocalypse, they'd be grateful."

I shrugged. "Maybe. A lot of people can't see past their bigotries. Doesn't matter how much you do or how many times you prove yourself. Some people see fangs and cast judgment. Nothing else matters."

"Meanwhile, they enjoy a fragile world without giving a second thought to how different their world would be without the contributions of those they hate and fear."

"That couldn't be any truer than it is now that you're a guardian of the convergences here," Annabelle added. "It's a thankless job."

I shrugged. "I don't need recognition. Some people do, but whatever. I know what I've done, the sacrifices I've made. People can express their gratitude by not being dicks to each other. That would be a nice start."

Annabelle chuckled. "If you expect people not to be dicks, don't hold out a lot of hope. I don't do what I do for them, though. When I fight something that threatens our community, I do it for the people I love. Everyone else can suck it."

I chuckled. "Especially us vampires. We like to suck it."

Annabelle smirked. "Not in the way I meant it. But yes, I've told Mercy to suck it more than once."

I laughed and shook my head. "Half the time, you realize she did things to get under your skin just because she found your reactions amusing."

Annabelle rolled her eyes. "That's the worst part. I knew she was doing that, but I couldn't help myself. That vampire really knew how to push my buttons."

I shrugged. "But you two made a pretty formidable team when duty called."

Annabelle grinned. "That we did. Now that she's up in Rhode Island, though, I can't say I'm too disappointed to be fighting the latest world-ending threat at your side instead."

"What can I say? Blondes know how to have fun."

"Amen, sister!" Ellie piped up.

Annabelle cocked her head. "Shut up, Ellie. You're a redhead. A little bleach doesn't make you a real blonde."

"It doesn't matter what's natural! How you look can change how you act. I'm a fun blonde now."

Annabelle snickered. "Do the curtains match the drapes?"

"None of your business!"

I turned around and grinned. "So you're only fun from the waist up?"

Ellie folded her arms in front of her chest. "Shut up."

"How about everyone shuts up?" Holland mumbled. "I'm trying to sleep back here."

Connor yawned and rubbed his eyes.

I squeezed his hand. "I thought you were still on vampire time."

"Mostly. I think it's less the time of night and more the activity. Staring at the same houses and streets and cars for so long with no change is more exhausting than you'd think."

A door opened from a black car that was parked across the street. It had been there as long as we were, but no one had entered the car the whole time.

"What the hell?" I asked.

Connor sighed. "He's in a uniform."

I rolled my eyes. "Shit."

"Just be cool," Annabelle said.

The cop strolled over and knocked on the driver's side window. He held his badge up to the window. Connor pressed a switch on his door and his window slid open.

"What can we do for you, officer?" Connor asked.

"You've all been sitting here in your car for a while now."

"So have you!" I piped up. "In yours, I mean."

"I'm an officer of the law. What I'm doing isn't your concern. I have reason to be concerned about anyone suspicious here."

I tilted my head. "You're spying on Savanna?"

"I'm not *spying*. Are you spying on someone?"

Annabelle cleared her throat. "He's probably here on protection detail, Hailey."

I shrugged. "Oh! You're here to protect her from the psycho boy who killed all those people."

"I'm not at liberty to speak about that."

I waved my hand through the air and winked at the cop. "Right. Not at liberty." I pointed at the cop, then back at myself. "You and me, though. We're here for the same reason. Same team."

"It doesn't work like that, miss."

"Pffft! Right. But you know, just between us, it works that way."

"Hailey," Annabelle whispered. "What are you doing?"

I turned back over my shoulder. "I'm trying to use my allure or whatever. Mercy's so much better at this shit than me."

The officer cleared his throat. "Would you all step out of the vehicle, please?"

"Why?" I asked. "We're just parked here. It's not like we're breaking the law."

"We should do as he asks," Annabelle muttered.

I rolled my eyes. "Alright. We're getting out. Don't shoot, okay?"

The cop furrowed his brow. "I just asked you to step out so we could all have a conversation rather than have you all whispering back and forth. I'm not arresting anyone. At least that's not on my agenda yet. And I don't plan on shooting anyone, either."

"Holland!" Ellie said. "Get up. Cop!"

Holland snorted. "Tell the pig to kiss my ass. I'm sleeping."

Annabelle turned around and back handed Holland on the leg. "Get up. You can go back to sleep later."

Holland grunted. "Fine."

Connor got out of the car first. "Need my license and registration?"

"This isn't a ticket. Just a conversation."

I stepped around the front of Connor's Escalade with my hands in the air. "Like I said, don't shoot. I'm cooperating."

The officer took a deep breath and shook his head.

Annabelle and Ellie each got out through the rear doors on either side of the vehicle. Holland stumbled out after them.

"Now, what are you all doing here?"

"Isn't it obvious?" I asked. "You're worried that Daniel Branham is going to come after Savanna. So are we. We're here to make sure he doesn't."

"That's not your concern. The suspect in question is dangerous and probably armed."

"And you're one dude," I said. "No offense, but we know what he did to the last cops who tried to arrest him."

"I wouldn't engage him alone. I'd call for backup."

"Why are you here? Why do you think Savanna is a target?"

"I told you already, young lady. I'm not at liberty to discuss the case."

"Well, like I said. We all want the same thing. And we have every legal right to sit in our legally parked car for as long as we want."

"Are you friends?"

I looked at Connor, Annabelle, and the other two mambos. "Yeah, we're friends."

"I meant are you Savanna's friends."

I bit my lip. "Ehh. Ish."

"You're friends-ish?"

Annabelle stepped up. "My apologies, officer. We don't intend any harm here. Why don't you call your chief? Tell him Annabelle Mulledy is here. He knows me."

"You know the police chief? How? Do you go to the same church? Are your parents friends with him?'

"My parents are dead, sir. And I'm not as young as I look."

"Me neither!" I piped up. "I don't really age."

Annabelle narrowed her eyes and glared at me. It was as if she was trying to tell me to shut up. I had to admit; I wasn't doing my best with my allure. If I was out on a hunt, looking for a meal, it was easy to capture a man's attention. I'd have him enthralled in moments. I wasn't trying to feed. I was full on bishop blood. My allure wasn't as instinctual as it would be in other circumstances.

Besides, the whole idea of using my allure on a cop felt weird. Maybe it was my anxiety that was holding me back. I was considering turning it up a notch, locking my eyes with his, licking my lips. It usually worked on most dudes when I was on the prowl.

I took a few steps back and gave up on my attempt. Annabelle was making better progress. If she really had a relationship with the police chief, it could help. I didn't know she had connections with law enforcement. It shouldn't have surprised me. She was basically the steward of all the supernaturals in New Orleans. They were her responsibility. If something came across an officer's desk that reeked of non-human or magically induced activity, he must've passed it along to Annabelle. If she came across conventional, run-of-the-mill, human criminal activity, she could turn it over to the cops. Win, win.

"Tell the chief that this is my kind of case."

The cop narrowed his eyes. "Excuse me?"

"Just tell him. See what he says."

The police officer returned to his vehicle. He got inside. I imagined he was on his radio. He came back out a couple of minutes later.

"I don't know who the hell you people are, but I was told to leave you be and return to the station."

I reached up and patted the cop on his shoulder. "That's a good boy."

The cop shook his head in confusion. "I don't know what is going on here, exactly, but be careful. This kid doesn't look like much, but he's dangerous."

I smiled widely, not even realizing that I was showing my fangs. "Danger is my middle name."

The cop gasped and turned around. He returned to his vehicle.

Holland laughed. "That was corny as hell."

"What was?" I asked.

"Cliche is your middle name, Hailey."

I giggled. "Alright. I admit it. Total cheese balls. But it worked."

"If scaring the shit out of that man was what you were going for, sure."

"You really shouldn't show your fangs to cops," Connor said.

I smirked. "I know. But hey, he's out of our hair now."

"Thanks to Annabelle and her connections!" Ellie piped up.

I nodded. "Right. And because I smooth talked him. Great team effort."

Annabelle laughed a little under her breath. "Get back in the Escalade, Hailey."

Chapter 11

We got back in the Escalade and resumed waiting and watching. We didn't have to wait long. It was almost as if Daniel knew a cop was watching and was waiting for him to leave. If what we knew about him was accurate, he didn't *want* to kill cops. He wanted to kill his classmates, the ones who never noticed him, the ones who mocked him and made his life hell.

A massive shadow appeared in the driveway of Savannah's family's home. It was almost half as tall as the house itself. From what we'd seen of the shadows so far, that didn't mean much. It could get larger or smaller at will. Until it materialized, it was frightening as hell, but mostly harmless. We had to get to it before it hurt Savannah.

We were taking a different approach this time. Before, when we tracked the stick-figure shadow, we didn't know that the bishop was its host. Even the bishop didn't realize it. I didn't know it, myself, when I had a parasite. Not until the clown tried to kill me and, even then, it was only because of Holland that we knew it was attached to me.

This was different. We knew who the host was. If all we did was stop the shadow, we'd save Savanna, but we wouldn't learn anything. This shadow was responding to Daniel. He knew about it and was using it. If they were communicating somehow, he was the best chance we had so far to learn something about these shadow monsters. Where did they come from? How many were there? Where was the convergence they used to travel to our world? Maybe Daniel would know those answers, maybe he wouldn't.

He was also different from the bishop, who was an unwitting host for his parasite. Daniel knew what it could do and *wanted* it to kill. He wasn't an innocent bystander. I certainly empathized with what he'd gone through. Being bullied sucks. That didn't excuse murdering people.

I took a deep breath. "We should split up. The priority is protecting the girl. We also need to learn what we can. And there might be a better way to stop the parasite than using my blood prison. If we can get to Daniel, we might convince him to call it off."

"We know where Savanna is. Connor, use your wolf sniffer to track down Daniel. You are our best chance to find him quickly."

"I think I should go with Connor," Ellie said. "If the monster is using Daniel's angst and hatred, I can use Erzulie's power to counteract that. Love always conquers hate!"

Holland rolled her eyes. "Tell that to the people Daniel killed. Sometimes hate wins. Next time someone tries to murder you, give them a hug and see how that goes."

"People rarely try to murder me, Holland."

"Really? I would have thought it happened to you on the daily."

I cleared my throat. "I might also need you, Ellie. If my succubus nature gains strength when I cast the blood prison and I use the bishop's blood, Erzulie's aspect is my best shot at fighting it off."

Annabelle shook her head. "If Ellie is right, if she can reach Daniel, you might not even need to cast the blood prison. Don't do it except as a last resort."

"My abilities are also more useful with the boy," Holland said. "The parasite manifested when I probed Hailey's mind before because it felt threatened. I'm not sure there's anything I could do to help Hailey protect Savanna."

Annabelle nodded. "Hailey isn't going in there alone. I'll go with her. If her blood prison fails, I still have my soul-blade as a last resort."

The shadow monster was still lurking outside of Savanna's home. I didn't know what it was waiting for, but we needed to move.

We jumped out of the Escalade. Annabelle took off toward the house.

Connor shifted into wolf form. He had better senses, even in human form, than average. As a wolf, though, he could track almost anything. He didn't have Daniel's scent, but if there was anyone lurking in the shadows, he'd find them. Given the late hour, there weren't many people outside. I knew Connor would find the boy.

The shadow monster had giant wings, just like Trevor's ghost described it. It was no wonder that Daniel thought it was an angel. Daniel wanted an angel of vengeance. An angel of death. Like the one from the book of Exodus that flew through Egypt and slew the first-born male in every home not marked by sacrificial blood. The parasite took that form because that's what Daniel expected. If he thought the thing was an angel of death, that's what it would become.

The shadow angel passed right through the front of the house.

I sighed. "Ever kick down a door?"

Annabelle nodded. "Once or twice. You've got that vampire strength. You do it."

I nodded. "Nothing like breaking and entering to save someone's life."

I charged the front door and blasted it with a hard front-kick. The door exploded off its hinges.

The security system went off. A loud siren sounded.

"So much for being discreet," Annabelle huffed. "We need to find Savanna."

"Hold it right there!"

I shook my head. A man holding a rifle approached us from his living room. "Sir, we're here to help. Your daughter is in danger."

"Where are the police? They're supposed to be keeping watch."

Annabelle took a step forward. "Lower your gun, sir. We believe that something is already in the house and is going to kill your daughter. We don't have time to explain."

"Something? What do you mean by *something*?"

"Do you want me to explain or do you want me to help Savanna?"

A girl screamed from somewhere upstairs.

"Go! It's the first door upstairs on the right!"

I climbed the stairs using my vampire speed. The poor girl's father was probably freaking out, but we'd worry about explaining the reality of vampires and supernatural monsters to him later. I heard footsteps behind me. Annabelle and Savanna's father were following me. I burst into the girl's bedroom.

Savanna was still screaming. She was in her bed and had her covers pulled up over her for protection. As if a few blankets would save her from the monster.

The creature was still a shadow. It spread its wings out wide and arched over the girl.

Until it manifested, I couldn't do much. I dove through the shadow monster and landed on top of Savanna.

"I'm a friend. I'm here to help."

The girl was shaking and crying. I was lying on top of her. I rolled over and aimed my wand at the monster. The second it materialized, I was ready to blast it. I had my blood prison spell ready to go. All I had to do was unleash my power. Doing it like this, with it so close to us, would not be easy. I needed a little space between myself and the creature.

I grabbed Savanna, still holding my wand in one hand, and wrapped one arm around her. I rolled with her out of the bed. We landed on the floor with a thud.

It gave us just enough space. If only the damned thing materialized, I could take it out.

It didn't take corporeal shape. It stopped and hovered in the air above us.

The monster turned its head toward the wall. It took off fast and passed through a closed window.

I turned to Savanna. "Are you okay?"

Savanna was still shaking, but she nodded her head.

"I've got the girl," Annabelle said from the doorway. "Go after that monster. The others must've found the boy."

I sprung to my feet and took off out of the room. I bumped into Savanna's father a little harder than I intended, but he was in the way. I don't think I even touched one step as I leapt down the stairs.

When Connor, Ellie, and Holland found the boy, he must've called the monster back for protection. He felt threatened. The monster responded to his angst, maybe even subconsciously. It was the boy's emotions, not necessarily his commands, that directed the parasite. His fear of my friends must've superseded his desire for vengeance.

I stopped in the driveway and listened. I didn't know where they were. Connor sniffed out the boy quickly, but my sense of smell wasn't strong enough to lock in on him.

Wolf shifters aren't especially adept fighters. They're basically wolves. They aren't like werewolves with extra strength. They can heal when they shift back and forth, provided they aren't dealt a mortal blow. All he had were a couple of mambos, neither who whom were adept at fighting. Annabelle's primary aspect—she had a few—was from the Loa of War. She was suited for battle. Mambos with the aspects of love and death weren't exactly equipped to take on one of these monsters. So far, the only two ways we knew that worked to stop them were my blood prison and Annabelle's blade. At least she was still with Savanna in case the monster came back.

This shadow monster took down a bunch of cops. Connor, Ellie, and Holland stood little chance. My heart raced in my chest. It was an odd feeling. Usually, as a vampire, my heart only beat a couple of times a minute. Now it thumped like it used to when I was human, if I'd just gone for a run or was anxious about something.

All I could think about was Connor. All I wanted when I told him to stay away from me was to keep him safe, now I'd let him right into the path of a murderous otherworldly monster.

I couldn't lose him. I wouldn't lose him.

I didn't know what was happening to me. I took off running. I instinctively turned a corner. I didn't know why. Something was pulling me, tugging at me through my pounding heart.

I saw them in the middle of the street about three blocks down. Ellie was knocked out cold. The beast materialized for a split-second, just in time to slap Holland with one of its wings. She flew into the grass of someone's home. Connor was running around, still in wolf form, evading the monster. He growled at the beast. The monster wasn't intimidated.

It was a shadow again. The way it kept phasing in and out of material form, I couldn't get a lock on it with my wand. I ran as hard as I could. With my speed, it only took a couple of seconds to get there.

A young boy with stringy brown hair and a black trench coat stood there. "Stay back!"

I wasn't about to engage the kid in conversation. He was too dangerous. All I could think to do was knock him out with brute force. If he was unconscious, maybe it would quell his emotions. It would pacify the beast. At least temporarily.

The shadow angel flew at me as I took off toward Daniel. It was fast. I was faster. I grabbed Daniel by his shoulders. I was going to slam him to the ground when my heart stilled. A tingle swelled in my body and a pink light appeared on the kid's face. It was coming from me—from my eyes.

I turned my head just in time to see the angel disappear. It was like his shadow turned to smoke and dissipated in the air.

"What are you?" Daniel asked.

I didn't answer him. Connor was running toward me. Ellie approached behind him, rubbing her head. I looked the other direction and Holland was also getting back to her feet.

"You did it!" Ellie exclaimed.

"What did I to? I'm not sure."

"Erzulie's aspect. You used it. You touched this kid, and it overwhelmed his emotions."

"Let me go!" Daniel shouted. "The angel is coming back. He protects me."

I shook my head. "It's not an angel. It's a parasite."

"What are you talking about?"

I looked at Daniel and flashed my fangs. "You're coming with us."

"You're a— No, vampires aren't real."

I tilted my head. "Reconsider your worldview. Hate to break it to you, but I'm very real. And you've been a very naughty boy."

Daniel gulped. I grabbed him by the shoulders and tossed him over. I grabbed him by his wrists with one hand and pulled him to his feet by the back of his coat with my other hand.

Holland stepped up behind me. "Want me to do my thing? You can kill it now."

I shook my head. "Not yet. I pacified his emotions for now."

"What did you do to me? I feel... different."

"I'll keep him in check," Ellie said. "What did you do, Hailey? How did you pull it off?"

I looked down at Connor, still in wolf form. "I thought about him. I was afraid for him."

"It was your love for him. It allowed you to access Erzulie's aspect."

"Mind if I give you a quick read?" Holland asked. "I'm curious."

Ellie took Daniel. She kept one hand on his back. Holland put her hands on my head. I braced myself for the piercing cold. I winced as the chill spread from my head through my body.

"Holy shit," Holland said. "You did it."

"I did what?"

"Using Erzulie's aspect. It purged the demon's essence from you. You're free!"

I gasped. "Say what?"

"I said you're free. No more succubus."

Connor resumed his human form. He was totally naked. I didn't mind. I wrapped my arms around him and kissed him on the lips.

"I missed that," Connor said.

I smiled. "Me too."

"You people are freaks!" Daniel shouted.

I laughed. "You don't know the half of it."

Chapter 12

CONNOR FOUND HIS CLOTHES. It was mildly disappointing, but then again, I didn't want Ellie and Holland staring at my man in the buff. Annabelle met us back at the Escalade.

Savanna was safe. Traumatized, but alive. Her father was confused. Annabelle said she'd have to pay them a visit later to give them the standard talk. It wasn't the first time she had to explain the supernatural world to outsiders. This wasn't her first rodeo.

We tied Daniel's wrists and ankles together with his own shoelaces and tossed him in the back seat. Ellie sat next to him and maintained contact. She was using her aspect to keep the parasite within him from accessing his angst.

"Where to?" Connor asked.

"We can't bring him into Vilokan while that parasite is still inside of him. It's too risky."

I nodded. "Go to Casa do Diabo. We'll question him there."

We arrived at mine and Mercy's mansion in the French Quarter. Tommy jumped up when he saw us walk through the front door. "You brought home food!"

I glanced at Daniel. He gulped.

"That wasn't the idea but, what the hell?"

Daniel struggled against his shoe-string bindings. Ellie kept her hand on his shoulder.

"Where's Sarah?" I asked.

"In her room, I think. Probably reading a book."

I nodded. "She isn't much for socialization. Comes with the territory. She lived by herself for a century and a half."

"Mind if we take the couch for a bit?" I asked.

"Can I have a bite first?" Tommy asked.

I smirked. "We'll see how cooperative he is."

Annabelle and I pulled over a couple of dining chairs and set them in front of Daniel and Ellie. I don't think Daniel blinked once. It would have been terrifying for almost anyone to be in his situation. Even more so for a kid who'd barely scratched the surface of puberty. His age wasn't an excuse, though. He knew what he was doing. At least he thought he did. He didn't understand the risks involved, or nature of the creature he thought was his dark angel. Still, he wanted those people to die. The shadow monster did his bidding because of his angst and, unlike others who hosted these ethereal parasites, he *wanted* his monster to kill. So far as I was concerned, giving the kid a bit of a fright was letting him off easy.

"That's Tommy. He's my progeny. He's thirsty. There's something you should know about young vampires. They have a hard time knowing when to stop during a feed."

Daniel's lip quivered. "Please let me go!"

"So you can go back to killing people?" Annabelle raised one eyebrow. "I don't think so."

"What are you going to do with me?" Daniel asked.

I smiled as widely as I could. I wanted to make sure he saw my fangs. "That depends on what you can tell us. We've been tracking these shadow monsters all over the city. So far, you're the only one who is sending out his monster on purpose. Everyone else, the monster acts on its own. It latches on to some kind of negative emotion and does its own thing. Then it kills the host."

"My angel defends me. He wouldn't kill me."

"Do you know that for sure?" Annabelle asked.

"You wouldn't understand. It's beyond you."

Annabelle snorted. "Excuse me? I'm the Voodoo Queen of New Orleans. I've communed with the Loa. I've faced a lot worse than you."

Daniel shook his head. "Have *you* been to the Aeon of Barbelo?"

I tilted my head. "Isn't that in Spain?"

Annabelle rolled her eyes. "You're thinking of Barcellona. Barbelo is a tripartite realm described in gnostic writings."

"Have you been there?" Daniel asked. "I have."

Annabelle shook her head. "I don't think that's a place you can go."

"Are you sure about that?"

I sighed. "How did you go to Barbelo?"

Daniel shrugged. "I don't know. I died, and that's where I went."

"Wait." Annabelle shifted in her chair. "You *died*?"

"I stabbed myself in the neck."

I winced. "That's one way to do it."

"My blood fell to the floor. The puddle opened up some kind of door. When I collapsed, I reappeared in Barbelo. My wound was healed."

I bit my lip. "Where did this happen?"

"In the bayou. I didn't want anyone to find me and try to save me."

"Which swamp?" Annabelle asked.

"Manchac, I think. There was a patch of dry ground and what looked like a burned out tree."

I pressed my lips together. "A convergence. That sounds like the place where Cain confronted Nachash, the serpent from the Tree of Knowledge."

Annabelle nodded. "It's also where Julie Brown first tore a hole into the void. It makes sense the veil between realms would be thin there. A prime location for a convergence."

"All my life I didn't fit in. The Aeon of Barbelo gave me a chance to come back and be something special."

"All your life?" I huffed. "You aren't that old. A lot of people have had awkward teenage years. I did, too."

Daniel rolled his eyes. "You're a pretty girl. Don't tell me you had it as hard as I did."

"I did," Ellie piped up. "I wasn't always pretty. I was an awkward girl when I was your age. Ever have your face shoved in a toilet?"

Daniel nodded. "It happened once."

"Try every freaking day in the eighth grade."

Daniel looked at the ground. "Then you know how I felt."

"But I never killed people, Daniel."

"I'm sure you wanted to."

"Wanting to do something and actually doing it are two different things."

Daniel sighed. "When I got to Barbelo, I encountered a being who called himself Kalyptos."

Annabelle nodded. "The hidden one. The highest sub-aeon within the Aeon of Barbelo."

"He said he was what allowed all things to exist. He was potential itself."

"What did he do to you?" I asked.

"He called an angel. He said I'd be its vessel. He called the angel Protophanes."

Annabelle crossed her arms. "The first appearing one."

"I brought Protophanes back to earth. Kalyptos said it would change the world. He said that those who are troubled, those who suffered like me, would have power. Their suffering would take form and manifest to exact justice in the world. When I woke up again in the swamp, I puked. Not food. My angel, Protophanes, released a thousand shadows into the world."

Annabelle pinched her chin. "The Autogenes. The self-generated. They're the parasites, the shadow monsters that self-generate beings that accord with a host's angst."

"Any pain, bottled-up, was supposed to become real. No one like me would ever have to suffer again. My angel told me his children would change things."

I snorted. "One of them infected me. It took the form of a clown and tried to kill me. How is that justice?"

"My angel said that he'd cure people of fear. Those who succumbed to fear might die by their fears. The only way to overcome was to defeat our fears. Those who were hurt, the victims, would realize vengeance at the hand of Protophanes' children."

I furrowed my brow. "How many of these children did you release?"

"The first of many. More will come in time. Eventually, no more fear. No more bullies."

I cleared my throat. "You realize, by killing these people, there are many people who see you as the bully now. You're the enemy who has to be stopped. Do you think the parents of the children you killed don't want justice?"

Daniel shook his head. "I was dead already. They sent me back to change things."

"By killing people?" I asked.

"Only people who deserve it!"

Ellie sighed. "Bullies are cruel. But most of them are young. They grow up. They change. Nothing that happens when you're young is permanent. If you knew that, you wouldn't have turned to suicide."

Daniel shook his head. "It was the best decision I ever made."

"You need serious help," I said. "I'm not just talking about seeing a shrink. This creature isn't your friend. It will kill you eventually."

"It needs me! I'm the one who brought it here."

"It hitched a ride on your spirit, through your body. That doesn't mean it needs you. These parasites, whatever they are, can attach themselves to just about anyone. You aren't special."

"I am special! For the first time ever, I am!"

Three loud knocks on the front door interrupted our conversation.

"Who the hell is visiting at this hour?" I wondered out loud.

"Newsflash." Annabelle chuckled. "You're a vampire, Hailey. Do you usually get visitors during the day?"

I sighed. "It's probably another vampire looking for Mercy."

"I'll get it." Annabelle stood up and approached the front door. She unlocked the deadbolt and opened the door.

"Mister Higbee?"

I gulped and stood up. Savanna's father was standing there, his eyes darker than before. "You followed us?"

Higbee nodded. He pressed himself into the foyer, past Annabelle. I met him half-way between the door and the living room. "Your daughter is fine. What are you doing here?"

"Why are you keeping him safe? He murdered people. He tried to kill my girl!"

"Calm down, sir. We're just trying to get information out of him. We're not protecting him."

"Then stand aside!" Higbee shouted.

He opened his mouth, and a giant shadow formed in front of him. It was the same shadow monster that we *thought* possessed Daniel. All I could figure was that when I used my aspect and silenced Daniel's angst, the parasite left him. It attached itself to Savanna's father. Now it wanted vengeance.

The monster—the one Daniel called Protophanes—flew past me. It arched its wings over Daniel and took corporeal form. It was no angel. Its body was reptilian, littered with scales. Its wings were more like a bat's than a bird's.

Daniel screamed as Protophanes snarled, drooling a green ooze on the boy's chest.

I grabbed my wand and blasted it with a blood prison. It surrounded the monster. "Get him out of here!"

Sarah ran down from upstairs. She and Tommy grabbed Mister Higbee and pulled him outside. If I were to guess, he was about to become a youngling's meal.

I wasn't worried about that. This creature was stronger than the one that possessed the bishop. It fought against my blood prison.

Annabelle, Ellie, and Holland grabbed Daniel and headed out the door. Connor followed with his keys in hand.

"Meet us back at my office!" Annabelle shouted.

"Ellie! Get to Higbee!"

I didn't know if she heard me. I knew I couldn't hold this thing forever. The last one suffocated in my blood prison. If this monster was the first, the one that spawned all the rest, it made sense that it was stronger.

I could only hold the prison so long as I had enough blood, could draw enough power from it, to hold it. I didn't drink much from the bishop before. It was just enough to get back on my feet and calm my cravings.

My blood prison faded. I ran out of juice. Protophanes charged at me. Before it could materialize, it disappeared in a puff of smoke—just as it did before.

I turned around. Sarah was holding Higbee. Blood dripped from Tommy's chin. Ellie had her hand on the man's head.

"It's gone for now," Ellie said.

My stomach turned. I used up a lot of blood. Maybe all of it. My arms were shaking. I couldn't even hold my wand. It fell to the ground at my feet.

"She's going feral!" Sarah shouted. "She needs blood!"

I tried to scream. It came out more like a snarl. Flesh hit my fangs. I bit, and I drank. It calmed my mind. My body stopped convulsing. Mister Higbee was drained, and lying on the floor. I rubbed my brow. "Damn it!"

Sarah placed her hand on my shoulder. "If you heal him, he might turn. He's lost too much blood."

"I can't let him die. He was only protecting his daughter."

"It's your choice," Sarah said. "But you aren't the only one who bit him. Tommy did as well."

I picked up my wand. I cast a healing spell over the man's body. It reflected off him.

"I'm using the power from his blood to heal him. It's not working. His body is rejecting it."

"Use other magic," Sarah said. "You aren't *just* a blood witch."

I kneeled down. My wand was incanted with other spells that would do the job. I pressed my wand to Higbee's chest. I was about to speak an incantation when I saw the man's ghost standing in front of me.

"He's already dead," Tommy said. "I can see him."

I took a deep breath and released it. “I see him, too. It’s too late. I can’t turn him.”

Higbee’s ghost stared at me in horror. He saw his body. He saw what happened. A tear fell down his cheek. “Look out for my daughter. You owe me that.”

My eyes welled up as I nodded. “I will. I promise. I’m sorry.”

Chapter 13

ELLIE STAYED WITH ME. We walked to Vilokan together. She wasn't her usual bubbly self. I wasn't much for cracking jokes at the moment, either. An innocent man died—not only because of these monsters, but because, in my effort to stop one of them, I nearly turned myself feral. He just happened to be there.

Tommy had bitten him already. He only took a few gulps. I couldn't fault him for it. I was the one who lost control. I'd *never* lost control feeding before.

Then again, I'd never cast a spell that nearly turned me feral. Most blood spells didn't require so much power. They weren't nearly as draining. Most of the time, a blood prison didn't take so much out of me. It took everything I had to hold these monsters. It nearly killed me.

Going feral was as good as death. Other vampires knew that if there was a feral on the loose, staking it was the only option. Maybe two or three percent of vampires who ever went feral came back from it. I liked my chances better than most. As a blood witch, my powers might have helped my odds, but there weren't any guarantees.

It's also pretty rare that a vampire goes feral. The cravings will overwhelm a vampire before it gets that bad. I'd turned several ferals with an exsanguination spell in the past, but short of that, if a vampire went feral, it was usually because there weren't any humans nearby. It happened from time to time when vampires were punished by the church, by the powers-that-be, or even the old vampire council, by being buried alive. They used to seal vampires in coffins and sink them in the ocean. It was a condemnation to an eternity as a feral, bound to a coffin he couldn't escape. It was a fate worse than death.

There's nothing worse than knowing you killed someone to save your own ass. That wasn't how I thought about it at the time. When a vampire was drained like that, it didn't matter how old the vampire might be. It was as automatic as gasping for air when you reached the surface after swimming underwater.

That didn't take away the overwhelming sense of guilt. Sometimes I wished I could have been like Mercy. Back when I first met her. She had more of a conscience now than she used to. There was a time when she could feed, kill, and forget about it before sunrise.

Maybe it was what Holland described when she analyzed my spirit. Maybe it had something to do with the fact that I had more of a soul left than most vampires. Baron Samedi didn't have mine. He didn't carry it around as a cigarette in his satchel.

More than that, I should have figured it out. We should have asked Holland to read Daniel's condition before we dragged him off the street and took him home. If we did that, we would have known that the parasite left him. We wouldn't know that it had attached itself to Savanna's father, but we would have suspected it before he burst into our house. We could have been prepared. Ellie could have neutralized his parasite before it manifested.

Ellie said little as she walked beside me. Not for the first couple of blocks, anyway. Tommy and Sarah were dealing with the body. Mercy would have known how to handle it. She could make it look like an accident. That way, the family could get the body back and have a little closure. It was better than the missing person eventually presumed dead approach. Knowing is always better than not knowing. Sarah was older than even Mercy. She didn't have Mercy's experience, and she was more of a recluse than a leader, but I hoped she'd figure something out that didn't involve burning the man's body to ash or tossing him into Lake Pontchartrain.

Ellie waited until St. Louis Cathedral was in view, shortly before we turned down Pere Antoine Alley to say something. "At least now we know what to do."

"Do we, though?" I didn't look at her when I replied. I kept walking.

"There's only one of those things we have to kill. I mean, kill all of them eventually. But to stop the shadow monster apocalypse? If

Daniel was right about what he told us, Protophanes is the only one that can reproduce."

"Maybe. I'm still worried about the convergence. Just because this particular Protophanes might be responsible for the others, if that convergence is still connected to the Aeon of Barbelo, who is to say another one might not make its way through?"

"It sounded to me like Protophanes needed Daniel. It had to hitch a ride in his body. The offspring, the Autogenes, also require hosts to manifest. When we separated these things from their hosts, when I overwhelmed their emotional matrix with Erzulie's power, they didn't take a different form. Nothing that we could see or interact with. They disappeared."

"Until they latched on to another host. I'm not even sure at this point if I actually killed the one Holland exorcised from the bishop. My shield didn't cut if off from Barbelo. It cut if off from the host."

Ellie nodded. "You're probably right. Your blood prisons and Erzulie's power might do the same thing, just from a different angle. The prison cuts off the monster from the host by surrounding it with blood magic. Erzulie's power does it by making the host uninhabitable."

I nodded. "All that means is that we might not have a way to kill Protophanes at all. It might keep jumping from host to host every time we force it out of someone."

"What are you suggesting we do? Do you have any ideas?"

"Let's get back to Vilokan and check in. If what I'm thinking is going to work, I'm going to need some help."

"What are you thinking, Hailey?"

"If Protophanes' spirit needs to hitch a ride to pass through the convergence, there may be only one way to send it back to the Aeon of Barbelo."

Ellie shook her head. "Daniel opened the gate by shedding his own blood. We don't even know where Protophanes is now, much less are we likely to find many volunteers who are willing to kill themselves. Say they could come back, like Daniel did. Protophanes could come right back with them."

"Not if I do it. I can use blood magic to flood the convergence. If that's what it takes to open it, that's not a problem. The trick is going to be convincing Protophanes to possess me before I go back."

Ellie nodded. "And you can use Erzulie's aspect to kick him out when you get there."

"That's the plan. Let's just hope I can find my way out again. So long as no one else sheds their blood over the location of the convergence, we shouldn't have to worry about it coming back."

Chapter 14

ELLIE AND I MADE it to Annabelle's office. Holland and Connor were already there waiting.

"Where's Daniel?" I asked.

"Holland double checked to make sure he was free of the parasite. We took him to the Vilokan Asylum."

"Are you going to turn him in to the secular authorities?" Ellie asked.

Annabelle shook her head. "I'm in contact with the Chief of Police. He understands that this is something the secular judicial system isn't prepared to handle. Chances are, given the condition of the bodies, and the lack of a murder weapon, there's little more than circumstantial evidence to convict. Even if they convicted him, somehow, they'd probably lock him up. He wouldn't get much help. That's sort of the problem with our judicial system. We lock away pretty much anyone for anything, even non-violent crimes, as if incarceration is the only way to achieve justice. There are more creative and fitting ways to penalize criminals, but our system isn't that thoughtful. Then we give them very little rehabilitation while they're there."

"So he's committed to the Vilokan Asylum. What happens after that?"

"That depends on him and how much progress he makes."

I took a deep breath. "Higbee didn't make it. I need to tell Savanna."

Ellie tilted her head. "Let someone else do it. Tell Annabelle your plan."

Annabelle squinted. "I'm sorry to hear that."

"I promised Higbee I'd take care of his daughter. I'd make sure she's safe."

"Let me hear this plan."

I cleared my throat. "Connor isn't going to like it."

"Why wouldn't I like it?"

I sighed. "I have an idea to defeat Protophanes. I want to send him back to the Aeon of Barbelo."

"How do you intend to pull that off?" Annabelle asked.

"The convergence was opened by blood before. If I can lure Protophanes into me, I can take it there. I can use Erzulie's aspect to expel it. Then, hopefully, I can get back."

"Why do you have to do this alone?" Connor asked.

"Because I'm the only one, apart from Ellie, who can come back sure that she's not possessed by another parasite from Barbelo."

Annabelle sat on top of her desk. "There will still be more parasites here."

I nodded. "But if Protophanes is the only one that can reproduce, we can contain the problem. We might not be able to stop all the Autogenes, we still need a better way to get rid of them. I'm not sure my blood prisons were killing them like we thought."

"Did you need Connor before to activate Erzulie's aspect."

Ellie shook her head. "Her love for him is what will bring her home. It's what will give her the strength to fight through whatever she has to endure in Barbelo. So long as that's what's front and center in her mind, Erzulie will protect her."

Connor stood up and took me by both hands. "You can do this. I know you can."

I nodded. "There's just one issue we have to address. somehow we have to find Protophanes. I have to keep Erzulie's aspect isolated so it doesn't kick the thing out of me. If it's even possible to convince that thing to bind itself to me."

Annabelle narrowed her eyes. "Angst attracts the thing like shit does flies. It needs something to latch on to, to use as a catalyst to manifest. If it doesn't sense something like that inside of you, I don't think it will come to you."

"I just drained an innocent man. A man who was only trying to protect his daughter. Perhaps that will be enough."

"Are you sure about that?" Annabelle asked. "How would something like this manifest in response to an emotion like that? It's not directed toward anyone except yourself."

I nodded. "That's it. The clown came after me because it was fear that drew it to me. It's not like I live every day thinking about clowns. It's not an all-consuming fear, but it was enough. It used that to manifest and attack me, to realize my fear."

Connor cleared his throat. "You want to use self-loathing and regret to convince this monster to bind itself to you and try to kill you?"

I nodded. "That's what I'm thinking. I've thwarted this thing already. With all of you helping me, of course. But I have the magic that threatens it. If it has a chance to eliminate me, and use my regret against me, perhaps that will be enough."

"You shouldn't hate yourself," Connor said. "You didn't kill that man on purpose."

I shook my head. "I don't hate myself. But a part of me fears what I am, what I might be capable of if I'm pushed to the limit. I'm afraid of losing control and killing everyone around me."

Annabelle cleared her throat. "If this thing binds itself to you, Hailey, it might not try to kill you. If your fear is that you might one day kill people you love, that's what it will do. It will manifest and try to kill all of us."

Connor shook his head. "Not if she drags the thing into Barbelo first."

Holland was sitting on a chair in front of Annabelle's desk. She had her feet crossed on top of it. She uncrossed them, put them back on the ground and stood up. "I'll go with you."

"I can't ask you to join me in Barbelo."

"If you can't cast the thing out on your own, I can do it. For some reason, these things feel threatened by my abilities."

"Which is why you have to stay here. If I don't come back, we need everyone who has a chance of stopping these things to take out the others. We still don't know how many are out there and how many people might die if we don't eliminate them all."

Holland pursed her lips. "Perhaps. The parasite probably jumped to a host nearby. We know when it left Daniel, it found Higbee. He was the closest, most distressed person in the area. That means it's likely inside one of us."

Annabelle nodded. "That's a good point. You checked Daniel when we arrived and we know it didn't go back into him. The question is which one of us is harboring the parasite."

"Tommy and Sarah were also there," I added. "If we're going to do this, I say we go out to the swamp. Holland will have to check all of us."

Annabelle narrowed her eyes. "Fair enough. Still, how are you going to ensure that Protophanes will attach itself to you once Holland exorcises it from the host?"

"Another blood prison. This time, I trap myself inside of it. I don't give it any other choice. If I cast it right over the convergence, I'm hoping it will be enough to force open the door to Barbelo."

"You couldn't hold it at Casa do Diabo," Connor said. "What if it refuses to bind itself to you and your prison fails?"

I shook my head. "I didn't have a lot of blood to draw on before. All I had was what I took from the priest, which was barely enough to get back on my feet."

"Do you need more blood now?" Annabelle asked.

I shook my head and sighed. "I was close to feral. When I started drinking from Higbee, I couldn't stop. I am as full as I could possibly be."

Ellie smiled and took my hand in hers. "Then his sacrifice wasn't for nothing."

I shook my head. "I will reflect on that when this is done. For now, if I have any angst at all about killing him, I need it to attract Protophanes."

Chapter 15

We only had a couple of hours left until sunrise. We also risked Protophanes manifesting in whoever it possessed. It could have been any of us. I already had some angst about killing Higbee. The monster knew I was the one fighting it. I had angst, but I was a threat. I couldn't say for sure, but I doubted it was inside me.

It was hard to tell if one of those things was inside of you. It was sort of like the end of a night with an unfortunately endowed date.

Not to mention, one of those bastards attached itself to me because I had a phobia of clowns. It was a relatively minor issue so far as angst went. The bishop had suppressed lust. Who doesn't have lust? The monster could be attached to any of us. There way no way to guess which one of us it could be. Add to that, we didn't know how intelligent these things were. Perhaps it bound itself to whoever had the most angst or, if it was strategizing against us, it might have chosen someone we wouldn't suspect.

We hurried out of Vilokan, returned to the Escalade, and picked up Tommy and Sarah from Casa do Diabo. Three vampires. Three mambos. With Erzulie's aspect, I suppose I was a bit of a mambo in training. Annabelle, Ellie, and Holland were Voodoo Academy graduates. At most, I was dabbling.

Connor drove us to the edge of the swamp. I glanced at the moon. It was nearing the horizon. It was a crescent. If it was a full moon, there'd like be werewolves in the swamp. It was where they usually went to run through the night.

This wasn't my first trek through the swamp. It wasn't pleasant. Of all of us, Ellie had the hardest time. All her pink clothing was covered in algae and muck. We moved across broken trees where we could, but there was no way to make it to the convergence without getting wet and muddy. There were also alligators and snakes, not to mention mosquitoes. The swamp wasn't a pleasant place to take a stroll.

It was a wonder that of all places, Manchac Swamp was where Daniel attempted to kill himself. He said it was because he wanted to be so far off the grid no one would find him and try to save his life.

I was beginning to wonder if the kid didn't know something. If all of this was more than an unfortunate coincidence. There were plenty of locations in the swamp he could have stopped before reaching the small patch of land where the convergence was supposed to be. There was no point questioning his motives. He told us where it was, after all. Maybe he was afraid that I'd bite him if he didn't tell the truth. Then again, what if he led us out here on a wild goose chase? We wouldn't know until we knew. All we could do was proceed with the plan.

We finally reached the spot. As a witch, I could feel the energies all around. The air was thick with residual magic. Was it pouring through the convergence at that moment? Was it from Barbelo or another realm? It could have been whatever was left from when Daniel opened the portal there before.

We gathered on the hill. One by one, Holland started probing our minds. I went first, just to be sure that the monster wasn't already attached to me. If it was, well, it would have made things easier. We weren't so lucky. I didn't think it would have been me, but it was worth checking.

Holland checked Tommy and Sarah next. They were clean.

Ellie went next. Holland placed her hands on her head. "You ready, Pepto?"

Ellie snorted. "You realize, just for calling me that, the monster might come after you if it is in me."

Holland smirked. "Well, you're clean. So I'm good."

Annabelle took a deep breath. "My turn."

Annabelle stood next to me as Holland grabbed her head with both hands. Annabelle winced when the cold Ghede power flowed from Holland's finger times into her skull.

Holland lowered her hands. "The spirit of Isabelle is within you. I don't think the parasite could attach itself to you if it wanted to."

Annabelle grunted. "Well, so much for that."

Holland checked Connor next. She nodded and lowered her hands. I was relieved. I don't know why. We were going to cast the thing out of whoever it possessed but for some reason I didn't want it to be Connor. Maybe I was being a helicopter girlfriend. Keeping him safe, no matter how much he wanted to fight alongside me, was an urge I had to be aware of. I was too hawkish, I'd only damage the relationship.

"There's one person left," I said. "Holland?"

"I can't do it on myself."

Ellie grinned. "Then I guess we have to do it my way. Time to show you the love!"

Holland huffed. "Great. Get it over with."

I had my wand ready. The power welled up within me. It was the sixth time I'd prepared to cast the prison and if this didn't work, we'd be back to square one. There'd be no telling who Protophanes might have gone to after it left Higbee.

When Ellie pressed her hand to Holland's chest, a pink magic enveloped both of them. Holland screamed in pain. "Love sucks!"

I chuckled a little. That it hurt must've been a good sign. Erzulie's power didn't hurt. The monster must've been holding on to Holland's spirit, resisting its expulsion. So much for Holland playing the tough girl. She might have had a thing for the macabre. She may have even enjoyed low levels of pain. An ethereal beast tearing at someone's soul, though, must've been agonizing.

Ellie contorted her face. This wasn't pleasant for her either. It was almost like the monster was shooting blasts of painful energy back through Ellie's magic. It was trying to fight her off so it could hold on to Holland.

It wasn't surprising that the monster might choose Holland. She had more than her share of vices. She embraced her own agony, wore it like the latest fashion trend. How would the monster manifest if it had a chance? Would it emerge as the world's most vicious torturer?

Two black wings burst from Holland's back. The monster stepped out of her body and immediately took a human form. It showed itself as a beautiful woman with long black hair.

Holland gasped. "Mother?"

"That's not your mom!" Annabelle screamed.

"I love you, Holland."

I almost choked on my tongue. Was love really the source of Holland's agony?

"You never loved me!" Holland screamed. "You loved no one more than the bottle. You showed more love to men, different men, every fucking night while I went without dinner."

"I love you so much, Holland!"

"Holland!" Annabelle screamed. "Ignore it! It's not your mother."

Holland narrowed her eyes. She kicked the monster in the chest. "Fuck you, asshole!"

Holland took off running. I didn't waste any time. I blasted the beast with a blood prison and pulled it around both of us.

Protophanes turned and looked at me. Its eyes were as black as the night sky. "What a clever witch."

I held my wand tight. I continued channeling power to the prison. "I could hold this thing for hours."

"You don't have hours, vampire. The sun will rise soon."

The monster was right. If this was a waiting game, I'd lose eventually. The canopy above us wasn't thick enough to shield me from the sun. There was only one way I knew how to draw something into myself. When I fed on a human, I fed on their soul. The creature was in the flesh, not a shadow. I didn't know if the monster bled like the human being it showed itself as, but it was the only move I had.

I lunged at Protophanes and sank my fangs into her neck. What filled my mouth wasn't blood. It tasted more like bile and ash. I choked it down. The monster screamed. It tried to release its material form, but it couldn't escape my bite. It was as if feeding from the thing connected us. Until I finished, until it attached itself to me, Protophanes couldn't escape. It couldn't take another form.

Every instinct I had told me to let her go, to spit it out. My stomach turned in revulsion, but I had to keep going.

Having the succubus in me was more tolerable than this. The demon's blood was oddly delicious. This wasn't meant for vampire consumption.

I had to focus. I needed to channel more blood into my spell. If I swallowed all this shit and absorbed Protophanes but couldn't drag it back into the Aeon of Barbelo, all this would be for nought.

I released more magic into the prison. I needed to try something else. Casting two spells at once wasn't impossible. I'd done it many times before. It took a lot of focus—to exsanguinate myself while maintaining the prison *and* drinking from an otherworldly monster might have been the most difficult maneuver as a witch I'd ever attempted. Even more, I couldn't totally exsanguinate myself. What if I emerged in Barbelo as a feral vampire? I'd lose my wits. I'd become a monster fueled by pure instinct—the craving for blood. I'd never be able to tap into Erzulie's aspect.

I gave myself a quick pep-talk. Not out loud. My mouth was busy drinking monster shit.

My name was Hailey Bradbury. I raised Moll from the dead. I kicked Corbin's ass more than once. I was the underestimated youngling who bested Count freaking Dracula. I was a badass blood witch and a badass bitch. I could do this.

I jammed my wand into my gut. I had to hope the prison would hold or, at least, that I'd swallowed enough of the monster that it couldn't escape if it did.

I cast an exsanguination spell into my body. I'd never performed a partial exsanguination, before. Usually when I used the spell, the goal was to eliminate a vampire, turn him feral and make him easier to kill. A partial exsanguination spell would only turn my target hungrier and more vicious.

I only used about half the magic I usually channeled into the spell. Blood burst from all my pores and splashed on the surrounding ground.

Annabelle and all the others were shouting and screaming, but the sound was muffled. I couldn't tell what they were saying. Maybe it was on account of blood loss. Whatever the case, it worked. The puddle of blood turned black and swirled with power.

The material body that Protophanes took before—the form of Holland's mother—withered into the shape of a dessicated corpse. I drank the last drop and what was left of the body fell into a pile of ash. My feet fell into the portal as the ground beneath felt as though it had disappeared under me.

For a moment, everything was black. Then a flash of orange light, almost as if the portal had taken me straight into the sun.

Chapter 16

THE AEON OF BARBELO was bright but shadows surrounded me. When the first parasite was attached to me, it manifested as a shadow before it materialized. Now there were dozens of them. Was it Protophanes within me or were there separate shadow beasts now surrounding me to antagonize me on their home turf?

I didn't know how long the portal would remain open. It was a relief to know it was still there at all. Portals come in all kinds of magic and they can behave in different ways. Some stay open indefinitely, others remain open so long as whatever energy is powering them is sustained, and others close the second someone passes through. When Annabelle forged gates to Guinee, they often dissipated after she went through. Since other realms exist outside the fabric of time that governs the earth, going through a portal that doesn't remain tethered to earth can be problematic. Even if you manage to open another portal home, there's no guarantee *when* you'll emerge on earth.

That was how Niccolo the Damned became the first vampire. He went to Guinee in the twenty-first century. He spent an immeasurable length of time fighting with the red aspect of Baron Samedi before agreeing to allow the Loa to transform him in exchange for sending him home. Little did Nico realize that when he got home, they wouldn't have smartphones, electricity, or even realize that the world was round. He managed to travel back to the future, but in the old-fashioned way. One year, one day, one hour at a time. It took centuries.

If I didn't get back through the same portal, I'd have no choice but to try to find a way to make another one. Perhaps I'd have to appeal to the natives of Barbelo. They sent Daniel back—but only so they could hitch a ride. Then again, Daniel might have returned through the same portal he made when he arrived in Barbelo. If these creatures couldn't traverse the realms without a host, there was no reason to believe they had the power to open trans-dimensional gateways.

The shadows blasted around me. When they got close, they took the darkened shape of terrible monsters. They must've been drawing inspiration from my mind. Perhaps Protophanes was projecting all of this. I didn't know. This place didn't operate according to the natural laws that governed the earth.

Some of them blasted past me as giant snakes, alligators, or angry dragons. Then came a host of shadowy clowns, chortling maniacally.

They were using my fear. Protophanes was communicating to his kin, inspiring them with whatever he could pull from my mind. It didn't take a genius to figure out what was happening.

Protophanes was doing its best to terrify me. My fear gave it something to hold on to. I had to use Erzulie's aspect to expel the ethereal parasite. To do that, I needed to focus. I wasn't a mambo. I was a witch, a vampire who happened to have a Loa's aspect. It was a potential power I'd only started to explore. There are many people with natural talents who never put in the work to refine them. Many people had good singing voices but wouldn't ever grace Carnegie hall without training. There were many people with natural athletic ability, but unless they trained in a sport, they'd never go pro. Not that I didn't want Erzulie's aspect. Until this incident, it just never seemed all that useful to me. Why would I want to go around and mess with people's affections? I had access to a lot of powers far more practical than what the aspect offered. Playing cupid just wasn't very high on my list of interests. Now, though, I needed it. Without the ability to focus, to channel not only my thoughts but my emotions, I couldn't access Erzulie's power. If I couldn't access her power, I couldn't expel the parasite. I couldn't go home.

Protophanes knew it. Hence the swarm of clown-shaped shadow monsters. It went downhill from there. It was a silly phobia. My deeper fears were more profound.

They're just shadows, Hailey.

It's one thing to know something isn't real, that it isn't an actual threat. It's another thing to ignore it when it's staring you in the face. Ever wear one of those virtual reality headsets? You can do a plank walk on that thing. It makes it feel like you're walking on a narrow board thousands of feet above the ground. It didn't matter that I *knew* I was standing on a solid surface and couldn't fall. The sensation of fear as I tried to navigate the plank was real. When Mercy pushed me, and the program in my headset made it look like I was falling, I actually screamed in terror. Overcoming one's senses, instincts, and natural fears with knowledge isn't easy. It doesn't matter how artificial the threat might be. The fear was real. That's all Protophanes needed to hang on, to send me screaming in terror back through my portal with the monster still attached to my spirit.

Face your fears, Hailey.

I swung my fists at a shadowy clown that appeared in front of me. The shadow infused itself with color. It wasn't material—I didn't think anything in Barbelo had a corporeal body of its own. It looked real. My punches passed right through the thing's ridiculous over-painted face.

I didn't hurt it. I couldn't hurt it. That wasn't the point. I wasn't battling these monsters, I was fighting my fear. If I could face whatever these creatures threw at me, if I could conquer the fear and activate Erzulie's aspect, I could kick Protophanes out of my body and go home.

These monsters imitated not only the appearance of my fears, they added an audio track. It was the sound of the clowns and their stupid laughter, their squeaking noses, and all that crap that made it worse. Every swipe I took, the more I fought, the less terrifying it was.

The world around me changed. The orange light took shape. I was in the old city market. They used to sell slaves there, like how cattle are sold at a livestock auction. Now, though, the place was mostly a bastion for hobbyists trying to sell their trinkets. It was also a farmer's market. Some people sold other wares, like handmade soaps, screen printed t-shirts. I knew the place well. It was where I was turned. I'd gone there because Moll told me to. I'd raised her from the dead, my great-great-great grandmother. She tutored me in the craft. She sent me to the market and arranged for a vampire to attack me. Moll's agenda was clear. She wanted me to become the most powerful blood witch ever. As a vampire, with my natural talents in the craft, she knew I'd be able to wield the power latent in blood in a way other witches couldn't. It worked. What wasn't expected was that it was Annabelle who arrived to heal me after the vampire bit me. The rest was history.

For the first time since it happened, I saw my sire approach. A young vampire. He was bloodthirsty, and I was his ideal meal. It was the one and only time I ever met the guy. He wasn't a real sire. Just a bite donor. As brief as the encounter was, as much time had passed since it happened, it surprised me I recognized him at all.

It was ancient history. Still, it was the most terrifying thing I'd ever gone through. I didn't even know my sire's name. There was no point asking him. This wasn't real. It was a projection from my memories, created by the monsters of Barbelo.

I knew what I had to do. I also knew what I couldn't do. If I succumbed to the fear, Protophanes would have something strong to hold on to. I had to face my fear.

My sire approached. He was pale-faced, his eyes wide with fear, like many younglings who had to feed and didn't know how to control their urges. He flashed his fangs and grabbed me by my shoulders.

When it happened, I was just a sixteen-year-old girl. It was terrifying. I screamed.

Not this time. I kneed him in the balls. He stumbled back, clinging to his crotch. Then I flipped him off.

The world around me shifted again. This damn parasite was going through my memories, bringing out the greatest hits of my most traumatic moments and forcing me to live them all over again.

I faced Moll again. The first time I realized she'd betrayed me, that I was just a tool, a witch she manipulated to gain more power for herself. I kicked her imaginary ass.

Every villain I'd ever faced—with Mercy, Annabelle, or alone—appeared again. Some of them at the same time. The shadow monsters appeared as demons and devils. Asmodeus. Legion. Even Lucifer, who appeared as the Horned God, chasing Mercy and me as he inaugurated the wild hunt. This time, I didn't let them chase me. I fought them off. I clawed at their projected forms. I faced Corbin again—first in his natural form, as he fed and bid me to join him. I didn't. Not this time. I fought him off just as I had the demons before. Fighting off his dragon form was more intimidating. When I defeated him like that, I had dragons of my own to counter his assaults. I blasted through it like everything else before.

I faced Mug Ruith and the succubus, Leann, at the same time. The unseelie Minerva joined in. What else could Protophanes throw at me? I tore through every enemy who ever threatened me in the past. I didn't even hesitate. The more I faced these things the less frightening they were.

The world around me changed again. I was in Casa do Diabo. I saw *myself,* but I wasn't myself. I was feral. My skin was pale, my cheeks sunken, and my eyes were plastered open and bloodshot.

I stood there alone in the room. Higbee wasn't there to satiate my hunger. The door opened and Connor was there. My feral self didn't hesitate. He was nothing to feral Hailey but a blood bag.

It was my worst fear. That I'd lose control and hurt someone I loved.

That damn parasite was cruel. It was also a fool. My heart fluttered in my chest when I saw Connor. The last time I thought he was in danger, I accessed Erzulie's power. This time, my fear wouldn't win. I screamed and charged my feral self. Pink energies enveloped my body. The light from my eyes destroyed the shadows all around me.

Protophanes blasted out of my body as the orange glow of Barbelo returned. The shadow beast shrieked as it struggled to hold on to me. Erzulie's power blasted from my form like a nuclear explosion.

I turned back to the portal. The blood swirling in front of me still had a subtle glow to it. The energies sustaining the portal flickered as the pink magic emanating from my body overwhelmed Barbelo.

The entire realm was collapsing on itself. A darkness expanded over the magic that continued pouring out of my frame. The darkness concentrated into a shadowy blast. It struck me in the back. The force threw me into my portal.

A thousand impressions flooded my mind at once as my body hurled through darkness. I could see the other end of my portal at a distance. The shadowy blast followed me. It spider-webbed through the void. Thousands of convergences, the shattered gates that connected earth to the other realms, all glowed like orbs around me.

Kalyptos

The name flooded my mind like an earth-shattering scream. It was the hidden one, the primary emanation of Barbelo. My pink energy held me on course. It connected me to the convergence that led me back to earth. It was the only one that Kalyptos couldn't reach. Erzulie's power repelled it, but I couldn't stop Kalyptos from dividing its essence, from pouring itself through the other gates.

I hit my original gate face-first and tumbled across the dry ground and into the swamp waters.

I pulled myself back to land and laid on my back. Dozens of black pillars, the essence of Kalyptos, shot into the sky from convergences scattered around the region. They were miles apart. How many more convergences, spread through the world, did Kalyptos invade? All of them? I didn't know if Kalyptos was like Protophanes. How would its energies change the world? What monsters were we going to face next?

Annabelle ran to me and helped me to my feet. A half-second later, Holland grabbed my head. It took me off-guard. The frigid magic pierced my skull, but it didn't last.

"She's clean. She did it!"

I shook my head. "Look to the skies."

Annabelle gasped. "What happened, Hailey?"

"I destroyed Protophanes. My magic infected all of Barbelo. Kalyptos followed me through the gate. His form splintered through the void into hundreds of spider legs of dark energy. It hit other gates."

"How many gates?" Annabelle asked.

I sighed. My shoulders sunk. "All of them?"

Connor wrapped his arms around me. He had tears in his eyes. "I don't know what that means, but you're back. That's all that matters."

I kissed Connor on the lips. "I couldn't have done it without you."

"You're cold. You don't look well."

"I'm famished. I need blood."

Connor lifted his wrist to my lips. "I need a fix, anyway. I'm still addicted to the bite."

I grabbed Connor's wrist. "I don't know. I can't do it. You don't know what happened. When I was there, I had to face my worst fears. I saw myself. I was feral. I was going to kill you."

"It wasn't you," Connor said. "It was an illusion. I trust you."

I bit Connor's wrist. I took two gulps of blood. It was all I needed to sustain myself. I released his wrist and cast a small healing spell into the wound.

Annabelle, Ellie, and Holland stood in the clearing with their eyes fixed on the sky.

I looked up again in time to see the black pillars of Kalyptos disappear. "What are we going to do?"

Annabelle shook her head. "Kalyptos is the hidden one. If he lives up to his name, it might be a while before we can figure it out."

Tommy and Sarah stepped up beside me. "It's almost morning. We need to get back to Casa do Diabo."

I closed my eyes for a second and took a deep breath. "What a night. For the first time in I don't know how long, I'm relieved the sun is rising. I'm exhausted."

"Do you need more blood?" Connor asked.

I shook my head. "It's not that. It's more like coming down from an adrenaline high. I'm *emotionally* taxed."

Connor nodded. "Well, before we go back and tuck into bed, what do you say we take a shower?"

I smirked. "Together?"

Connor smiled widely. "Why the hell not?"

Chapter 17

IT WAS AN UNEVENTFUL day. After the night before, I needed a whole lot of nothing. Connor and I had our fun, of course, but we were both exhausted. If not physically, then mentally and emotionally. Sarah and Tommy dealt with Higbee's body. I wasn't sure how they handled it. I'd suggested they drop it off with Jeanne at the funeral home. Annabelle told me she'd talk to Savanna, which was a major relief. Telling that poor girl about her father wasn't something I thought I could handle. Not after the rollercoaster of emotions I'd gone through all night, especially in Barbelo.

I turned on the television to check the evening news. I wasn't much for television news. More often than not, it wasn't news at all. A lot of jerks with opinions. Opinions are a lot like assholes. Everyone has one. Most of the time, it was better to keep it to yourself. Still, if there were any earth-shattering events, they'd report on it. Given the emergence of Kalyptos, I suspected *something* was happening. According to the talking-heads, though, nothing of note beyond the usual nonsense was going on around the world. Maybe Annabelle was right. Kalyptos might make his presence known in more subtle ways, hidden from plain view. At worst, he'd transform the world into a new Barbelo. At best, his presence was another mystical energy among dozens of others that insidious and stupid folks would eventually lean into and misuse.

I was supposed to meet Annabelle back at her office after nightfall. More to debrief over the previous night's events than anything else. I told her about my experience, but I didn't dive into a lot of details. I was just too tired to get into it.

We didn't take the Escalade. Connor and I walked to Vilokan. It was a delightful night. Weather wise, not that different from the night before. There wasn't so much chaos stirring in the world. If there was, it was hidden—courtesy of Kalyptos. Until we knew more, the lingering feeling that the other shoe was about to drop was bound to persist. All we could do, though, was keep living our lives. Keep fighting the good fight. I was still a guardian. There were other monsters, other creatures from other realms with capacities I had never considered, who could appear at any time.

I interlaced my fingers with Connor's. "It's funny. The air just feels lighter now."

Connor chuckled. "It's mostly in your head. It's New Orleans. It's always humid."

I snorted. "I read somewhere that New Orleans has the highest average humidity among major cities in the country. It doesn't feel so bad, though. Maybe it's just me."

"It's just you. Sometimes I think I'd be better off if I were a fish shifter. At least, then, I could breathe through my gills."

I leaned my head on Connor's shoulder as we followed the sidewalk. "I had fun last night."

Connor snickered. "Well, you didn't devour my soul. I'd say that all things considered, we're better off tonight than we were twenty-four hours ago."

"It's funny. It hasn't even been a week since I was in the faerie realm, and I bit that damned succubus. It feels like it was a lifetime ago."

"You realize, Hailey. When you went to Exeter, you didn't even say goodbye. You left me sleeping in the bed."

I sighed. "Yeah, sorry about that. I've done a lot of dumb things. I should have kept you in the loop. About everything. I learned while fighting these monsters something I should have realized a long time ago. Being with you isn't a liability. It isn't a weakness. You are my *strength*."

Connor kissed me on the cheek. "I get it, Hailey. I'm not as powerful as you are."

"Not true. Your powers are different. Just because you can't cast spells doesn't mean you don't have power."

Connor smiled kindly. "Thank you for saying that, but seriously? You might be the strongest witch ever. And you're a vampire. Add to that this Erzulie stuff you've got going on. Face it, all I can do is change my shape. I can sniff butts better than anyone around, but that's not a superpower I'd say compares at all to what you can do."

I shrugged. "Sometimes it's not the size of the power that matters. It's how you use it."

Connor tilted his head. "We're still talking about supernatural abilities now, right?"

I giggled. "Of course we are, big boy!"

The staircase descending into Vilokan was always the worst part of the trip. It was steeper than normal stairwells; the steps were damp and slick, and it was a claustrophobic nightmare. I'd made the trek up and down the stairs so many times that I might have had the best butt in New Orleans. Yeah, vampires had super strength, but that didn't mean we couldn't tone and tuck. It also didn't mean vampires couldn't let themselves go. Staying in shape didn't take half the effort that it did for humans—a steady diet of blood is inherently ketogenic—but it still took intention.

Annabelle's office was inside the Voodoo Academy. Annabelle changed the sign a while back to "Voodoo University," but no one called it that. She was trying to get supernatural accreditation or some shit. She took over what used to be the old headmaster's office. Back in the day, Papa Legba himself ran the academy. After that, Erzulie. Now, Annabelle ran the school and the entire city of Vilokan. On top of being the policewoman for supernatural shenanigans in New Orleans, it was a marvel she could keep up on everything. She was like the waitress who carried eight plates of entrees to a table with only two arms. Except, in Annabelle's case, she wasn't balancing meals. She was balancing the wellbeing of Vilokan, New Orleans and, technically, the world. I was a powerful witch, but Annabelle had multitasking superpowers every bit as valuable as my best spell.

Holland and Ellie were sitting next to each other on a bench just outside the academy. I approached them and tilted my head. "You two are talking to each other?"

Ellie nodded her head three times fast. "She's so cool! I think we're going to be besties now!"

Holland cleared her throat. "Pepto isn't so bad."

"I'm even starting to like the nickname! It's growing on me!"

I chuckled. "I suppose your aspect functions as cure for heartburn, even if not in the literal sense."

"Are you going to enroll?" Ellie asked. "I'm not a student anymore. But I'd be happy to tutor you anytime!"

I shrugged. "Someday, maybe. I could certainly use a little more training in all things voodoo, including Erzulie's aspect. I'm not especially interested in attending classes or enrolling at the academy."

Holland cleared her throat. "Vampires have enrolled before. Every other vampire, though, has been a part of College Samedi."

I nodded. "Makes sense. I'm disinclined to accept another aspect. I have too many abilities swirling around in my spirit as it is."

Ellie pointed toward the elevator that led to Annabelle's office. "I think she's waiting for you."

I nodded. "Yeah, we took our time strolling over here. It's nice every now and again not to be in a rush to save the world."

Connor and I left the mambos to their girl-talk. I pressed the button to call the elevator to Annabelle's office. The doors parted with a ding and we stepped inside.

Annabelle had to approve our entry on the floor above. She had a closed-circuit camera in the elevator, so she knew who was coming to visit. She was expecting us, so it didn't take long before the doors parted and we stepped into her office.

A young girl was sitting on one of the chairs in front of Annabelle's desk. She turned and looked at me when I entered.

"Savanna?"

"Hi. You're Hailey, right?"

I nodded. "That's right. Look, Savanna. About your father—"

"He saved your life. Annabelle told me."

I gulped and looked at Annabelle. She nodded at me slightly.

"That's one way to look at it. I just wanted to say how sorry I am about what happened."

Savanna wiped a tear from her eyes. "It's all a little surreal. It's hard to believe he's gone, you know?"

I pressed my lips together. "I can't imagine what that must be like."

"I didn't have anyone else. It was just my dad and me. I don't know what I'd do without Annabelle."

I tilted my head. "What do you mean?"

Annabelle grinned. "We have an opening in the school. Sogbo is looking for a promising new mambo to sponsor."

"The Loa of storms, right?"

Annabelle nodded. "That's right."

"Pretty cool, right? I mean, the ability to change the weather! How badass is that?"

I smiled and touched Savanna on the shoulder. "I'm sure you'll do well. You never know. One day I might need your help."

"It's been several years since Sogbo sponsored a student," Annabelle said. "He's only recently taken a new host and is willing to resume his role in the school. Given what we're facing, I suspect Savanna's talents might be useful in the future."

"No offense. I agree that controlling the weather is neat. How is that going to help with convergences?"

Annabelle smiled. "Lightning. Ionizing the air. You'd be surprised how many kinds of magic it can neutralize."

I shrugged. "It doesn't affect me much."

"That's because you draw power from blood. Other witches, warlocks, and sorcerers often use nature as a source for their magic. With new powers in the air, and things we don't understand yet, it's just a matter of time before practitioners of various crafts start experimenting with new spells. It might take some time before she's ready, but Savanna will be a great help when the time comes."

"I'm not sure whatever Kalyptos is doing will be so easily managed with lightning."

"We don't know what Kalyptos can do," Annabelle said. "We need every power at our disposal so we can be ready for whatever happens next."

I nodded. "You're right. You know, Savanna. There was a time that, oddly enough, feels just like yesterday. Long story. I sort of had to relive some of my history recently. Still, Annabelle took me in when I had no one else. You're in excellent hands. She's sort of like a big sister to me."

"I guess that makes us sisters, too, right?" Savanna asked.

I smiled widely. "I guess it does, in a way. Is there a funeral scheduled for your father? I'd like to attend and pay my respects."

Savanna nodded. "It's all so fresh I haven't planned anything. It's overwhelming, really."

"I told her I'd arrange everything," Annabelle said. "We have a contact at a local funeral home. I hear the director there already has Savanna's father's body."

I sighed. "That's a relief. Everything happened so fast, I wasn't sure what Tommy and Sarah did to handle the situation."

"We all handled it," Annabelle said. "I was at your place early in the morning. By the sound of it, though, you and Connor were rather busy. So much banging. Were you building something?"

I chuckled. "Steel erections! We're really into construction."

Connor rolled his eyes and shook his head. "Thank you for respecting our privacy and handling the situation."

Annabelle grinned. "You two deserved some time together. You've been through a lot. All of us have been."

I nodded. "Again, Savanna. My condolences. If you need anything ever, Annabelle can get you in touch with me. Not to mention, I have a feeling I'll be around her a lot in the near future."

"Why do you say that?" Annabelle was scrolling through the screen on her computer examining her feed through her extremely slow dial-up connection. "I see nothing out of the ordinary going on right now."

I shrugged. "Ellie said she'd give me a few lessons. Help get me up to speed on all this voodoo stuff. I think after what we've been through, given that Kalyptos is still out there and is probably vulnerable to the same magic as the other shadow monsters, the more I can learn about managing Erzulie's power, the better."

Annabelle chuckled. "After all these years, you've never once shown much interest in my tradition."

I shrugged. "It's not that I wasn't interested. I just had a lot on my plate. Mastering bloodwitchery. Figuring out how to be a vampire without becoming a serial killer. You know, minor distractions."

"Understandable! You can trust Ellie. Despite her many eccentricities, she's a talented mambo."

"What about Daniel?" I asked.

Savanna winced. "Burning in hell, I hope."

Annabelle folded her hands on her desk. "He's not dead. But that's another matter we need to discuss."

I shrugged. "He's at the Vilokan Asylum, right? Freud should have the matter handled."

Annabelle raised her hand. "He does. He isn't a threat. Not right now, at least. The doctor did manage to get him to open up about what he did. I don't think you'll find it entirely surprising that he didn't open the gate to Barbelo by accident."

"I suspected as much. That spot isn't easy to get to in the swamp. There were plenty of places he could have committed suicide without interference if that was his goal."

Annabelle turned her computer around. The image of a tall man with dark hair in a long black cloak was on her screen. "This is Daniel's father. He left a long time ago. He only returned to town a few weeks ago."

"Creepy looking dude. What's his deal?"

"I told you we might have to worry about sorcerers or warlocks who could tap into Kalyptos's power. Daniel told Freud that he was the one who told him how to open the gateway, that it would solve all his problems. He said he'd survive and, well, obviously, he did."

"Who is this guy? Is he a warlock?"

Annabelle nodded. "Baladan Branham. His first-name means 'the son of death,' and given his reputation, it's fitting."

"Sounds like the sort of enemy we might need Holland's help to stop."

Annabelle nodded. "Freud only sent this information over about thirty minutes ago. I'm still gathering information. Given what Baladan put his own son up to, the notion that he works with death magic is fitting. Given how much power the convergence released from Barbelo, if there's anyone with an insidious plan up his sleeve to use that power, he's the prime candidate."

I shook my head and laughed. "This is too much."

"Why are you laughing?" Connor asked.

"This shit never ends, does it?"

The Blood Witch Saga Continues in...
Wraiths and Warlocks

THE BLOOD WITCH SAGA

THEOPHILUS MONROE

Cover Design by Deranged Doctor Design

Proofreading/Editing by Mel: https://getproofreader.co.uk/

For information:

www.theophilusmonroe.com

Chapter 1

I GRIPPED MY PUTTER with both hands. I tried to hold back but vampiric strength was hard to control. I hit the ball. It bounced off a spinning windmill and came right back to me.

Holland chuckled. "You suck at this."

"Be nice!" Ellie piped up. "These obstacles are meant to be challenging."

"Shut up Pepto. It's called talking shit. It's all a part of the game."

"Talking shit in miniature golf?" Ellie rolled her eyes.

I chuckled. "It's alright, Ellie. Holland isn't wrong. Don't worry, though. Sucking at putt-putt golf doesn't break my cold vampiric heart."

Ellie giggled. "I suppose as a vampire you're used to *sucking.*"

I sighed. "If I had a dollar for every 'vampires suck' joke I've heard over the last eight-plus years since I was turned, I'd be rich enough to purchase a small country."

"Watch and learn." Holland placed her black golf ball on the tee—if you could call the little green pad where you were supposed to set the ball a tee—and widened her stance. She tapped the ball. It also struck the windmill.

"Now who sucks!" Ellie piped up.

Holland narrowed her eyes at Ellie, but said nothing. As a Mambo who specialized in the Ghede, who had the aspect of Baron Samedi, being on the other end of her piercing gaze was bone chilling.

Ellie took her shot. Her pink golf ball passed through the damned windmill, bounced off an angled barrier, and landed about two inches away from the hole. "Almost!"

"Nice shot, Pepto."

It took me three tries to get my ball past the stupid windmill. It wasn't a real windmill, anyway. Wind wasn't turning it, but electricity, which was exactly the opposite of what real windmills were supposed to do. This windmill existed for the sole purpose of being a pain in the ass. When I got it into the green surrounding the hole, I kept overshooting the damn thing. I lost count of my strokes. Ellie didn't. Eventually I got my red ball in the hole.

"Eleven strokes!" Ellie marked down my score on a small card.

Ellie made it in only two. Holland in four. It was only the first hole, and I was going to spend the next seventeen holes trying to catch up. More likely, I'd only solidify my status as the resident putt-putt loser.

Miniature golf was one of only a few recreational activities that didn't involve bumping and grinding I could do, given my aversion to light.

Annabelle suggested we spend a little time together. Ellie was still helping me master the aspect of Erzulie, the Loa of Love. I was usually a quick study in matters of magic. With all that voodoo shit, I struggled. It probably had to do with me not having much reverence for the Loa, or any deity at all. As a witch, we had our gods and goddesses, of course. A lot of old-school witches made "working" with the old gods central to their craft. I think I'd just met too many so-called gods and goddesses over the years that revering them didn't appeal. Half of them were dicks. The other gods and goddesses were stubborn and set in their ways. Of all the deities I'd ever encountered, only the Morrigan had earned my respect. Not that I'd had much occasion to work with her over the last few years. If I ever needed the help of a goddess, though, she'd be the one I'd call.

Working with Ellie took a lot of patience. She was more bubbly than a flooded shampoo factory. If it wasn't for Ellie's pretty face and long, wavy, dyed-blond hair, she'd look just like the Pink Panther, or Malibu Barbie. That was why Holland nicknamed her Pepto—only in Ellie's case, she didn't cure nausea; she was more likely to cause it.

In many respects, Holland was the exact opposite. She reminded me of Wednesday Addams in both her appearance and attitude. She wore a lot of stylish clothes—but every item in her wardrobe was black. Although she was stunning, she didn't care much if anyone noticed. She didn't look for or even desire the approval of others. If anything, she got her kicks out of making people squirm.

The two mambos were like oil and water. At least on the surface. Deep down, though, they were more alike than either of them cared to admit. They were both among the most skilled mambos in all of Vilokan. They both had insecurities stemming from their childhoods. Ellie was bullied as a teen. Holland was raised by an alcoholic mother who went through men like I went through pairs of socks.

It was their wounds from earlier in life that I suspected made them such a good pair, despite their external differences. They shared a mutual respect. They'd even come to become friends, in a way. They also took more shit from each other than a porta-potty at a music festival.

The night sky was totally clear. There was a cool breeze that offset the usual humidity that typically plagued New Orleans. I didn't even sense any magic in the air which was something since only three months earlier I'd inadvertently destroyed the Aeon of Barbelo and released some kind of spirit-energy into not only New Orleans, but through every mystical convergence spread around the world, that could probably be harnessed in ways I didn't even realize. Beyond that, if our encounter with the shadow monsters from Barbelo taught me anything, it was entirely possible this new energy could create brand new horrors, birthed from the combination of the energy of Kalyptos, the hidden personification of Barbelo's power, and old-fashioned human angst.

We even knew of at least one warlock—Baladan Branham—who was primed to do something nasty with all the power I'd spilled into our world. He was primarily responsible for opening Barbelo to begin with. He'd convinced his own son to actually kill himself over a mystical convergence to do it. Any man who could do something so diabolical was capable of anything.

All that made the three months of calm nights both surprising and also disturbing. I know it's a cliche, but the whole "calm before the storm thing" usually proved true in my experience. When things cooled down, it was like the universe was biding its time to take a shit on the world.

I also learned to enjoy the peace while it lasted. I hadn't gone miniature golfing since I was human. My performance on the course was consistent with my lack of experience. It wasn't about that, though. Ellie was certainly in it to win it. Holland was more entertained by messing with Ellie than she was by the game. I was just enjoying a night out with the closest thing I'd had to girlfriends who weren't vampires almost twenty times my age.

We were about halfway through the course. I was somewhere in the neighborhood of seventy-five over par.

A rain drop struck my cheek. I looked up and saw a single dark cloud hovering just over us. Then a deluge poured down on top of us.

Holland laughed and spread her arms. "Finally, some gloomy weather to make this dreadfully clear night more tolerable."

Ellie held her hands over her head as if she thought she could block the rain. She ran around the course on her tip-toes, shrieking as if she was afraid she'd melt.

The rain didn't bother me. I didn't much like it, either. I might have been a witch, but contrary to the lore of Oz, witches don't melt from water.

I heard a giggle. I turned and saw Savanna Higbee strolling toward us with a wide grin and her nose turned up in pride. "See what I did?"

"You did this!" Ellie shrieked.

"Impressive." Rain dripped from Holland's nose and chin and it didn't phase her in the least. "You've only been studying under Loa Sogbo a few months and you already mastered localized storms?"

Savanna snapped her fingers. The rain quit falling and the cloud above dissipated in the breeze. "Haven't quite mastered thunder and lightning, not to mention tornados, but a rain cloud is easy as pie."

Holland bowed her head slightly. "Like I said. Impressive."

Ellie was wringing the water out of her shirt and hardly noticed. "It wasn't funny."

I chuckled. "It sort of was. I thought you were too busy to join us tonight?"

Savanna shrugged. "Loa Sogbo and I wrapped up about an hour ago. Too late to pick up on the back nine?"

I shrugged. "I don't see why not."

"Impossible," Ellie huffed. "It's not fair to join half way through. It'll mess up the scorecard."

Holland rolled her eyes. "Who gives a shit? Grab a putter."

Ellie's jaw dropped. "Seriously?"

"It doesn't really matter who wins, Ellie. That's not why we're here. If you insist on keeping score, double her score on the back nine."

"Or don't count my score at all," Savanna said. "I just wanted to come hang with my girls!"

"You're a first-year student," Ellie said. "We're graduates. We aren't your girls."

"Show some love, Ellie!" I grinned. "That's your aspect, after all. And I'm not even a student at all. It doesn't matter one bit."

Holland smirked. "No need to be a competitive prick, Pepto."

"I'm not a prick!" Ellie grunted. "I don't even have a prick!"

I tilted my head. "You're sort of acting like a prick. No offense."

Ellie reached over to a small pedestal next to the ninth hole tee. She grabbed the score card and shook it off. "Damn it! All the ink is running. Savanna! You ruined our game!"

I laughed and patted Ellie on the shoulder. "She ruined nothing. We'll just have to play the last nine holes for *fun.*"

Chapter 2

THREE OF US WERE soaking wet. Savanna, of course, didn't form a rain cloud over herself. She only stepped on the golf course *after* she'd sufficiently drenched us. I didn't mind too much—except for the squishiness in my shoes. It was a pleasant night. Despite my overall suckiness on the course, it was fun.

We finally reached the eighteenth hole. The last hole doubled as the ball return. Hit it in the gator's mechanical mouth and it was game over. Hit the ball up the narrow ramp, jump the gator, and hit a single hole set on a slope and you'd win a free game.

Probably not for the entire party. A free game for one person meant everyone else would have to pay again. At least, that was my assumption. Then again, it wasn't like our presence on the course cost them money.

I secretly hoped no one made the shot. Not that I wasn't having fun, but eighteen holes, ten to fifteen strokes each hole, got a little old. Besides, unless they had another course, I wasn't looking forward to being conquered by the same obstacles a second time.

I wasn't worried about making the shot myself. I aimed straight for the gator's chomping mouth and watched him gulp down my ball. Poor gator. He really sucked a lot of balls.

Holland was equally indifferent to the matter of scoring a free game. She gave it an honest try but missed the free-game hole, overshooting it by about two feet. When her black ball rolled back down the ramp, it didn't even get close. The ball didn't return. The bottom of the ramp had an opening that I imagined dumped the ball into the same track that probably passed through the gator's mouth, out of his ass, and down a series of tubes leading to an overflowing ball repository.

It was Ellie's turn. She kneeled down next to the tee like she was Tiger Woods, trying to score a birdie and win the Masters.

I cheered her on even though on the inside I was secretly rooting against her. I didn't want to deal with another round of Ellie's competitive dickery. I wanted to go dancing on Bourbon Street.

Connor was hanging out with Tommy for the night. I think they were going to go catch some kind of action flick, then probably go out for a beer and a game of pool or darts. Or they'd go back to Casa do Diabo to play video games.

This was a girls' night/boys' night out situation. We didn't do that sort of thing often. We were usually too busy kicking something's ass to have any fun. Not that ass kicking wasn't enjoyable, but it was also stressful. Mostly because people's lives, and sometimes the fate of the world, depended on it. And also because any time you go out ass kicking, there's always a risk that your ass is the one that will get whooped.

Maybe that's why I couldn't bring myself to care much at all about who won a game of miniature golf. The stakes just weren't high enough.

Then again, I never minded *high* stakes. That meant they missed my heart.

The point was, I'd been through so much shit that I needed to have a little fun. I *deserved* a chance to cut loose. The problem was that nothing seemed to matter. Everything seemed trite and meaningless. When you've had the weight of the world on your shoulders for so long, once it's taken off, you're likely to go flying aimlessly off into space. Into the great wide nothing.

Could vampires suffer from post-traumatic stress? I didn't see why I couldn't. Especially since Holland discovered that, unlike most of my kind, my soul was still intact. Then again, perhaps it was a simple case of operant conditioning. You know, that experiment by Pavlov where he taught dogs to associate the ringing of a bell with their meals until just the sound of the bell made them salivate. In my case, it was simply existing that gave me a looming sense that some kind of supernatural shit was going to hit the fan at any moment. It didn't make me salivate. It was more like a general sense of meaninglessness, a reluctance to enjoy anything too much because I knew it wouldn't last. The second

I let loose and allowed myself to invest totally in something personal, I was sure that Branham warlock, some monster from another realm, or some dick of a vampire, would turn up and I'd once again be the only one who stood between them and the fate of the world.

"Fuck balls!" Ellie exclaimed.

She missed her chance at a free game.

I tilted my head. "Did you just say *fuck balls?*"

Holland furrowed her brow and tilted her head. I was expecting some kind of sarcastic response. She opened her mouth for a moment, as if her lips sprung into motion before her mind gave them the message. "I've got nothing."

"What next?" Savanna asked. "Off to a bar?"

I snorted. "You're sixteen. So, no."

"Weren't you sixteen when you became a vampire? You don't look much older than me."

"But I am. I was turned eight years ago. My driver's license still makes me legal in twenty-one-and-over bars. Yours doesn't."

"What else is there to do?" Holland asked. "I'm not big on the party scene, anyway. Mostly because I care little for humans."

Ellie had cooled off a little. "You *are* a human, Holland."

Holland raised an eyebrow and smirked. "You sure about that?"

Ellie wasn't paying attention to Holland anymore. She was easily distracted—usually by whatever was going on inside her squirrelly mind. Her eyes widened. When Ellie's hot-pink lips parted, I knew whatever she was about to say was bound to be absurd.

"Let's go rollerskating!"

I wasn't wrong.

"I don't skate," Holland said. "What's the point? If I wanted to travel around and around in a circle, I'd walk."

Savanna smiled. "I think it's a great idea. It's a lot of fun. A lot of cute boys go there too."

Holland snorted. "Prepubescent cuteness isn't really my thing."

"I should hope not!" I shook my head. "It's illegal."

"The age is only half of it," Holland said. "I'm only attracted to men who have experience with suffering."

Ellie shook her head. "You're so warped."

Holland smirked. "Proudly, but this is a perfectly rational position. I appreciate men who have wisdom. Wisdom doesn't come through classrooms or learning. It's gained through suffering."

"I'd say it comes through love," Ellie added.

Holland narrowed her eyes. "If you really love something, you'll eventually suffer for it. Suffering also teaches a lot of lessons about love. It has a way of clearing the air, showing us what we truly love, or at least revealing what we have that's worthy of love. That's why love isn't about rainbows, hearts, and teddy bears. That sort of shit shows up in a relationship when people still don't know if they love each other. It happens when they're merely *infatuated.* The tears shed in a graveyard or a funeral come from genuine love."

Ellie tilted her head. "You don't date much, do you?"

"No. Not really."

"Well, heaven forbid a nice young man brings you flowers."

"Flowers are fine. When you pick a flower, it's already well on its way toward death. When a man gives me flowers it's like he's saying 'here, watch these die.' It's sweet."

We moved away from the golf course, dropped off our putters on a rack near the front desk, and headed back out to Connor's Escalade. Yes—he let me take it for the night. He and Tommy were hanging out within walking distance of Casa do Diabo. We had more exotic adventures planned—like miniature golf.

Savanna had a car of her own. "Where we meeting up? What did we decide? Going roller skating?"

I tilted my head and pinched my chin. I couldn't think of anything we could do that also included a sixteen-year-old. There wasn't much of anything appropriate for underage folk in the French Quarter after dark. Night was when the boobies came out to play.

We could have caught a movie, but the whole point of this excursion was to get to know each other better on a personal level. Annabelle insisted on it and I agreed it was a good idea. I was technically the protector of the region, the guardian of the mystical convergences in and around New Orleans. There might not have been a place on earth with more convergences than New Orleans. Southern Louisiana's landscape was riddled with more thin spots ready to pop than bubble wrap—and it was a lot less fun to play with. When you messed with convergences, nasty things came through.

We decided to go roller skating if for no other reason than that we could think of absolutely nothing else to do that included Savanna.

We had to wait in a line that stretched along the front of the building to pay the entry fee. Eventually, we made our way to the front, paid for our skate rentals and admittance, and headed in. The whole place smelled of puberty. A combination of body odor, Doritos, and cheap body sprays.

The skates themselves looked dated. They had well-worn orange rubber wheels. The leather boot portion of the skates had random shiny spots. I scanned the place. There was a concession area that served sodas, popcorn, and candy. You could also buy neon glowing necklaces, bracelets, and probably a few other wearables.

The rink itself was well polished. The crowd had changed little since the last time I'd been skating. Multicolored lights, a lot like the dance floors at most of the clubs. A disco ball hanging over the middle of the floor. Most of the skaters were between the ages of eight and sixteen. There were a few stragglers who rolled carefully and awkwardly in a counter-clockwise direction around the floor. There were some who clearly knew what they were doing. Then, there was the standard middle-aged man in tight jeans who was skating backwards, showing off his skills to the kids who were probably half his age.

"What, is there *always* a creeper at the roller rink?" I asked.

Ellie shrugged. "Maybe he just likes to skate."

Holland, Savanna, and I all looked at Ellie with incredulous expressions. "Seriously?"

"What? He's clearly got skills. Look at how he moves those hips?"

I snorted. "No man's hips should move like that. And what's up with the mustache? That guy looks like he jumped through a convergence straight out of 1985."

Savannah chuckled. "Those styles are in again, you know."

I raised an eyebrow. "Seriously? I mean, the nineties. I could dig a grunge revival. But the eighties? Not that I was alive back then, but I've seen *Stranger Things.* No, thank you."

Savannah grinned. "Maybe that's why the style is back. Wait until a hit show or movie takes audiences back to the nineties and maybe we'll see a similar revival."

I tilted my head. "They did do that! In *Captain Marvel.* They had Blockbuster Videos and everything."

Holland shook her head. "Not a terrible movie, but it was one Marvel movie in an expansive franchise. *Stranger Things* is really popular, and they set the entire show in the eighties."

I rolled my eyes. "Whatever. Who wants to head out there to show off their skills?"

"You're on!" Ellie said. "If I can remember how to do this. I was the limbo queen on the rink in the sixth grade."

"Aren't you almost thirty now?"

Ellie darted her eyes back and forth. "Hush. It feels just like yesterday."

It had been so long since I skated I didn't know what to expect when my wheeled feet left the carpet and hit the slick polished floor. I was never a great skater, but I wasn't awful either. When I was a human girl, back in school, my modus operandi was to blend in and not do too much to draw unnecessary attention. Life was just easier that way. Especially since, at the time, I was attending a religious school while dabbling in witchcraft on the side. If anyone in the school found out about it, I'd have been showered with out-of-context bible lectures about the dangers of a practice they didn't even care to understand. Even when I could excel at something, I preferred in those days to keep a low profile, my nose in a book, and avoid unnecessary attention at places like roller rinks.

It took a little time to steady my feet under me, but I was gaining confidence by the minute. Before I knew it, I was keeping up with the crowd. Everyone except tight-jeans weirdo who weaved around me, doing a little spin, as the smell of too much cologne wafted around me.

A nervous boy, probably fifteen, skated up beside me. He blushed a little and waved. I just raised an eyebrow. Sometimes I forgot I looked so young. With my vampirism, I'd learned to carry myself in a way that made me pass for my early twenties. There wasn't any *need* for that on the roller rink. That kid must've thought I was about his age. One look at my red irises or my fangs and he'd regret it—but I wasn't there to frighten children. I was supposed to be having fun and bonding with the mambos.

I picked up the pace as the D.J. started the most cliche dance floor song of all time: Y.M.C.A.

I tried to sing along. "Young men. Blah blah blah blah. Young men. Na na na na na."

That was all I really knew, apart from the chorus.

I wasn't about to do the hand motions. Arms were still integral to my sense of balance. I lost track of my friends. It was surprising because I assumed Ellie would do everything she could to get the attention of as many people as possible. Finding Holland would be harder—mostly because she was dressed in black and didn't care at all what other people thought of her, much less if they noticed her. I caught Savanna out of the corner of my eye. She wasn't on the rink. She was on the bench talking to some boy. The way she touched his leg periodically, and the two were laughing, suggested they knew each other.

Savanna still attended human school during the day. She had a couple of years left. She had to commute from Vilokan where she studied her voodoo aspect with Sogbo and took evening classes with the hougans and mambos employed by Annabelle in the academy. It was a rigorous schedule for a girl of her age. I knew what it was like to have my youth cut short. I had little choice. She still had *some* say in it all. Still, with her father dead, and Annabelle the closest thing she had to a mother, it was tempting to push aside anything trite or recreational in lieu of getting lost in study.

Seeing Savanna still have contact with someone from her former life she knew was both nice and reminded me a bit of what I'd lost when I was turned.

Everything happened so fast. It was several years more before Connor and I reconnected. My parents didn't even see me for a half decade plus after I went mysteriously missing. A few hiccups through the years gave them hope and they sent private investigators my way on the regular. All that stopped when I reconnected with them some months back—shortly after Connor and I got together. They knew a little about what had happened to me, what I'd become, but I still kept them at arm's length.

Savannah didn't become a vampire. She didn't have to stay away from the people she knew in life out of fear she might accidentally bite and kill them. She had lost more than I had in one sense—my parents weren't harmed when I was turned. But she didn't lose her life. Not completely.

I had a new life now. I was happy as I could be with it. Still, a part of me looked back on those days and regularly wondered what could have been.

Nothing like a night at the roller rink to cook up a little nostalgia and a tinge of regret.

After Y.M.C.A. came the limbo. I finally spotted Ellie. She was in line doing side-bends to stretch out her spine. This was going to be a sight. Limbo isn't all that fun of a game without rollerskates. On skates, it's almost impossible.

I watched as girls skated under the bar one-by-one, some of them eliminated, as the bar lowered one peg to the next. Some girls were doing the splits and folding their bodies forward while skating under it.

Ellie couldn't bend like she used to. The pole grazed over her front as she tried to bend back. She only came in fifth and looked thoroughly disgusted with herself on account of her showing.

I was about to suck it up and roll my way over to console her before the next free-skate started and another song picked up when I felt a hand grip my arm hard.

I turned. It was hard to judge from Holland's grim countenance what she had to say. She always looked that way. "What's going on?"

"Something in my aspect is stirring. Something to do with the convergences."

"Something your aspect picks up that's coming *through* the convergences? You mean dead people?"

"I don't know. This isn't the kind of feeling I can interpret. It's just an energy. If it's awakening the aspect of Baron Samedi and the Ghede, though, and someone's drawing it out of a convergence, I doubt its anything pleasant."

"Right. It's never unicorns and rainbows."

"I was thinking pleasant like guillotines and whips, but to each her own."

I sighed. "I hate to break up all the fun here. I'll shoot Ellie a text and let her know we're going to check out something and will be back."

Holland raised an eyebrow. "You sure she's alright? I haven't seen her this distraught since the last time she broke a nail."

I took a deep breath and did my best to maintain a blank expression. "She *lost* at limbo. This one might take some time to get over."

Holland smirked. "Of course she did."

Chapter 3

HOLLAND AND I PUSHED ourselves through a wall of tweens. It was sort of like swimming upstream in a river of irrational angst and acne. Even at this time of the night, probably ten o'clock give or take thirty minutes, there were more people arriving and crowding into the roller rink than leaving—which was unusual considering the average age of the roller skating patron and the time of night. Then again, the folks arriving appeared to be a few years older than those already circling the floor. Creepy jeans guy excluded.

Holland took my hand and dragged me through the crowd. I had to utter a few "excuse me's" and "sorry about that's" as I bumped into people along the way. Some folks looked at me with such appalled, wide-eyed and jaw-dropped expressions you'd think I'd just ran over their family pets—all of them, at once. I wasn't trying to be rude, but Holland was so determined to press through the crowd and her vice grip on my hand made it clear I wasn't getting free without using my vampiric strength, that whatever her Ghede power was picking up must've been serious.

We finally got outside. We weren't supposed to take the rented skates outside, but there we were in the roller rink lot as Holland took me to find out what she thought had come out of the convergence.

I cleared my throat. "We're still in skates. Where are we going?"

Holland looked to her right, and then to her left. "Not far. There's something nearby."

"Define 'something.'"

"I don't know, Hailey. If I knew what it was, I'd say something. All I know is that it has my Ghede aspect all riled up, like an alarm going off in my soul."

I scanned a tree line on the opposite side of the roller rink parking lot. The only reason I looked that direction was because that's where Holland was looking. She wasn't surveying the tree tops like I was. She was more focused, almost like she knew exactly where whatever it was she sensed was coming from.

Holland stuck out her arm across my shoulders, as if she was trying to stop me from taking a step forward. "Something's coming. We need to get back."

I reached into the pocket sewn into the thigh of my leather pants. Every pair I owned had a pocket for my wand. I had to be ready at all times. Even before I was a guardian of the mystical convergence, I'd faced enough nastiness in my brief life as a vampire that I knew bad guys rarely waited for me to go home to get supplies so we could have a fair fight. Bad guys were *bad* guys, after all. In the world of supernatural brawling, the only rule was there were no rules. Take whatever advantage you have and do whatever you can to win.

"It's moving fast."

"*What* is moving fast, Holland?"

Holland pursed her lips. "I don't know."

"Is it a Loa?"

Holland shook her head. "Definitely not."

Something wispy and black shot up over the trees. It paused for a half second before it turned to me. Then it shot straight at me like a missile.

I threw up a quick blood prism, basically a shield forged from the power drawn from my most recent feed. The figure struck it. The prism deflected it over the roof of the roller rink.

"It's coming back," Holland said. "What the hell was that thing?"

I huffed. "I know exactly what it is. It's a wraith."

"The warped and deceased spirit of a condemned vampire?"

"Never seen one outside of hell."

I assumed the wraith was doubling back to take a second shot at Holland and me. I set up a second blood prism, but it flew straight past us and into the chest of a man smoking a cigarette next to a rusted Dodge minivan.

The wraith blasted out of the man. Blood exploded out of him like it did when I cast an exsanguination spell. The wraith gathered all of it, turned and looked at Holland and me, and for a brief moment, it took the shape of a man.

His cheeks were pale and sunken in. His hair was long and shiny. I'd killed him—that must've been why he came after me.

"Who the hell was that?" Holland asked.

I snorted. "Count fucking Dracula."

"You can't be serious."

"As serious as a funeral. I killed him a few months back."

"He's not the only one. There are more wraiths all over the city."

"We need to get out of here before someone finds the body of that man. There's nothing I can do for him. If they find an exsanguinated man here, and someone connected to law enforcement can place me at the scene, there are folks in the police department who know all about our kind."

"We need to get back to Annabelle," Holland said. "She knows the chief of police."

"And she might have an idea or two about how to stop these things."

"You really don't know how to kill a wraith?" Holland asked.

I shook my head. "They're supposed to be dead already, confined to vampire hell. You don't generally kill things that are already damned. I'm not sure any of my spells will do the trick."

Holland nodded. "Get the Escalade started. I'll go get Ellie and Savannah."

"Hurry. If Dracula really was coming after me looking for vengeance, he'll be back."

Holland grabbed my arm. "The real question is how did he know you were here? He must be able to sense you like how I sensed him. If that's the case, it doesn't matter where we go. He'll be back for you, eventually."

I nodded. "Let's hope the magic that protects Vilokan will shield us while we come up with a way to deal with them."

Holland ran inside. I stepped in and pressed the ignition button. The Escalade was fancy. It knew I had the key in my pocket, so I didn't have to turn it in the ignition to start it.

While I waited, I called Annabelle. She had a phone line in her office. If she was in Vilokan, she had to be at her desk to hear it ring. If she was outside of Vilokan, in the city, the call would redirect to her cell. She didn't pick up. That meant she was most likely in Vilokan, but not in her office. As the Voodoo Queen of New Orleans, she usually knew when nasty shit was happening before I did. I hoped she'd already started working on a plan.

These were vampire spirits. They were ethereal wraiths. That meant they didn't have hearts we could stake. Given Dracula's behavior, the wraiths still had a taste for blood. It gave Dracula enough power that it allowed him to resume a ghostly form that resembled his former physical body. How many more souls would he and the others feed on? How powerful might they become if they got more blood? I didn't know, but I suspected we were about to find out.

Chapter 4

THE DOOR TO VILOKAN wouldn't open. Not for me, Holland, Ellie, or Savanna. We all had the aspect of a Loa. It should have worked.

Holland crossed her arms and leaned against the exterior wall of the St. Louis Cathedral. "The city is on lockdown. I can sense the wraiths inside."

I placed my hand on the wall. "It's more than that. There's magic in there. Someone's casting something I've never encountered before."

Ellie huffed. "Baladan Branham. It has to be that damned warlock."

I clenched my fists. "He's probably going after his son."

Savannah nodded. "Daniel is at the Vilokan Asylum."

"That place is seriously warded," Holland said. "It'll take a lot to get in there, not to mention the warlock won't be able to cast any spells."

I nodded. "I know. I've been in there a few times myself. There are only a few places in the asylum where any magic will work, a few gaps in the wards. If Baladan doesn't know where they are, it won't help. He'd have to get in first."

I shook my head. "If he's controlling the wraiths somehow, that might not be enough. They warded the asylum against magic. I don't know enough about these wraiths to know if they can get past the wards or not."

Holland grabbed my hand. "Come on. There's another way in. Hidden in the tomb of Marie Laveau."

Ellie tilted her head. "How do you know about this?"

Holland shrugged. "I'm Annabelle's favorite."

"Are not!" Ellie huffed. "I'm her favorite!"

I sighed. "We can argue about who mommy loves best later. For now, we have to get in and try to stop these things before they overrun the city."

"How are we going to do that?" Ellie asked.

"She's right," Holland said. "We don't know how to stop these things."

I pressed my lips together. "We'll figure something out. We can't just stand here and do nothing."

Holland nodded. "They are vampires at their core. Their nature is bound to the power of Baron Samedi. I may be able to exert some influence over them."

"That's a start. Anything you can do, Ellie?"

Ellie rubbed her brow. "If they're motivated by vengeance, I might cloud their resolve with Erzulie's power. I don't know. This is unlike anything I've ever tried."

"We are all in this together. We don't have a choice but to try. My blood prisms can hold them off. Perhaps between the three of us, we can make something work."

Savannah cleared her throat. "I can rain on them."

Holland smirked. "Unless you can rain holy water, I don't think that will help. Give us space to work. Stay back and stay safe."

We ran to the cemetery. I used my vampiric strength to break open the locked gates to St. Louis Cemetery No. 1.

Marie Laveau's tomb was also padlocked. The triple X's that marked the stone surface of the tomb were from pilgrims. People believed if they marked the tomb, spun around three times, and made a wish, the dead queen would grant their requests from the beyond. If Marie Laveau granted their wishes, many returned and circled their X's. I didn't have time to bother with superstitions. We needed more than a few wishes to deal with the wraiths and the warlock.

I thrust my shoulder into the door.

"Move that slab," Holland said. "The entrance is beneath it."

I pushed the slab to the side. It was heavy, even for me. Before I knew it Holland jumped right in to what looked like a long chute.

"What the hell?" Ellie paced back and forth as much as she could in the small tomb. "A freaking slide?"

"You going to go in or not?" I asked.

"Fine." Ellie grunted and jumped in. Savannah followed. I went in last. The slide was long and lined with cold metal. It was also dark.

It was steep and wound around in several directions. Eventually, I slid out on my ass in a small room.

Holland and Ellie were standing next to a door on the other side of the room. An electronic panel with several keys was on the wall next to the door. Savannah was still sitting on her butt, rubbing her tail bone.

"Do you know the code?" I asked.

Holland nodded and typed in a series of numbers. With a click, the door popped open. "We're behind Annabelle's office. If the wraiths are going after Daniel, we need to get to the asylum."

We hurried through Annabelle's office, down her elevator, out of the lobby of the academy and into Vilokan's streets. It was like a ghost town. A siren sounded overhead, indicating the place was on lockdown. So far as I knew, it was the first time the new early-warning system had been employed.

"If we encounter Baladan, I'll deal with him. If you can manage the wraiths, I'll help after I eliminate the warlock."

The three girls nodded. I *almost* told Savannah to stay in Annabelle's office. It wasn't only that she was a young and inexperienced mambo. I also felt responsible for her. I didn't *mean* to kill her father. I was short on blood. A parasite from Barbelo that manifested as an angel of death possessed her father. I used every ounce of blood in my body to prevent the thing from killing his son. It nearly turned me feral—and Savanna's father was there. Tommy and Sarah gave me his blood and in that condition, I couldn't stop.

Savanna didn't see it that way. She didn't blame me for killing her father. Annabelle spun the story a little different. From Savannah's perspective, her father *saved* my life. It was true—it just wasn't the *entire* truth. Still, almost entirely exsanguinated, I couldn't help myself. Savannah's dad was in the wrong place at the wrong time. Still, she thought of him as a hero. Maybe she knew the truth deep down, but she wasn't letting it on. Thinking of her father as a hero, and thinking of me as the one he saved rather than his killer, was an easier perspective to manage. Telling her any different wouldn't change things. If I told her the truth, it would be more to assuage my conscience than anything else. It wouldn't help Savanna. It was one of those rare circumstances when telling the truth was selfish.

That didn't mean I didn't have an obligation to keep her safe. I promised her father's ghost as he left his body and moved into the afterlife that I'd watch out for her. I *should* have said something, locked her up in the Voodoo Academy, maybe in the warded gymnasium if not in Annabelle's office.

Then again, if those locations weren't entirely safe from the wraiths, and something happened to her when I wasn't there to protect her, that would be just as bad.

I had to protect her and I could—I was pretty sure—so long as she stayed back and didn't get too involved.

We ran as fast as we could across Vilokan's empty streets. I saw a few citizens of the voodoo underworld peek out from windows in the buildings around us. The blue hue of the magical firmament above that held back the water table and prevented the city from flooding still cast a light over everything and everyone that made a vampire like me take on the complexion of cookie monster.

I didn't see any wraiths in the streets. I wasn't sure how they'd appear under Vilokan's strange light. When we encountered Dracula's wraith at the roller rink, I wouldn't have spotted it at all if it weren't for the parking lot lights. I suspected black wispy wraiths under the blue light were more difficult to spot. We had to be ready. If those things were feeding on people, we were all vulnerable. I had blood—most of it wasn't my own. The three mambos were like meals on legs.

We didn't know how much good Holland's or Ellie's aspects might be against them. I could have run ahead using my enhanced vampiric speed. I stayed close. The one thing I knew was that my blood prism could deflect a wraith if it came after us.

When we arrived at the Vilokan Asylum, a tall man with dark salt-and-pepper hair, dressed in a long black trench coat, holding a crooked wand and surrounded by a shield of wraiths backed out of the door. He held a boy in a hospital gown—his son, Daniel—with his free arm, while he used his wand in his opposite hand to deflect a series of green blasts.

I knew the magic flying out the door at Baladan. It was Annabelle—the magic she could draw straight from Guinee courtesy of her familiar, Isabelle.

Her magic sizzled when it struck the wraiths protecting the warlock. It wasn't clear if it was killing the wraiths or even weakening them a little. There were so many spinning around the warlock we could barely see through them. The only reason we saw anything at all was because the greater concentration of wraiths was in front of him. He didn't know we were there. It was the best chance I had to strike—if I could hit the warlock without also hurting Daniel.

I'd never met a witch, warlock, or sorcerer of any sort who I couldn't beat. Not trying to brag, but most practitioners of magic didn't have a fraction of my power or skill. I wasn't going to risk underestimating the warlock. Especially since I didn't recognize the brand of magic that he was using.

I couldn't get to him to bite him. Not with the wraiths spinning around him. My best shot was a forceful blast that could get past the wraiths and incapacitate the warlock.

He had a semblance of control over the wraiths. Killing him outright wouldn't only free the wraiths and leave them free to go after anyone they found nearby. Right now, Baladan had the wraiths devoted to protecting him and his son from Annabelle's attacks. Even incapacitating Baladan was risky. I couldn't kill him. I couldn't knock him out. If I could connect to the power in the warlock's own blood, I could temporarily seize his peripheral nervous system. I could force him to let his son go. I could make him drop his wand. Most practitioners didn't *need* wands to cast, but it was a lot more difficult. If his wand was what he was using to control the wraiths and I could disarm him, our best shot was to seize him and force him to send the wraiths back through a convergence to hell.

That was my on-the-spot makeshift plan. Any plan that hinged on "forcing" someone to do something they didn't want to do was dubious. It depended on how susceptible one might be to influence—or torture. Most practitioners of different schools of magic have ways to guard against a vampire's allure. I could try that, or whatever kind of torture I might come up with. It would have to do.

Even my best laid plans in the past needed revision on the fly. Things never went the way I expected.

"Do your thing!" I shouted. "Both of you!"

Holland's eyes glowed red. Ellie's pink. They were channeling their aspects, attempting to seize or at least slow down Baladan's wraiths.

The warlock snapped around and aimed his wand at me. I raised a blood prism. He cast a dark spell—something that flowed almost like a sparkling black ooze from the tip of his wand. My prism held up, but just barely. How could I possibly strike him if I was putting all my energy into blocking his spells?

The wraiths broke rank, spiraling over Baladan's head, and inched toward us. Both Holland's and Ellie's magic slowed them down. They were fighting against the voodoo magic that the two mambos unleashed, like salmon swimming against a vigorous current.

With the wraiths moving toward us, I could finally see Daniel in Baladan's grip. The boy was limp, almost like he was asleep, but his eyes were open. His eyes looked like two miniature eight-balls, resembling his father's spell.

Annabelle charged Baladan with her soul-blade in hand. It glowed a brilliant green. One wraith met her and struck her in the chest. It didn't kill her. Isabelle and her green magic prevented the wraith from entering her the way it did the man back at the roller rink.

It pounded against her repeatedly, trying to work its way in.

If I dropped my prism, my shield, the warlock's spell would hit me. I didn't know what it would do. Maybe it would kill me. Perhaps it would open me up to possession by a wraith. If that was something they could do. Whatever his spell was, its effects were bound to be unpleasant, if not deadly.

How could one warlock and a bunch of dead vampire spirits overpower two mambos, the voodoo queen, and *me*?

The sound of thunder cracked above. I turned to see Savanna behind us, her arms extended toward Vilokan's firmament.

"No!" I shouted. "If you break the firmament, everyone will drown!"

It had happened before. The last time Vilokan flooded, more than half the city's population perished.

Savanna didn't respond. This was beyond what she knew she could do. A small rain cloud, maybe, but a full-fledged storm? She was tapping into a dimension of her aspect she hadn't yet mastered.

A series of dark clouds formed above us—but below the firmament. The clouds collided. When they did, more thunder sounded. It was so loud that if my hands were free, I would have covered my ears. Then lightning struck all around us.

The wraiths screeched at such a high pitch, it would have made Connor bark.

Then they dissipated—almost like the electricity neutralized their energies.

A look of panic struck Baladan's face. He pulled back his spell, but the ooze-like magic remained connected to his wand like a leather whip.

I charged after him. If I couldn't strike him with a spell, I'd bite him and drain him unconscious.

Before I got to him, he spun his wand over head and wrapped himself and Daniel in his magic. The ooze formed a cocoon around him, then melted into a puddle where he stood.

Baladan and Daniel Branham were gone.

"What the hell?" I asked. "Where did he go?"

Annabelle struggled to her feet. "I don't even know how he got into Vilokan. What kind of magic was that?"

I shook my head. "I don't know. It was what you'd expect if they made tar and glitter in the same factory and the whole place exploded."

Annabelle moved past me and took Savannah's hands in hers. "That was impressive."

"Thanks!" Savannah giggled a little. "I wasn't sure it would work, but I had to try something."

I nodded at Savannah. "He was beating us. You might have saved all of us."

"You may have saved all of Vilokan." Annabelle smiled widely. "Now we know those wraiths are also susceptible to electricity."

"It didn't kill them," Holland said. "I would have known if it did. It just took them out of phase with our world for a time. They'll be back."

"It's still something," I said. "If we can stop them even temporarily, it gives us a chance to stop them from hurting people."

"How many wraiths might there be anyway?" Ellie asked.

I shook my head. "We're talking, potentially, every vampire who has ever been staked over the course of several millennia. If Baladan drew all of them out, we might face thousands."

"They aren't all under Baladan's control," Holland said. "Dracula came after you of his own volition."

"That isn't necessarily good news," Annabelle said. "All that means is that Baladan released more wraiths than he can control. Perhaps that's why he abducted his son. He needs more juice to harness their power."

"I'd say we should go after him, but I don't have a clue what his magic can do, much less how to stop him. My blood prism held up against his spell well enough, but it took a lot of strength. I'm going to need to feed before I face him again. We don't want a repeat of what happened, you know, the last time."

"When you fed from my father?" Savannah asked.

I winced. "Right. I can't protect anyone if I'm not at full strength. We're already facing potentially thousands of dead vampire wraiths. The last thing anyone needs is a feral Hailey on the prowl."

Chapter 5

NOW THAT WE KNEW the wraiths were vulnerable to electricity, we had a way to protect Vilokan. We didn't need Savanna to do it. Annabelle sent her to train a little more with Loa Sogbo to refine her abilities. That was the first time she'd pulled off a storm like that, and she wasn't sure she could duplicate it on a whim. Knowing *how* to do it and refining one's abilities to the point that they were second nature took practice. No matter your school of magic—be it witchcraft, voodoo, sorcery, or druidry—the only way to really become a master of your craft was through repetition.

Savanna needed not only to make sure she could cast another storm if we needed her, but she needed to expand her repertoire of lightning-producing abilities. According to Annabelle, Sogbo could maintain a low-level electric charge in the atmosphere of Vilokan. Something virtually undetectable to most of the citizens, but hopefully strong enough to repel the wraiths or weaken them if they came back.

"We need more ways to fight these things," Annabelle said. "Electricity works, but it's not perfect."

I scratched the back of my head. "These are vampires at their core. They may not have hearts, but the wraiths may still be vulnerable to sunlight."

"I should be able to tell if they go dormant or something come morning," Holland said. "Still, as every vampire ever knows, you can wreak plenty of havoc, even if you only have the nighttime to do it."

I rubbed my brow. "The Order of the Morning Dawn used to carry enchanted crucifixes imbued with celestial power. Alice used to carry one. I'm pretty sure she left it with Nicky back in Kansas City."

"Who is Nicky?" Holland asked.

I let out a soft laugh, my lips curling into a smirk. "A nymph of Guinee, aka Annwn or Eden. A shapeshifter and a total diva. She used to be one of the Neck back when she was corrupted. Alice bit her, trapped her in human form, the two made up later, and later Nicky purged herself of the curse."

Holland tilted her head. "You're talking about Nyx?"

I nodded in confirmation, my hair brushing against my cheeks. "Right. That's the name most vampires know her by. She's pretty deadly with a stiletto heel. Her friends call her Nicky."

Annabelle's heels clicked against the tile floor as she paced behind her desk. "She's also married to a warlock. Devin might have insight into Baladan's strange magic. Good call, Hailey. I'll ring them up and see if they're willing to help."

"I haven't spoken to Nicky in at least a year. Given her deadliness when it comes to vampires, myself excluded since I'm in her circle of trust, the entire Kansas City area has been a vampire-free zone for a while."

Annabelle nodded. "She's still singing. Her club sells out almost every night. Her daughter Lily headlines the show as much as Nicky does these days. I'm sure she can cover for her if we need Nicky's help."

"Even if Nicky and Devin are willing to help, it's a good day's drive. We need to get a handle on this as best we can until then. We at least need to make it through the night."

Holland rubbed her brow. "I can sense these things, but it's vague. I'd like to invoke Baron Samedi and perhaps a few other Ghede to see if they have any insights into how we might bottle up these wraiths again and send them back to hell."

I bit my lip. "I'm going back to Casa do Diabo. Sarah's ability might come in handy here. She can usually connect to vampires in a region, see through their eyes. Since her abilities started with feeling and sensing when vampires died, she might be able to pick up the wraiths as well."

Annabelle grabbed a spiral notebook out of one of her drawers. "Ellie, come with me. We're going to do a little research."

Ellie rolled her eyes. "Holland gets to go talk to the Ghede. Savanna is going to go train with Sogbo. Why do I have to be a research assistant?"

Annabelle grinned. "Because you might be the best chance we have to stop Baladan. If we can't figure out how to counter his power, or discover where it came from, your abilities might be able to alter his temperament."

"Then I should be out there looking for him!"

Annabelle cleared her throat. "Like I said, if we can't figure out how to stop him, altering his emotions might be a way to get to him. It's still risky because we don't know what protections he's working with, how he might resist your influence, or what he could do to you if he hit you with that nasty magic he's wielding."

Ellie plopped down on one of Annabelle's office chairs. "Fine."

I chuckled. "Let me know if you hear back from Nicky. I'm going to head out. I'm also a little nervous about Connor and Tommy."

"Boys' night out?" Annabelle raised her eyebrows.

"Exactly."

Annabelle smirked. "Sounds like trouble to me. You're sure Tommy is ready for a night out on the town without you?"

"He's doing well and managing his cravings. Tommy has shown remarkable restraint. He still misses Mel. I was afraid that the whole long distance relationship angst might stoke some emotions that could make a young vampire volatile, but so far, so good."

Annabelle smiled at me. "Just remember, he isn't you. He's not a blood witch. You had a few advantages that other young vampires don't. Also, given his unique abilities, there's no telling how a bunch of dead vampires flying around might affect him."

"So far I haven't picked up anything unusual. You forget, I turned him. I cycled his Haley Joel Osment sixth sense and can see and talk to the dead as well."

Holland let out a deep, gruff sound, then pursed her lips together. "You're usually suppressing those abilities, right? His abilities are innate. He can't turn them off."

"You're right. I haven't opened up those abilities completely since before this started. The wraiths we've seen, though, are already visible."

"At the very least," Holland said. "Any sensitivity to the dead could be both an advantage and a liability."

"Keep an eye on him," Annabelle added. "Until we know more about what we're dealing with, we can't be too careful."

Chapter 6

I COULD HAVE WALKED back to Casa do Diabo. Connor would be upset if I didn't bring back his Escalade. When you drive a luxury SUV, leaving it parked in random places in the French Quarter practically invites vandals and thieves. The truth was that Connor wasn't rich at all. He'd made his money doing jobs for vampires and witches before we reconnected. Now that Corbin was burning in hell he didn't get as much work as he used to. Now and then Alexandra, a local witch, paid him a fee equivalent to the earnings of a Grubhub driver to pick up a few exotic ingredients for a spell she was working on. He barely made enough doing that to pay his cellphone bill. It didn't matter much. I had Mercy's credit card. She inherited the riches of her sire and the first vampire, Nico, when he decided he'd had enough mouth breathing and ended his life. Then again, he didn't have to breathe at all and he was already dead. Sort of. You get the idea.

I'd encountered his ghost once or twice since then. I had to wonder if he was among the wraiths. Last I knew, his spirit hadn't devolved into wraith status. He wasn't in vampire hell, technically. He had a special place where he and a few other vampires could dwell eternally. It was the only good thing Corbin did when he took over hell by binding himself to Lucifer. Long story—I've told that one before. Needless to say, I didn't have any reason to believe he was back with the wraiths. Unless Lucifer abolished "vampire heaven" when he retook the throne of hell. I had little reason to suspect that happened.

Lucifer never bothered much with vampire hell at all. Baron Samedi exerted more influence over that realm.

I also now possessed Nico's sire status. I probably wasn't the vampire he'd choose for that if it was up to him. It was how I beat Corbin. It meant any vampires Nico sired were beholden to me if I ever exercised it. It probably applied to a few of the wraiths, but certainly not all of them. Since Nico was the first vampire, technically, if I could fill out his family tree, I could compel those he sired to use their sire bonds to influence others and so forth. Since the wraiths didn't register with Ancestry DNA, it wasn't really a viable option. Especially since most of the wraiths were so warped they probably didn't even know their own names, much less have the wherewithal to exercise sire bonds over other wraiths. Even if I could pull something like that off, there was no guarantee it worked on wraiths at all, or that a sire bond could overpower whatever magic Baladan was using to enthrall them.

I parked Connor's Escalade outside Casa do Diabo and went inside. Connor and Tommy were playing beer pong at our kitchen table. Tommy had two young, attractive, dark-haired females at his side. They looked full of color, which meant, so far, he hadn't fed from them.

At least Connor was faithful—no girls at his side. He was losing the game. Wolf shifters could get drunk. Vampires could, too, but to pull it off, we had to drink about three times as much as humans did. It also didn't last long. We sobered up fast. Beer had a low enough alcohol content that it was virtually impossible to drink enough fast enough to get anything more than a slight buzz. It wasn't worth it—mostly because of all the peeing.

Connor could sober up at any time. Shifting back and forth between wolf and human form naturally healed the body. Since alcohol was technically poison, shifting negated the effects. He clearly had no interest in that—at least not until the night was over.

"Baby!" Connor stumbled over to me. "You look hot tonight."

I smirked. "Thanks. What have you two been up to tonight?"

"Lots of beer!" Connor spit a little as he laughed. "Beer is so *good.*"

I glanced at Tommy. "You doing alright?"

Tommy smiled and nodded. "A little bummed I can't get drunk, but it's probably for the best."

I grabbed Tommy by the arm and pulled him aside. "Does Mel know you brought girls home?"

"They're just hanging out. I'm not going to sleep with them. Was waiting for you before I took a bite. I'm too afraid of losing control."

I nodded. "That's smart. You guys see anything unusual tonight?"

"Yes!" Connor piped up. I wasn't talking to him, but as a wolf shifter, his hearing was acute. Even while he was drunk, apparently. "There was a woman at the club with three nipples!"

Tommy chuckled. "It's true. Very weird."

"I have a double-jointed thumb!" one of the dark-haired girls held up her hand and bent her thumb back to her forearm.

"Congratulations!" I pulled Tommy into another room. Talking about vampire wraiths and warlocks probably wasn't the sort of conversation suitable for intoxicated humans. "Baladan attacked Vilokan. He has an army of vampire wraiths."

"Those are dead vampires, right?"

"Have you seen anything like that? Since they're dead, I thought you might be extra sensitive to them. They're hard to see otherwise."

Tommy scratched his head. "I'm not sure. I see a lot of ghosts. They blend into crowds."

I heard a loud bang coming from upstairs. "Have you seen Sarah since you got back?"

Tommy shook his head. "She's up in her room, I'd guess. Like usual."

"I'll be back. Don't bite anyone."

Tommy smiled widely and nodded. "I was waiting for you, anyway. I can wait a little longer."

I took off up the stairs. I knocked on Sarah's door. She grunted but didn't exactly invite me in. I opened the door anyway.

Sarah had her blanket pulled over her head. Her lamp was on the floor. She must've knocked it over. That was the sound I heard from downstairs. "Sarah?"

Sarah rolled over and started punching her pillow. "The voices won't stop!"

"You're hearing the wraiths, aren't you?"

"Wraiths? Dead vampires. That makes sense. I can't turn it off."

"What are they saying? That warlock pulled them out of hell. He's controlling them. I need to know what he's planning."

Sarah pulled her pillow over her face. "Too many voices. So much pain and rage. I can't make out any words. Just screams."

"Your ability works through psychic energy, right?"

"What? I can hardly hear you over all the noise."

"Psychic energy. That's what channels the voices into your mind, right?"

Sarah sat up and rested her face on her clenched fists. "I think so."

"I think I can help. I'll be right back."

I hurried out of Sarah's room and went to mine. I had a collection of ingredients sufficient for casting almost any spell. I wasn't big on wards. They came in handy from time to time, but I wasn't the kind to sit behind wards and hide from magical attacks. I could usually overpower any witch who came after me. Not that many dared try. Until I knew how to beat Baladan, though, warding might be wise. Then again, the wards at the Vilokan Asylum didn't stop him from taking his son. Warding against the warlock's magic was just as uncertain as any attack I might lob at him. I knew a few warding spells that could dampen psychic energy though. It wouldn't stop the voices in Sarah's head completely, but hopefully it would help.

I grabbed a bunch of sage, a vial of horned toad blood, and a jar of bone dust collected from a staked vampire. Pig urine was recommended, but not strictly necessary. I didn't keep bottles of piss on hand because, *ew*. Without it, the ward would only last a day or two. With the urine, it might endure for a week. Worst-case scenario, I'd have to cook up the spell again in a couple of days. By then, hopefully we'd have a handle on the wraith and warlock problem.

I grabbed a porcelain bowl and mixed the ingredients in it, stirring it with the sage. With the sage covered, I took my wand and channeled a little magic into it. It didn't take much. Wards usually just needed a tiny touch of magic to catalyze the spell.

I grabbed a lighter from my dresser drawer and took the sage to Sarah's room. She was writhing in her sheets. She didn't appear to be in pain, but that many voices that wouldn't shut up would drive her crazy, eventually. She was halfway there already.

I lit the sage and drawled it around the perimeter of Sarah's room. She had a small bathroom connected to her bedroom. I wafted the sage over her toilet, sink, and shower. Sage didn't smell bad. It was nice. The ingredients mixed with it made the odor more pungent. It would have been a lot worse with the pig piss.

After I saged the room, I grabbed an empty vase off of Sarah's dresser and put the sage in it so it could burn out.

Sarah laid still. She was breathing deep. "That helped. Thank you."

"Can you make any sense at all of what you heard?"

Sarah shook her head. "Sorry. I wish I could. Some of those wraiths have languished in hell for centuries. They don't have any coherent thoughts left."

"Dracula is out there. I saw him."

Sarah rolled off her bed. She took my hands. "Dracula? Can he still steal your abilities?"

I shook my head. "I really don't know. He killed a man. Pushed his form right into him and exsanguinated him before he absorbed every drop of that man's blood out of the air. For a second, he appeared as I remembered him. He came after me, but then he flew away."

"He hasn't been dead long. I might be able to tap into his thoughts."

I shook my head. "You need to rest your mind. You've been through too much."

"I can do it. The ward worked. The voices aren't coming at me like before. But I think I can still use my abilities."

"Like I said, it's not a total ward. It just subdues the psychic energy you're picking up."

"Was he under the control of the warlock?"

"I can't say for sure. I don't think so. He wasn't there in Vilokan with Baladan."

Sarah bit her thumb. "In that case, he might not reveal much. I can't probe his mind. My abilities don't work that way. I can only hear what he's thinking at the moment."

I pinched my chin. "Are you sure you can do this? You don't look well. You've been through a lot."

Sarah stretched her arms out over her head. She stepped into the bathroom connected to her bedroom, moistened a washcloth, and patted her face. "I appreciate your concern. We still need to know what we can learn about the wraiths. I will manage."

Sarah dried her face on her bath towel. Hopefully, she didn't use the same portion of the towel for her face that she usually used to dry her ass or her lady parts. I've always been anal about that—pun not intended. I change my towel out between every shower. Weird? Yeah, well, maybe. But at least if I need to wash my face I don't have to dry it off with butt towel.

Sarah strolled back to the side of her bed. The sheets were soaked in sweat, probably from her episode earlier. Old vampires like Sarah remembered days going back to their human lives when people used to only shower intermittently. Even older vampires, those sixteenth century bloodsuckers, remembered the days when they bathed only a couple of times a year. Some of them still maintained those habits. Sarah wasn't *that* old, but she had lived the better part of a couple of centuries in a small shack without electricity and running water. She'd come a long way since. She used her shower. Doing laundry on the regular was a work in progress.

Sarah's bare feet were flat on the floor. She rested her hands on her thighs and took a series of deep breaths. Her eyes shot open.

"He's here!"

"I know. I saw him at the roller rink."

Sarah grabbed my hand and squeezed it like a vise. "He's *here.* Dracula's wraith is in Casa do Diabo."

Chapter 7

PLAYING HIDE-AND-SEEK WITH A wraith isn't fun. I searched the whole damn house. Connor was still drunk and wouldn't shift to help look. He was quickly progressing beyond the annoying and ridiculous phase to the sit-in-a-daze about to pass out stage of intoxication. He was sitting on the couch examining the ten or fifteen fingers he probably saw on his right hand.

The girls Tommy brought over for a late-night meal were still there. Why didn't they just leave? He probably had them enthralled by his allure. They weren't entirely zombified. They still had their own thoughts. The allure, though, made Tommy so attractive to them that they wouldn't and couldn't leave even if they wanted to.

He scanned the rooms. I had the same ability turned on, too, just in case it helped me spot Dracula. Sarah insisted he was there—somewhere. If a thought crossed his mind relevant to his surroundings it would help Sarah locate him.

"He's focused," Sarah said. "All he's thinking about is blood."

I gulped. "Tommy, we have to get those girls out of here."

Tommy nodded like a good boy. He probably wasn't thrilled about it—he was hoping to enjoy two girls at the same time. For dinner—not in bed. When it came to feeding, variety was the spice.

Tommy led the two girls toward the front door. He was about to lead them out when a black wispy form darted out of the floor vent and blasted through both of them. Blood exploded in the air.

Tommy screamed. I grabbed my wand as Dracula appeared just as I remembered him.

"Good evening."

"Step back, fucker. I killed you once and I can do it again."

"Who are you talking to?" Connor stumbled into the room.

I grunted. "It's Dracula."

"I see nothing." Connor pinched my butt.

I swiped his hand away. It wasn't the time. "Go shift and sober up."

"But Hailey—"

"Now!" I screamed.

Dracula cackled. "You were saying you intended to kill me? Well, I'm already dead."

"I can see him," Tommy said.

"I can't," Sarah added. "But I can hear him."

"Still don't see shit!" Connor piped up.

"I told you to sober up!"

"He wouldn't see me," Dracula added. "Only those with an affinity for death can, now that I've regained my wits and can appear as a regular ghoul."

An affinity for death. Certainly not something you'd put on your dating profile. It explained why Holland could see it when he attempted to regain his form after he killed the man at the roller rink. Tommy and I shared an ability that allowed us to see the dead. Sarah could hear his thoughts already, but couldn't see him. Connor couldn't see shit. Holland specialized in the Ghede, the death loas, and had the aspect of Baron Samedi. A different *kind* of affinity for death. Everyone in our present company, Connor excluded, had some kind of death-related skill set. Even the two poor girls—who were actually dead.

I'd have to clean up that mess later. You don't tidy up and hide your bodies when you're face-to-face with the ghost of Dracula.

"I take it you're not vulnerable to stakes."

Dracula shrugged. "I'm a spirit. No heart."

"But you *can* kill."

"A wraith is like a feral vampire without a body. Blood fuels us in death even as it does in un-death."

I snorted. "I could exsanguinate you again."

"You could. You're a talented blood witch. I still envy your talents."

"I'm not giving you shit."

Dracula waved his ghostly hand through the air. "Our unique abilities do not persist beyond the stake. They reside in the flesh."

"You just killed those people!"

Dracula looked at me with a blank stare. "Hello. I am Dracula."

"What the hell are you doing here? You could have gone after me before, back at the roller rink."

"I wasn't trying to harm you. I was trying to speak to you. I didn't yet have enough blood to restore my spirit."

I rolled my eyes. "Yeah, right. I staked your ass and burned out your heart. My friend sensed your rage."

"It was not directed at you. At least, not all of it. This is an 'enemy of my enemy' situation. I am certainly less than grateful that you killed me but, at the same time, I respect you. Do you know how many young vampires have attempted to kill me through the centuries?"

I shrugged. "I'm sure more than a few."

Dracula bowed his head slightly. "You demonstrated impressive skill and resolve. It is why I've come to you now. The warlock is as great a threat to me as he is to you."

"I doubt that. You're already dead. What can he do to you?"

"He seeks to bind all of us to his will. His magic is powerful. Still, he is but a human. His body can only channel so much. He is recruiting more warlocks, loyal to his cause."

I tilted my head. "That's why he rescued his son."

Dracula nodded. "I've been observing him the best I can. He's taken wraiths who've been dead for centuries, those without any mind or will to resist his compulsions. If he grows his coven, I fear even I will be vulnerable to his influence. If he cannot enthrall me or the others, he will send us back to hell."

I shrugged. "That's not my concern."

"It is your concern. You saw what he could do with the wraiths he had in his thrall. What do you think Baladan might be capable of if he builds an army of warlocks and wraiths?"

"Why would he build an army? What is his end game?"

Dracula pinched his chin. "Power, perhaps. I do not know precisely. Whatever his plan is, I doubt you'd like to see him realize it."

I narrowed my eyes. "You're probably right. What do you propose?"

"Help me stop him. In exchange, leave me be. Send the rest back to hell if you like. I get to stay."

"Stay and do *what,* exactly?"

"I have no aspirations beyond my desire to stay out of hell."

I huffed. "Forgive me for doubting your sincerity."

"Believe me or don't." Dracula straightened the collar on his cloak. "I must feed occasionally to maintain my form, not to mention my sanity. I will not pretend to require anything less. Still, one vampire ghoul taking the occasional victim is certainly less of a threat to humankind than Baladan and an entire army of wraiths and warlocks."

I snorted. "Can you feed without killing people?"

Dracula shook his head. "I wish I could tell you I could. Consider it a token of trust that I tell you the truth. I could easily lie to you and promise to only feed in small amounts. Perhaps I'll learn moderation in time. I do not know. This is a unique experience."

I paced across the foyer. I stopped and extended my index finger. "If we do this, you only feed on bad people."

"Define 'bad people.' I can certainly find enough bad in anyone to justify making them a meal."

"Death row inmates. People on their deathbeds already. Criminals and scoundrels."

Dracula raised an eyebrow. "Politicians?"

I shrugged. "Most of them. Sure."

"Republicans or Democrats?"

"Like it matters."

"Fair point. Very well. I will limit my feeds to people who are near death already or deserve it."

I extended my hand. "Alright. You tell me a good way to stop Baladan and we have a deal."

Dracula chuckled. "I am a ghost. I cannot shake your hand. You'll have to take my word."

I tilted my head. "You can't even pinky promise?"

Dracula sighed. "I'm sorry. I cannot."

I nodded. "Alright. It's a deal. But if you feed on good people, I'll send you back to hell myself. Now, tell me what you know about Baladan. How can we stop him and get control of these wraiths?"

"The sire bond persists even in death," Dracula said. "Perhaps you should feed the wraiths. Use Niccolo's bond to control them."

"Already thought of that. First, I'm not feeding innocent people to vampire wraiths. Second, organizing something like that is impossible. I'd only be able to exert direct influence over those Nico turned, himself. Ever play the game of telephone?"

Dracula cocked his head. "The *game* of telephone?"

"Right. You sit in a circle. One person comes up with a message and tells it to the person beside them. That person passes it around, so and so forth, until it gets all the way around. The fun of the game is to see how much they change the original message in the process."

"Choose your commands wisely," Dracula said. "It is true, a sire's bond relies on commands, and crafty vampires often find loopholes in those commands to exploit. They find clever ways of fulfilling the command while undermining it at the same time."

"Add to that the fact that these wraiths are all warped in the head. Well, the ethereal equivalent of their heads. I don't think it would work."

Dracula bowed his head slightly. "Perhaps you're right. Still, you are a blood witch. You may find a way to feed wraiths enough that you can exert some influence over them."

"I wouldn't even know which wraiths to target."

"I could help with that. I can see their true identities."

"Alright. Well, we could try. That still doesn't help me figure out how to stop Baladan. What do you know about the strange magic he's casting?"

"What I can say is that it is not of this world."

"No shit, Sherlock."

"I am not Sherlock. I am Dracula."

"It's just a saying. If his magic had origins on earth, I'd know about it."

"You really believe you know every kind of magic there is in this world?"

I shrugged. "Pretty much."

Dracula laughed. "Perhaps some humility is in order, child. You can only know what you've encountered. There are powers you've never considered that flow into and through this world. It's the point an old friend of mine, perhaps you've heard of Immanuel Kant, once made. No one can say that all crows are black because no one can be certain that he's seen every crow there is. There could be an albino somewhere else in the world that you've simply yet to meet. The same is true of magic, young witch. You don't know what you do not yet know."

"Fine, I get your point. Still, I have a lot of experience. It's pretty clear that what Baladan is using is from somewhere else."

"He was the one who first opened the convergence to the Aeon of Barbelo, is he not?"

I bit the tip of my thumb. "Yeah. He convinced his own son to kill himself to do it. What a dick, right?"

"He is indeed. If I were to guess, the power he's wielding now is from Barbelo. Did you bring something back with you when you went there?"

I sighed. "I inadvertently destroyed the entire realm. I'm pretty sure everything native to Barbelo spilled out on earth through the convergences."

"According to the lore, Kalyptos is *potential* existence. The primary force that undergirded all of the Aeon of Barbelo. If that's the case, Baladan's magic could be anything. Using Kalyptos, he could devise a whole new magic of his own. Something rooted deep within the confines of his soul."

I huffed. "Make your own magic? What a nightmare. Magic has rules. If you can make up whatever the hell you want without rules or limits, it might not have any weaknesses, either."

"Everything has limits. What was your experience with Barbelo before?"

I grunted. "The first things that we discovered were the autogenes, produced by Protogenes. They manifested as monsters rooted in someone's angst or fear."

"I presume you had to face me again, then?"

I smirked. "I killed you, dude. You're not my greatest fear. I had to fight a clown!"

"Seriously?"

"Don't judge. Clowns are every bit as creepy as Count Dracula."

"Perhaps. What if it wasn't a monster that was produced by someone's fear or angst, but a power, a force, that someone who tapped into Kalyptos's power could manifest? What would it look like?"

"That depends on what motivates or terrifies Baladan."

"Then that's the answer. You need to learn as much about the warlock as possible. What makes him tick? What's his history? Does he have a vendetta he intends to exact, or is he some kind of sociopath who kills simply because he can?"

"I was hoping you'd have answers to those questions."

"I'm avoiding him as much as you are. I don't want to get caught up in his scheme any more than you do. I have a few progeny of my own who are among the wraiths. If I can get them a little blood and awaken them, even if they are connected to Baladan, I might be able to find out more."

I shook my head. "No killing innocent people. That's the deal, remember?"

"Of course not. You are a blood witch, though, are you not? Perhaps there's something you could do that would have the same effect. A spell that might infuse them with the power latent in blood just long enough that I can reach them."

I bit the inside of my cheek. “I will figure something out.”

“I’ll work on tracking down those I can find. In the meantime, find out what you can about Baladan.”

“Annabelle recognized him before. She probably knows more than I do. I’ll also do the usual search.”

“The usual search” Dracula raised an eyebrow. “Do you think there’s something in the libraries that might help?”

I raised one eyebrow. “Libraries? Please. What year do you think it is? I’ll Google him. I’ll scour his social media if he has it. I’ll see what I can learn about his past that might help figure out what angst fuels his magic. Diagnose the source, then I can figure out how to counter it.”

Chapter 8

BEFORE I LEFT, I had to deal with the bodies. Blood splashed on Connor when Dracula exsanguinated the girls. He went upstairs to shower.

Working with Dracula made me sick to my stomach. In a matter of hours, I'd seen him murder three people. I'd say he did it in cold blood, but he took their blood warm. There may have been more victims I didn't know about. If it took three or more bodies full of blood to allow a wraith to become a vampire ghost like Dracula, what kind of spell could I possibly perform to animate the wraiths of Dracula's vampire offspring?

All I had was Dracula's word. *Dracula's* word. It was probably less reliable than a Wikipedia article. It was also the only thing I had. Even if his intentions were impure, he was right about one thing—our motives aligned for the time being.

I needed to go to Annabelle and see what she and Ellie came up with in their research. If Dracula was right, if Baladan's magic was something new born from the combination of his angst and Kalyptos, there wouldn't be much in her books that would describe exactly his nature. Annabelle already knew quite a bit about the Aeon of Barbelo—perhaps there was something from that angle that could be of use. If Baladan had developed a new kind of magic that depended on Kalyptos, maybe there was a way to sever the connection.

If there wasn't, I needed to learn what I could about Baladan. I sure as hell would not use Annabelle's dial-up connection in Vilokan to do my research.

I sat on the couch. Sarah was back in her room under the protection of the sage ward. Tommy sat next to me and pulled out his phone. He started searching Facebook. I started with Google.

"Not finding anything on Baladan Branham."

Tommy shook his head. "Me neither. There is a Daniel Branham."

"Right. That's his son."

Tommy showed me his phone. A man in his fifties—the warlock but in a polo shirt, khaki shorts, holding a golf club. He was also wearing white New Balance tennis shoes with socks pulled halfway up his shins. "I think Baladan's son is a junior."

I narrowed my eyes. "He must go by Daniel. Baladan could be shortened to Dan. Dan could be expanded to Daniel. It makes sense. Annabelle said that Baladan Branham had a reputation. She also predicted, as Dracula confirmed, that he was primed to use the energy released from Barbelo."

"There's nothing on his profile about being a warlock."

"That's definitely him. Sounds like he has a double life. Baladan the warlock by night. Daniel the dad by day."

"This guy posts nothing but memes."

I chuckled. "He's a dad. Dad's love memes. Ever since I reconnected with my parents and gave them my number, it's been nonstop memes by text message."

"I didn't know you had regular contact with your parents."

"I don't. The number is for emergency purposes. I never respond to their texts. They don't even know for sure that I'm getting their messages, but that doesn't slow down the memes."

Tommy shrugged. "At least you have a father."

"I didn't mean to—"

"It's not your fault. I'm not the only foster kid who grew up bouncing from family to family. I'm just saying, maybe you should send him a thumbs up or something from time to time. All he's trying to do is connect, even if it is in a superficial way. My guess is he sends memes just so you know he's thinking about you, but he's also trying to respect your privacy. That's why he doesn't send anything too personal."

I swallowed hard. "My family issues can wait. We need to stay on task. Is there anything apart from memes that suggests any kind of angst or any intense emotion at all?"

Tommy shrugged. "His relationship status says divorced."

"Can you see his photos?"

Tommy shook his head. "Friends only."

I did a Google search for Daniel Branham. It's crazy how many sites there are that log people's addresses, history, and personal connections. "Check out Mary Ann Branham. If that doesn't come up, try her maiden name. Mary Ann Redstone."

Tommy typed on his phone. "There's a Mary Ann Redstone-Branham."

I looked over Tommy's shoulder. "Check out her feed."

Tommy scrolled through Mary Ann's feed. She posted a lot. At least she had until about three months ago. That made sense. That's when Daniel opened Barbelo at his father's behest. Mary Ann posted nothing about all of that. Daniel had used a shadow monster to kill people—even the police who came to arrest him. The mood to post status updates must've faded. Before that, though, she posted several times a day. Pictures of her meals. Random status updates about her general mood, more pictures of her food, and several with her son—Daniel. He didn't look too thrilled about being photographed. He was a troubled boy—that much was established.

"Keep scrolling. There has to be something of substance, eventually. This woman posts every damn detail about her life."

Tommy scrolled through maybe a thousand posts. It only took us back about six months and she hadn't posted anything during the last three. Then I saw it.

Divorce is final today! I have full custody of Danny!

There were more than a hundred comments and twice as many likes.

"That could be it," Tommy said. "Recently divorced and a custody battle on top of it."

"Sounds like a recipe for angst. Surely she knew that Baladan was a warlock. After all that's gone on, especially given her sudden silence over the last few months, she's probably distraught."

"Maybe you should go talk to her. She's probably worried about her son."

"It's the middle of the night. Maybe if it were nine or ten o'clock, I could stop by and pay her a visit. It's three in the morning."

Tommy shook his head. "It's not like you can catch her after sunrise."

I pressed my lips together. "I'll pass this along to Annabelle. She can visit her in the morning. Right now, I should get back to Vilokan and see if she and Ellie turned anything up we can use."

Tommy pocketed his phone. "We still have a couple of bodies to deal with."

"Connor is still in the shower. He'll help you take the bodies to Greenwood Funeral Home. I'll have Annabelle call ahead and explain the situation."

Tommy raised an eyebrow. "The situation? Two girls are dead. They didn't deserve this."

"You're right. If we don't stop Baladan and these wraiths, two girls will be a drop in the bucket."

"Will the funeral director even be there at this time of night?"

I shrugged. "I don't know. Like I said, Annabelle will take care of it. This isn't the first mess we've had to clean up as of late. I think Annabelle has the funeral director's personal number."

Chapter 9

I HURRIED BACK TO Vilokan. I didn't see Dracula or any wraiths on the way. I didn't encounter Baladan. I suspected I wouldn't. If there was a bright side to any of this, for once we were confronting an enemy who didn't have staking me at the top of his to-do list. He abducted his son. He probably thought of it more as a rescue. I had no reason to believe that I was on his radar. He was *benefitting* from my defeat of the Barbelo shadow-monsters. If anything, he should have sent me a thank you card.

Hallmark probably didn't have a card that said, "Thank you for destroying a mythic realm and giving me the power I needed to threaten human existence." A general thank-you card would have to do.

I went to Annabelle's office. There were a few books stacked on her desk. One was wide open and Ellie was using it as a pillow. She was snoring. A half-empty mug of coffee rested next to her.

It wasn't the first time the living struggled to keep up with me during my waking hours. Three in the morning isn't usually the best time to do research. If I was still human, it would have put me to sleep, too.

I hesitated a half-second before I grabbed Ellie's shoulder and shook. She didn't budge. I shook her again. She swiped away my hand. "Go away," Ellie whined.

"Where's Annabelle?" I asked.

Ellie looked up at me, squinting. "Oh, hey Hailey. I think she's looking for more boring books on Barbelo."

"I'll check the library."

Ellie dropped her head back on her arm. I think she fell asleep again before I even got into the elevator.

I was always a bookish girl. After I first became a vampire and Annabelle took me in I spent more than my fair share of time in the Voodoo Academy library. They were short on fiction. I don't think they had anything published in the last fifty years. They had a collection of short stories by Edgar Allan Poe that I'd read a dozen times. Probably not the best fodder for a brand new vampire. It passed the time. They also had several grimoires. The vodouisants didn't use them much other than for research, but I picked up a few spells I didn't know.

I found Annabelle behind a shelf with her arms full of books.

"Would you mind grabbing that Crowley volume from the top shelf?"

I snorted. "Crowley?"

"His works might surprise you. That man dabbled in just about every kind of magic he could get his hands on. If there's ever been a connection to the magic of Barbelo before, there's a good chance Crowley tinkered with it."

I got up on my tip-toes and grabbed the volume. I added it to the top of the stack in Annabelle's arms.

"Mind lightening my load?" Annabelle asked.

"Right. Sorry." I took half of the books. The weight wasn't the problem so much as the awkwardness of trying to manage so many books at once without dropping them. "Find anything we can use?"

Annabelle shrugged. "Ellie's looking into the books I've found. It's hard to say what we've found."

I snorted. "Yeah, well, Ellie is sleeping on a book as we speak."

Annabelle sighed. "I made her coffee. I hoped that would be enough."

"People need sleep. I don't think the wraiths will be active during the day, but Baladan will still be out there. I have a theory about how his magic might work. A partial theory, anyway. We have a lot to discuss."

"Talk while we walk. We need to get these books back to my office and get to reading."

I told Annabelle about my conversation with Dracula, what Tommy and I found on social media, and explained how I thought his angst over the divorce and custody battle might fuel the new magic he forged from Barbelo's energies.

"By the way, I need you to call Jeanne."

"The funeral director?"

"I told you about Dracula. He killed two women at Casa do Diabo and used their blood to manifest. Tommy and Connor are taking the bodies to the funeral home."

"I wouldn't trust that dead vamp if I were you."

"I don't trust him. Dracula cares only about himself. At the moment, his self-preservation and probably ours share an enemy."

"Can you get to work on these books?" Annabelle asked.

I grunted. "Probably. It's a lot to go through—"

"Good!" Annabelle turned and added her stack to mine. I almost dropped them all. "I'll call the funeral home when I get to the surface. I'm going to check on Holland. Working with the Ghede still might be our best shot at dealing with the wraiths."

"What about Nicky?" I asked.

"Caught her just as she was wrapping up one of her shows. She and Devin will leave first thing in the morning. They should be here before tomorrow night. That means we only have to deal with the wraiths another three hours before sunrise."

"After that, I need you to follow up with Daniel Branham's mother. I won't be able to do it for obvious reasons. When the sun rises, I won't be any help at all, but I suspect Baladan will still be out and about."

"Why isn't Holland in Vilokan? Can't she summon the Ghede here?"

Annabelle nodded. "She can and she has. Holland reached out to Baron Samedi himself. He thinks he might help—but he needs a host and I did not incline Holland to offer herself."

"Probably for the best. When a Loa takes a host, they usually hang around a while."

Annabelle tilted her head. "You said Connor and Tommy were taking those bodies to the funeral home, right?"

I nodded. "That's right."

Annabelle pinched her chin. "The Ghede don't require a *living* body as a host. So long as they haven't started to decompose, either will do. Perhaps we'll give the Baron his choice between the two."

I scratched my head. "That's still two girls who will be missing. Someone out there is going to be looking for them."

Annabelle took a deep breath. "What's done is done. This isn't the first time I've had to clean up a supernatural homicide. All I need to do is contact the chief of police and explain the situation. He'll handle the rest with the girls' families."

Chapter 10

ANNABELLE HAD A SMALL bar refrigerator in her office. I grabbed a bottle of water, opened it, and poured it on Ellie's head.

Ellie jumped up and screamed. "What the fuck, Hailey?"

"Rise and shine. Well, no shining. I don't do well with that part."

"You're one hilarious bitch."

I chuckled. "We need to dig into these books. Annabelle is out and about helping Holland summon Baron Samedi."

"Do you at least have a towel?"

I shrugged. "That's what shirts are for."

I wasn't sure why Annabelle picked some of the books we searched. The Aeon of Barbelo was mostly accounted for in gnostic texts. It looked like Annabelle also gathered every volume she had on vampirism in the academy library. Since Baron Samedi originally made vampires, it made some sense that the voodoo community had done quite a bit of work on the subject. It was the same reason Holland was summoning Baron Samedi. What the voodoo community could only theorize about vampires and how we were made, what happened to us after we died (again), or anything else about our kind, Baron Samedi knew the truth.

Baladan's name meant "the son of death." Was there some connection between him and the Ghede? Of all the creatures from innumerable realms he might draw through the convergence to form his army, why wraiths?

The wraiths and Baladan weren't two separate enemies. Maybe a part of the problem was that we were treating Baladan's strange magic and the wraiths like two unrelated weapons at his disposal. What if they were linked? How could they be? That's what we had to find out.

Ellie and I pored over the books. Since there was probably a lot in the books that Ellie didn't know, but I did, I focused on vampires. I needed to figure out if there was anything about my kind that might link us to Barbelo, or if there was any record of wraiths coming to earth, how they might be controlled, or what power they contained that might be different from flesh-and-blood vampires. Ellie had a much smaller collection of books, but almost all the material was foreign to both of us. Books on the ancient gnostic philosophy and the religions that adopted their worldview. Even Christianity had gnostic sects in the early years.

"Check this out," Ellie said. "It's from the Gospel of Judas. Judas himself tells Jesus, 'I know who you are and where you've come from. You've come from the immortal realm of Barbelo, and I'm not worthy to utter the name of the one who's sent you.'"

I shrugged. "Doesn't mean much. The gnostics didn't actually know Jesus. These gospels they wrote were an attempt so far as I understand it to co-opt the popularity of the Christian message at the time with their peculiar philosophy. This text doesn't tell us much about Jesus, so much as it tells us about the gnostics. Look for anything in there that might speak of a magic power, or something possibly connected to vampires."

Ellie continued reading, tracing her finger down the page, as I flipped through page after page of details about vampires that I already knew. Whoever wrote these books had a unique ability to take something that could have been said in just a few words and make it fill dozens of pages. It read like something that might be published in an academic journal, complete with footnotes and big words I didn't know.

Ellie cleared her throat. "Check this out. Most of this book is nonsense. I don't understand most of it. Here, though, Jesus is describing the moment when the world was created. Some of it's like Genesis, but there's a lot more here about twelve realms and twelve angels who were sent to rule over something called Chaos."

"Anything about Barbelo or vampires?"

"I'm getting to it. Listen to this: 'And behold, from the cloud there appeared an angel whose face flashed with fire and whose likeness was defiled by blood. His name was Nebro, which means 'Rebel.'"

I shook my head. "I don't know what that means. We know that Baron Samedi used the succubus demon's essence somehow when he turned Nico into the first vampire. Creating something new, though, isn't the sort of thing the Ghede Loa typically are about. Can you find anything else about this Nebro character?"

"Well, reading a little before that section, Nebro was one of twelve angels who came into being to rule over chaos and the underworld."

I shook my head. "His appearance was *defiled* with blood. Interesting if this is some kind of creation account. Where'd the blood come from?"

Ellie pursed her lips and grabbed another book. "This is all about gnosticism. Apparently, they believed that the God who created the universe was too pure to create the world directly. He created Barbelo as a sort of first emanation of his being, an intermediary realm, where the agents of creation that gave birth to everything else could work and reside."

I shook my head. "I'm not going to say I agree or disagree with all that philosophy or theology about God and whatnot. It doesn't matter. I've been to Barbelo. I fucked the place up with your love magic."

"It wasn't *my* love magic. It was Erzulie's aspect and she gave it to you, same as she did me."

"I meant the magic you taught me how to use. Why would love magic destroy a place like Barbelo?"

"Beats me. Love doesn't usually destroy things. It builds things up."

I smirked. "I suppose you've never read the Iliad. How Paris's love for Helen of Troy led to a ten-year siege and the eventual fall of Troy."

Ellie blushed a little. "Brad Pitt was hot in that movie."

"That's just a dramatization of Homer's Iliad. And ew, Brad Pitt is old!"

"But he wasn't always! And he's still hot for an old guy. Not that he's even that old."

I took a deep breath. I wasn't inclined to entertain the hotness of men old enough to be my father. "Here's a thought. I wonder if there's a connection between Nebro the Rebel in the gnostic writings and Ghede Nibo. The names are similar enough that the difference could be on account of translation."

Ellie shrugged. "Or it could just be a coincidence. Isn't Ghede Nibo the one who Holland summoned before so you could talk to that dead boy?"

I nodded. "Back at Greenwood Funeral Home. It was the ghost of that boy brought back by Ghede Nibo, who led us to Savanna so we could save her from Daniel Branham."

Ellie narrowed her eyes. "What I know about Ghede Nibo, not that I'm an expert on the Ghede at all, he was a man who was killed violently. I think in some kind of uprising or revolution. Baron Samedi and Maman Brigitte adopted him as a Loa."

I tilted my head. "The Loa can turn humans into other Loa?"

Ellie shrugged. "It's not altogether common. Technically, though, La Sirene was once a human. You know her as Joni Campbell. Marie Laveau was also adopted by Papa Legba which was why she was able to live and rule as the Voodoo Queen for more than a century after her human life ended."

I narrowed my eyes. "But *how* do they change a mortal into an immortal?"

"I don't know. Baron Samedi did it when he made vampires. Maybe it's a similar process to how humans can be turned into Loa. They'd need to access a power that they don't typically wield to pull it off. What about a power that's capable of creating new reality? What if the Loa used emanations or angels like Nebro from Barbelo to do it?"

Ellie closed the book in front of her. "That's an interesting theory. It doesn't explain why Baladan would use power from Barbelo to harness the wraiths, or to give himself a new kind of magic."

I scratched the back of my head. "I was just reading a book here on theories of the vampire's spirit. Most of us don't have souls. I'm an aberration. Probably because of my witchcraft. Most vampires lose their souls when they're turned. Baron Samedi claims their souls, but we still have a spirit of a sort. That's what's left after a vampire languishes in hell and lets go of all his or her connections to the world. They become wraiths. What if the wraith is that part that came from Barbelo, the pure energy that can be manipulated and changed to make something completely new."

"If that's the case, Baladan isn't forming an army of wraiths. He's using them to manipulate their power in an attempt to forge something else. Maybe they're the source of his new magic he wields. Letting Kalyptos free into the world, along with all the energy of Barbelo, might be what Baladan needed to mold the wraiths into whatever he intends to turn them into."

The corded phone on Annabelle's desk rang. I picked it up. Annabelle had an update. Holland succeeded. Baron Samedi took one of the bodies of the girls as a host. He wasn't the only Loa who

Holland summoned. Ghede Nibo took the other body. They were at the convergence in Manchac Swamp—the same one I passed through when I entered and destroyed Barbelo. I hung up the phone.

"We'll find out soon enough if our theories are correct. Baron Samedi and Ghede Nibo are here. They want us to meet them at the convergence in the swamp."

Ellie sighed. "I hate going into that swamp. It's so messy!"

I smirked. "Get used to it, honey. Take it from me. I've had to learn from experience. Saving the world is *always* messy."

Chapter 11

Ellie offered her vehicle. Connor and Tommy already took the Escalade when they hauled the bodies out of Casa do Diabo and, apparently, to Manchac Swamp.

We left Vilokan and found her truck parked a few blocks away. It was an old beat-up farm truck. From the look of the body style, it was manufactured ages ago, probably in the seventies. It was a marvel that it still ran at all.

Ellie tossed me the keys. I caught them. "You should drive. My license expired five years ago."

I tilted my head. "Five years ago?"

Ellie shrugged. "I don't drive much. Annabelle takes me most anywhere I need to go and most everything I need is in Vilokan."

"Does this thing even run?"

Ellie shrugged. "It did the last time I used it."

"How long ago was that?"

"It's been a couple months. Without a license, I try to avoid driving whenever I can."

"You could just renew it. It's not that hard to do."

"The truth is, I don't enjoy driving. I get in a lot of accidents. That's why I got the truck. This thing is indestructible. Might as well keep the keys. I have another set. Use it whenever you need it."

I tilted my head. "Thanks. I guess."

The keys didn't have a fob attached. I had to use the *actual* key to unlock the door. I had to reach across to manually unlock the passenger door for Ellie. It was pretty much the exact opposite of Connor's Escalade. I could get in and out of his luxury vehicle and even start it without taking the key fob out of my pocket. The ignition was also sluggish. I had to give it a little gas to force it to turn over. The truck still ran, but it sounded like a dying alligator.

It also had a manual transmission. I learned to drive on a stick. My dad was old fashioned that way. He believed it was important to learn to drive with a stick. That way, I could drive anything I wanted. I thought it was dumb at the time. Who drives a stick anymore? I suppose my dad was right. Heaven forbid, if I didn't know how to drive a stick, Ellie would have to drive with an expired license.

I drove out to the swamp. We only had an hour and a half until sunrise, so this was going to have to be a quick meeting. Given that we were short on time, and Ellie wasn't eager to go trouncing through the swamp, she stayed with the truck.

I could move through the swamp a lot faster without her. That didn't mean I'd get to the convergence clean and dry, but it could have been worse.

I found Annabelle, Holland, and the two Loa in the bodies of the two girls Dracula killed standing over the patch of weeds where the convergence was located.

"Glad you could make it." One girl bowed her head. "I'm Baron Samedi. I've been curious about you for some time."

"Why is that? Because I still have my soul?"

The Baron nodded his, or her, head. I wasn't sure which pronouns were appropriate given the situation. "You aren't the first witch who has ever been turned."

"Right. Mercy is a witch, too."

"You're the only one whose soul is not in my possession."

I snorted. "I'd say I'm sorry about that, but I'm really not."

"If I look you boys, or girls, or whatever you are in the eye, y'all won't mount me, will you?"

"No need," the second girl, who must've been Ghede Nibo said. "We have bodies. They're pretty, right? I've always been a dandy, but never a real girl."

I smirked. "Congratulations. I don't have a lot of time on account of the impending sunrise. What can you tell me about what we're dealing with?"

"We're here to reclaim my wraiths." Baron Samedi tucked his long, dark hair behind his ears. "Given your unique... condition... not to mention your gifts, you're uniquely suited for the task."

"Can't you gather the wraiths yourself?"

"Unfortunately, I cannot. When a vampire devolves into a wraith in hell, I still hold its soul. That much is true. However, the wraith is a primordial kind of energy that I cannot wield if it does not feed."

"Dracula fed. Can you take him?"

Ghede Nibo chuckled. "We could seize him and take him back to hell. From what we understand, however, he may also be of use to us."

I grunted. "Ellie and I have a theory. These wraiths are a kind of energy born in Barbelo."

"Yes and no," Baron Samedi said. "When I made Niccolo, I used energy from Barbelo and mingled it with the blood of a demon to turn him into the first vampire. Your kind is special. You can reproduce. The wraiths have never been in Barbelo, but their energy is the same as the kind I first drew from that realm when I created the vampire."

I was smiling on the inside—if only because Ellie and I were right. I enjoyed being right. Who doesn't? It struck me that all our research was for nothing, though, since the Baron now confirmed what we suspected. Then again, would he have explained it if I hadn't already put the pieces together?

Annabelle cleared her throat. "Excuse me. How exactly do you think Hailey can help? From the sounds of it, these wraiths need blood. When they do, you'll be able to re-exert your influence and pull them back to hell."

Baron Samedi bowed his head slightly. "The soul coheres in the blood. Every vampire knows this. They can taste it. It's the soul, not the hemoglobin, they crave."

I nodded to confirm the Baron's words. "But those pesky hebo goblins are necessary. Can't have too much protein."

"Since I have the vampire's souls," Baron Samedi continued, "I can attach the soul to the blood they absorb and regain control."

Holland stepped up. "We're going to need to get a lot of blood."

"How *do* we get so much blood?" Annabelle asked. "And how much does it take?"

"More than you'd think," Baron Samedi explained. "The wraiths don't have bodies. Blood doesn't give them a real, material, body."

I sighed. "Dracula killed at least three people and absorbed their blood before he was able to regain the appearance of his former body."

"Do we really need that to happen?" Annabelle asked. "How much blood does it take to attach a soul to it?"

"The spirit must be receptive," Baron Samedi said. "Many of these wraiths have been dead for some time. The longer they've been dead, the more blood will be required."

I gulped. "Dracula hasn't been dead that long, and he needed to kill three people."

Ghede Nibo smirked. "There are plenty of humans to spare."

"We're not going to commit mass murder just so we can take people's blood."

Holland cleared her throat. "How about a blood drive?"

I sighed. "We'd need a shit ton of donors to pull that off. No one donates the entire contents of their body."

"Can you do something, Hailey?" Annabelle asked. "Can you use blood to make more blood?"

I shook my head. "Blood doesn't make blood. Blood is made from cells in bone marrow. Getting bones with healthy marrow is harder to do than it is to just take people's blood."

"Find a crowd," Holland said. "Exsanguinate them all and channel their blood into barrels."

Annabelle raised an eyebrow. "Can you partially exsanguinate an entire crowd?"

I bit my lip. "Maybe. I've only done a partial exsanguination once, and that was on myself. It's harder to do than a total exsanguination. I can't think of any way to pull something like that off if I targeted a whole crowd at once. I could go around town and zap the blood out of people, but trust me, pulling the blood out of a person through the pores hurts like hell. It would also take a lot of energy on my part. I'd have to consume some of the blood just to maintain my ability to cast so many spells."

"Is there another option?" Holland asked. "Didn't you and Dracula have a plan already, Hailey?"

I rubbed my brow. "He's trying to find the wraiths of the vampires he sired. He can use his sire bond over them to control them. If I'm able to get the wraiths of the vampires who Nico sired directly through the years, I can exert an influence on them. They can do the same to the wraiths of their own progeny."

"Do the wraiths still need blood for the sire bond to work?" Annabelle asked.

Baron Samedi shook his head. "I have the souls. The sire bond works because the energy of Barbelo that *makes* a vampire is passed from one vampire to another. Only a vampire's sire can control a wraith."

I pinched my chin. "It won't take as much blood to do that. Attracting the right wraiths won't be easy, and I'm not sure I can trust Dracula to do the job. He might identify and take control of the vampires he made who also died, but that's not all of them."

Baron Samedi nodded. "The lineage is also discontinuous. They are not all wraiths. Some of the vampires needed to maintain the connection from sire to progeny as progeny to sire will necessarily involve many vampires who still walk the earth."

Ghede Nibo smiled widely. His host had a pretty smile with perfect teeth. "If that's your intention, you'll have to gather nearly every vampire who has ever sired another. Especially since so many wraiths barely lived beyond their first few nights before their potential existence ended in literal heart break."

Annabelle shook her head. "Even if we *could* somehow convince all the world's vampires to make a pilgrimage to New Orleans, it would take too long to gather. I'm assuming the power of a sire bond doesn't have a long distance plan."

I chuckled. "Long distance plans aren't really a thing anymore. But you're right. A sire bond is only effective when the progeny hears his or her sire's voice. It's not especially strong if exerted by telephone. Ideally, the vampires should be face-to-face."

Annabelle checked her phone. "You need to get back home, Hailey. On the bright side, the wraiths should be dormant during the day. That gives you some time to try to find a spell that we can use. Gather as much blood as safely as possible, or find a way to use the chain of sire bonds to control them."

I raised an eyebrow. "On the bright side?"

Annabelle smirked. "Right. That doesn't have the same positive connotations for you as it does for the rest of us. On the dark side, then."

"Will you come back with us to Vilokan for the day?" Annabelle asked.

"I'm assuming Connor and Tommy already headed back to Casa do Diabo."

"I believe they did," Annabelle said. "After they dropped off the bodies. The boys had to carry them through the swamp. They needed to shower."

"I need to get back home. I have plenty of books of my own I can dig into. Dracula will have to retire somewhere and I have a sinking feeling he'll be at my place. Connor can leave at any time. I'm not going to leave Tommy there with Dracula's ghost."

"I'll send Ellie over with more books," Annabelle said.

"Let that girl sleep," I chuckled. "She's exhausted. She's probably in her truck sawing logs right now."

"I can bring you whatever you need," Holland said. "I can go between Vilokan and Casa do Diabo during the day, no problem."

Chapter 12

HOLLAND CAME WITH ME. So did the two Loa. When you have death deities coming to visit, it's good to have a specialist on hand. I took Ellie's truck. Ellie rode with Annabelle in her sparkly purple Camaro.

The truck wasn't meant to sit four, but Holland and the dead hosts taken by Baron Samedi and Nibo were petite. So long as they didn't crowd into the stick shifter, I could manage.

I hadn't heard from Dracula all night. Tommy texted and said he was in the house. Connor was there, too. I didn't know if Connor could see him. He could see wraiths, but if Dracula was an *actual* ghost, he couldn't. Whatever the case, leaving Connor in the house with nothing but my young progeny and a half-baked Sarah to defend him if Dracula got thirsty made me anxious.

I pushed that old farm truck as hard as I could. The thing needed a serious tune-up. At the very least, it was probably due for an oil change. At least it ran well enough to get us from point A to point B. With only a few minutes until sunrise, I couldn't risk a breakdown. If we stalled out on the side of the road, I'd have no choice but to bury myself in the ground. I'd done it a few times before. There's no worse way to spend a day than in a makeshift grave.

The sun was just cracking on the horizon when I pulled up in front of Casa do Diabo. I'd normally be more hospitable and casually let my deathly guests through the door first. Steam was already rising from my skin. Burning vampire flesh doesn't produce a pleasing fragrance.

It wasn't enough to leave any wounds or scars, but every second mattered. I blasted through the front door. If Baron Samedi thought I was being rude, tough. He made me this way.

Once everyone was inside, Holland locked the front door. Dracula was seated at my dinner table. He didn't appear as a ghost. He was sipping on a glass of red wine—or perhaps some freshly drained blood. Ghosts don't eat and drink. Not from glasses, anyway.

Dracula smiled at me widely. "Good morning."

I turned to Connor, who was seated at the table. "You can see him?"

"Of course I can."

I rubbed my forehead. This wasn't the first time a ghost had materialized in something like a body. Julie Brown, Mercy's half-sister in life and a caplata, had taken a body despite being a ghost. How many more people did he drain overnight to accomplish it? I didn't know and at the time I didn't *want* to know. Did he stick to our agreement and limit his consumption to scoundrels and criminals? Probably not, but I knew he'd lie to me if I asked.

Dracula saw the two Loa beside me. He stood and tilted his head. Then he looked at me. "You turned them?"

"We are not who we appear," Baron Samedi said. "I am the maker of your maker and every maker before."

Ghede Nibo shrugged. "And he's my adopted father."

Dracula raised one of his bushy eyebrows. I'd say he looked as though *he'd* just seen a ghost, but he always looked that way given his complexion. "Baron Samedi, I presume?"

The Baron bowed his head slightly. "You've always been a clever one, Count. I'm curious how you managed to reforge your body."

"It was not merely from blood." Dracula stood up and did a turn. "Call it an experiment. I've some news on what the warlock, Baladan, is up to and my embodiment confirms it."

I gulped. "You didn't drain more humans to do this. You consumed a wraith."

Dracula laughed and pointed at me with his longer-than-natural index finger. "Clever girl! I knew I liked you. That whole killing me matter aside, of course."

"You harnessed the energies of Barbelo," Baron Samedi said. "You used it to make yourself a new body."

"With a few improvements, of course." Dracula grinned from ear-to-ear exposing his fangs. "I'll tell you what Baladan is doing, but then I must be on my way."

I snorted. "It's early morning. You can't go anywhere."

Dracula licked the fingertips of each of his hands and slicked back the hair around his ears. "I told you I made improvements."

"You can walk in the sun?" I asked.

"Why couldn't I?" Dracula asked. "I have a body now. It's remarkable, really. Our usual vulnerability to sunlight must've been a part of our design."

Baron Samedi grunted. "If I did not create your kind with limitations, you would have dominated the world. You would have become like gods!"

Dracula stood up and straightened the collar of his coat. "I know, right?"

I aimed my wand at Dracula's chest. "We had an agreement."

"And I intend to fulfill my side of the bargain. I have no desire to slaughter the thousands I might. I do not wish to dominate the world like some kind of vampire emperor. I am not Corbin. Who wants that kind of responsibility?"

"Then what are you planning, Dracula?" I asked.

Dracula smirked and paced around the table even as I kept my wand directed at his body. "I thought I might take a cruise. Maybe spend some time on the beach. Maybe I'll go on an expedition in the Amazon. My only plans are to do things I never could before."

I snorted. "Sorry, Drac. I don't believe you. You were always out for power. You stole Mercy's compulsion ability. You tried to steal my telekinesis."

"I no longer possess those abilities, nor do I have the ability I once did to steal the abilities belonging to other vampires. All I've ever wanted was freedom."

I raised one eyebrow. "Freedom for what?"

"To do whatever the hell I please! The way I see it, you have a choice. You can lower your wand and listen to me. I'll tell you what you want to know about Baladan. Or, you can exsanguinate me and take your chances with the warlock."

Holland placed her hand on my arm. I lowered my wand. "Listen to what he has to say. If the vampire is not telling the truth, we'll deal with him later."

"You should listen to the mambo," Dracula said. "I have no current intentions to harm you or your friends. I could have simply left, after all. Instead, I came here because I agreed to help you."

I took a deep breath. "That's a fair point. Alright, Dracula. What is Baladan up to and how do we stop him?"

"He's not forming an army of wraiths. Sure, he uses them to protect him when he must. He can *control* them. Some of them, at least. He is forming a coven of warlocks not so he can harness all the wraiths and use them, but so that they can *absorb* their energy. All I can do with this new body is endure the sunlight. That doesn't make me a god. If Baladan succeeds, however, he will use the power of the wraiths to make anything he wishes. Weapons, creatures, new forms of magic. Literally anything."

Connor tilted his head. "He'd be like the Green Lantern. But without the ring and his creations would be black rather than green."

"They can be whatever color he intends," Dracula said. "The colors don't matter."

I narrowed my eyes. "Quick question. The wraiths can't go out in the sunlight. How were you able to use one to give you a body that could?"

"The energy within them is malleable, but it requires an intelligence to manipulate its shape. Most of the wraiths were vampires in life. They are still conditioned to their former limitations. When I took a wraith, I could alter its essence however I intended. That's the whole point, Hailey. Once the wraiths are pulled into a body, be it Baladan's, his son's, or anyone else's, the power can be molded like clay into virtually anything."

"You said you could tell us how to stop him."

Dracula cracked his knuckles. "Every wraith can only be repurposed once. There are thousands of wraiths out there, but they aren't easy to find or harness. Baladan has developed a spell to do it. If you want to beat him, it's simple, really. You need to gather and harness more than he does."

"I can sense the wraiths already." Holland craned her neck around. She was sitting next to Tommy on the couch, pretending to watch him shoot someone on a video game. She didn't give a rat's ass about the game. The mambo was listening to my conversation with Dracula as best she could, even if her head nodded up and down from time to time. It was a long night, and it had exhausted her as much as the rest of my human friends. "If it's a simple numbers game," Holland continued, "and the wraiths can't be out and about during the day, it's basically a race to see if we can get more wraiths faster than he can."

I shook my head. "He's gathering more warlocks to harness as many as he can as fast as he can. How is he training his new warlocks to do it?"

"Simple," Dracula said. "He's using wraiths to create the magic he knows, and he's giving the wraiths to his recruits."

Baron Samedi huffed. "Once he turns one into magic, anyone who holds that magic can absorb more wraiths. Just because the warlock can only hold one unpurposed wraith at a time doesn't mean he can't hold on to whatever power he used the previous wraiths he absorbed to make."

"Let me get this straight. Baladan can only harness one at a time, right? The same principle applies to as many warlocks as he gathers. They can't absorb all of them at once, but he needs them all. That means he must be using them to create something huge."

"I've told you all I know," Dracula said. "Now, if it's no difference to you, I think I'll be going."

"Where the hell are you going?" I asked.

Dracula did a spin. "Aruba? Jamaica? Off the Florida Keys, there's a place called Kokomo. That's where I wanna go."

Connor chuckled. "Alright, Brian Wilson."

"Like hell!" I shouted. "We need your help to do this!"

Baron Samedi grabbed my arm. "Let him go. I have another idea."

Dracula waved at us. "See ya! Wouldn't wanna be ya! Muahahaha!"

The Count took off and left through the front door. I turned to Baron Samedi. "What's your plan?"

"Dracula gave me an idea. Tell me, Hailey. You still hold Nico's sire bond, do you not?"

I nodded. "Yeah. Don't use it much. We already thought about using it to attract the vampire wraiths. It's just not practical."

"Would you be willing to return it to its owner?"

I tilted my head. "You're talking about resurrecting Nico? You don't have his soul anymore. You gave it back to him before he died so he could move on."

Ghede Nibo laughed. "I know where to find him."

"Dracula always had ambition," Baron Samedi said. "He also lacked vision. If he could alter the body he made using the power of Barbelo within the wraiths, we can do that with Nico. Only this time, we'll give him a better body. One that can use his sire bond to not only seek out the wraiths and compel them one by one to return to him, but one that draws them in."

I shook my head. "Nico has had several chances to return from the dead. Every chance he's had, he turned down. He doesn't want to live in this world anymore."

"He won't live in this world. I will make him one of us. A new Ghede Loa. Any wraith might help us do as much. We need to go bigger. We need to harness Kalyptos. It's the energy of the demiurge that will form Nico's new being."

"If Kalyptos is a part of him, does he even need his sire bond back?"

Baron Samedi shrugged. "That depends how many wraiths are left unclaimed by Baladan when we finally find Kalyptos."

Chapter 13

I WASN'T SURE HOW I felt about resurrecting Nico as a demigod. I tried to call Mercy for her opinion, but I didn't get an answer. That whole underground vampire world in the sewers of Exeter was high tech, but it had shitty cell service.

What was it about my mentors and their living arrangements? Both Annabelle and Mercy lived in underground communities now.

Ultimately, it wasn't up to Mercy. Still, since she was Nico's favorite progeny, I thought it might be a good idea to let her know her maker might be coming back from the dead and could be a Ghede Loa the next time she saw him.

The choice had to be Nico's alone. I sure as hell would not help Baron Samedi turn him into a Loa without Nico's consent. At the same time, though, it was the best plan we had. He could use his sire bond once I returned it to him to gather as many wraiths as possible. Those who didn't respond or he couldn't reach, we could fight off—ideally with Nicky and Devin's help.

Ghede Nibo left to retrieve Nico's spirit from wherever he was. Apparently, Ghede Nibo was some kind of usher who could lead dead souls in and out of the land of the living. He was the Baron's errand boy. Having a host must not have limited his powers.

They didn't limit the Baron's powers either. He had his host's bare feet crossed on my table. He wiggled her toes. "They're so pretty, aren't they?"

I snorted. "They're toes."

"Toes can be pretty. Just like candy! There's a beauty to everything in creation. You simply need the eyes to see it."

I furrowed my brow. "What about buttholes?"

Baron Samedi tilted his head. "Certainly not candy in any sense. Though, a Baby Ruth or a Tootsie Roll might be in the ballpark. The beauty of a thing isn't always in its appearance. Sometimes it's in its function."

I stared at the Baron blankly. "I know what buttholes do. It isn't helping your case."

"Suppose I used the power of a wraith to create a body without an anus. How do you think that would go for a person after a day or two? Trust me, there's a beauty to *everything.*"

"What about disease? What about cancer?"

"As an immortal, there is a beauty to mortality as well. It's a gift that you used to know but no longer do. Why do you suppose Niccolo wanted to die after walking the earth for thousands of years? Most people don't want to die, that's true. But without mortality, things lose their urgency and meaning. There *is* beauty in that, in cherishing every moment precisely because you never know if it might be your last."

Connor chuckled. "Kind of ironic, isn't it?"

I tilted my head. "Connor!"

"He's right. I am the primary Ghede, a Loa of death, but I can never die."

I tilted my head. "But you have a dark side. Annabelle and Holland raised you in your green aspect, but I know you have a red aspect, one that we'd never summon if we could avoid it."

Baron Samedi shrugged. "That's not the point. It's necessary. Death is pervasive, angst-ridden, and relentless. It's also liberating."

"Still, I know what it's like to have another side to yourself. To live fearing that it might one day take over and turn you into something you don't want to be. While vampires *can* live forever, we can be killed as well. The wraiths prove as much. Even if I were to live forever, though, I still cherish every moment because things change. Moments are fleeting. The present is always perishing. Why live worried about the past or the future when all anyone ever has is now?"

Baron Samedi extended both of his host's hands. Her red fingernails matched her toes. He formed a flask in one hand and a cigarette in the other. After he took a swig from his flask and set it down, he lit his cigarette with a flame that appeared on the tip of his thumb. Mercy wouldn't be pleased to know we allowed someone to smoke in the house.

I cleared my throat. "We don't usually allow smoking in the house."

Baron Samedi chuckled. "This isn't just tobacco. It's a soul. I'm drawing my host's soul back into her body. When I leave, she'll live again. It's the least I can do."

I furrowed my brow. "I wasn't aware you held human souls as *cigarettes.*"

Baron Samedi bowed his head. "It's efficient. My satchel grants me access to any soul I require. Should I desire to commune with one's soul I need only take a puff. Anyone who is killed by a vampire passes through my hand on the way to the afterlife. The host will revive—but she will be a vampire."

Tommy was on the couch in the living room. He craned his neck around and smiled widely. "Yay! I won't be the baby anymore!"

"She'll be Dracula's progeny, not mine."

"Both of them will be. Ghede Nibo will do the same for his host before this is done. You were not raised by your sire, Hailey. A sire's bond to his or her progeny is sacred as a parent's bond is to their child. There's more to being a sire, or a parent, than bringing someone into the world. I'd like nothing more than if you took care of these girls. They'll need a strong vampire like you who has heart and wisdom to guide them."

I rubbed my brow. "No offense to Tommy, but siring young vampires is a lot of work."

"But it's worth it, is it not? These vampires will be like you. They will retain their souls. Perhaps it is time that I cut my children loose."

"Why did you make vampires to begin with?" I asked.

"Vampires were to be my eyes and ears in the world. My connection to the land of the living. Anything any vampire has ever seen or done I can witness if I wish. After all these centuries, though, I'm wondering why I ever desired such a thing? Seeing all you've accomplished has opened my eyes."

"I thought you couldn't see through my eyes."

"I cannot. But I've seen what Mercy, Sarah, and Tommy and many others have witnessed. Withholding souls from my vampires was misguided. You said before you sometimes feared what the darkness in you might do. That's unique."

"How so? All vampires have a darkness, a craving for villainy."

"As do most humans! That you *fear* becoming a monster is exactly why I'm sure you'll never be one. I cannot return the soul to every vampire who does not ask for it, but I can ensure that from here on out new vampires will be different."

Tommy stood up from the couch and cleared his throat. "Can I have mine back?"

Baron Samedi laughed. He formed another cigarette in his hand and flicked it to Tommy across the room. "Smoke it and live."

Tommy caught the cigarette in his right hand, held it in front of his face, and examined it. Then he chuckled. "I always knew the surgeon general was full of shit."

Baron Samedi laughed. "These are not typical cigarettes. They're still hazardous to human health. For you, though, it's life. Real life."

Tommy placed the cigarette between his lips. "Have a light?"

Baron Samedi waved him over. The Loa of death extended his painted thumb and formed another flame. Tommy lit his cigarette and for a half-second, his eyes glowed a golden hue.

"I just smoked my soul. How about that!"

I tilted my head. "Feel any different?"

Tommy narrowed his eyes. "I'm not sure. I think so. It's subtle."

Baron Samedi nodded. "The difference between good and evil is always subtle. The boundary between life and death is not as cut and dry as some assume. Sometimes, though, it's the small things that make all the difference."

Ghede Nibo stepped into the room. The ghost of Nico followed him. I could see him. Tommy could, too. Connor couldn't.

Nico stepped up to the table. "We were in the other room and heard what you said, Baron. You've changed."

Baron Samedi laughed. "If you don't change, you die. Ironic for me, perhaps, but I intend to keep evolving. Will you accept my proposal?"

Nico grinned. "Are you going to get down on one knee?"

"I'm not proposing marriage! Though, this host is quite pleasing, is she not?"

Nico laughed. "She is, indeed."

"Pretty enough to eat!" Tommy piped up. "That's why I chose her. Before all this happened, I mean. Seems kind of weird to say it now."

I rolled my eyes. "You think?"

Tommy smiled widely. "Weird is sort of my thing these days."

"You and me both! Now, Mister Samedi—"

The Baron cleared his throat. "Baron Samedi. I didn't spend three thousand years in Baron school to be called 'Mister,' thank you very much."

I bit the inside of my cheek. "Sorry, I didn't mean—"

"No offense taken. Just don't let it happen again."

I sighed and nodded. "Presuming Nico will do this, how do we get Kalyptos?"

"Kalyptos is not a person. He's a demiurge."

"Don't get me wrong. I've been trying to learn what I can about all that gnostic shit. I've seen that word, but don't have a clue what it means."

Baron Samedi laughed. "The gnostics made their writings difficult to understand on purpose. Their obsession was with secret knowledge. Get that knowledge and they believed you could ascend to divinity through Barbelo and Kalyptos. None of them ever made it. You can't become divine through knowledge. Knowledge might elevate the ego, but it doesn't do much for the spirit."

"Good to know," Nico piped up. "I was afraid I'd have to pass a test before you'd make me a Loa."

"You've passed through more than your share of trials," Baron Samedi said. "The power of Kalyptos can only be channeled by a god or one equal in power. I believe this warlock we're dealing with intends to do exactly that. Dracula said as much. He wants to absorb as much power as he can through the wraiths so that he becomes *like* a god. Powerful enough to master Kalyptos. I've chosen you, Nico, not because of your intelligence. It's because of your character. Now that Barbelo is here, mingled with this world, whoever becomes the vessel of Kalyptos will be unstoppable. That kind of power should not belong to a fly-by-night warlock who has gotten a bit too big for his britches."

"I'm not sure I should have that kind of power," Nico said. "No one should."

"That's why you're suited for it. It's precisely because you have no desire for such power that I can trust you will wield it responsibly, if you choose to use it at all."

Nico shook his head. "Power like that corrupts even the best of us. If I do this, I will not use the power. I will keep it safe. That is all."

"You will be bound to this world," Baron Samedi added. "You will be one of the Ghede, but what vampires have done for me for so long, you will do in my stead. You will ensure that the dead may continue to rest in peace by protecting the afterlife from those in the land of the living who would threaten it."

I cocked my head. "What does that mean?"

Nico turned to me. "What the Baron means to say is that the power of Kalyptos could be used to remake the world and overthrow the natural order. It will be my task, as it has always been the responsibility of the Loa, to maintain the balance, the natural order of the universe."

"Without using the power of Kalyptos to do it?" I asked.

"It would be easier if you did," Baron Samedi said. "With the gates between worlds shattered and convergences opening between this realm and every other, someone needs to represent the interest of the Ghede here. Regardless, Niccolo, if you can do that without using the power I'm willing to give you, that's your choice."

"What if he can't do it?" I asked.

"He will do it," Baron Samedi said. "If he does not, I'll have no choice but to resume my collection of souls from those who are turned."

"First things first," Ghede Nibo said. "We have to stop the warlock. We cannot permit him to take Kalyptos."

I stood up from the table. "Then what are you waiting for? The warlocks could have all the power they need already."

"They do not or we would know it," Baron Samedi said. "Kalyptos is the *hidden* one. The demiurge will not be easy to find, even for me."

"Wish I could help. Not much I can do while the sun is out. Besides, I wouldn't know where to start."

"Ghede Nibo, Niccolo, and I intend to leave and begin our search for Kalyptos. If we have not procured the demiurge come nightfall, do whatever you can to thwart the warlock. Holland has my aspect and can sense the presence of the wraiths. If this friend of yours from up north has something that might be of use to destroy them, hunt down as many as you can lest they fall into the warlock's hands."

I nodded. "I get it. Slow the warlocks down. Buy you enough time to find Kalyptos before Baladan gains enough power to claim the demiurge for himself."

Baron Samedi stood from the table and took a swig from his flask. "Precisely. Do whatever you must. We will handle the rest. Once we locate Kalyptos and vest Niccolo with his power, the warlocks will have no choice but to abandon their ill-fated project."

Chapter 14

CONNOR WENT TO SLEEP in my bed. I laid beside him for a while. He didn't need to stay in during the day, but when you're dating a vampire, it really screws with your sleep schedule. With our blackout curtains, it was just as good as night in Casa do Diabo.

Holland had said little since we got back from the swamp. She was playing the role of a quiet observer—when she wasn't nodding off on the couch while Tommy sat there playing video games.

I let her sleep as long as she needed to. Sarah could let me know more or less the status of the wraiths. She just couldn't leave her room without losing her mind. Holland would have to come with me come nightfall so we could go wraith hunting. If all went according to plan, Nicky and Devin would be there to help. I still didn't know if Devin knew any spells that could help. Last I saw him, he wasn't especially powerful. He was a run-of-the-mill warlock. He could throw some fire around and such, but I'd never seen him do anything on Baladan's level. I'm not saying Devin wasn't formidable. What he lacked in raw power, he made up for with heart. Still, it had been a while since I saw either him or Nicky.

Connor sometimes whimpered in his sleep. Just like a dog. Side-effect of being a wolf shifter. Once he was asleep, I rolled out of bed and snuck over to Sarah's room.

I knocked on her door and she let me straight in. "The sage ward still holding up?"

Sarah nodded. "So far, so good."

"What can you say about the wraiths? Have you been listening in at all? I need to know how many of them are with Baladan."

"Hardly any. The strangest thing. There were a bunch all together, they just stopped making noise. I can't hear them at all. I figured it had to do with the sunrise."

I sat down on the edge of Sarah's bed and rested my head in my hands. "That might be it. I doubt it, though."

Sarah nodded. "You think the warlocks are stealing and repurposing their power?"

I laughed and shook my head. "You were listening in on my thoughts earlier?"

Sarah nodded. "Be careful, Hailey. I wasn't only listening to you. Dracula isn't going to Kokomo."

I tilted my head. "But that's where he said he wanted to go?"

"He's after the same thing the warlocks seek, the same thing Baron Samedi is after."

"He wants to turn Nico into a Loa."

"That's what he says. Are you sure that's his true intention? Why would Baron Samedi, the most powerful of all the Ghede, create another Ghede more powerful than he is?"

I shrugged. "Desperation, perhaps."

"He gave Tommy back his soul. He was currying favor and trust. He made grand promises. I highly doubt if he infuses this Kalyptos into Nico's spirit that he will not do so in such a way that leaves Nico beholden to him. He would, in effect, be Nico's sire."

"He wants me to transfer Nico's sire bond back to him."

"Because you have a soul. The Baron can't control you, Hailey. Maybe the Baron's intentions are genuine. I could not read his thoughts, only yours as you spoke with him."

I sighed. "WWMD."

Sarah laughed. "What would Mercy do?"

"Damn straight. I think I know the answer."

"She'd kick these things' asses without having to rely on a demigod who is every bit as dangerous as he is powerful. At the very least, she'd find a way to use the Loa to her advantage."

"The enemy of your enemy isn't necessarily your friend. Not if the enemy of your enemy was your enemy before. After all, if the principle applied in such a situation, your enemy could call your enemy's enemy a friend as well. Then who would the enemy be? Your enemy's enemy or the enemy of your enemy? And whose enemy would you be but everyone's enemy, even while everyone else was an enemy, too?"

I stared at Sarah blankly. "My head hurts now. That's a lot of enemies."

"More enemies than a colonics convention."

I tilted my head. "Good joke, but you said it wrong. More *enemas* than a colonics convention. It helps if you say it with an accent. All I know is that I don't want to be anybody's enema. The enema of my enema is an asshole."

Sarah scratched her head. "I'll have to think about that one. I'm not sure it makes sense."

"Don't dwell on it. I appreciate the advice. I don't know why my conversations as of late end up circling the anus, but that's life when the universe is constantly shitting on you."

Sarah laughed. "Is that what you think's happening? First, the universe doesn't take shits. Black holes aren't anuses. At least not *that* kind of black hole. They suck things in but don't spit things out. The anus can do both. Second, I wouldn't call what you've been doing lately getting shat upon. If anything, the universe is telling you that you matter. It needs you. That's why it keeps dumping so many of its enemies on you."

I smirked. "Dumping enemas? That's sort of how they work."

Sarah rolled her eyes. "You know what I mean. You aren't the universe's toilet. You're more like the universe's toilet paper."

I laughed and shook my fist in the air. "Gee, thanks! Charmin strong!"

"What I mean is to say you're the universe's hero. Have you considered what the world would look like today if you never became a witch and a vampire?"

I shrugged. "Maybe Mercy and Annabelle would have figured it out without me."

Sarah huffed. "Yeah, right. They have their gifts. But there are things you can do that they never could. Everything happens for a reason, Hailey. The world might not shower you with gratitude or throw parades in your honor, but if they knew the truth, you'd better believe they would."

"I wouldn't want that attention. It's not entirely selfless, either. I just don't want to live in a world where millions of people suffer for one jerk's ambitions. I'd also like to enjoy myself a bit. What good is it to be potentially immortal if you don't get to have fun?"

Sarah smiled. "I have plenty of fun."

I tilted my head. "You do? Since when?"

Sarah reached under her bed. She pulled out a ball of yarn and half of a sweater. "It's called crochet! It's a blast!"

I stared at Sarah blankly. I tugged at my earlobes. "I think something is wrong with my ears. I could swear that you said crochet is your ideal way of spending eternity."

"What's wrong with that?"

"Sounds more like a hobby an inmate might pick up to pass the time than a happily ever after."

"Everyone loves a nice sweater! Not to mention blankets, stockings, handbags, and just about anything else. It's thrilling. I'll teach you how to do it if you'd like."

I smirked. "I appreciate the offer. No offense, but once this is over and I have time to enjoy myself, crochet won't be my first hobby of choice. Maybe I'll try skydiving. Cliff jumping. I could kick serious ass in MMA."

Sarah shrugged and poked her crochet hook through a loop of yarn. "Suit yourself. I'll keep listening in on the wraiths and will let you know if I find anything out."

There was a knock on the door downstairs. I half suspected it was a Jehovah's Witness. Wouldn't be the first time. You'd think after I showed them my fangs on their last visit, they'd stop knocking on my door. I knew it was risky. If they told anyone about me, it wouldn't turn out well. Who really listens to those JW's anyway? Maybe I'd invite the gentleman in for a bite.

"Who is it?" I asked.

"Annabelle! Open up!"

I grunted. I unlocked the door and took a few steps back to avoid the flush of sunlight that would follow. "It's unlocked. Come in!"

Annabelle stepped in and wiped her shoes on the rug. "I won't be long. Just wanted to let you know I stopped by to find Mary Ann."

I rubbed my brow. "Damn. I almost forgot all about that. How was she? Did you learn anything?"

Annabelle shook her head. "Nothing at all. She was gone. Her house looked like no one had been there in a while. That, or she didn't dust often and regularly invited insects to a pool party in her toilet."

"Maybe she took a trip after the divorce was final. With her son missing, though, I'd think she'd be looking for him. At least she'd stay in town to press law enforcement on the search."

"I also checked with Doc Freud at the Vilokan Asylum. Daniel didn't mention anything in any of his sessions about his mother leaving town or anything like that. It surprised him as much as it did me that she wasn't around."

"Maybe she's just staying with a friend. Then again, if Baladan needs more warlocks, who is to say she didn't pick up a few spells during the time they were married? I don't think she'd go with him willingly, but if he had their son, she might have left for his sake."

Annabelle scratched the back of her head. "I had the same thought. Anyway, I wanted to let you know the status of that, which I realize wasn't much status at all. If you need some kind of emotional situation to imagine what might be behind Baladan's power, going with the divorce and custody battle is as good a guess as any."

"Thanks, Annabelle. You should get a little rest. I have a feeling it's going to be another long night."

Annabelle smirked. "That's what energy drinks and coffee are for."

Annabelle let herself out. I locked up behind her.

I kicked back on the couch and rested my eyes for a couple hours. I didn't need to sleep, but sometimes it was nice to zone out or snooze a little to pass the time during the day. I'm not sure how long I was out. I woke up and noticed the sun was now cracking around the windows on the west side of the house. I checked my phone.

I headed back up to Sarah's room. "Sunset is rapidly approaching. I won't be here for more than a couple more hours. Pick up anything during the day from the wraiths?"

Sarah shook her head. "Nothing at all."

"Need anything before I leave? I know sitting in your room all this time sucks. Maybe a book from the shelf? A DoorDash delivery boy? Anything at all?"

Sarah slipped her crochet hook through a loop of yarn and pulled the string through. She did it several times at an impressive pace. "I need nothing at the moment. I'll shout for Tommy if I need anything later, presuming he'll still be here."

"I'm not taking him with me tonight. He's too young to get involved in a fight like this. The last thing I need is to pull him off someone's neck while I'm throwing down with Baladan Branham or whatever monsters he might repurpose the wraiths into becoming."

"I'll text if I hear anything of use from the wraiths. Remember, though. Only trust those you know you can trust. This demiurge everyone is after is too powerful to trust in the hands of Baron Samedi. He very well might use it to make Niccolo a Loa, but I doubt it will come with the kind of freedom he expects. Don't trust Dracula, either. He has his own ambitions. You don't need to rely on them to do what you have to do. You need to rely on your actual friends. Together, I imagine, you won't need your enemy's enemies to stop the warlock."

Chapter 15

THE SUN WAS JUST setting. I could tell from the amber glow around the window shades. The internet will tell you if you search for it what time the sunset is supposed to be. A nice advantage for modern day vampires. Even so, the actual sunset time and when vampires are safe to come out and play can vary by a few minutes. Older vampires could go out earlier and even stay out a few minutes longer. That wasn't a universal thing, though. Every vampire's sun tolerance was different. Some would burst into flames the second they stepped into sunlight, others could endure it for a few minutes without ill effect. I was somewhere in the middle. I'd been scorched once or twice. Without magic, I'd still have the scars. I usually waited about five minutes after what the internet told me before I braved dusk. There was usually a red glow on the western horizon which was the closest thing to seeing the sun I could endure. The glow around the windows also helped confirm that all was well. Sometimes, on an overcast evening, I could go out earlier.

Holland slept most of the day. So did Connor. Tommy spent half his day on Minecraft. The rest of the day was on Fortnite. I didn't get either game. Neither one seemed to have a point other than building crap and killing. Then again, killing things was the point of most video games. They never made video games that allowed someone to level-up by doing virtuous stuff like working at a soup kitchen, raising children, or helping the elderly. Video games rewarded vice. Mostly war and slaughter. If you have to get your homicidal tendencies out of your system, best do it in a virtual world.

I did a little digging through my grimoires during the day but didn't come up with much that I didn't know already or I thought might be helpful.

I shared Sarah's concerns about the two Ghede with Holland, but she wasn't worried about it. She assured me it wouldn't be a problem. I wasn't sure why she was so confident about it but she had more experience working with the Ghede than I did.

I heard a loud rumble approach from down the street. It stopped in front of my house. I knew the sound of that motorcycle. It was Nicky's Thruxton RS. I pulled the curtain back to confirm. Devin was riding bitch behind Nicky.

Nicky's long silver hair glistened under the streetlights. So did her red knee-high boots that were pulled up over her leather pants. Her stiletto heels were probably nine inches long. Nicky had all the fabulousness in the relationship. Devin was a jeans and t-shirt kind of guy—sort of like Connor.

Nicky had a large bag strapped to her back. She was a hunter, remember, on top of being a shape-shifter and a nymph from the garden groves of Annwn. She traveled with supplies. Last I knew, a crossbow was her weapon of choice. Effective against most vampires. A wooden bolt was basically a flying stake. If she wasn't wielding a wooden stake directly she used her stiletto heel to down a vampire. As a fire warlock, Devin burned out their hearts to finish the job. They called it a stake and bake.

Nicky—feared by most vampires under the name of Nyx—wasn't like any hunter I'd ever met. Most of them were bigots. They killed vampires for what they were without any consideration for who they were. For years, trapped in a male body, Nicky knew what it was like to be on the other side of a bigot's gaze. The funny thing was that while she could shift into virtually any shape she wanted, she'd come to love who she was. All that effort to reclaim her lost powers, only to realize she didn't need them to be happy. She chose to stay in the same body she was in when Devin fell in love with her.

I opened the door before they could knock. Nicky's diamond ring sparkled under the porch lights.

"Damn, girl! That's some kind of rock!"

Nicky hugged me. "It's been too long!"

Devin smiled and waved. "Hey there, Hailey."

"These your friends from Kansas City?" Holland was standing behind me.

"Yes. Holland, this is Nicky and Devin. Guys, this is Holland. She's a mambo. Pretty badass when it comes to the Ghede and all that death magic shit."

Holland raised an eyebrow. "Death magic *shit*?"

I smirked. "Sorry. You know what I mean. If you want to call my craft 'blood magic shit', I won't take offense."

Nicky reached into her bag. She pulled out a golden crucifix. "I think this is what you needed. It belonged to Alice, the nightwalker who used to be with the Order of the Morning Dawn."

I nodded. "Right. I know who Alice is. That's why we called you."

Nicky tossed the crucifix back in her bag. "I can use it. Took me a while to master. It channels celestial power. If these wraiths you're hunting are vulnerable to sunlight, this stuff burns twice as hot."

I turned to Devin. "We're also dealing with warlocks. They have a spell that they're using to harness the wraiths. They're converting their energy into a primal force that *we think* they intend to amass so they can grab the big kahuna."

"The big kahuna?" Nicky chuckled. "I've fought my share of evil, but no one has ever gone by something so silly."

"That's not what he's called. It's not really a he. It's a demiurge, a power that God, or the gods, or whoever first created the world, used to make everything that exists. If these warlocks get Kalyptos, the demiurge, they'll be unstoppable."

Nicky blew a stay strand of silver hair out of her face. "Blast the wraiths. Keep the warlocks from getting stronger. No problem. Know where we can find the wraiths?"

"I can lead us to them," Holland said.

"Any clue what kind of spell they might use to absorb their power?"

Devin shook his head. "I'm not sure."

"They've also used wraiths to create a new magic I've never seen before."

"If we're hunting wraiths, perhaps I can try a few things before Nicky blasts them with celestial light. It won't matter, though, if we kill enough wraiths to stop the warlock from getting the power he requires."

"We could be too late already," I said. "It's nighttime now so the wraiths are out and active. It means Baladan is hunting them just as we are."

"Anything else we need to know?" Nicky asked.

I nodded. "You've heard of Dracula."

Nicky grunted. "Who hasn't?"

"He's trying to do the same as the warlock, we believe. He wants to claim the demiurge as well."

Nicky smiled widely. "Hunting vampires is my speciality. No offense, Hailey."

"I killed Dracula once. Thing you need to know is that he doesn't have a heart. He came back as a wraith himself, then absorbed enough blood and a few wraiths to make himself a new body. He's also immune to sunlight."

"A vampire who can't be staked and isn't vulnerable to light?" Nicky raised an eyebrow. "Sounds like a challenge."

"Do you have any idea at all how to kill a vampire like that?"

Nicky shook her head. "Can you exsanguinate him and turn him feral?"

I nodded. "I think so. That won't kill him, though."

"An ancient vampire like Dracula relies on his intelligence as much as his natural abilities. Turn him feral, and he'll be as mindless as any feral. We still won't be able to kill him, but we can chain him up, seal him in a tomb, and sink him to the bottom of the sea."

I chuckled. "Remind me never to get on your bad side."

Nicky laughed. "You're one of the good ones. You have nothing to worry about. It's been a while since I've had a vampire to hunt. They steer clear of my area these days."

I chuckled. "I wish I could say the same thing. The bad guys seem to swarm around me like flies to shit."

Nicky cracked her knuckles, then checked her fingers to ensure she hadn't chipped a nail. "Honey, I sing in my club every night. I love what I do. But there's a side of me I haven't let loose in months. What do you say we go kick the shit out of these bastards together?"

I grinned. "That sounds fantastic."

"Correction." Nicky did a little spin. "It sounds *fabulous.*"

Chapter 16

"HOW CAN WE HELP?" Connor asked. "Tommy and I aren't sitting around here while you guys go hunting."

"You probably should—"

"I'm with your boyfriend," Tommy added. "We have to do something."

I shook my head. "You aren't doing nothing. We can't be all together. It's too risky. Stay here with Sarah. She can use her abilities to check on us. She can see through the wraiths. If we're in trouble, Sarah can't leave the ward in her room. She may not be able to reach Annabelle or Ellie if they're in Vilokan. That means if we get in over our heads, we'll need you to rally reinforcements."

"So we're backups. Sitting on the bench."

"I get it," Tommy said. "Remember that NFC championship game when the 49ers ran out of quarterbacks against the Eagles?"

Connor smirked. "I remember. It wasn't that long ago. I didn't realize you were a football fan."

"Of course I am. Who isn't? The point is that a good backup can be just as important as any other player on the team."

Connor kissed me on the cheek. "Alright. We've got your back."

I raised my hand and traced Connor's jawline with my knuckles. "You always do. You've always been the unsung hero. Without you, I never could have beaten Corbin. I couldn't have accessed the power I needed to stop Protophanes without you. I'm not asking you to ride the bench, Connor. I'm asking you to have my back because there's a damn good chance I'll need you to take the field."

Connor laughed. "Now you're on board with the football analogies?"

I chuckled. "I don't watch a lot of games, but I'm not a complete recluse. I watch the Super Bowl every year."

"You watch it for the halftime show and the commercials."

"But I still watch it!" I kissed Connor once on the lips. "All I have is the night and I don't intend to spend another day helpless while Baladan and Dracula are out there getting stronger."

"Love you, Hailey Bradbury."

I blushed a little. "Love you too, Wolfie."

Holland sighed. "That's all very sweet. It really touches me. Not in the heart, but in my turning stomach. The wraiths are on the move. We need to get going."

Holland and I took Ellie's farm truck. Nicky and Devin followed behind on her motorcycle.

Holland's eyes emanated a subtle red glow as I drove. "Turn right."

I turned. "How are you doing this? You sensed them before, but it was different."

"With two Ghede on earth, my aspect is stronger than before. The wraiths are coming from all over. They're all converging on one location."

I raised an eyebrow. "The convergence?"

Holland shook her head. "Not the one in Manchac. I don't know if there's a convergence where they're going at all, but I'm guessing that's where we'll find Baladan."

I shook my head. "If they're all going to him, how are we going to stop them? We'll have to fight these things while Baladan is sucking them up."

Holland was still staring straight ahead with her glowing eyes. I wasn't even sure if she could see through her magic. "Baladan does suck, but I don't think sucking is the process he uses with the wraiths."

"Whatever power he used before to enthrall them must be what he's using now to draw them in."

Holland took a deep breath. "He's stronger now. These aren't the same wraiths we saw in Vilokan. I think he already absorbed those. The more wraiths he and his warlocks take, the more they can draw."

I clenched my hands on the farm truck's cold rubber steering wheel. "That means he's getting stronger exponentially. The more power he gains, the more wraiths he absorbs, the faster he can gather the rest."

Holland rubbed her brow. "There are so many I can't focus on all of them. There must be a thousand. Maybe more. They're all heading to the same place."

"Try to focus on the place, the spot. Not the wraiths themselves. Where are we going, Holland?"

"Turn left. First chance you get."

"*Where* are we going, Holland?"

"I don't know! I'm just following the flow of the wraiths."

"They have to be gathering at one place. That's the destination."

Holland shook her head. "That's just the thing. They're all moving into an area, but I can't sense them at all once they get past a certain point. It's like the hole in a donut."

"How large of an area are we talking?"

"I don't know, Hailey. It's not like my abilities show me a map. It's all flashes, glimpses, and there are so many of them it's hard to put it all together."

"Is it in the city or out of the city?"

Holland shook her head. "I don't know!"

"Are they going into Vilokan? Maybe that's why you can't sense them. The firmament might block your power."

"They aren't going into Vilokan. I sensed the wraiths there before. Turn left!"

I took the next turn. I checked the rearview mirror to be sure Nicky and Devin were still there. Holland wasn't giving me a lot of notice to turn. Thankfully, Nicky knew how to trail someone. She kept enough distance that she could react to my turns but didn't put so much space between us that she'd lose track of us.

"We're almost there!"

I looked ahead at a row of houses on each side. I didn't see anything of note. "Are you sure?"

No sooner did I say it and something like a wall of light blasted down the street and enveloped the truck. It was as if the sun itself had set itself down in the neighborhood. The light didn't burn my skin through the window thankfully.

"What the hell just happened?" Holland asked.

I stopped the truck and got out. Nicky and Devin pulled up behind us and dismounted her motorcycle. Holland got out of the truck and stepped up behind me.

"I know what this is. I've been here. A place like it, at least. This is Barbelo. Or maybe New Barbelo. And it's not in another realm through a convergence. It's here, on earth. In the middle of New Orleans."

Chapter 17

"I DON'T SENSE THEM anymore." Holland scratched the back of her head.

I sighed. "You wouldn't. They aren't dead here. They're pure energy."

"How is this even possible?"

I shook my head. "That must be how Baladan intends to lure Kalyptos. I forced the demiurge out of Barbelo. By creating a new reality on earth that's like Barbelo I suspect he's trying to lure Kalyptos so he can use the energies he's gathering to absorb the demiurge as well."

Nicky stepped up beside me. "If they aren't *vampire* wraiths here, I don't think celestial light is going to do us any good."

I snorted. "So much for that plan."

"We need to leave," Holland said. "If Baladan is using the wraiths he's gathering to grow this fake Barbelo, we have to stop them from getting here."

"The bigger this realm grows, the more likely it is to attract Kalyptos."

"Are you sure the demiurge isn't here already?" Nicky asked.

I shook my head. "If Baladan already had Kalyptos, I suspect we'd know it. The entire world would know it."

I was about to climb back into the truck when Nicky grabbed my arm. "We have a better chance at stopping this if we attack from within and from without. My crucifix isn't any good in here. I can kill wraiths out there so long as I can find them."

"I'll go with Nicky," Holland said. "Can you two stop Baladan and whatever warlocks might be in here?"

I shrugged. "I'm still not sure what kind of magic he's wielding, but I like my chances."

"I'll stay here with Hailey," Devin said. "I'll be of more use here than I could possibly be chasing wraiths. Especially if you still want me to try to figure out what magic the warlock used to start all of this."

I nodded. "He must've used something more conventional, or at least natural, before he took a wraith and used it to make whatever magic he's casting now."

"If we can figure that out," Devin added, "we might be able to do something similar. I'd say fight fire with fire since that's my specialty, but I don't think fire magic had anything to do with it."

Nicky and Devin kissed before Holland hopped on the motorcycle behind Nicky and they took off in the direction we came from. They disappeared further away than I thought we'd driven since we arrived. That meant that New Barbelo was expanding by the minute.

"Got a wand?" I asked.

Devin extended his hand and snapped his fingers. A wand formed right in his palm. "Of course I do."

"What the hell? How did you do that?"

Devin chuckled. "It's a warlock thing. Couldn't always do it. Only learned how a few months back. With no major threats in Kansas City, I've had more time to focus on my skills."

I pulled my wand out of my pocket. "Some of us still need pockets. We don't know how many warlocks we might be dealing with, but we'll probably be outnumbered. There's also no telling what they're capable of. These wraiths give them the power to literally create whatever they imagine."

Devin nodded. "Our best bet is to spy on them from a distance. Watch and see how they're doing all of this."

I sighed. "I wish I'd had time to confer with Annabelle before all of this."

Devin raised an eyebrow. "Annabelle. The Voodoo Queen?"

"She was trying to track down Baladan's ex-wife. She went to her house, but she wasn't there. Looked like she hadn't been home in a while. We were hoping to learn more about Baladan, so we'd know how to counter his new magic."

Devin tilted his head. "How would that help?"

"I have a little experience working with entities from Barbelo. The power they use manifests in connection with deep seated human emotion. Usually some kind of angst or fear. If he created a new kind of magic, it's tied to whatever angst he used to make it. If we want to dispel his magic, we have to counter whatever emotion it's tied to. That's the theory, at least."

"Would that undo anything he's made through the wraiths?"

I shook my head. "I don't know. He's working with a coven of warlocks including his own son. I don't know how we could possibly psychoanalyze everyone and counter all their emotions. The more warlocks he has who are responsible for this new version of Barbelo, the more difficult it will be to figure out how to dispel. I'm sure that's by design."

"One warlock at a time. Even if we can only disarm one of them and neutralize their power, it will slow this down and lessen the chance that they'll be able to attract the demiurge."

I nodded. "That's the best hope we have. I'm not sure how we would counter Baladan's angst. Most I've been able to learn is that he was divorced a few months ago and his wife got custody of his son. He kidnapped his boy from the Vilokan Asylum. Long story."

"How did you destroy Barbelo before?" Devin asked.

"I used Erzulie's aspect. I don't know why I didn't think of that. If it worked, before, maybe we can take this whole thing down just like I did the original Barbelo."

"If it works, we'll still have warlocks to deal with. We might not be able to fight them off."

"The truck is still running. If we have to run, we can peel out like a banana."

Devin chuckled. "Like a banana?"

"It's the only thing I could think of that peels. Except for sunburnt skin, but I try to avoid that for obvious reasons. Besides, it's gross."

Devin shook his head, laughing. "Give it a shot. If it doesn't work, it doesn't work. We go back to plan A and try to track down the warlocks."

I took a deep breath. To access Erzulie's power, the only thing I'd found that worked was to focus on Connor. I'd practiced with Ellie a lot in recent months. It wasn't as difficult as it used to be.

Butterflies fluttered in my stomach. The same sensation that I suspected Holland might mistake for nausea. You might call it the power of love. All courtesy of Erzulie and her warm-n-fuzzy aspect that welled up within me and blasted out of my eyes and hands with concussive force. Devin took a few steps back. I didn't want to infect him with my love magic and find myself on the other side of Nicky's wrath.

I didn't think it worked that way. I wasn't really sure *how* it worked or how I could manipulate it. What I knew how to do was unleash the raw, unrefined power of Erzulie. I shot my love all over the place. Like a teenage boy with a computer in a locked room. I really didn't have any control. The bright orange light of New Barbelo flickered. For a split-second, I saw the New Orleans neighborhood around us, but it disappeared again once the light resumed. Only the farm truck remained—probably because it was close to us. Maybe the road, the houses, the bushes and the trees were there and I'd see them if I was as close to them as I was to the truck. This light didn't have an external source. It was in the atmosphere itself, so bright but also thick that it obscured most of the physical world. At least I knew it was there.

"Is that what you expected to happen?" Devin asked.

I shook my head. "In the original Barbelo, I released just as much power, but it infected the whole place and forced the entire realm through a portal and into the various convergences scattered around the earth."

"This felt more like a rolling brown out during a storm."

I sighed. "This isn't identical to Barbelo. Apparently when the warlocks forged this primordial atmosphere, they made a few upgrades to prevent me from taking it down."

Devin pressed his lips together. "Or maybe not. You said this energy responds to human emotion or angst."

"Right! Before, when I was facing the shadow monster parasites, Erzulie's power worked to exorcize it from a person. So did Holland's death power."

"I doubt the original Barbelo was attached to anyone's emotion. What if you *gave* it emotion that it latched onto? You didn't so much as destroy Barbelo as you gave the energy of that place something to attach itself to. Your power isn't exactly focused."

I pinched my chin. "You're right. It's raw magic. I can't even access it if I'm not thinking about my boyfriend."

Devin tilted his head. "The wolf shifter?"

"Of course. He's the only boyfriend I've got."

Devin sighed. "It's not *raw* energy, Hailey. Not entirely. You may have more experience with this kind of magic, but my kind of sorcery is deeply intertwined with human emotion. You can't use something to access your magic without giving it focus."

"You're saying my connection to Connor drove the power I released in Barbelo back to earth because he was the focus of my magic?"

"Just a theory."

"Wouldn't it all come through one convergence? The one closest to Connor?"

Devin shrugged. "Maybe one convergence isn't big enough for that. Did you see where exactly this demiurge went through?"

I shook my head. "I think it divided like the rest of Barbelo."

"Which is why looking for Kalyptos isn't Baladan's strategy. He isn't just drawing the demiurge here. He's recombining its divided essence. If it was Erzulie's power that drove the demiurge out of Barbelo, and it's that same kind of power it seeks here, you might have just set off a beacon to draw it here faster."

I twirled my wand in my fingers. "We don't know that. Let's assume the worst. What if we did call Kalyptos? Baladan might not be ready for it. Harnessing a demiurge requires god-like power, and I'm not sure he has enough here."

"It won't take long, depending on how many warlocks he has working with him in here. You said we should assume the worst. That means anticipating that Baladan will have total control of the demiurge. That its essence was divided before might mean he doesn't even need the entire force of Kalyptos. We don't even know if having all of what used to be Kalyptos in the original Barbelo is any stronger than his divided essence now. When you're talking about unlimited power, basically infinity, it doesn't matter how much you divide it up. Half of infinity is still infinity."

I grunted. "We have a warlock, Count Dracula, and two Ghede all trying to harness Kalyptos. I thought it was a race to see who could get to the demiurge first. What if *all* of them get a piece of Kalyptos?"

Devin shuddered. "I don't know, but I don't know if I'd want any of those candidates to have so much power, much less all of them. If they turn against us, or against each other, there's no telling how destructive it will be. The demiurge is the power that created the universe. Give limited beings with narrow and self-centered ambition that kind of power and we'd be lucky if they used it to create a new universe or another planet somewhere. I'm guessing they won't be that creative."

"Whatever the case, we can't stop everyone at once. Let's hope Nicky and Holland are making progress. If we get in too deep, Connor will reach out to Annabelle and she'll come out to fight with Ellie and Savanna. Ellie can use love magic the same as me, but with a lot more skill. Savanna can create storms. Electricity seems to neutralize the wraiths. I'm not sure if it will have the same effect on Kalyptos. Either way, we have friends out there. Let's focus on stopping the warlocks. Baladan is the one who started all this crap. It won't break my heart if he's the first one to bite it. In this case, though, if we can't stop his magic, biting *him* might be my best option."

Devin tilted his head. "That's how Nicky lost her shapeshifting power a long time ago. A vampire's bite. What if—"

"You think this power that Baladan is wielding works like that?"

"You can absorb other powers with a bite."

"Sure, but I also have to cycle the blood I consume. The power has to be attached to the soul."

"Worth a shot. Maybe you can take whatever magic he's using."

"I don't know why Nicky lost her powers from a vampire bite. Usually, the bite doesn't steal the power in someone's soul so much as it spreads it or replicates it."

"This isn't attached to the soul. It latches onto emotion. Does emotion also impact the blood."

I nodded. "It can change the flavor. It's not just emotion. It's more like a person's disposition."

"Still, it's worth trying. Maybe it won't work. Worst-case scenario, you get a snack."

"Worst-case scenario is I get killed trying to take the bite."

"True. It's just an idea. What would happen if you died, anyway? Would you get to come back with the other wraiths?"

I huffed. "I'd rather not find out."

"I don't blame you. It does make one curious, though, what would happen to any new vampires who die now given the situation. Is hell still wide open, or did it just purge the wraiths and close up shop again?"

I took a deep breath. "We'll have to deal with Dracula one way or another. If we have any luck at all, the gates of vampire hell are shut again. If I end up killing him twice, well, the third time might be his charm."

"Let's hope we can stop Baladan. And let's hope you can harness his power and put an end to this before Dracula or the Loa become a problem."

"We're grasping at straws as it is. If I can get a hold of the new magic Baladan forged from the wraiths, at the very least I'll be able to examine it. Maybe I'll find a weakness or something we can exploit."

Chapter 18

WHEN YOU HAVE A whole slew of bad guys all after the same power, probably for entirely different reasons, the only strategy at your disposal is to divide and conquer. Presuming, of course, you have capable friends who can split up to do the conquering.

Then there's the whole stronger together strategy. I think a bunch of politicians have used that as a campaign slogan. You know, when they're still trying to convince voting folk that they're cooperative and reasonable people who are willing to work with variously minded people to come up with better solutions than either side has alone. Then, of course, you find out that stronger together only means together with the folks they agree with, fuck everyone else. That's why I didn't often feed on politicians. It's why Dracula wasn't exactly thrilled by the idea. They usually tasted like shit. That's because they always said "stronger together" when they really meant "divide and conquer." They didn't realize the two strategies didn't work together. It's one or the other.

Divide and conquer or stronger together. Which strategy was the right one at the moment? Most of the time, dividing and conquering only worked when you were conquering something that wasn't all that dangerous. Like shopping at Walmart.

Then again, there's no telling what creatures might lurk between the aisles of Wally World. Especially when I went shopping. It was one of the few twenty-four-hour establishments available to vampires during our waking hours.

We were doing the best we could. Annabelle was the Voodoo Queen. Ellie and Holland were powerful mambos. It was better that they be out in the world where the Ghede may or may not be a threat. Annabelle had killed her share of vampires through the years. Her soul blade could send them straight to vampire hell, even if she didn't hit the heart. Nicky had staked so many vampires that she'd lost count years ago. Dracula wasn't your run-of-the-mill vampire, and he was immune to most of our vulnerabilities. Nicky had a plan, and I was pretty sure Annabelle's soul blade would still be effective.

Devin and I were also the two best suited to take on the warlocks, all things considered. We were facing potential enemies that we really needed to conquer one-by-one as a team. The situation didn't make that possible. If any of them got Kalyptos, and if Sarah was right that the Ghede had ulterior motives, we couldn't allow any of them to harness the power of the demiurge.

I knew I could trust Nico—but not if it was Baron Samedi who used the power of Barbelo to make him into a Loa beholden to the will of the other Ghede.

Devin's theory was intriguing. If the power of Erzulie's aspect was what drew the energies of Barbelo to the world, and if the magic I'd just released was drawing Kalyptos to New Barbelo faster than Baladan wanted, there might be an opportunity to use it to our advantage. If Kalyptos was coming to me, and everyone else including Dracula and the Ghede, were looking for Kalyptos, they'd all end up in New Barbelo eventually. If they were together to fight over Kalyptos, my friends would be together again, too. Divide and conquer could *become* stronger together.

Devin and I pressed forward through the light. The farm truck disappeared from view after only taking a few paces. The atmosphere of Barbelo was light, but it was light that shone only upon itself. It didn't illuminate the material world around us. The laws of particle physics didn't apply. After all, the Aeon of Barbelo predated the existence of physics and the physical world.

"Do you have any idea how many warlocks we're facing in here?" Devin asked.

"All I know is that Baldan and his son, Daniel, are probably here. I'm guessing there are others, but a guess is all it is."

"It may not be necessary that all of the warlocks have the same unique magic. When warlocks band together with other warlocks, or any other practitioner, we can channel each other's power and amplify it as if it was our own."

"So you don't think Baladan is investing the other warlocks with his new magic?"

"I don't know. All I'm saying is it might not be necessary given his goals. Together they can use the magic originating from Baladan to do the same thing, as if they all wielded the same power independently."

"That's not necessarily a bad thing. That means if I can subdue Baladan, presuming he's the one who holds the power, I might be able to disarm all the warlocks."

"Possibly. It's one reason warlocks tend to work in covens."

"Witches often work in covens as well."

Devin nodded. "For different reasons. Witches certainly bring unique abilities together and are stronger as a group than they are as individuals. They share knowledge and hold one another accountable. Warlocks come together because each one of them is stronger when they're in a coven. Every power that any warlock brings to the coven, all of them share. That makes a coven quite formidable. It also means that if you remove a single warlock from a coven, you also reduce the power of all of them, since they'll no longer be able to use whatever unique power that warlock supplies to the group."

"And I thought warlocks were just witches who supported the patriarchy."

Devin laughed. "Warlocks tend to take a more domineering approach over the elements they wield. Rather than working *with* the spirit of an element, they subdue it. If you want to call that the M.O. of patriarchy, I won't argue with you."

"Is that how you work? You dominate the spirit of fire and make it your bitch?"

Devin laughed. "No one makes fire his bitch, Hailey. Most warlocks are their own worst enemy. You can only dominate the spirit of an element so much before it turns on you. I work more like a witch than a warlock, even though I learned most of what I know from warlocks rather than witches. I've seen more than one warlock who got in over his head, who pushed his power too hard, and was consumed by the power he thought he'd mastered. Since the element I know the best is fire, if I were to push it beyond what I should, I'd burn alive. A responsible warlock respects the spirit of his element and learns to work with it rather than dominate it. Put another way, good warlocks must eventually become more like witches if they wish to both grow more powerful and survive."

I pressed my lips together. "If Baladan is pushing this new magic too far, and the magic was born from a wraith, I wonder what that would do to him."

Devin shook his head. "I don't know. If you bite him and take his power, though, be careful. It may be dangerous. Use what you must and no more. Not until you learn more about the volatility of his magic."

As Devin and I navigated our way through the orange light, I noticed that the light got more intense when we moved in certain directions, and it dimmed when we walked in others. We used the brightness of the energy like a compass. The brighter it was, the closer we were to the core, the heart of New Barbelo, and probably to Baladan and the warlocks.

The light got so bright that it hurt. I wasn't accustomed to bright lights at all. The brightest thing I ever saw was a florescent bulb. They say you shouldn't look straight at the sun. It can blind a person. It can kill a vampire. Walking through this energy was like taking a stroll through the core of the sun itself. The only difference was it didn't burn. It wasn't hot at all. If anything, it was soothing, like taking a warm bubble bath. Without the water or the bubbles.

All at once, the light faded. Devin and I were standing in a clearing. The light formed a dome over us. We were in the middle of a park. Based on our location in the city, I guessed it might have been New Orleans City Park just south of Lake Ponchartrain but north of the Mississippi River. We were in the St. Bernard area when we lost sight of the real world. We must've crossed Bayou St. John while inside New Barbelo and didn't even realize it. How we got through dry, I couldn't say.

Baladan was standing in a circle surrounded by a dozen people in long black robes. Daniel was standing on his right and a woman who must've been his ex-wife was on his left. No wonder Annabelle couldn't find her.

Wraiths flew down into the circle and poured their forms into random warlocks. After each one settled within them, an orange energy flowed around the circle above their heads, then shot into the sky above. That was how they were expanding New Barbelo.

Daniel and Mary Ann looked like they were in a daze, their faces devoid of expression, and their eyes as black as coal.

"It took you long enough!" Baladan exclaimed. "Welcome to my new creation!"

I tilted my head. "You're Baladan Branham."

"Call me Dan. Please, Miss Bradbury, join me."

I gulped. "I'm not here to join you, *Dan.* I'm here to stop you. You can't harness this kind of power without consequences."

Baladan smiled widely. He had a kind face, all things considered. In my experience, most bad guys didn't look the part. Not like you might expect if you watched a lot of movies. Based on Hollywood, one might think that being ugly was the driving force that led people to turn to evil. Villains tended to be either extremely attractive and seductive or repulsive. There was very little in-between in television or film. In reality, though, the worst villains were neither ugly nor beautiful. They looked like your next-door neighbor, or the guy who worked at the convenience store on the corner. Baladan Branham could have worked at Home Depot and I never would have thought, "why isn't this guy trying to murder people or take over the world?" He could have helped me find door knobs or house paint and I'd have thanked him for his assistance.

"We've never met," I said. "How do you know who I am, anyway?"

Baladan chuckled. "Who doesn't know the great Blood Witch? Everyone who dabbles in magic in these parts knows who you are. Who is your friend? I sense a power within him."

"The name's Devin," Devin said. "What is your game here?"

"This isn't a game. It's an opportunity."

I snorted. "That sounds like a euphemism for a diabolical plan."

"I'm not evil, despite what you may have heard. My intentions are modest, even if my means and methods are a bit over the top."

"Over the top? You don't say. You're using the power of creation, the primordial forces of Barbelo, to pursue a *modest* opportunity?"

Baladan nodded his head slightly. "I'm a modest man."

"That's not what I've heard."

"What have you heard about me?" Baladan asked. "I suppose you've been told about the exploits of my youth, the havoc I caused as a young warlock. Nothing too dreadful, mind you. I haven't done half the things that you and the other vampires like you in the city have accomplished through the years."

"You realize that you've drawn out vampire wraiths from hell? At least one of them, Dracula, has killed and absorbed enough power from the other wraiths to take a body again."

Baladan sighed and shook his head. "That was not my intention. I admit, I underestimated the capacity of the wraiths and overestimated my ability to keep them in check."

"Then you realize he intends to harness Kalyptos, same as you?"

"I don't wish to *harness* Kalyptos. Do you think I'm a fool?"

I tightened my hand on my wand. "Do you really want me to answer that question?"

"I simply wish to use Kalyptos to make a few slight adjustments to my reality. To patch up a few of my personal mistakes. After that, well, you're welcome to cast this entire realm into a convergence, to reform Barbelo outside of our world, and send Kalyptos back with it."

"What kind of personal mistakes are you trying to fix?" Devin asked.

"I just said it's personal."

"You welcomed me here like you were expecting me," I said. "If you want my help at all, you'll tell me what you're doing."

"I've gathered more warlocks than I need and we've absorbed plenty of power. I've even forged a magic that no other power on earth, including your blood witchery, can overcome. You will help me draw Kalyptos here so I can do what I intend, or you can fight me here and the show of power will surely draw him in anyway. After all, Hailey Bradbury, it's you and the power within you that the demiurge craves."

"The power of Erzulie?" I asked.

"The force you used to overwhelm Barbelo before is now the power that Kalyptos follows, like a wire channels an electric current. You nearly brought him with you a moment ago. All I need is for you to do what you did once more."

I clenched my fists. "Tell me what your plans are."

"I have no intention of making anything new. I only wish to bring back what was."

"Stop talking in riddles and spit it out!"

"I made a mistake. I broke my family. I'm going to set the world back to what it was six months ago. Before everything fell apart."

I stared at Baladan blankly. "You've got to be kidding me."

"I'm telling the truth. I have no high aspirations to remake a different world, or change anything all that significant. I simply want my family back!"

I paced around the circle. "Let me get this right. You stuck your pecker somewhere it doesn't belong. Now you want to erase six months of the entire world's history just so you can go back to before you nailed the next-door neighbor?"

"It wasn't my next-door neighbor. She lived three doors down! And... she was my wife's cousin."

I scratched my head. Back in the day, if you did something like that, you went on Springer. Now? You harness the primordial power of creation and remake the universe. "You're insane. You screwed up.

Everyone screws up. This isn't a video game. You can't just reboot the universe every time you make a mistake. Man up and deal with your shit!"

Baladan shook his head. "It's too late for that. The power is here. It has to be used and directed."

"You told your son to kill himself to open up Barbelo. In what version of reality did you think that was the way to fix your mistake?"

"It's too late to turn back now!"

"What would you have done if I hadn't gone to Barbelo and destroyed that realm?"

"I already had access to the power. I just needed to get strong enough to pull it through. You accelerated my plan. But when you did, you bound Kalyptos to the magic that sent it here. That's why I need you, now. Help me, or someone else will take the power and do much worse than I intend."

"Do you really expect us to believe that all of this was to fix your little mistake?" Devin asked. "There must be more to it than that."

"Believe me or don't!" Baladan screamed. "You don't understand what it feels like!"

"You can't possibly reset the entire world to exactly as it was. Billions of lives moving on that you don't even know about. You can't possibly change things back for them. It's not fair, either, to put the world through that just because you're a cheating bastard!"

"That's not the only reason! It started with my affair, I confess! But it's bigger than that now."

I aimed my wand at the warlock. He didn't seem all that phased by it. He could probably block almost anything I threw at him. Then again, maybe he couldn't. Either way, he didn't exhibit any fear. "Spill it, Danny boy!"

"I thought I could use the autogenes to fix my affairs only. I'd read about the power of the Aeon of Barbelo and learned how to access it. Especially now that the veil between worlds is thin. I didn't expect to draw out more than a little energy, a single entity from Barbelo, who could make my wife forget. What came through was much bigger than I expected."

I huffed. "Protogenes."

Baladan nodded. "Then you blew Barbelo to hell and the power of that realm pulled the wraiths straight through the convergence. It wasn't a surprise. I didn't know these creatures, or vampires at all, had a connection to Barbelo. I don't even know how Kalyptos drew the wraiths through. Once it happened, though, I knew there was only one way to fix this. I had to take control of Kalyptos and turn back the clock, to fix my mistake. Not just my adultery, but that would be fixed too. I had to undo my attempt to open Barbelo as well."

I rubbed my brow. "Haven't you ever seen *Back to the Future?* Or any movie at all on time travel? You change that, how you opened Barbelo, by using the power from Barbelo it will create a paradox. You can't use Kalyptos to undo the first thing in a chain of events that led to Kalyptos being here. It will break reality!"

"You don't know that! Maybe it will just be ironic. Nothing has to break."

I shook my head. "That's all beside the point. I don't buy it. You're telling me you convinced your son to sacrifice himself to open Barbelo just to make him forget?"

"He wanted to do it. When I told Daniel about the angels, he wanted one of his own."

"Those monsters were *not* angels."

"Still, it was a way to solve his problem and mine, to fix our family, to set things right! How was I supposed to know that vampire hell would open up and spill out thousands of dead vampire spirits on the earth? When that happened, I did the right thing. I knew I could use those wraiths to remake Barbelo, and I hoped that I'd draw you in to this mess because you have the power to send this new Barbelo back through a portal once all the energies from that world were drawn in to the power!"

"What the hell is this new magic you made?"

"Something vampires can't thwart. Something I can use to whip the wraiths into shape and make them obey. I used a wraith to make the magic that I'm using to control the wraiths. That is ironic. I really do think!"

I tilted my head. "No comment, Alanis. How did you harness a wraith to begin with? You needed a wraith to give you its power to create a magic that could control the others."

Baladan shook his head. "I cannot tell you that. One of the wraiths attacked me when I was attempting to fight them off. It entered me and I felt its raw power. I turned it into something else. I didn't even mean to do it. It just happened. I discovered I could use the new power it gave me to defend against the others, to do pretty much anything at all. It's how I fended you off in Vilokan when I rescued my son."

"What about your son and your wife and the rest of these warlocks? They're not even conscious."

"Isn't it obvious? They're using the wraiths I gather to spread this realm until it's big enough to contain all that used to be a part of Barbelo. Then, as I told you already, my hope is that you can siphon all this energy and all the beings within it back through the gate."

I shook my head. "After you turn back time?"

"*If* I could turn back time... if I could find a way. I'd take back those things that hurt her and she'd stay!"

"Did you seriously get this idea from a Cher song?"

Baladan shifted his eyes back and forth. "Does it matter?"

"You really made a mess of all this, you know. Why do you think a wraith entered you to begin with?"

"I don't know, but it didn't hurt me. Not in the least. It gave me a chance to fix this mess I made."

Devin took a deep breath. He grabbed my arm and pulled me aside. "Maybe this is the best option we have. Baladan is clearly insane."

"You think?" I chuckled.

"I'm not saying we let him use the demiurge to erase the last six months. We can't let it get that far. Still, you have to admit, his plan to send Kalyptos back through a portal isn't bad. Let Kalyptos reforge the Aeon of Barbelo elsewhere. If you can push it into the void, then the new realm can be born out of the void and into its own new space. Just as it was before."

I shook my head. "That's not as easy as it sounds. I'm not a gatekeeper, Devin. I can't guarantee that anything I send through a convergence will go to the void."

"How did you open the convergence before to Barbelo?"

"A blood offering. I partially exsanguinated myself and it worked."

"Then do it again. If that's what used to be the key to opening a gate to the Aeon of Barbelo, and if Barbelo no longer exists, that gate will by definition open into the void."

"Then how do we direct this realm into it?"

"I think that's what Baladan is using the other warlocks for. We can kick Baladan's ass and throw him in supernatural jail after this is over. For now, though, his plan isn't horrible."

"It's a risk to go along with this knowing we can't allow him to do what he's wanted all along. If we don't let him use Kalyptos before we try to toss the demiurge and New Barbelo back through a convergence, he'll try to stop us."

"Then we deal with that at the time. These things never resolve themselves without a fight."

I sighed. "You're right. I suppose the alternative is letting Kalyptos fall to Dracula or the Ghede."

Devin nodded. "It's worth a shot. We need to tell Nicky and Holland to stop fighting the wraiths. We need to help Baladan gather the power he needs to prepare New Barbelo to accommodate the demiurge. After that, we'll fight like hell to stop him from using Kalyptos and do what we can to force all this energy back through a convergence."

I scratched my head. "If I can find the convergence. I can't even find the damn farm truck in here. Let's hope New Barbelo expands far enough by then to encompass Manchac Swamp and that the convergence radiates some kind of energy we can follow. If not, well, we'll have a fully empowered Baladan ready to harness a demiurge and fuck up the world."

Chapter 19

ALL THIS TIME, I thought Baladan was some kind of evil genius. That couldn't have been further from the truth. He was a complete dumbass. If that was all he was, I might have a little pity on him. He was still a psychopath who convinced his own son to lean into his depression, kill himself, and unleash the primal forces of creation on the world.

I'd say it was a nice change of pace to find myself facing off against a moron for once. Idiots with power, though, can be just as dangerous as the most conniving villain.

I wasn't entirely sure what to make of Baron Samedi and Ghede Nibo. Sarah thought they were up to no good. Holland assured me it wasn't an issue. Dracula was a real son of a bitch who'd lied his way into convincing me to work with him for a while just so he could make himself an almost invulnerable body and, if that wasn't enough, he wanted to claim the power of the demiurge.

Devin and I took off through the light. There was no sense looking for the farm truck. Everything in New Barbelo looked the same. It was an expanding ball of light. The only thing other than pure orange light that we could see were the black wraiths soaring overhead. The only way we even knew which direction to go was to run the opposite way to the wraiths. The more wraiths that joined the warlocks, the more New Barbelo expanded. Could we even run fast enough to catch the expanding borders? As a vampire I could run a lot faster than Devin, but I didn't want to leave his side, otherwise I wasn't sure I'd be able to find him again.

Devin stopped and clutched at his side. He was panting for air. "I can't keep running. I need a break. I need water."

I took a deep breath. "It's no use. I can try to carry you, but even at full speed, I don't know if we can run fast enough to reach the end of this. There are too many wraiths flying into this place."

Devin pulled out his phone. "No signal in here. We can't even reach Nicky or anyone else to tell them the plan."

The surrounding light flickered again. This time, it didn't reveal the city around us. Instead, it flickered from bright orange to a bright white light. "That might be Kalyptos."

I heard a loud rumble in the distance. I tilted my head. My sense of hearing was more acute than Devin's. "Do you hear that?"

"Hear what?"

"I think it's Nicky's motorcycle."

The sound got louder. "I hear it now. She's coming this way."

A shadow emerged from the light. It was Nicky with Holland on the back. Nicky skidded her bike to a halt.

"You're here!" Devin exclaimed.

Nicky parked her bike and hopped off. "It's not just us."

A couple of seconds later, Annabelle's purple Camero emerged. She stopped and got out. Ellie got out of the passenger side and Savanna squeezed out behind her. After that, Connor's Escalade arrived. I wrapped my arms around him before his feet hit the pavement.

"Tommy is still back taking care of Sarah, but we're here. Sarah said she lost track of you and nearly all the wraiths were here. I was worried sick. I'm glad you're alright."

I kissed Connor's cheek. "We have a plan. I think Kalyptos is here. We need to send *this* Barbelo back through the convergence."

"Where's my truck?" Ellie asked.

I chuckled. "Can't find it. It's in here somewhere."

"Any news on Dracula or the Ghede?"

Holland shook her head. "Haven't seen them. I think they're on the way. If not, I can bring them here at any time if we need their help."

"You're leaving them out there on their own?" I asked.

Holland rolled her eyes. "I'm not an idiot, Hailey. I didn't summon the Ghede to leave them free to do their shit."

"What are you talking about?"

Annabelle laughed. "We made an offering when we summoned them."

Holland nodded. "I bound them to my will. Tell me what you want. Should we cast Kalyptos out through the convergence, or should we give it to Nico?"

I scratched my head. "I don't know. What does Nico want? I have a feeling he's doing this only because he thinks he has to."

Devin coughed in his hand as he stared up at the sky. "We might have to do both. Kalyptos isn't one entity. I think the power is spreading throughout New Barbelo."

I looked up. Devin was right. The white light was shooting around in different directions, like a series of comets soaring above. "We might not have time to get to the convergence. I'm not even sure how to find it, given how far this has spread."

Devin nodded. "We need to get back to the warlocks. I don't trust Baladan."

"What is Baladan going to do?" Annabelle asked.

"He wants to remake the world, the entire world, as it was six months ago."

"He can't possibly do that. He doesn't know how the whole world was six months ago. He only knows what the world was like for him."

I nodded. "Exactly. Baladan isn't the brightest crayon in the box. I'll explain later. He's trying to fix a *personal* mistake and he'll probably screw the universe in the process."

"Get in the Escalade," Connor said. "Tell us where to go."

"We'll follow," Nicky said as she re-mounted her motorcycle. Devin climbed up behind her. Holland and Ellie got in the Escalade with me, and Annabelle followed all of us in her Camaro.

"Follow the flow of the wraiths. It should lead us to the warlocks."

Connor nodded. "I'll do what I can. I'm not going to crash into anything in here, am I?"

"I don't think so. This is sort of a hybrid between earth and Barbelo. It's Barbelo *on* earth. Everything from the physical world remains intact, but it's almost like it's behind this energy. So long as we're moving through the light, we should be fine."

We drove through the orange light of New Barbelo in one caravan. Stronger together.

This time, though, white lights were shooting through the sky above.

All the light got brighter the closer we got to the middle.

We pulled into the clearing, the dome of clear air where the warlocks were gathered before.

Connor slammed his brakes. "Shit."

I stepped out of the Escalade. Nicky pulled up beside me. Annabelle pulled up behind us.

The warlocks were dead. Every one of them stacked in a pile. Blood was everywhere.

Baladan's body flew out of the pile and Dracula climbed up on top of them. The Count kicked up his feet and crossed his legs, treating the pile of warlock corpses like a La-Z-Boy recliner. Dracula looked at me and narrowed his eyes. He laughed as he wiped the warlocks' blood from his chin with the sleeve of his shirt. "Good evening."

I clenched my hand on my wand. Devin ran up beside me and summoned his wand in his grip. Nicky ran up and shot a crossbow bolt at Dracula.

Dracula pulled the bolt from his chest and tossed it aside.

I shot an exsanguination spell at the Count. He waved his hand through the air. A black and sparkling wall of magic—the same magic that Baladan wielded before—formed in front of him and deflected my spell.

I lowered my wand. "Fuck."

Dracula raised his hands into the air. Three wraiths flew into his body. "More! Join me, my brothers and sisters! Let us be as one!"

The Count tilted his head to the sky. He opened his mouth as one wraith after the next flew into his throat.

"So much for going to Kokomo."

Connor grabbed my arm. "We have to get out of here. We can't stop him."

I shook my arm out of Connor's grip. "If we don't stop him, if he takes more wraiths into his body, he will *become* New Barbelo. He'll attract Kalyptos. There won't be any place we can run. He'll remake the world however he sees fit."

Chapter 20

SAVANNA PUSHED HER WAY past me.

"What are you doing? You can't take him!"

Savanna raised her arms. She formed a dark storm cloud. Lightning flashed around. The wraiths flowing to Dracula dissipated.

"Brilliant!" Ellie screamed. "Keep going! Everyone, keep Savanna safe!"

We formed a wall around Savanna. Dracula stood on top of the dead warlocks. He clapped his hands. "Bravo! Good show! You realize you're only delaying the inevitable?"

I took a step toward Dracula. "You can't harness Kalyptos. You're not a god!"

"Not yet. I'm getting there."

Dracula waved his hands through the air. Black magic followed the path of his arms.

Annabelle pressed herself past me. Her eyes glowed green with the power of the Tree of Life, the power she wielded through Isabelle. She formed a wall of green magic just in time as a blast of Dracula's power blasted against it.

"Holland!" Annabelle shouted. "Do it now!"

"I'm going to need your help," Holland said to me. "Yours too, Ellie."

"My help?" I asked.

Holland nodded. "Baron Samedi! Ghede Nibo! Come and harness Kalyptos!"

The two Ghede appeared, still in their hosts, in a cloud of black smoke. Nico's apparition appeared between them.

Baron Samedi turned to me. "We cannot do this alone. Kalyptos came to this world through the power of Erzulie. To harness Kalyptos and infuse the demiurge into Niccolo will require far more power than it took to cast Kalyptos out of the Aeon of Barbelo."

I nodded. "Got it. Ellie, can you help?"

"Hell yes I can!"

Annabelle was still holding off Dracula. Savanna still had her storm brewing overhead. I didn't know how long they could keep it up.

Devin grabbed my hand. "As a warlock, I can amplify your power as well."

Baron Samedi nodded. "Good. We need as much power as you can gather. Enough to equal the power of Erzulie, herself."

I only knew one way to tap into Erzulie's power. I fixed my eyes on Connor. He looked as though he was preparing to shift and take a bite out of Dracula himself.

The pink glow of Erzulie's power filled my eyes and cast a hue over everything in front of me. Ellie released her power as well.

"I can't hold this storm!" Savanna shouted. "I barely have control over it as it is!"

"If he gets any more wraiths, I don't know if I can hold him either," Annabelle screamed.

Baron Samedi and Ghede Nibo stood in front of me with Nico between them. The white light of Kalyptos swirled above them. It mingled with Erzulie's power.

"It's mine!" Dracula screamed.

The storm faded. A dozen more wraiths blasted into Dracula's gaping mouth and he forced another blast against Annabelle's shield. The Voodoo Queen crashed into the ground at my feet.

A blast of Kalyptos filled Nico's ghost. The demiurge's energy divided into three more streams. One of them hit Dracula. Another struck Connor and still another filled Nicky.

The orange light of Barbelo faded away. We were standing in the park.

Nico took material form. He was a Ghede Loa—but he wasn't under the Baron's control.

"Nico!" Holland shouted. "I command you! Kill Dracula!"

Nico nodded and leapt over Annabelle as she was struggling to get to her feet. Dracula and Nico collided in mid-air. They clawed and bit at each other.

Connor shifted into a wolf. He glowed with the power of the demiurge. He dove at Dracula and took a bite out of his leg. Nicky was also enveloped in the power of Kalyptos. She charged after Dracula. Nico held the count as Nicky delivered a swift kick with her stiletto heel into Dracula's chest.

He still didn't have a heart. It didn't kill him.

I aimed my wand at Dracula and unleashed the strongest exsanguination spell I could cast. Blood blasted out of the Count's body and with it the light of Kalyptos flowed out of him and into Nico.

Dracula snarled as his flesh shrank against his bones.

"He's feral!" I screamed. "We have to subdue him!"

"Fuck that," Annabelle grunted. "Beli!"

Annabelle's soul blade formed in her hand the second she screamed its name. She charged Dracula's feral body and stabbed him in his gut.

What was left of Dracula blasted apart in green energy.

"Back to hell with you!" Annabelle shouted.

I lowered my wand. I ran over to Connor. He was shaking on the ground, still in his wolf form.

"What's wrong with him?"

"Nicky!" Devin screamed as he caught her in his arms. She was also seizing.

Nico approached Connor first. He placed his hand on Connor's furry head. The power of the demiurge left him, but Nico didn't absorb it. It shot up into the sky. Nico did the same with Nicky.

"I don't understand," I said. "Why couldn't you take the power?"

"That part of the demiurge was harnessed with Erzulie, not the Ghede," Baron Samedi said. "Niccolo will not be able to harness it."

Nicky held on to Devin's shoulders. "It was too much. My body is resilient, but it was more than I could hold."

Baron Samedi nodded. "You're a nymph, but not a god. The wolf shifter is also strong, but he couldn't hold it for long either."

Connor shifted back into human form. I found his pants and quickly retrieved them. Connor slipped into them. "Is it over?"

I kissed Connor on the lips. "I couldn't have done it without you."

"It wasn't just me," Connor said.

I stood and looked at my friends. "We really are stronger together. Every one of you played a role here tonight. If any of you weren't here to help, we couldn't have beaten Dracula."

"There is still unrestrained power out there," Nico said. "I'll stay as long as I can to help assure that no one else misuses it."

I nodded. "I think we can find room for you at Casa do Diabo. You might have to share a bed with Tommy, though."

Nico tilted his head. "You're kidding, right?"

I laughed. "Maybe Sarah?"

Nico tilted his head. "Sarah, huh? If she's willing. Otherwise, I'll take the couch."

I turned to Savanna. She was catching her breath. That storm took a lot out of her. "Good work. You bought us just enough time to stop him."

Savanna smiled. "Thanks, Hailey."

I rested my hand on Annabelle's shoulder. "We have a lot of bodies. I think it's time to call the funeral home."

Annabelle shook her head. "Baladan Branham. What a moron."

I shrugged. "A dead moron, now. I just feel bad for Daniel. That kid didn't deserve this."

"He killed people too," Savanna said. "Tried to kill me."

I nodded. "You're right. He was a troubled kid. The whole thing is a tragedy."

"We'll assure the dead reach the afterlife in peace according to what is just," Baron Samedi said. "Ghede Nibo?"

"The spirits are with me," Nibo added. "If we have fulfilled the purpose for which we were summoned, I request our leave."

Holland nodded. "I release you. Both of you."

The two women that Baron Samedi and Ghede Nibo possessed gasped for air. Their eyes widened in confusion and fear.

I took their hands and met their eyes with mine. "You're safe, both of you. Don't panic. You're both vampires.."

I wasn't good at using my allure when I wasn't feeding. It was even more tricky using it on vampires. It only worked on younglings, those whose minds hadn't yet caught up with the changes in their body. I wasn't sure what they could remember from the time they were possessed, or how they'd respond once I released them from my allure and they saw a giant pile of bodies. These girls weren't just vampires. They were orphans. Dracula was technically their sire. Thankfully, whether my allure worked or if they were just in shock and a kind voice gave them solace, the girls calmed down.

"Come with me, ladies." Annabelle piped up. "We have a place that is well-experienced helping new vampires adjust."

I didn't release the girls from my allure until they climbed into Annabelle's Camaro. The Vilokan Asylum of the Magically and Mentally Deranged would be their temporary home. Fresh blood, warm and ready. They had donors. They'd get the help they needed to adjust to their new existence. How much did they know already? How much did the Ghede tell them and show them while they were possessed? All stuff they'd have to work through with Siggy Freud. I had a feeling, though, that I'd be playing the big-sister role eventually. Annabelle helped me when I turned but, eventually, I needed Mercy's guidance to totally understand what it meant to be a responsible vampire. I wasn't Mercy Brown. I didn't have the benefit of nearly two centuries of existence. But I wasn't the crappiest sire out there. Tommy was doing well. With Annabelle's help, and mine, the girls would be alright.

Chapter 21

I INVITED NICKY AND Devin to stay with us to rest. Nicky insisted they leave straightaway. She wanted to get back in time for her show. A part of me was disappointed. We hadn't really had much time to talk and reconnect. I spent a little time with Devin in New Barbelo, but hadn't spoken much to Nicky since she arrived.

"Next time you're in Kansas City, come to Nicky's for a show. Drinks are on the house."

I snickered. "Including my kind of drink?"

"No feeding on my fans!" Nicky laughed.

"Lately, it seems like I've been jumping from one crisis to the next. With the convergences blasted open all over the city, there's no telling when the next shit show will open its curtains."

"I know you asked me to guard Kansas City. There are a few convergences there but so far nothing out of the ordinary has cropped up."

"Stay vigilant. It's just a matter of time."

Nicky took my hand and kissed my cheek. "You know me. I'm always vigilant. Thanks for calling me."

"Thanks for coming to help! We couldn't have done this without you. Besides, it's always a treat to see Nyx in action."

Devin chuckled. "We've been saving a lot on stilettos. You wouldn't believe how many pairs she goes through when we have vampires in town."

I laughed. "I bet! Talk about a way to go. A heel to the heart. Damn."

Nicky winked at me. "Never screw with a chick in heels."

Nicky and Devin took off. Her Thruxton RS motorcycle rumbled in the distance even when they were far beyond my view.

Annabelle took Holland and Ellie back with her. Connor and I drove around for darn near an hour before we found the farm truck. It was Ellie's truck, but she practically gave it to me. I guess we were sharing it. I followed Connor home.

Nico rode with me.

"How does this work? Are you still a vampire?"

"I think so. I'm also a Ghede Loa. I'm not really sure how this is going to work but so long as there's anything left of the demiurge out there, I'm here with you."

"I'll have to let Mercy know you're back. She'll want to come see you."

Nico chuckled. "I'd love to see her. She really moved back to Exeter?"

I nodded. "She's working with Prince Ladinas. Apparently Ramon became a vampire again and is on some kind of tear."

Nico shook his head. "Sounds like Ramon."

We drove for a couple of minutes in silence. "How are you with all of this? I know you didn't want to come back."

Nico shrugged. "The afterlife is the afterlife. One chapter closes, another one opens."

"Want your sire bond back? I'm not using it much."

Nico chuckled. "That's the last chapter. Perhaps a time will come when it will be of use to you. That you haven't used it suggests it's in excellent hands."

We got back to Casa do Diabo. A thumping sound blasted from within the house.

"Is that bass?" Nico asked.

I shook my head. "Freaking Tommy. We were gone, and he threw a party?"

Nico laughed. "Younglings. Am I right?"

I burst through the front door. The whole place smelled like booze and weed. Tommy was on the couch with two women. Blood was smeared down their necks across Tommy's chin. Sarah had a tall man in her arms and was grinding with him to the beat of the music.

"Sarah? What's going on?"

Sarah laughed. "Hey, Hailey! Want a bite?"

"You didn't answer my question. What is going on here?"

Sarah shrugged. "I was stuck in my room for the last couple of days. Tommy and I were hungry. I figured it's better to feed here than out on the streets."

Nico stepped through the door. Sarah gasped and released the man she was dancing with. He stumbled toward the couch but fell on the floor in front of it when he noticed there wasn't a seat available.

"Niccolo?" Sarah gasped. "I don't sense you. I had no idea—"

"I'm back. I'm different, now."

Sarah giggled like a schoolgirl. She wrapped her arms around Nico. "I missed you!"

"This is still my house. I think it's time to send our guests home."

"Of course!" Sarah jumped up and down in excitement. I'd never seen her like this. She was always so mousey. I wasn't sure if it was more because she was cooped up in her room for a couple days, because the voices she'd heard before had warped her mind, or if she was jovial because Nico was back.

I helped up the two girls that Tommy was feeding from. "Are they sufficiently intoxicated that they'll forget?"

Tommy nodded. "Should be."

I bit each of the girls and drank enough to make sure that their blood alcohol content was sufficient to ensure they'd forget. I needed to feed, anyway. Two birds with one stone—or two girls with one feed. Girls weren't usually my flavor of choice, but the blood hit the spot.

"Come on, Tommy. We're taking them back to where you found them."

"Am I in trouble?" Tommy asked.

I sighed. "I don't have the energy to be angry. You didn't kill anyone, right?"

"No bodies. These are the only two I drank from."

"Good enough for me. You were with Sarah. You weren't unsupervised. No harm, no foul."

Tommy smiled widely. "I should probably wash the blood off my face before we take the girls back to the bar."

I pressed my lips together and nodded. "Probably a good idea."

The girls needed help to walk. Tommy and I walked them back to the bar where he found them. They'd find their way home from there.

I updated Tommy on all that happened on our walk home. He never knew Nico before. I explained that he was the first vampire and should be paid the appropriate respect. Especially now that he was also a demigod.

We got back to Casa do Diabo. Tommy yawned. "I think I'm going to retire for the day."

I grabbed Tommy by the arm. "Not so fast."

Tommy sighed. "I drank a lot of blood. I'd like to take a nap."

"You're a vampire. You don't need to sleep. You can take a snooze *after* you clean up the house."

Tommy grunted. "I will clean it up tomorrow. After the sun rises. We have all day."

I narrowed my eyes. "As your sire, I command you. Clean the damn house."

Tommy stomped his foot in protest, but he couldn't resist. He picked up a couple of beer cans from the floor and took them to the trash.

"Freaking sires," Tommy muttered under his breath.

Nico was standing in the corner, laughing. "You can't buy this kind of entertainment."

Sarah nuzzled up against Nico's chest. "You can share my bed if you'd like?"

Nico smirked. "Help the youngling clean the house. I've been at rest for years. I think I'll catch up on my shows. I never caught the end of *Game of Thrones.*"

I chuckled. "You might be disappointed."

Sarah shrugged. "I'll watch it with you. I didn't want to go back to my bedroom, anyway."

I took Connor's hand and led him upstairs to my room. I kissed him softly on the lips.

"What would you like to do with the rest of the night?" Connor asked.

I shrugged. "What did you have in mind?"

"Want to have some fun?"

I kicked off my shoes and hopped on the bed. "How about a foot rub?"

Connor laughed and sat on the edge of the bed. He rubbed the arch of my foot with his strong thumbs. It probably wasn't his idea of *fun*, but I needed it. After all I'd been through, all I really wanted to do was relax with the man I loved.

The Blood Witch Saga Continues in...
Shifters and Shenanigans

FOR NICKY/NYX and DEVIN'S STORY check out...
THE LEGEND OF NYX

THE BLOOD WITCH SAGA

SHIFTERS & SHENANIGANS

THEOPHILUS MONROE

Cover Design by Deranged Doctor Design

Proofreading/Editing by Mel: https://getproofreader.co.uk/

For information:

www.theophilusmonroe.com

Chapter 1

NICO LIFTED THE FRONT of the farm truck and I slid a stack of bricks under each front tire. The only light we had was from the street lamps above. It didn't matter. I was a vampire. Nico was the *first* vampire, now a Ghede Loa. We could see better in the dark, anyway.

"How long has it been since you changed the oil on this piece of crap?" Nico asked.

I chuckled and shook my head. "This is Ellie's truck. We share it. Knowing Ellie, she probably hasn't changed the oil once."

Nico grunted as he slid on his back under the front of the truck. "Slide me the oil pan."

I took the wide aluminum pan that we'd bought at the auto store, along with several pints of 10W-30 engine oil. I kicked the empty pan toward Nico.

Nico didn't have tools. He didn't need them. He was strong enough to unscrew the oil plug with his fingers. It took him a few minutes to get it loose. I heard a plop as the first of the old oil hit the pan. "Damn. This shit is as thick as crude oil. It's a wonder this truck ran at all."

"Ready for the new filter?"

Nico grunted. "Yeah. Toss it to me."

I grabbed the box labeled *Fram* and reached under the truck. I set it in Nico's waiting hand. "I don't know how you ladies got along without a man in the house all this time."

I huffed. "Excuse me?"

"I'm not saying women don't know how to do this kind of thing."

"That's exactly what you were saying."

"Fine. I shouldn't have said it. I'm sorry. Still, would you have done this at all if I weren't here?"

"It's not like there are many places you can get your oil changed after dark."

"My point exactly. It's not because you're a woman. You just weren't taught how to do this kind of thing."

"We have Tommy. He's a guy and he doesn't know shit about cars."

"That's my point. What I meant to say before is that it's a wonder you got along in this house so long with no one who knew squat about fixing shit, or doing basic maintenance. How long has it been since you changed the furnace filter in the house?"

I gulped. "The furnace has a filter? Shit."

Nico sighed as he slid back out from under the truck. "We'll take care of that next. It's ready for fresh oil. You bought a funnel, right?"

I bit my lip. "I had Ellie buy this shit during the day. She brought it over. I forgot to mention a funnel. I think we have one in the kitchen."

Nico grabbed a pint of oil and twisted off the cap. "Never mind. I'm a man. I know how to aim."

I chuckled. "The spots on the toilet rim say otherwise."

"That wasn't me. It was Tommy after he drank all that beer. You'd think he'd figure out by now that beer is the least efficient way for a vampire to get a buzz."

I chuckled. "Blame it on the youngling."

"I don't think I've pissed but twice since I came back from the dead. I've only fed once and don't drink much at all."

"You're right. It was probably Tommy. Once again, though, you equated your ability to aim with being male."

"I have a penis. Aiming is a necessary skill."

"Which has nothing to do with pouring oil into an engine."

"It was a joke, Hailey. Relax."

"I'm just giving you shit, man. You know, since you're a misogynist. You relax."

"I'm not a misogynist! I'm the one who willed my entire estate to Mercy over Corbin."

"Yay!" I clapped my hands. "You picked a qualified woman over a male psychopath. You deserve a medal."

Nico finished pouring the first pint into the truck and grabbed another one. "I'm helping you out here, you know. You could at least be polite about it."

I scratched the back of my head. "You're right. I'm not trying to be a bitch."

Nico chuckled. "Could have fooled me."

"Hush! I'm trying to apologize here. I just don't do well with authority figures. I've been running the show here ever since Mercy left for Exeter. Even then, she treated me more like an equal than a subordinate. I'm not really accustomed to doing as I'm told."

Nico finished pouring the second pint of oil into the engine block and grabbed a third. Before he unscrewed it, he took a deep breath. "You're right. Old habits die hard. You're still a young vampire. What you've accomplished, though, in my absence has been nothing short of impressive."

I tilted my head. "Niccolo Freeman. Was that a compliment?"

Nico laughed. "Don't get used to it. My compliments aren't like Halloween candy. I don't hand them out to anyone who comes knocking. They're more like artisan truffles. They cost a pretty penny, and I only give them out on meaningful occasions."

"Your compliments *cost* something? That's some kind of hubris."

Nico laughed. "You're spunky. I like that about you. That's another truffle for you, by the way."

I gulped. "I have a boyfriend. If you're flirting—"

Nico smiled widely. "You think I'm flirting with you? You just insulted me twice."

I furrowed my brow. "I didn't insult you."

"You called me a misogynist, and you accused me of arrogance."

"Those weren't insults. They were observations."

Nico cracked open the third pint of oil and poured it into the small hole. I doubt he got it all in. I don't care how many times he'd peed over the thousands of years he walked the earth. No one has a perfect aim. He finished pouring it in. "I wasn't flirting."

"Sure you weren't. Most men are masochists at heart. They find women who treat them like shit undeniably attractive."

Nico snickered. "That's not unique to men. I still wasn't flirting with you."

I smirked. "Good. If you were, Sarah would be jealous."

Nico sighed. "That proves my theory. I barely give her the time of day, which, I suppose, is a good thing since she's a vampire. I don't give her the time of night, either. The more I ignore her, the more she comes on to me."

I chuckled. "She wants your wiener, dude."

Nico shook his head. "Could you be any more crass?"

"What? It's the truth. Why mince words about it?"

"I'm not interested in romance. When you've lived as long as I have, and had as many lovers as I have, human and vampire alike, it all gets rather tiresome."

"Who said anything about romance? A woman has needs, same as a man. Sarah might not be as ancient as you are, but she's been around a long time. Do you really think she hasn't had her share of lovers as well?"

Nico raised an eyebrow. "Someone has to go out and meet people to find lovers."

"Don't sell Sarah short. She might be a bit of a homebody, but she gets around from time to time. Sarah's stronger than you think. She's pretty, too, don't you think?"

"Of course she is. I'm not saying she's not attractive. Casual sex never really works for me. Especially with vampires. Women tend to get attached."

I snorted. "Because you're the first vampire, the infamous Niccolo the Damned?"

Nico tossed the empty pint bottle in a pile with the others on the sidewalk. "Something like that."

I shook my head. "There's that arrogance, again."

"It's not arrogance. It's a fact. You wouldn't understand. I don't sleep with vampire women *casually* because I don't want to disappoint them when they realize that's all it is."

I rolled my eyes. "Because what woman could possibly resist the idea of being *with* the original vampire, not to mention a demigod?"

Nico took a deep breath and wiped his oil covered hands on his overalls. "When you say it like that, it sounds bad."

"It really does, doesn't it?"

Nico chuckled and shook his head. "She deserves better than what I can offer."

"So you're a shitty lay? You'd think after thousands of years you'd pick up a few things."

"Hailey! That's not what I mean."

"I thought you weren't interested in relationships? Tell me, Nico. Is it really about Sarah deserving *better* or is it that you don't think you deserve happiness?"

Nico cocked his head. "I thought we were talking about casual sex. No strings attached."

"That's what *I* was talking about. Then *you* started talking about what Sarah *deserves.* Do you want to know what I think?"

Nico sighed. He bent over and grabbed a fourth pint of 10W-30. "I'm not sure I do."

"I'm going to tell you, anyway. I think you've lived for thousands of years, then you died, without ever knowing genuine happiness."

Nico snorted. "You're wrong. I've loved and been loved by many. That's the problem, I suppose. It's not that I never had a chance at happiness. It's not even that I haven't had moments, years, even decades of happiness. Every pleasant night eventually turns into a scorching sunrise. Every good thing comes to an end. I've had more than my share of happiness through the centuries. It always ended, eventually. I choose to remember the good times I've had and do my best to forget the pain."

I pressed my lips together. This conversation wasn't going how I expected. All I was trying to do was convince Nico to go to bed with Sarah. They were both too uptight. They needed to get laid. My motives weren't especially deep. Now, Nico was treading into territory where a shrink like Dr. Cain or, perhaps, Dr. Freud, was better equipped to accompany him. "You're afraid of heartbreak?"

"I wouldn't say I'm *afraid* of it. I've had my share of meaningless sex. I've also known the passion of a woman who held my dead heart in her hands. I've given my heart to others. I have little left to offer. At the same time, when you've loved like I have, a fling doesn't satisfy. I cannot sleep with a woman I do not love. I don't have any love left to give."

"That's tragic."

Nico laughed. "Is it, though?"

"Is that why you decided to die?" I asked.

Nico rubbed his brow. It left a trail of black oil on his forehead. "That's a good question. It was a part of it. I suppose you could say I'd lived as much as anyone could, longer than anyone should. Some men are called to celibacy. They take vows of chastity and find their fulfillment in prayer. I've known many such men. I've spent hours with the likes of mystics like Meister Eckhart and John of the Cross. The latter spoke of what he called the dark night of the soul. He passed through it and found God. I entered it and never left."

"So, this is all some kind of spiritual thing?" I asked.

"I thought if I could not pass through the dark night as a vampire, my only recourse was to recover my soul and pass through the dark night that we all meet in the end. Peace, not to mention the God I sought, still alluded me. Now, I'm here. I'm back. I'm something of a demigod myself, but that's little more than a label. Divinity itself still chides me like a bitter schoolmistress."

I swallowed hard. "That's cool. If you don't want to fuck, you don't want to fuck."

Nico laughed. "Just when I think we'd moved our conversation to something a little deeper..."

"So deep. Deep and hard. Two bodies in the thralls of passion. So warm. So moist."

Nico shuddered. "Yuck."

I raised an eyebrow. "Seriously?"

"You used the M-word."

I chuckled. "Moist?"

"Stop! I can't stand that word. Just hearing it—"

"Moist, moist, moist, moist, moist, moist, moist, moist, moist!"

Nico plugged his ears with his index fingers. He'd probably need a cue-tip and witch hazel to get the oil smudges out. "Do you want me to finish helping you change your oil or not?"

I covered my mouth with my right hand in a futile attempt to suppress my giggles. "Sorry. I'm in a weird mood today."

"I'm not sure if you're trying to convince me to give Sarah a chance, or turn me off to the idea completely."

"I don't understand how a word can evoke such a sense of disgust. It's just a word, Nico."

"It's not just a word. It's moi—. Ugh, I can't even say it."

"Moist?"

"Stop it!"

I chuckled. "Niccolo the Damned has his kryptonite, after all."

"I don't need kryptonite. I have all the regular weaknesses that any vampire might have . Well, I used to. I'm not sure all that applies now that the power of Kalyptos is coursing through my body and I'm supposed to be some kind of death god."

"How does it feel? Having all that power in you, I mean."

"Well, that I can go out during the day without being afflicted with a fatal sunburn is nice. My body is mostly as it was before. Since I was a hougan in my earthly life, already a student of the Ghede, it's not all that different. Before I could tap into the power of the Ghede by borrowing it, appealing to the Loa. The only difference now is that I can skip that step. I just have to appeal to myself!"

I laughed. "That won't be a problem!"

"What is that supposed to mean?"

"Nico loves himself some Nico. That's all."

"I tried to explain that it's not arrogant. If anything, it's a deep-seated disdain for myself that's the problem."

I shrugged. "Arrogance and self-loathing are not mutually exclusive. Most cocky dudes are insecure at the core. It's not a bad thing. To love yourself, I mean. It balances out the other side of that coin."

I hadn't even noticed that Nico had finished pouring the fifth and sixth pints of oil in the truck. He checked the dipstick. "How about that? Right in the zone."

"Thanks, Nico. Sorry for being a bitch."

Nico laughed. "Honestly, it's refreshing. Most people tread on eggshells around me. It's nice to talk to someone who doesn't give a shit."

I grinned widely. "It's not that I don't care. I'm just not intimidated by much at all. If you're going to be living with us, taking shit from each other comes with the territory. It's how we show our love."

Nico chuckled, and he lowered the farm truck hood. "I must be really loved, then! Mind pulling out the blocks when I lift the truck?"

I tilted my head. "Watch this."

I grabbed the front bumper and lifted the truck myself. "I am vampire woman. Hear me roar!"

Nico laughed and kicked the bricks out from under each of the two front tires. "Impressive strength for a youngling."

"I'm not a youngling!" I dropped the truck back on its front wheels. "I'm eight years a vampire!"

Nico raised an eyebrow. "Compared to me, you're barely a baby."

I shrugged. "Well, this *baby* has officially killed Dracula twice, now. I kicked your progeny's ass in hell. Corbin didn't stand a chance. Plus, I've got killer magic."

Nico patted me on the back. "I'm not questioning any of that. You may be a kickass baby, but you're still a baby."

Chapter 2

I WAS STILL TRYING to get a handle on the dynamic between Nico and me. We gave each other crap, which was par for the course in any friendship I'd ever had, but I still wasn't sure if he really respected me. He respected some of the things I'd done, that's for sure. As a person, as a vampire, he treated me more like a child than a woman. As a witch, he was a little standoffish. He didn't know what to make of my power—especially my bloodwitchery. I think it made him uncomfortable.

As far as respect went, it didn't help that when I first brought Nico back home to Casa do Diabo Tommy and Sarah were throwing a party. They left the place a mess. He told me to get my "youngling" in line. In his view, I was little more than a child raising a child.

I will not pretend I'm the best sire in the world. I didn't have an actual sire. As a vampire, I was raised by the collaborative effort of Mercy and Annabelle. The way I saw it, if the worst thing my progeny did was throw a party when I wasn't home, with the supervision of Sarah, who was way older than me, he was doing well. Most younglings leave a body or two in their wake the first week. Tommy had been a vampire for months now, and hadn't killed anyone. In a short time, he endured romance and heartbreak. He and Mel didn't break up. I don't think they really made their relationship exclusive. Still, since Mel moved back with Mercy to Exeter, I worried the heartache might manifest in a few unsavory vampiric behaviors. So far, though, so good. I deserved a freaking medal.

I knew three of Nico's offspring. Mercy turned out well. Corbin was a homicidal psychopath. Merrick turned to sorcery and devised a spell to emancipate himself from Nico's sire bond.

The way I saw it, when it came to our success as sires, Nico was one for three. I had a damn near perfect record—so far, at least. Never mind the small sample size. That's *beside* the point.

Apart from bossing us around from time to time, Nico was a welcome addition to our house. Mostly because he didn't demand his room back—which was mine. He didn't need a room. Most of his old things were still in storage. He hadn't opened a single box. That was his *old* life. He was something else now. A vampire, but also a Ghede Loa. He was earth bound. Baron Samedi said his responsibility was to monitor the left-over energy from Kalyptos, the parts of the demiurge that had struck Connor and Nicky. Even as shifters—albeit different kinds of shifters—their bodies weren't resilient enough to accommodate Kalyptos. The primal force of creation requires a nearly indestructible vessel—like Nico's reforged body.

The energy of the demiurge was out there, somewhere, and if anyone dared tap into it and use it for anything insidious, Nico was there to stop them. Since Kalyptos was the primal force, the mediating energy harnessed by whoever God was when *she* created the world, anyone who harnessed the power could use it to make anything at all. A billion dollars. An army of zombies. It could give someone the powers of freaking Superman, or remold the planet into a cube rather than a sphere. The only limit to what it could do was what one could imagine. Thankfully, Nico absorbed the bulk of it. He refused to tap into it. Whatever was left, once it was used, couldn't be repurposed. It was sort of like a genie in a bottle, without the bottle. Use up however many wishes the power allows, and that was that.

Maybe it would be harnessed by someone with modest desires. A noble man in Ethiopia who wanted an endless well of clean water for his village. A sixteen-year-old who wanted a Lamborghini. A middle-aged woman who needed a butt lift or a gym rat who wanted to get swole. The problem was that anyone who had the kind of power to harness something like the demiurge needed to know about it, have access to a magic or method to harness it, and a body resilient enough to contain it. Anyone who had those qualifications probably wasn't interested in something trite like modifying their figure and probably wasn't noble enough to use it to provide for the hungry or thirsty.

It had only been three weeks since we stopped Dracula from claiming Kalyptos, and the warlock Baladan Branham from harnessing the power in his fool-hearted attempt to turn the clock back six months on the entire planet. In my world, a three-week respite from some kind of world-threatening crisis was the closest thing I ever had to a vacation. When you're one of the designated guardians of the mystical convergences, the breaches between worlds and dimensions, you can't take a break. You have to be ready because at any given moment, something nasty and previously unimaginable could break through into the world.

Three weeks also gave Connor a chance to get his sleep schedule back to normal. Annabelle gave him a job. He worked the counter at a head shop called Marie's on Canal Street. Annabelle's predecessor, the Voodoo Queen Marie Laveau used to have a room in the back where she met with folks who sought her services, engaged in business deals on behalf of Vilokan, and performed her summonings and rituals. Annabelle didn't use the space, but the shop was still there. It was one of a dozen or more business establishments that Annabelle inherited from Marie Laveau. The proceeds helped support the voodoo community in Vilokan. As such, Annabelle needed people she trusted to run her businesses. She had an opening at the head shop, and Connor needed a job.

It was a perfect arrangement—except for the fact that it gave Connor and me very little time together. He worked during the day and after he closed up shop in the evening, we had a few hours to spend together before he had to get to sleep so he could function at work the next day. He usually stopped by Casa do Diabo before his shift after sunrise. The head shop didn't open until nine o'clock. That gave us a little more than an hour after I went inside for the day and he woke up before he had to leave for work.

Connor had his own apartment, but he usually spent his nights sleeping in my bed while I got out of the house to either grab a snack or patrol the area for convergence-related shenanigans. It was a way to maximize the time we spent together before we went our separate ways.

I made Connor breakfast while I waited for him to wake up. Cooking might not be my strong suit, given my personal dietary considerations, but I made a *killer* bowl of Cap'n Crunch. I went all out. I also made him my world-famous Pop Tarts and had a steaming pot of Maxwell House waiting.

Nico was out and about for the day. He took the farm truck with him. I didn't have any use for it during the daytime. He said he was going to get new tires—the ones still on the truck were threadbare.

Tommy and Sarah were still up. Sarah was in her room working on her latest crochet project—a hat and gloves for Nico. Tommy was on the couch, dicking around on his phone. He used Tinder the way most people used Grubhub. Swipe right, and if he had a match, he also had breakfast come nightfall.

We'd come a long way since my days as a fledgling vamp. We had no choice but to evolve once they shut down the "casual encounters' on Craigslist. Survival of the fittest.

Mercy thought all of that was dumb. She was an old-school vampire. She still believed that we met the best meals face-to-face in the real world.

Mercy had a point. The last time I used social media to find a meal, the "gentleman" presented in his mid-twenties with a baby-oiled chest and a six-pack. The man who showed up was fifty-plus, had a beer gut, and had week-long whiskers. No baby oil on his mid-section, but his hair was greasy, and he smelled like Long John Silver. That's what you call a "catfish." I bit him anyway. I had to pinch my nose and hold my breath while feeding, but I choked it down.

The sound of a fart let me know Connor was up. Apparently, we were at that point in our relationship. When we first started dating, he held them in. When did we move beyond the romantic gesture phase and gas pains being worth enduring for the sake of wooing the other?

It reminded me of my dad. I nicknamed him the "toot man" when I was five. Why do men feel the need to blast ass first thing in the morning? And when they're going up the stairs? Or when they're brushing their teeth? Connor even did it when he was shifted. Wolf farts are the worst.

Connor stumbled down the stairs in his pajamas. His gourmet bowl of cereal and his platter of Pop Tarts were waiting next to his full mug of coffee on the table.

"You shouldn't have!" Connor exclaimed, seeing the smorgasbord of goodies awaiting him.

"What can I say? I slaved over it all night."

Connor sat down and took a bite out of his first Pop Tart. "Mmm! Delicious! I don't know how you do it."

I smirked. "It's a secret family recipe. I'd tell you how, but then I'd have to bite you."

"Please do! I could use a fix, and you deserve breakfast, too."

Connor held out his wrist. I pulled one of our high-backed dinner chairs next to him and sank my fangs into his flesh. I took two swallows, released his wrist, and wiped my mouth with a napkin. "Scrumptious! You taste different."

"It's the vitamins. The guy at GNC said men shouldn't take iron supplements, but he didn't realize that I was dating a vampire."

I grabbed my wand from my leg pocket and pressed it to Connor's wrist, healing the two wounds my fangs left behind. "Just like new."

"Voodoo" by Godsmack sounded from my phone that was plugged in on the kitchen counter. It was Annabelle's ringtone. Fitting, right? I re-pocketed my wand, stood up, and picked up my phone. It was a strange time to call. She was a late sleeper.

"Annabelle?" I asked.

"Is Connor with you?"

"Of course he is. Do you want to talk to him?"

"I could have called him. I need to talk to both of you. Where were you two last night?"

I furrowed my brow. "He slept through the night. I took a walk then came back and Nico helped me change the oil on Ellie's truck."

"Are you sure about that?"

I pressed the speaker-phone button and set my phone on the table. "What's going on, Annabelle?"

"Turn on your television. It's on all the local channels."

I sighed. "Don't tell me something *else* showed up from one of the convergences, freaking people out again."

"I don't know what I'm seeing. Maybe you can explain it."

I hurried across the room, grabbed the remote from the end-table next to the couch, and switched on the television. It was already tuned to the local morning news.

A freeze frame of my image taken from a security camera was on the screen. The caption below said, "Young woman and wolf wanted for attack on Bourbon Street."

"What the hell?"

Connor tilted his head. "And a wolf? I was here all night!"

"You're telling me you had *nothing* to do with this?" Annabelle asked.

"I didn't go to Bourbon Street last night. That's not *me.* It looks like me, but you have to believe me—"

"I believe you. The problem is that the Chief of Police is demanding I turn you over. Both of you."

"He knows about Connor and me?"

"Of course he does," Annabelle said. "He and I communicate about anything involving supernaturals in the city. If I don't give you to him, he's threatening to come after us."

"What do you mean, *come after us*?"

"I don't know. A SWAT team in Vilokan, probably. I'm sort of between a rock and a hard place, here."

"Tell him it wasn't us!"

"He won't believe me. That looks like you, Hailey. It's not even a fuzzy image. I don't know what I can say that will dissuade him."

Connor grunted. "Kalyptos."

I sighed. "That must be it. When we harnessed Kalyptos, and parts of it struck Nicky and Connor, what if it molded itself to their abilities?"

After about two seconds, Annabelle exhaled. "Nicky can shape-shift. Connor is a wolf-shifter. It's possible, but Kalyptos can't do this alone."

"Right, the demiurge isn't a *person.* It's more like a force. Someone must've harnessed that power and is framing us!"

"Who would do that?" Annabelle asked. "Do you have any ideas? If we don't give the cops something soon, they'll come for you."

I picked up several footsteps approaching the front door. "I think it might be too late for that."

With a loud bang, someone kicked open the front door of the house. A half-dozen men in black, with helmets and face shields, bullet-proof vests, and rifles poured into the house. Tommy sprang up from the couch.

Before I could even react, the SWAT team had Connor and me surrounded.

I could have fought them off. Their bullets wouldn't hurt me. Connor didn't have that luxury. I also couldn't let them arrest me. The sun was out. If they took me outside, I'd fry.

The men tossed both of us on the floor. They handcuffed Connor. I wouldn't allow them to pull my hands behind my back. "Get off of me!"

"You're under arrest for the murders of fifteen people on Bourbon Street last night. You have the right to remain—"

"Fuck you!" I screamed. "I didn't do it!"

They'd probably heard that before. Not just the F-bomb, but the denial. They ushered Connor out of the house while the rest of them struggled to hold me down. Once he was in the clear, if I fought back, he'd be safe. At least, I hoped he would.

I sprang to my feet, sending three of the officers flying against the wall. I flashed my fangs and hissed. What can I say? It was instinct.

"What the fuck!" one cop screamed, taking two steps back.

"Grab her!" another officer screamed.

They didn't stand a chance. I yanked the gun out of one of their hands. I ran around the room, disarming them one-by-one. They couldn't keep up. I resisted the urge to bite. If someone was framing me, the last thing I needed was to add "assaulting an officer" to my charges. I didn't commit the murders, but I would be guilty of that. I could deal with resisting arrest. The alternative was a deadly sunburn.

One of the SWAT members had Tommy at gun point. My progeny stood against the wall, shaking. He wasn't under arrest. I had to wonder, why did they think Connor was involved? The news said a wolf was there—did they know Connor was a shifter? The Chief must have known and gave them his name. Proving he was guilty, though, wouldn't be a straightforward task. Not without exposing what he really was to the world. Even then, there was no way to prove that the wolf who helped the imposter kill those people was Connor. That's the thing about wolves. They look a lot alike.

I couldn't kill these men. I also couldn't leave the house.

Officers went flying as a force pressed between them. It was like Moses parting the Red Sea. The force moved so fast that even with my enhanced senses, I couldn't make it out. Something flew over my head and grabbed me tight. I was in a blanket and whatever held me was a lot stronger than I was. My feet left the ground. The next thing I knew, my body thudded down on something metal. I didn't dare move. I could tell from the sounds all around me that I was outside.

The sound of a door opening, an ignition turning over, and the rumble of an engine helped me put the pieces together. There was no mistaking that sound. No one else I knew drove a vehicle with a death rattle. It was the farm truck. That meant the figure who took me was Nico. My racing heart slowed from a rapid ten beats per minute to my usual two or three.

All I could figure was that Nico saw what was happening, parked a couple blocks away, and ran at a speed that only a vampire as ancient he was could. He rescued me. What about Tommy? Sarah was in her room when everything went down. I could only hope she'd find a way to help him through the situation. After the officers were thrown around the house like rag dolls, I doubted they'd play nice with either of them.

I wanted to tell Nico to go back for them. Riding in the back of the truck, with the wind blowing over me, and several layers of thick light-tight cloth over me, I wasn't sure Nico could hear me even with his enhanced hearing.

I couldn't call or text him. My phone was sitting on the dinner table when the SWAT team broke in. Annabelle must've heard everything. I could only hope that she'd take care of Sarah and Tommy since Nico was occupied. Sarah was stronger than me. She was older than me. She was even older than Mercy. She could fight them off. Tommy was stronger than the average human, but probably couldn't overpower a SWAT team alone. I was worried that the situation would push his limits, put a strain on the control he maintained over his bloodlust.

If Annabelle didn't get there fast, Sarah and Tommy might not have any choice. Vampires are like snakes that way. They won't usually strike if they aren't hungry—unless they're threatened. At the moment, the cops had them cornered. It was a recipe for a bloody massacre.

Chapter 3

WE MUST'VE BEEN ON the road for an hour. Thankfully, the farm truck was registered to Ellie. There was no reason to suspect that the cops knew I had access to it.

The police were the least of my concerns. With that video out there, it was only a matter of time before hunters got wind of the incident. Hunters who knew how to slay vampires.

I didn't have any sense of direction since I couldn't see and didn't dare peek beyond the blankets. They were all that was keeping me safe from the sun. All I had was the sense of momentum and the vibrations of the road. The farm truck slowed down. Nico was exiting the highway. He made a series of turns. The sound of crunching gravel and the bumpiness of the drive suggested we'd left the paved streets. My body bounced around the truck bed. It didn't feel good but, as a vampire, I didn't bruise easily. Eventually the truck squealed to a stop.

The truck door opened and closed. Footsteps. Then my body was dragged in the blanket out of the truck bed. Nico slung me over his shoulder.

"Nico, is that you?" It had to be. Who else could toss me around like that or had access to the farm truck? Presuming it *was* the farm truck. Who was I kidding? Most people wouldn't be caught dead driving that thing in the city. Since I was sort of dead anyway, I guess it didn't bother me that much. It was transportation. Most of the time, it functioned.

Nico didn't respond. He chuckled, though, enough that I recognized his voice. I heard a door open. It squeaked and from the sound of it the door rubbed on the ground of whatever building he was taking me into.

Nico flung me back over into his waiting arms, then dropped me on the floor.

"Ouch!" I shouted.

Nico laughed. "There aren't any windows in here. You can come out."

I rolled around. I couldn't tell how many times he'd wrapped me in this cloth. He did it so fast and I was in a bit of a panic when it happened. I didn't really notice. I hit the wall.

"A little help, please?"

"What was that?" Nico asked. "I can't hear you. Too many blankets."

"Unroll me, asshole! I feel like the beans on the inside of a burrito."

"I just saved you, Hailey. What's up with the name calling?"

I sighed. "Will you please help me get out of here?"

"Glady," Nico said. The next thing I knew, my body tumbled around and around three or four times. He must've grabbed the edge of the blanket and pulled hard. I found myself laying on my back in what looked like an abandoned log cabin.

I rubbed my forehead. "Gentleness isn't really your thing, is it?"

"You're a vampire. You can take it. Besides, I thought you liked it rough."

I pushed myself into a seated position. "Like you'd know anything about that."

Nico laughed. "The sounds that come from your bedroom in the evenings make it clear."

"Connor is in trouble. Tommy and Sarah—"

"The situation is under control."

"Seriously? A SWAT team busting into Casa do Diabo doesn't sound like an in-control scenario to me."

"The police don't have any solid evidence to pin anything on Connor. I assume you know why the police came this morning since it was all over your television set when I ran in."

I nodded. "Annabelle called me a few minutes before the cops showed up."

"They won't be able to hold Connor for more than twenty-four hours without charges. We'll get him into hiding once it's safe."

"What about Sarah and Tommy?"

"I knocked out the cops. Hopefully, I bought them enough time to hide."

"To hide? You really think they could *hide* from a SWAT team? They'll tear that place apart looking for any evidence they can find. There won't be a corner of that house they *can* hide."

Nico grinned widely. "That's not true. There's a small chamber encased in cement under the floorboards of the kitchen. I built it a long time ago for situations just like this."

"Seriously? I've lived there for a couple of years now and Mercy never mentioned it."

"Mercy knew it was there. I suspect she never had occasion to bring it up."

"An emergency panic room might be something she'd mention given all the shit that the universe likes to throw our way."

"I slipped a note under Sarah's door explaining what to do."

"When did you do that?"

"Before I saved you. I'm fast. You might have noticed."

"What's the plan? They hide in the panic room until nightfall?"

"I gave her coordinates. I'll pick them up there and bring them here tonight."

I looked around the cabin. It wasn't much. Cobwebs covered what looked like a turn-of-the-century bronze chandelier. A thick layer of dust coated everything. There was one antique square table against the wall and what looked like a couch covered in clear but dusty plastic. "What is this place?"

"One of my safe houses. I suppose Mercy owns it now since she inherited all my property. I wasn't entirely sure it was still here. I haven't come here in almost twenty years."

"You own a cabin in the woods and you never went there?"

Nico laughed. "I owned a lot of properties back in my time. This wasn't exactly a spot I frequented."

"Where are we exactly?" I asked.

"Close to Bayou Chene in St. Martin Parish."

I bit my lip. "You're telling me we're in the middle of nowhere?"

"It wasn't always like that. Sure, the community that used to be here is now buried under about twelve feet of silt. About a hundred years ago, nearly five hundred people lived in a small community here. Then, there was the Great Mississippi Flood of 1927. They rebuilt after that, but most of the area was abandoned in the fifties. No one has settled here since. Given the condition of my cabin, I don't think anyone's been here since I was, decades ago. It's about as safe a place to hide as there is in the entire state."

I stood up and stretched out my arms. "I can't stay here forever. Annabelle and I were talking just before the cops showed up. We think that the power from Kalyptos that hit Connor and Nicky must've absorbed their power or mimicked it somehow."

Nico nodded. "Kalyptos definitely has something to do with it. I'd say that's a sound theory. The question is, who would want to frame you and Connor for a mass murder?"

I shrugged. "I don't know. Most of the people I've known who wanted me dead ended up dead themselves."

"Nicky and Connor couldn't hold the power. You saw what it did to them."

I nodded. "A common warlock or witch couldn't harness the demiurge, either. Even Baladan needed to recruit a dozen other warlocks when he was trying to seize Kalyptos."

"My best guess is that vampires are involved. Not younglings, either. Only an old vampire has the fortitude to use a power like that. The question is who it could be and what kind of magic they used to attract Kalyptos to themselves."

"Can you use the power of Kalyptos to track them down?"

Nico shook his head. "I don't know. I meant what I said before. No one should wield that kind of power, myself included. The power is inside of me, but even if I knew how to use it, I wouldn't."

"Come on, man. Someone is framing me. There has to be something you can do."

"I saved your cute little butt. I am doing something."

I smirked. "I do have a cute butt, don't I? One of my better assets."

Nico smirked. "*Ass*ets."

I rolled my eyes. "You're hilarious."

Nico winked at me. "The good news is that any vampire old enough to use power like that is someone I probably know. When I meet up with Sarah, we should be able to use her power to identify the culprits."

"Nice thinking. Then it's easy. We track them down and stake their asses."

"Hearts, Hailey. Some vampires might enjoy getting their asses staked, but it won't kill them."

"There you go with your jokes again."

Nico laughed. "I'd say I'll be here all week, but I have things to do. It won't be so easy as staking them, either. That won't get the fuzz off your back, and it certainly won't dissuade the hunters, who are probably already on their way from every corner of the country looking for you."

"Killing bad guys is usually the way I handle this kind of problem. If we can't kill them, what do we do?"

Nico smiled from ear-to-ear. After all the crap I'd given him, and how I'd resisted his attempts to exert his authority over us since he came back, he was enjoying this more than he should have. "The way I see it, we have no choice but to bait the vampires responsible into taking your shape again. We catch them on camera, or with credible eye witnesses from the police present, and bust them. Once the Chief of Police knows shifters were responsible for what happened, it should clear your name."

"How exactly do you plan to do that?"

Nico scratched the back of his head. "I'm still working on that."

I bit the inside of my cheek. "I need my grimoires."

Nico raised an eyebrow. "They're at Casa do Diabo. We can't go back there. The cops will be watching the place twenty-four seven."

"Sarah and Tommy are still hiding there, right? My phone is on the table, but you should be able to get hold of them. You have a phone, right?"

Nico reached into his pocket. "One of the first things I got when I returned to the land of the living. You can't survive in the twenty-first century, even as a vampire, without one."

"Tell Sarah to channel my thoughts. I can let her know which books to grab. There are a few spells that can use someone's blood to temporarily seize control of a person."

"You don't know those spells by heart?" Nico asked.

I shook my head. "The spells are complex and require exotic ingredients that are hard to come by. Mastering spells like that takes time—which I haven't had as of late."

Nico shrugged and tossed me his phone. "You text her and tell her what to do. Good luck getting service out here."

"What's your passcode to unlock it? I can't use your thumbprint or facial recognition."

Nico's eyes darted back and forth. "1, 2, 3, 4."

I stared at Nico blankly. "Seriously?"

"What? I don't leave my phone lying around. It's not like anyone is going to break into it."

I unlocked Nico's phone. "Damn. You're right. No service."

"Wait until dark. Hopefully, Sarah and Tommy will still be in the house. If you head due north, you'll hit Interstate 10. You might pick up a signal near the highway."

I furrowed my brow. "If the cops are watching the place, how are Sarah and Tommy going to leave without being noticed?"

"That's a good question. I hadn't thought of that."

I smirked and started typing out a text. "I'm going to ask Annabelle to get them out of there and get my books."

Nico rolled his eyes. "Annabelle Mulledy."

"I know you two aren't the best of friends."

Nico laughed. "Our history is complicated. Even so, I don't think she can teleport in and out of the house."

"She can't. Pauli can. He can get everyone in and out of there and no one will know the difference."

Nico grunted. "I was really hoping we wouldn't have to get them involved."

"You were all classmates at the Voodoo Academy back in the day, right? Before you got lost in Guinee, became a vampire, and were sent back to earth a few thousand years earlier."

Nico nodded. "That's right. For me, it's ancient history, I suppose I can suck it up and work with them."

Nico headed for the door. "Don't go anywhere."

"It's the middle of the day. Where the hell am I going to go? More importantly, where are you going?"

"I'm going to head back to the crime scene and see what I can find out."

"You're taking the truck? How am I going to use it to get into cell range?"

Nico chuckled and tossed me the keys. "I don't need the truck. I'm faster on foot, anyway."

Chapter 4

STAYING AN ENTIRE DAY in a dusty old cabin was only marginally better than the few occasions when I'd had to hide in a makeshift grave until nightfall. I had Nico's phone but he didn't have any entertaining apps and I needed to save his battery so I could contact Annabelle once I got into a service area.

I pulled the plastic off the couch. It could have been the ugliest couch I'd ever seen. Why was the color of vomit so popular back in the day? I'd spent enough time in Corbin's temporary mansion and his castle in Romania to know that some old world vampires had Victorian tastes. I could appreciate that. Why was Nico stuck in the seventies? He was older than they were, but apparently his modernizing sensibilities died with the eight-track and Betamax.

At least he had the latest iPhone. He probably didn't have a clue how to use it other than for sending texts and receiving calls, but it was a step in the right direction.

I dug around in the seat cushions because I had nothing better to do. I found a wrapper from a Tootsie Pop. Why in the world was that there? Nico was a vampire. Maybe he was just curious to see how many licks it really took to get to the Tootsie Roll center. I checked the wrapper for the Native American and the star. There was a rumor that if you had that on your wrapper you could exchange it for a free one. I'd never tried it. I suspected the cashier at the grocery store wouldn't know what to do with it if I did. They didn't sell Tootsie Pops individually anymore. You had to buy an entire bag. Besides, these days someone would probably find the imagery offensive. Tootsie Roll and their damned cultural appropriation. Exploiting stereotypical imagery of First Nations people just to sell shitty suckers. Cancel the Tootsie Pop!

I also found a nickel under the cushions. Whoopee!

There was a small kitchenette on one side of the square cabin with two whole cabinets over a small, dirty countertop. I checked the cabinets and found a stack of old Polaroid photographs.

It's sad to admit it, but they provided the most entertainment I'd had in months. Most of them featured Nico, Mercy, and Ramon. They were dressed in early nineties attire. Mercy was wearing baggy printed jeans. Ramon was in tight-rolled jeans and a matching jean jacket. Nico was wearing the gaudiest baggy parachute-style pants I'd ever seen—and a bright green fanny pack. I don't know why they called them fanny packs. He was wearing it in the front. It had at least three zippers.

They were dressed the same in all the photos, which meant they were probably taken the same day. Obviously, the photos didn't have great light since all three of them were vampires, but they had enough light cast from artificial sources that I saw enough to make it all out.

Nico also had a mustache and a flat top—which was awesome.

Those were the "good old days," when vampires like Nico and Mercy had little more to worry about than where to find their next meal, how to avoid sunlight, and went about their routines without worrying about the next world-ending threat. It struck me that the photo must've been taken in the late eighties or early nineties. After Nico was born in the early nineties, Mercy and Ramon staked his older vampiric self. He couldn't exist at the same time on the same plane of existence twice. One of those funny rules about trans-dimensional travel. You could never take a gate or a portal to a time where you already were, or you'd end up getting dumped into the void. Mercy didn't remove Nico's stake until *after* his grown-up self was lost in Guinee, when the whole vampire origin story began.

One photo depicted a woodsman, passed out, with bite marks on his neck and wrists. Ramon was holding him up by the scruff of his flannel shirt the way a kid might who'd just caught a large fish. At least they found a meal out in these parts to sustain them. I had to wonder why they'd come out to the bayou to begin with. Perhaps it was a family trip, a chance to get away from the busy city and relax.

I realized I knew little at all about this time in Mercy's vampiric life. She talked a lot about growing up in Exeter, and the years when she and Nico first arrived in New Orleans. Maybe she didn't share much about these times because there wasn't much to say. It's funny how that works. We tend to remember and talk about the trying times in life, the struggles we went through, and forget about the moments when we had a chance to actually live and enjoy whatever life offered. For most people, the best part of life is also the most mundane. I was looking forward to that. A chance to do nothing meaningful at all except enjoy my time with Connor, feed when needed, and take vacations. Probably not to a cabin in the swamps, but vacations no less.

I suspected I'd never get that chance. Not unless we figured out a way to close the convergences again. Then again, the irony of the situation was that I had absolutely nothing to do while I sat in that damn cabin and was *eager* to kick something's ass. Preferably whoever it was who'd framed me for mass murder.

The entertainment value of the old Polaroids was short-lived. After that, it was back to sitting on my ass and waiting for the sun to set. I tried to sleep, but my head was spinning with rage. Someone out there had it in for me. It was probably a couple of old vampires who I'd never met but inadvertently pissed off somehow.

Since the cabin didn't have windows, I relied on Nico's phone to tell me the time. Checking the clock didn't drain the battery much. I knew the sun would set around eight-thirty. The last hour dragged on for what felt like another day.

When I knew it was safe, I left the cabin and got into the farm truck. The engine choked a little as it started. I was afraid it might not, and I'd have no option but to hoof it through the swamp until I found a signal.

Thankfully, the GPS function on the phone didn't require data to work. I didn't have access to all the features, but it was enough that I found my way. It was a good thing I had the farm truck. The roads were overgrown with high peaks in the center. A smaller vehicle would have bottomed out. Not all the roads that navigated the old bayou showed on GPS. They might have been whatever roads used to access the bayou town that used to be there. If no one had lived there since the fifties, it made sense that the roads wouldn't be on modern electronic maps.

Until turn-by-turn navigation kicked in, I used my orientation on the map to make sure I was making the right turns that led me north.

I was checking Nico's phone every minute or so. Once I had a signal, I could stop and call Annabelle. She and Pauli could get to Casa do Diabo, get my books, and help Sarah and Tommy get out of there without being seen by the police.

I was trying to keep track of my turns. I knew where the cabin was on the map, but since the roads weren't marked, getting back wasn't straightforward.

Eventually, I picked up a single bar on Nico's phone. I tried to call Annabelle but when I hit dial, I was stuck listening to silence. I drove a little further until I got two bars. This time my call connected.

"Hey bitch!" a voice answered on the other end.

"Pauli? What are you doing with Annabelle's phone?"

"What are you doing with Nico's phone?"

"You seriously call Nico 'bitch'?"

"I call everyone bitch, bitch."

I chuckled. "Fair point. You still didn't answer my question. Where is Annabelle?"

"She's right here. We're in her Camaro. She's driving."

"It's actually good you're there. I need your help. Tommy and Sarah are hiding under the floors at Casa do Diabo. Now that it's dark, we might be too late. If they leave and the cops see them—"

"Bitch, please. I brought them both to Vilokan hours ago."

I snorted. "You did?"

The volume of road noise increased. Pauli must've put the phone on speaker. "I heard what was happening on the other end of our call," Annabelle said. "I went and got Pauli right away to get you out of there, but you were already gone. Pauli teleported all the knocked out cops out of there then came back and grabbed Sarah and Tommy."

I took a deep breath and let it out slowly. "That's a relief. Thank you."

"I'm the one that's relieved! When Pauli said you were already gone and it looked like a tornado had blown through your living room, I feared the worst."

"That was Nico. He knocked out the cops and took me to an old cabin he owns somewhere in Bayou Chene."

"Damn it, Nico. Don't get me wrong. I'm glad he was there to help, but he could have let me know what was going on."

"You two never got along, did you?"

"That's because he's a bee-atch!" Pauli piped up.

"Maybe he was when you all were classmates in the academy. He's had the advantage of a few thousand years to grow up. Not to mention, the whole death thing and coming back as a god. It doesn't matter. Can you pick up a few things at Casa do Diabo and bring them to me along with Sarah and Tommy?"

"Send us a ping to your location," Annabelle said.

"A photo would also help," Pauli added. "I should be able to put two-and-two together to get there."

"The cabin is out of phone range, so you'll have to meet me where I am. I can take us back to the cabin. I think."

"What books do you need?" Pauli asked.

"I'll send you a list with the coordinates and the photo. Annabelle, any news on Connor?"

"We were on our way to the department to pick him up. They couldn't prove he was involved, and he certainly wasn't about to shift into wolf form to bolster their case."

"Any progress with the Chief of Police?"

Annabelle sighed. "I only talked to him once. He's not too happy about how things went down at Casa do Diabo. I tried to tell him it wasn't you, but I don't think he believed me. He suspects I was involved and was hiding you in Vilokan."

"Can he get *into* Vilokan?" I asked.

"I don't think so," Annabelle said. "But if he knows I'm coming to pick up Connor, it might be a trap."

I tightened my grip on Nico's phone. "It's definitely a trap. If he thinks you helped me escape the SWAT team, he could charge you with aiding and abetting."

I heard sirens through the phone.

"Speak of the devil." Annabelle sighed.

"Pauli, get her out of there."

"That will only make this situation worse," Annabelle said. "Pauli, go pick up Connor. Take my phone with you. Help Hailey and Nico solve this little problem."

"Annabelle!" I shouted. "You can't trust them. They might not release you like they did Connor."

"They don't have any proof of anything," Annabelle said. "Besides, I can escape at any time. Isabelle is with me. I have my soul-blade. You'd better take my phone with you, Pauli. There's lots of crap on there they could use against us if they're looking for an excuse."

"Annabelle! You've been working with the Chief of Police for years, brushing shit under the table. He probably has a whole file on you he can bring up as leverage."

"I'll be fine, Hailey. We don't have time. The officer is approaching the car."

"Call me back on her phone in five minutes," Pauli said. "I'm getting out of here."

Chapter 5

UNLESS ANNABELLE WAS PULLED over for speeding, she was going to jail. Connor was getting out. At least that's what we thought. What if they told Annabelle he was being released just to lure her out of Vilokan? Either way, Pauli could save them both. All he had to do was shift into rainbow patterned boa constrictor form, teleport to wherever they were being held, wrap himself around them, and take them with him when he teleported out.

Since we were likely dealing with shifters, it was handy to have a shifter of our own. Don't tell Pauli he was *handy,* though. He'd probably tell you that was one of his favorite things to do. Pauli was right, though. That the cops probably had a file of shit they'd turned over to Annabelle through the years. Supernatural mishaps, murders, and mayhem of any sort that they weren't equipped to handle all fell on the Voodoo Queen. They should have been grateful. This wasn't about Annabelle, though. Not really. It was about using her to get to me. She didn't even need Pauli to escape. She could use her dragon-soul-blade, cut a portal to Guinee, and summon the dragon in his beastly form there who could blast a portal back to earth with his breath. The dragons were the *original* gatekeepers of the realms. They could carry a person across realms without the need of a convergence. What we knew as convergences, though, were found in locations where such portals were created in the past. If she had to use Beli to make a jailbreak, getting home meant another portal which could easily become a new convergence. We already had more than we could manage in the New Orleans area.

Annabelle's ability to cut portals into thin air was one reason why. Annabelle couldn't do it at any time. She could only cut portals when Isabelle's spirit was with her. That was the only way they could summon Beli, the dragon-soul blade that could open new portals between worlds.

When Isabelle wasn't with Annabelle, she was the prime guardian of the crossroads along with her second and her love, a hougan named Mikah. Back when Isabelle and Annabelle were inseparable, Mikah was Annabelle's mentor in College Ogoun. This was when Annabelle was still a student, well before she became the Voodoo Queen. Isabelle fell in love with Mikah. Annabelle wasn't attracted to the hougan in the least. It made for an awkward romance. Annabelle had to allow Isabelle to take the reins so she could date Mikah.

It was a long story—I was involved in it, but I was closer to the enemy at the time. Another Loa, Kalfu, had deceived me into being his second in his attempt to take over the crossroads. Annabelle and Isabelle saved us—Isabelle and Mikah took over the crossroads. Now, Isabelle often went back and forth between guarding the crossroads with Mikah and inhabiting Annabelle. They could use Beli and forge gates together. They'd done it many times in their effort to save the world from the bad guys.

It wasn't her fault. No one ever told her that the era of the gatekeepers was coming to an end. It made sense. The gatekeepers were finite mortals—Merlin and Lilith. Even if they could use their gates to traverse the fabric of space and time, every finite being has its own time. They still aged. Without new gatekeepers to take their place, the gates between worlds and dimensions were vulnerable. In less than a year, we'd already seen several world-threatening entities and beings that could have brought the end of the world.

This wasn't a threat to the world. Not directly, at least. It was coming after *me* and if it was the power of the demiurge that the conspirators were using to frame me; it was only because I'd destroyed the realm of Barbelo and sent Kalyptos to earth. Just as Annabelle didn't know she was forging gates when she used her soul-blade to save the world in the past, I didn't know that using the power of Erzulie in Barbelo in an attempt to get him would destroy the aeon and cast the primordial energies through my exit-gate and through the convergences spread around the world. If I was up to my ears in shit in New Orleans, I had to wonder what they were dealing with in other places across the world where similar convergences thrived. Not all the convergences were as active as those in New Orleans. Nicky and Devin hadn't encountered much in Kansas City. Mercy had her hands full in Exeter, but she also had Wee Willie Winkie, the new Faerie King, guarding the transplanted Seelie Forest over an active convergence. I hadn't heard much from the druids in St. Louis, but Elijah and Emilie tended to take care of business like I did. They'd call in help if needed, but only if needed.

Bottom line—Annabelle allowed herself to be arrested and she wouldn't use her blade unless it was necessary. Was "escaping" a crime if you could prove that they held you unjustly to begin with? No clue. I was no lawyer. I didn't know many. I'd bit a few in my time, but it wasn't by choice. Their personality types soured their blood. Lawyers were the brussels sprouts of humans. The nutritional value was fine, but no one really craves them.

Given all of Annabelle's business dealings, I knew she had a lawyer. He was also a vodouisant who lived in Vilokan. I'd never met him and his name skipped my mind. Was he equipped to deal with criminal law, or was he one of those lawyers who only handled contracts and shit? I wasn't sure how much of a difference there was, but I suspected choosing the right *kind* of lawyer was like making sure you went to the right doctor. You don't want to get your dentist confused with your proctologist. Go to the wrong one looking to get your cavity taken care of and it could scar you for life.

I took a few photographs of my location. I wasn't sure how much it could help Pauli. Bayous are sort of like convenience stores. They all look about the same. There wasn't anything remarkable about my surroundings that set it apart from any other swamp I'd ever ventured into. The only difference I noticed was that Bayou Chene had more oaks and other deciduous trees while cypress trees dominated Manchac Swamp. I hadn't seen as many alligators in Bayou Chene. There were rivers running through the area while Manchac was more marshy.

So long as Pauli could get there with my friends and my books, I had no reason to question his methods. I sent him the photos and my coordinates. He sent back a clapping hands emoji. Two seconds later, he sent a random eggplant emoji. It didn't make any sense, but if anyone was going to send that emoji for no reason at all, it was Pauli. He was letting me know he was the person behind Annabelle's phone and was sticking to the plan.

I sat on the back bumper of the farm truck and waited.

Ever since the cops came to arrest me, it was a series of hurry-up-and-wait events. A bi-polar cycle of hurried crises and doing nothing at all. First it was escaping Casa do Diabo only to lay wrapped in a blanket in the back of the truck, then left in a cabin with nothing to do for a day. Then it was hurry and get a signal while Annabelle got arrested and I waited for Pauli to show up.

Chapter 6

FINALLY, A FLASH OF multicolored light signaled Pauli's arrival. He dropped a duffel bag full of my books in the bed of the truck. Pauli grabbed a change of clothes out of the bag as well—if Pauli didn't bring clothes with him, when he shifted out of boa constrictor form, he was stark naked. He was fine with that—I wasn't. For once, he was respectful enough to cover his naked body in my presence.

"My books? You got my books before you got Connor?"

Pauli sighed. "They didn't release him. It was all a ruse to get Annabelle to leave Vilokan."

My shoulders sank. "Of course it was. I was afraid of that."

"Annabelle suspected as much. She insisted on leaving anyway."

"You could break them out!"

"And what would that accomplish? She could break herself out if she had to. Annabelle is buying us time."

"But Connor did nothing wrong."

"Neither did Annabelle. They'll both be free soon enough. The police will question her. The Chief himself, I suspect. She'll make the case that you were not responsible for the murders."

I rolled my eyes. "I doubt he'll believe her. If it inclined him to listen to reason, he wouldn't have arrested her without just cause. He wouldn't have arrested Connor, either."

"Be that as it may, she is in a position to present the case. All we have to do is give him the evidence to prove that what Annabelle reveals is true."

"Nico is out looking for evidence as we speak. At least he was. He may be back at the cabin now. We should get back, then you can retrieve Tommy and Sarah."

Pauli shook his head. "You won't find the evidence you need out here in the middle of nowhere. The night is still young."

"If we go back to New Orleans and Nico doesn't find me in the cabin, he'll be pissed."

"Probably. Are you Nico's bitch?"

"Of course not! He's not the boss of me, but he did save me. He's still trying to save me."

"Since when were you a damsel in distress? You're Hailey fucking Bradbury. You're a badass blood witch bitch, honey. If someone out there is trying to frame you, you'd better believe they're looking for you the same as the cops. They want you out of the picture."

I shook my head. "Even if we find them, we can't just kill them. That's why I had you get the books. I need to work on a spell that I might be able to use to force the imposters to shift in plain view of the cops. Nico has a good plan. We can use Sarah to find the vampires responsible."

"That assumes they are vampires. Even so, I know where Sarah is. She's safe in Vilokan right now. You can take care of this now. Why wait for Nico?"

I sighed. "Fine. But first we go back to the cabin. If Nico isn't there, we'll leave."

"Nico is a Loa now. It makes him more powerful, for certain. It also makes him vulnerable."

"Vulnerable to what?" I asked.

"Just like Holland summoned Baron Samedi and Ghede Nibo before and bound them to her will, a vodouisant with the aspect of a Ghede can do the same to Nico."

"Why would we do that?" I asked. "He's on my side already."

"I wouldn't have suggested it if Annabelle hadn't mentioned it already."

"So, this is her idea? She wants us to bind Nico and use him like a dog on a leash?"

Pauli laughed. "The metaphor would be more appropriate for your boyfriend. I have to ask, Hailey. Have you and Connor ever done it doggy style?"

I smirked. "That depends what you mean. If you want to know if we've ever done it while he's shifted, then no. I'm not a freak."

Pauli giggled. "I am!"

"You'd do a dog?"

"That depends how well hung he is!"

"Shut up! You're not serious."

Pauli shrugged. "Technically, I'm a snake. That's my default form. I was born a man, of course. But my body was claimed by another Loa by the name of Kalfu. Aida-Wedo cast my consciousness into her personal pet, a Boa with rainbow scales. With her aspect, I can shift into any form I like. I'm still an animal at the core."

"You're a snake. What does that have to do with doing a wolf?"

"I can become a wolf, too. Is it any less natural to do a canine than it is for me to take a human form and screw a man?"

"You're reasoning is seriously fucked up, did you know that?"

Pauli smirked. "I just like watching you squirm. I wouldn't do a wolf. Please. That's not my style. A horse, on the other hand. Have you seen the size of of the—"

"I get the point," I interrupted, desperately hoping Pauli wouldn't finish his sentence. "My position is the same. Binding Nico to Holland wouldn't help us."

"Unless you need the power of Kalyptos that he refuses to wield."

"He has a good reason for not tapping into that power. I won't subject him to that."

Pauli shrugged. "It's just an idea. With his power, raw and unformed, you could stop the shifters. The power of the demiurge they absorbed was already purposed to the abilities of two shifters."

I scratched my head. "You can shift into *anything*, right?"

Pauli shook his head. "Not anything. I can't become an inanimate object."

"We already know that one of the vampires—if they are vampires, as we suspect—shifts into a wolf like Connor. That's because it was his power that shaped the power that struck him. The other one has shapeshifting ability taken from Nicky. I know that she can shape however she likes, but it wasn't always like that. Her powers have changed over time. If we want to know exactly what shapeshifting ability the imposter who framed me has, we need to talk to her."

"It can't hurt," Pauli admitted. "Give her a call?"

I nodded and climbed into the truck. Pauli got in the passenger side. I dialed Nicky's number on Nico's phone, switched it to speaker, and set it on the dash.

Nicky had just finished her nightly show at her club. I explained what was happening. I didn't go into too much detail. I gave her the Cliff Notes version. Enough that she'd know what I was asking and why I was inquiring about her abilities.

Surprisingly, I remembered most of the turns that would lead us back to the cabin. I was about eighty percent sure we were headed in the right direction.

"You can shift into anything, right? After you purged yourself of the curse of the Neck and embraced your identity as a nymph, your powers are basically unlimited, right?"

"They were," Nicky said. "Until a couple of months ago. My power to shift however I like isn't innate. It's connected to the essence of the wellsprings in Guinee."

"So whatever power the demiurge mimicked when it hit you is limited again?"

Nicky let my words linger in the air a moment considering the implications before she spoke. "My ability to shift at the moment is what it was before. I'm still a nymph, not cursed like the Neck, but my abilities reverted to what they were when I was among the Neck once the gatekeepers fell and I couldn't access the wellsprings the way I did before."

"Refresh my memory. How *exactly* do those powers work? I need to know what power the vampire who arrested the power of the demiurge has."

Nicky sighed. "I have to target someone. It's how I hunted humans when I was among the Neck. I focused my will on a person I intended to woo, you know, so I could lure them into my watery lair for dinner."

"I understand what you were and what that means. The form you took was based on what your target desired the most."

"That's right. If my target was in love with the Queen of England, I became the Queen of England. If he had an unnatural desire for Henry Kissinger, I'd look like Henry Kissinger."

"Why would anyone think about Kissinger like that? I've studied history."

"He was a brilliant man. Not everyone desires someone because of their physical traits. The point is that I can only shift into a form that my target most desires."

"So you target Devin and, with no desire to eat him, you still maintain your current form."

"It would work that way. It did work that way before. I haven't used my ability since the gatekeepers fell. If I try to draw on the wellspring, if the nearest convergence is more in tune with another realm, I can't access my true power. I don't have any desire to change my shape anyway. I love who I am, and Devin does, too. So I've stayed as I am."

"So whoever took *my* form has targeted someone who desires me."

"I'd say that's likely," Nicky said. "Do you suspect they targeted Connor?"

I sighed. "Maybe. There's another alternative I hadn't considered. We thought we sent all the wraiths back to hell. What if we didn't?"

"You're thinking the imposters might be vampires you've killed already?"

I nodded. "Not just any vampires. Corbin and Bianca. If Corbin absorbed the power that was shaped to match Connor's abilities, and Bianca targeted Corbin, who thinks he loves me, Bianca would look just like me."

"I've never encountered either Corbin or Bianca. As a hunter, though, I know who they are. Bianca was Corbin's most loyal subject, one of his progeny."

"It might not be her. It could be any vampire, really, but it makes sense she'd go along with his scheme."

"I wish you luck," Nicky said. "If there's anything you need, feel free to call."

"Thanks, Nicky. You were a tremendous help once again."

Pauli hung up Nico's phone. "You really think Corbin is back?"

I clenched my hands on the steering wheel. "I can't say for certain, but it tracks. My gut tells me it's true. There's only one way to know. If Nico isn't at the cabin, I need you to take me to Sarah."

Chapter 7

MY INTUITION WAS ALMOST always right. Mercy thought it was a vampiric gift, something I'd absorbed and inadvertently cycled from one of my past victims. When I had a gut feeling about something, something I couldn't shake, it was always right. If it was a vampiric ability, it wasn't the kind I could turn on and off. It was a latent ability, something that manifested instinctually, like the ability a human has to breathe or how the brain signals the heart to keep beating without a conscious thought. Maybe Mercy was right. Maybe she wasn't. Whatever the case, I *knew* we were dealing with Corbin and, probably, Bianca.

If I was right, it meant Corbin had become a wraith. He'd escaped Lucifer's hell, or was cast there by the devil as refuse. It also meant since Corbin was one of Nico's progeny, I could use Nico's sire bond to control him. As ominous as it was, the revelation also gave me a real way to control him, even without the spell I intended to master from my grimoires.

I made a few wrong turns but when the GPS showed I was moving the wrong direction, I backtracked and course corrected.

We made it back to the cabin. I stepped inside. It was vacant. "Damn it, Nico."

"He's not here. Are you really going to wait another full day cooped up in this place or are you going to come with me?"

"Nico could still come back. As you said before, the night is still young."

"Are you really willing to waste the night on the off chance Nico shows? He might *not* come back and with Annabelle risking her neck for you, buying you time, wasting the night would make all that pointless."

I took a deep breath. "Fine. Take me to Vilokan. We'll come back for the truck later."

"It's an old beat up truck. Is it really worth the effort?"

"It's not my truck. I can't leave it here. Besides, something about that old hunk of metal is growing on me. I like it."

Pauli rolled his eyes. "Fine. We won't leave your truck. I don't want to bother with it later. Get inside."

"You want to drive back?" I asked.

Pauli smirked. "I said get inside. Don't start the truck."

I got in obediently—mostly because I was curious about what Pauli was about to do. I climbed into the truck and fastened the seat belt. It was a habit. I always felt naked if I was in a car without my seat belt on. It was also a precaution because I suspected Pauli was going to use his ability to somehow teleport me within the truck. It could be a bumpy ride.

Sure enough. Pauli stripped down naked and tossed his clothes onto the passenger side of the bench-style seat. He closed the door before he shifted into his snake form and expanded his body. He grew until he was big enough to wrap his entire boa constrictor body around the truck. He coiled around until his massive face was staring straight at me through the windshield.

His forked tongue tickled the glass before a flash of multicolored light enveloped everything. The next thing I knew, I was sitting in the truck on the side of a street about two blocks from Jackson Square. Pauli shrank back to his normal snake form, slithered through the cracked window, and shifted again until his naked body was straddling me.

"What are you doing, you dirty girl?"

"This was your doing!" I laughed.

"My anaconda don't want none, honey!"

I chuckled. "Get off of me you perv!"

Pauli laughed and rolled back into the passenger side of the truck where he'd tossed his clothes.

Pauli quickly slipped into his fancy sequin decorated jeans and his frilly floral-patterned blouse. He zipped up his three-inch platform boots over his jeans.

"Let's go! We can walk from here."

"You can't just teleport us again?"

"You insatiable minx! I could do it, but do you know how much energy it took to do what I just did? Pauli needs a break and a Viagra before he gets any more action."

Pauli was an acquired taste. It wasn't hard to see why Mercy found him mildly annoying and Nico didn't have the patience to deal with his antics. Personally, I found him entertaining. No matter how tense a situation was, Pauli always had an inappropriate comment, or a dick joke, to lighten the mood.

I locked the truck with the key. It was an old truck—I had to lock it manually. We headed to Pere Antoine alley on the side of St. Louis Cathedral, and from there passed through the mystical doorway and down the steep staircase that led into Vilokan.

We found Sarah and Tommy, along with Holland and Ellie, hanging out in Annabelle's office. Ellie was on Annabelle's computer, looking at Hello Kitty paraphernalia. With Annabelle's dial-up connection, it seemed like an awfully inefficient use of time. Not to mention, Hello Kitty. Seriously? Ellie liked to party like it was always and forever 1999.

Ellie jumped up from her chair, pushed the bridge of her reading glasses with her forefinger to straighten them on her nose, and ran to me with her arms wide open. I reluctantly allowed her to hug me. When a tsunami is coming for you and you have nowhere to run, all you can do is hold your breath and hope for the best. In this case, it was a tsunami of fruity body spray, too much makeup, and giggles.

"What are you doing?"

"A little shopping! In between making arrangements. Erzulie is coming to town. She has a new host ready and willing. I'm so excited! She's going to teach some classes at the Voodoo Academy again and plans to sponsor a new student!"

I raised my eyebrows. "She was just here recently—back when she gave me her aspect. I take it that host didn't last?"

Ellie shook her head. "It didn't, but she couldn't stay away for long. Yay for us!"

"You're still hugging me."

"Sorry!" Ellie giggled.

Once I wiggled free of Ellie and her cloud of pear-scented fragrance, I turned straight to Tommy. "Are you alright?"

Tommy nodded. "As well as can be expected."

I patted Tommy on the cheek. I wasn't that much older than he was, vampiric years aside. His earthly life began only two years after mine. As his sire, the closest thing a vampire had to a parent, it was a little awkward. Most vampires had sires who were at least a human lifetime older than they were. Tommy hadn't let on that it bothered him at all. He respected me, and also pushed my limits, like a son might his mother.

Sarah was pacing back and forth behind Annabelle's desk. "Where is Nico?"

I tilted my head. "Don't you know? You can sense him, can't you?"

Sarah shook her head. "Not since he became a Loa."

I sighed. "I don't know where he is. He left me at a cabin in Bayou Chene and never came back."

I turned to Holland. "Can you summon him?"

"Maybe." Holland was leaning against the wall with her arms crossed in front of her chest. "He's a new Loa, there's no precedent, no recorded offering that might draw him to me."

"What would you need to do it?" I asked.

Holland shrugged. "Most of the Loa enjoy rum, cigars, or a variety of dishes. Nico was a vampire."

"He's still a vampire," I added. "He's just more than that now."

Holland nodded. "If I were to make a guess, an offering of blood might do it. There's just one problem with that. Blood offerings might attract any other number of entities who share his appetites."

"How does it work with other Loa? From what I understand, a lot of them have a taste for rum. How do you determine which Loa is going to show?"

"With a veve," Holland said. "A sacred symbol attuned to the Loa's essence. It's like a spiritual signature, unique to each one."

I rubbed my brow. "Serving on the vampire council, I've had the chance to examine several of the orders he issued while he was still chancellor, before he died and Mercy took over. He used a waxen seal on the envelopes that contained his orders. The seals were stamped with his ring, one he still wears. It looks a bit like a family crest but contains only his initials at the center."

"Can you duplicate it?" Holland asked.

"I think so. I can probably scribble out something similar."

"It's worth a shot."

Ellie reached into Annabelle's desk and retrieved a sheet of loose-leaf paper and a pencil. "Try to draw it."

I took the pencil. Before I started drawing it I turned back to Sarah. "By the way, Sarah. Have you sensed any vampires who might be the shifters responsible?"

Sarah scratched the back of her head. "I'm not sure. I've heard strange echoes, but nothing distinct."

"I have a theory. It might be wrong. I'm thinking it might be Corbin and Bianca, returned just as Dracula did before."

Sarah took a deep breath. "If that's the case, it might make sense. Both vampires were older than me. Since Corbin knows about my abilities, they could be taking precautions to block me from accessing their thoughts."

"What kind of precautions?"

"Something similar to the wards you used to dampen the psychic energy feed that was flooding my mind when the wraiths escaped hell before. My guess is some kind of magically imbued trinket. Older vampires are harder to sense already. The murmurs I'm picking up, though, are more elusive than usual."

"Start drawing," Holland said. "Nico is one of the Ghede now. Even if Sarah can't sense Corbin or Bianca, if that's who they are, Nico might."

I shook my head. "If he could do that, he would have already. He doesn't seem to know what kind of power he has as a Ghede Loa or how to use it."

Holland smirked. "When Nico was a student, he belonged to the same college I did. He vanished during his first year. I finished my education as a master of the Ghede. I can teach him a few things that might help."

I closed my eyes and took a deep breath. I was trying to recall the symbol on Nico's seal. "If I can get back into Casa do Diabo, I can dig into the files and find his seal."

"I can take you there, but the police are still watching the place. They were already inside. They could have the place bugged."

"Give it your best shot," Holland said. "If it doesn't work, nothing will happen. It doesn't hurt to try before we take that risk."

I took a deep breath. I drew what looked like a knight's shield. I wasn't sure of the exact shape, but I drew it the best I could recall. I knew the bottom of the shield came to a point. I wasn't sure about the angles that formed the top. The initials in the middle of the shield were equally complex. I knew it was an N.F. but it was in a flourished script I wasn't sure I could duplicate. Then there was something around the outside of the shield. A world-serpent wrapped around the shield and swallowing its own tail. Was the serpent's face on the right or the left, more toward the top or the bottom of the seal? I didn't remember. I scribbled out an image that vaguely represented what I thought I remembered, but I was sure I'd messed up a few of the details. I wasn't sure which details, but the seal was too complex for me to duplicate perfectly. I was no artist. Even if my memory was perfect, I doubted my ability to sketch it out exactly.

I handed the sheet of paper to Holland.

She looked at it and narrowed her eyes. "This looks like shit."

I chuckled. "Thanks. Shit was exactly what I was going for."

"I'll give it a shot. No promises. I doubt this is sufficient, but it doesn't hurt to try."

I cleared my throat. "If you summoned him, would he be bound to you?"

"That depends how I do it. Something like that, though, is risky. Attempt to bind a Loa but miss a single detail in the ritual tends to have the opposite effect one intends."

"You did it with Baron Samedi and Ghede Nibo."

"Right. They're well-known and often summoned Loa. I've practiced those rituals for years. Trying to do something like that with Nico could awaken a rage in him I doubt any of us would hope to experience if I weren't to do it just so."

"It's still possible," Pauli said. "Figure out how to summon him without binding him, then add the necessary incantations the next time you do it."

Holland nodded. "Once I'm certain I can summon him at all, it's possible. Is it really necessary? Nico is on our side already."

"He refuses to tap into the power of Kalyptos," I said. "Pauli thinks we might need to force him to use it to stop Corbin and Bianca, presuming I'm right that they're the ones framing me."

"Why would Corbin frame you?" Ellie asked. "You used Erzulie's aspect on him. He is in love with you."

I sighed. "Love is weird. He tried to kill me before to make me his queen in hell. Framing me doesn't seem nearly so drastic a measure."

Tommy cleared his throat. "It's possible he's simply trying to create chaos. He wants to unsettle you, force you to abandon everything and everyone you've relied on in the past. That way, you'd have to turn to him for help."

I snorted. "That sounds like a desperate move."

Ellie shook her head. "Unrequited love is desperate by definition. I think Tommy might be on to something."

"How long will it take for you to use this drawing as a veve and attempt to summon Nico?"

Holland smirked. "Give me ten minutes, fifteen at most. I'm not going to try it here. We don't have the supplies necessary. I'll need to go down to the gymnasium. That's where students of voodoo often practice such rituals. There are altars already set up for rituals like this. I'll just need to make a few modifications. I'll also need to shed a little blood. The blood I use, though, might give Nico a particular craving for the one who gives the blood."

"Use mine!" Sarah piped up.

"You're a vampire," Holland said. "Your blood isn't the kind that satiates a vampire's cravings."

"Right," Sarah muttered. "Still, I wouldn't object if he took a little extra interest in me."

Ellie giggled. "I could help you with that."

Sarah sighed. "I don't want that. If Nico is going to love me, I want him to love me for me. Not because of Erzulie's influence."

"Wise choice," I said. "Do what you can, Holland. If that doesn't work, I'll either have to go back to Casa do Diabo or we'll have to try to hunt down Corbin and Bianca on our own."

Holland grabbed my hand. "Come with me. This summoning will require blood."

"You have blood. Why do you need me?"

"You can awaken the power within my blood and greatly increase the power of the summoning. Our chances of success are far better with your help."

I tilted my head. "You want me to exsanguinate you? Partially, I mean?"

"That's unnecessary," Holland said. "I want you to activate the power within my blood when I shed it over the veve. I assume that's not a problem."

I smirked. "It's elementary, my dear Holland. Elementary."

Holland rolled her eyes. "Follow me. You too, Sarah. If I'm able to contact Nico, but he cannot manifest, your skills might help."

Chapter 8

HOLLAND TOOK MY CRUDE sketch of Nico's crest. Sarah and I followed her into the elevator that led down from Annabelle's office. Holland took us to the gymnasium.

There were a few students at the academy practicing their skills. Savanna was there with her patron Loa, Sogbo, who possessed the form of a gray-haired man in his early sixties. Three clouds floated in the air about six feet over Savanna's head. She was casting lightning bolts between the clouds that formed a triangle of electric light over her.

When we entered the room Sogbo raised his hand and the clouds and lightning vanished.

"Hey guys!" Savanna exclaimed. She ran over to us and touched my shoulder. A shock passed from her fingers to my skin.

"Ouch!"

Savanna giggled. "Sorry about that. I've got quite the charge flowing at the moment."

I rubbed the spot on my shoulder where she shocked me. It was sore like a sunburn. "Maybe don't touch people when you're electric like that."

Savanna winced. "Better you than someone else. You'll heal, right?"

I chuckled. The pain was already fading. "Perks of being a vampire."

Sogbo strolled toward us. "What are you doing here?"

Holland cleared her throat. "My apologies, Loa Sogbo. We're going to summon Ghede Niccolo. He's gone missing and we think it might be important."

Sogbo tilted his head. "Do you have his veve?"

Holland handed Sogbo my sketch. "This won't do."

"It's his crest. He uses something like it to seal his correspondence. At least he used to back in the day."

Sogbo cleared his throat. "Give me just a moment."

Sogbo pulled a charcoal pencil from behind his ear and flipped the page over. He started sketching a different veve. It was similar to the one I drew, but the shield was a little larger. The upper edge had a more concave shape than the flat line I drew. He added a script to the middle that had a few more curls at the ends of the letters and redrew the world serpent at the border with its mouth swallowing its tail on the opposite side.

"One advantage of being a Loa is that we knew one another's veves. This one is brand new, but I can assure you, it will be more effective than what you drew before."

"Thank you," Holland said. "I wasn't aware the Petro Loa were familiar with the veves of the Ghede."

Sogbo chuckled. "My brother, Bade, possesses this host with me. He wishes to tell you he finds your ignorance amusing."

Holland snorted. "My ignorance?"

"No disrespect," Sogbo said. "My brother can be brash. The point is simply that there is much to what we are, and how we relate to the other nanchons or families of our kind that not even the most astute mambos or hougans understand."

I raised an eyebrow. "So there are two demigods within you right now?"

"My brother and I are inseparable," Sogbo said. "Our abilities work in concert. Bade can harness the wind. I can spin his wind into a tempest."

"Technically," Savanna added, "I have the aspects of both."

"You're certain this veve will work?" Holland asked.

"Absolutely," Sogbo smiled widely. "Provided you give the young Ghede a suitable offering."

"Why are you helping us?" Holland asked. "It's usually against the rules for the Loa to work with students of other schools."

Sogbo shook his head. "You are not a student, you're a graduate. The rules don't apply. Besides, I'm aware of our queen's current predicament."

I gulped. "You mean that she's been arrested?"

Sogbo bowed his head slightly. "For your sake, no less. Anything that threatens our queen is a threat to all of us. The integrity of Vilokan and our continued existence without interference from the outside world depends on her success and yours."

"Mine?" I asked. "You mean, that I don't get arrested, too?"

Sogbo laughed. "More than that! You are a guardian, are you not?"

I nodded. "That's right. I'm supposed to monitor the convergences."

"Then you are to us as the gatekeepers were before. Our kind dwell in Guinee when we are not on earth. Our continued interest in this world has always depended on the cooperation of the gatekeepers. Now that you are a guardian, we expect you to cooperate with us in the same manner. Were you to be removed from the picture, and other beings took control of the convergence, it would not only be devastating to this world. It would compromise our ability to come to the aid of the mambos and hougans who depend on us."

I cocked my head. "If I was compromised, you would lose your power on earth?"

"Eventually, perhaps. Your purpose is greater than stopping whatever creatures might invade the earth from other realms. You must also maintain the connections, the balance, that the gates between worlds permit. If that balance was altered, or entities like the Loa, or even the angels, could no longer interact with the world, there's no telling the devastation that might result. There is much we do here that goes unnoticed by most. We prefer it that way. While our presence might not be widely known, our absence would surely be felt. Consider my skills, and those I'm teaching young Savanna to master. Even with my assistance and that of my students, the devastation caused by storms is profound. Our very city has suffered much in recent decades. Hurricane Katrina, for instance."

"You could have stopped it?"

Sogbo shook his head. "The earth itself has powers that exceed those that even the collective power of the Loa possess. We cannot stop every disaster from occurring, but without our gentle nudge, things would be much worse."

I scratched my head. "I suspect the same applies to the other Loa?"

"Think of a world where humans were unrestrained in matters of war? Ogoun cannot prevent every conflict, but he can help bring those that arise to a speedier resolution. How treacherous would the seas be without La Sirene? How would the world's ecosystems be impacted if La Sirene and Agwe did not defend marine life? Without

Erzulie, whose power breeds charity, how many millions would suffer? Without the Ghede, a peaceful transition to the next life would be impossible. Vengeful spirits and haunts would be a regular and recognized threat rather than fodder for the Travel Channel."

I brushed my hair out of my eyes and tucked it behind my ears. "I get it. You're important."

Sogbo bowed his head. "Indeed. That means *you* are every bit as necessary a presence in the world, along with the other appointed guardians, who are consigned to a similar fate of heroism without acclaim and risk without recognition."

I shrugged. "I don't know if I deserve any rewards. Saving the world, and continuing to exist in a place not ruled by a savage vampire, overrun by devils or dragons, or swarming with unseelie faeries and wraiths, is reward enough."

"Still, Miss Bradbury, you have my gratitude. We Loa recognize and value your contribution."

Holland snorted. "If you two are going to screw, screw. We have work to do."

I shuddered. "Ew!"

Sogbo tilted his head. "My host is not so repulsive."

"Your host is old, dude! You look old enough to be my father."

Sogbo grinned. "I have no desire for intercourse with you."

"Excuse me? *No* desire? I'm insulted!"

"That's not my point. You're lovely. I only meant—"

I interrupted Sogbo with a chortle. "I'm not offended. I'm giving you shit."

Sogbo furrowed his brow. "I do not desire shit. If you ever intend to summon me, shit is not an appropriate offering."

Savanna giggled and covered her mouth with her well-manicured French-tipped nails. "It's an expression, Soggie."

Holland tilted her head. "Soggie?"

Sogbo shook his head "That's what she calls me."

Savanna nodded resolutely. "Annabelle has her Oggie. I have my Soggie."

Holland smirked. "Hailey has her doggie."

I raised an eyebrow. "Connor is a wolf, thank you very much. He's not a dog. There's a difference."

Holland shrugged. "No judgment. Far be it from me to kink shame."

"What are your kinks?" Savanna asked.

Holland narrowed her eyes. "You're too young to know about the things I enjoy."

"I'm sixteen!" Savanna crossed her arms in front of her chest. "I'm practically an adult."

Holland narrowed her eyes. "If you tried to Google the things I enjoy, you'd get one response: WTF."

"We get it," Savanna said. "You are into whips and chains. Everyone knows you dig that sort of thing."

"Whips and chains?" Holland huffed. "Please. Try the Pear of Anguish."

"What the hell is that?" Savanna asked.

I shook my head. "You don't want to know."

"I'm surprised you know what it is," Holland said. "I'm impressed."

I snorted. "Oh, I didn't say I knew what it was. I'm content with my ignorance."

Holland shrugged. "To each her own."

Holland took the reworked veve toward an altar on the wall on the opposite side of the entrance to the gymnasium. There were several altars, stations, where students could practice their summonings. Nothing more than a curtain divided them. I didn't know how it worked, but I imagined the curtains were imbued with some kind of enchantment that silenced whatever magic might be swirling next door. Curtains were handy like that. Blackout curtains were a blessing to vampires who realized that living in windowless houses severely limited our options. Soundproof curtains were a thing—though I wasn't sure how effective they were. Magic proof curtains were new to me, but I didn't have any reason to doubt their efficacy. Annabelle ran this place, and she didn't half-ass anything when it came to the security of Vilokan and the safety of the voodoo underworld's citizens.

Sogbo—who was apparently joined by Bade within his host—and Savanna resumed their lessons. When someone is casting thunderstorms nearby, it can be distracting. Holland didn't seem to notice. She'd practiced her summoning in the gymnasium for years. Presuming the veve worked, and the blood offering would appeal to Nico, there was no reason to think Holland couldn't pull it off.

A part of me was anxious Nico would show up and be pissed. I didn't listen and stay in the cabin. For all I knew, he showed up there just after Pauli and I left. I had a feeling, though, he'd gotten tangled up in something. I doubted he was in any danger. How could Niccolo the Damned, now a demigod as well as vampire numero uno, ever be in real danger? Still, I had his phone. He didn't have a way to contact me—unless he used someone else's phone. He wouldn't do that, though, unless there was an emergency that required my assistance. I doubted he'd ever admit he needed my help. Nico wasn't the sort of guy who asked for help. He was the do-it-yourself kind of guy, the sort who would struggle to do a two-person job alone when a willing assistant was standing only a few feet away.

Holland scattered several items on the altar. The few summonings I witnessed usually involved a flask, a glass of red wine, or some kind of premium tobacco, usually cigars. Sometimes flowers were included. This time, though, all Holland scattered were a variety of dried herbs. I didn't need to ask her what they were for. As a witch, I worked with herbs on the regular. Arnica blossoms helped increase psychic energies and probably amplified the power of the summoning. Astragalus root offered protection from any harmful magical blowback. When you're summoning demigods, while not a part of my regular practice, it was probably a wise precaution. Citronella was supposed to attract friends. It made sense. Nico was a friend. In this instance, though, given the similarity between vampires and mosquitos, I wasn't sure if it was the best choice. It wasn't my spell, though. Meadowsweet was a staple for altar offerings across a variety of traditions. It ameliorated any kind of discord or disharmony. It was supposed to make the summoner seem more desirous and worthy to the summoned.

Pretty standard stuff. There were debates about the uses of some herbs and elements across traditions, but most of the basic uses were universal.

"What is Nico's preferred vessel?" Holland asked.

I tilted my head. "What do you mean by a vessel?"

"Does he prefer to drink from a glass, a mug, or a flask?"

I tilted my head. "He prefers to drink from the carotid or femoral artery. Occasionally the wrist."

"He never takes his blood in a secondary vessel?" Holland asked.

I shrugged. "I don't know. I haven't seen him feed more than once or twice. He tends toward high society. If he uses a vessel at all, a wine glass is far more likely than a flask."

Holland nodded. "Using my body as a vessel for this ritual is too risky. Besides, presenting my femoral artery is too forward for a first summoning. I rarely allow a Loa access like that until our second or third encounter, and even then, he has to work for it."

I pressed my lips together. "Just use a wine glass. I'll heal your wound when we're done."

"Very well." Holland took a small blade from a cabinet. She disinfected it over an open flame. She set a wineglass on the altar, then slit her palm over it, squeezing her fist as her blood drizzled into the bowl of the glass, the red hue reflected down the stem.

That was my cue. I recovered my wand and aimed it directly into the glass. I didn't need to channel extra magic into the glass. Drawing out a bit of Holland's soul, bringing it to the surface, added flavorful notes that a vampire like Nico would surely appreciate.

"Ghede Niccolo!" Holland shouted. "I bid you, come! Bless us with your deathly presence! Shower us with your favor."

I tilted my head. Showering with Nico hadn't ever occurred to me. I was pretty sure Sarah had entertained the notion once or twice.

As Holland made her appeal, the veve Sogbo drew glowed with vibrant red energies. As the magic pulsed through the veve, the blood faded from the glass, as if someone was sucking it out of the bottom through an invisible straw.

The veve exploded. The glass shattered. The force of whatever magic was released sent Holland flying to the ground, skidding more than ten feet on her back across the waxed gymnasium floor. I ran to Holland and helped her up.

"What happened?" I asked.

Sarah sighed. I'd almost forgotten she was there since she'd remained quiet since we arrived. "Nico happened."

"What do you mean?" I asked.

"He's not himself."

"She's right," Holland said, rubbing the back of her head. "We're too late. Someone *else* has already summoned him and bound him to their will."

Chapter 9

HOLLAND PACED BACK AND forth across the gymnasium floor. "Only someone with a Ghede's aspect could summon him. Anyone else couldn't overpower my summons."

I rubbed my brow. "So a mambo or hougan is involved?"

Holland stomped her foot. "It has to be. It doesn't make sense. If you're right, and Corbin and Bianca are the shifters, I can't think of anyone in the voodoo world who would take their side."

I rubbed my brow. "There are hougans and mambos who aren't members of Vilokan, right? Bokors and caplatas."

Holland nodded. "That's the only reasonable explanation. What I did before, when I bound Baron Samedi and Ghede Nibo to my will, that wasn't exactly accepted practice."

"You broke the rules? You rebel, you."

"It was with good reason. The rules are more like guidelines. Every rule has exceptions, especially when it comes to dealing with enemies who have no rules at all. Sometimes, for the sake of preserving the balance, we have to bend the rules a bit."

"Annabelle knew what you did. She was with you when you summoned the Ghede before."

Holland clenched her fists. "It was her idea!"

"We can't assume that whoever bound Nico is also working with the shifters. They may have bound Nico for unrelated reasons."

"That's a part of the problem," Holland added. "Nico is *new.* Few vodouisants even know he's among the Ghede now. We had to pull his veve out of our asses."

"Not exactly," I added. "Sogbo gave it to us."

Holland nodded. "Which means whoever is responsible likely got the veve necessary from another Loa. Since it had to be someone with a Ghede's aspect, it had to be a Ghede Loa who provided the veve."

I shrugged. "No problem. You summoned him before. Call up Baron Samedi. Ask him who did it."

Holland rubbed her brow. "I can't bind him, not like before. Not without Annabelle's authorization."

"I thought rules were meant to be bent when it was for the greater good?"

Holland placed her hands on her hips and took a deep breath. "You're right. We can't do it here. There are safeguards, wards in here, that prevent anyone from doing anything like that within Vilokan."

"Didn't you do it at the convergence in Manchac last time?"

Holland nodded. "Performing a summons near the convergence helped draw the Baron and Ghede Nibo to us. I can summon Nibo just about anywhere. He's less likely to have the information we need though. We should summon Baron Samedi, but he's notoriously difficult to call forth. The convergence increases our chances of success."

I nodded. "Alright. Pauli is still back in Annabelle's office. At least he was when we left. He can take us there."

"Alright," Holland said. "I don't like this. Annabelle has worked with the Baron in his green, or benevolent, nature before. If I summon and bind him, we might get his darker red persona."

"If he's bound, does it matter?" I asked.

"Binding a Loa is tricky. It's also not a hundred percent. Last time, despite binding them, they helped us because we shared a common interest. If the Baron is not inclined to help, bound or not, he can simply return to Guinee. I can't force him to help, I can only direct him to a point, so far as doing so doesn't piss him off. He may not be willing to assist us unless we agree to terms."

I sighed. "You mean he'll want to make a bargain?"

"Even if he appears in his green aspect, he isn't the sort who lends aid to mortals without something in it for himself. The last time, our plan to capture the wraiths and return them to vampire hell was enough. We don't have that kind of leverage anymore."

"I have a question," Sarah chimed in. "If a Loa can simply resist, even if he's bound, by returning to Guinee, why wouldn't Nico do that if whoever bound him is up to no good?"

Holland rolled her eyes. "Because Nico can't go to Guinee. He was made different. So long as the demiurge is out there, he's stuck here. When the other Ghede elevated him to Loa status, they did so for the purpose of thwarting anyone who might use the energy of Kalyptos to threaten the Ghede again. He doesn't have the luxury of resistance."

"It's the best shot we have," I said. "Do you need any supplies to summon the Baron?"

"I can grab what I need from here."

Holland picked up a handful of supplies from the cabinet near the altar station where we failed to summon Nico before. We left and returned to Annabelle's office.

Ellie was still surfing the internet on Annabelle's computer. Tommy had his feet crossed over Annabelle's desk. Pauli was gone.

"Where did Pauli go?" I asked.

Ellie looked up from the computer. "He said he had a sudden craving for kielbasa and left. What a strange thing to want at this time of night?"

I sighed. "For Pauli, that's code for something else."

Holland shook her head. "Fucking Pauli."

I picked up Annabelle's landline phone from her desk. Cellphones didn't work in Vilokan. I looked up his number on Nico's phone and dialed it.

It went straight to voicemail. His greeting sounded through the speaker on Annabelle's phone: "Hey, bitches! You reached Pauli! If you're calling for head, I'm currently booked through 2025. If you're calling for any other reason, leave a message."

I was about to tell Pauli to call us back ASAP when a female voice chimed in. "This voice mailbox is currently full."

"Well shit," I huffed.

"Fucking Pauli," Holland muttered for the second time in as many minutes.

I nodded. "We can take the farm truck. It's just a couple of blocks away. Ellie, can you stay here in case Pauli comes back?"

"Sure!" Ellie smiled widely. "I was just about to place an order. Check out this My Little Pony 'Friendship is Magic' t-shirt that's on sale!"

I stared at Ellie blankly for about two seconds. "Whatever. Tommy, you should probably stay."

Tommy huffed. "I can help. I know I'm only a youngling, but I'm still useful."

"We don't have enough seats in the farm truck. We need Sarah. She might have a better chance of picking up on the vampires involved outside of Vilokan. I know you're useful, Tommy. I'm not saying you aren't. It's just a matter of logistics. Three people in the front of that truck is already cramped."

"I'll ride in the bed of the truck! I can lie down. No one will know I'm there."

Ellie tilted her head. "I could use your company."

"You haven't said two words to me this whole time we've been sitting here."

"That's not true. Without your help, I might have settled on that Malibu Barbie backpack. Thanks to you, I have money left for this t-shirt!"

Tommy huffed. "Anything you show me, my answer is going to be the same. It sucks."

"Rude!" Ellie snapped.

Holland chuckled. "Bring him with us. I never thought I'd say something like this, but he doesn't deserve that kind of torture."

I took a deep breath. "Alright. You can come. But you have to listen to what I say. If the cops pull us over, run. If things get out of hand in the swamp, and we get in over our heads, you need to come back here and get help."

"Understood!" Tommy jumped up from his chair. "Let's do this!"

Chapter 10

We checked the security monitors before we left. Annabelle had an infrared camera mounted over the place on the side of St. Louis Cathedral in Pere Antoine alley where the door to Vilokan appeared to those of us who had access—usually it meant someone with the aspect of a Loa.

Ellie knew how to work the security system. The camera could turn to give us a view up and down the alley. I had to assume that the police were monitoring the area. They knew about Vilokan, but I wasn't sure if they knew where the entrance was. It wasn't supposed to be common knowledge, but when you have a community of hundreds, and people come and go through a doorway that magically appears and vanishes again, keeping it a secret was sort of a lost cause. It only took one person to talk, or someone to use the door without checking to be sure no one saw them do it, for word to get out. For most people, given all the supernatural lore surrounding New Orleans, the notion of a doorway on the side of the cathedral wasn't the most scandalous or even the strangest thing that circulated through the rumor mill. About half of the paranormal and supernatural activity that people believed existed in New Orleans was pure fiction. The rest, though? It would shock most people to learn exactly how much of it was real. The police knew about Vilokan. If word circulated about the location of the entrance, they'd certainly take note.

We didn't see anyone in the alley. That didn't mean the cops weren't watching just outside.

"It's too risky," Holland said. "I might be able to come and go just fine, but you can't. They're looking for you."

I sighed. "I need to be there."

"Why?" Holland asked. "You can't summon a Ghede."

I sighed. "You said that the Baron might require a bargain."

Holland nodded. "I did. You aren't seriously considering offering him your soul in exchange for information about Nico, are you?"

My eyes darted back and forth. "The idea occurred to me. Look, Baron Samedi told us before that he was going to allow vampires to be born with souls."

"I have my soul," Tommy said. "He gave it back to me. I haven't noticed much of a difference."

Holland shook her head. "He will not be all that interested in your soul. No offense, Tommy."

"But he would be curious about mine," I said. "He's never seen mine since, apparently, I held onto it when I was turned. He has to at least be curious why."

"Which is why you'd have to be an idiot to offer it to him," Holland said. "You don't know how it would affect you."

"I'm not an idiot. If I offer my soul, I'm going to need more than information. Everything has a cost, right? I can drive a hard bargain."

Holland shook her head. "No one gets the upper hand in a bargain with Baron Samedi. Even if you think you're getting the better end of the deal, you aren't."

I shrugged. "It doesn't hurt to see what we can find out through negotiation. I don't have to accept his bargain. He just has to think I'm considering it. We just have to get him talking. With a few leading questions, we might get a few clues, at the very least."

Holland sighed. "It's still not going to be easy to get you out of Vilokan unnoticed."

"They didn't see me when I came here."

"You don't know that," Holland said. "Maybe they saw you and now they're just waiting for you to leave."

"There's another way in and out of Vilokan. We used the slide from Marie Laveau's tomb before. I'm pretty sure the cops *don't* know about that."

Holland stared at me like she thought I was a moron. "That tunnel is steep, narrow, and slick. There's no way you can climb out of it."

"Tommy and I can. We have vampire skills."

"It's too damn slick, Hailey. Your speed will not make much difference."

I bit my thumb. Then I turned and pressed the door to open the elevator. "I have another idea."

"What are you thinking?" Holland asked.

I smirked. "I'm going to go tell Savanna to blow me."

Holland shook her head and chuckled. "If she has that kind of power."

"Sogbo said that Bade was also within his host, right? If Savanna can't do it, well, the gods can blow me instead."

Holland tilted her head. "I wouldn't phrase it that way. The Loa don't typically respond well to that kind of thing."

I rolled my eyes. "I wouldn't actually tell him to blow me. I have tact!"

"*You* have tact? Yeah, and I'm Miss Congeniality."

I chuckled. "I see your point. Still, Sogbo said he is duty-bound to help. All I have to do is ask."

Holland joined me as we returned to the gymnasium. Sogbo was still training Savanna. When we entered the gymnasium, a small tornado was blasting across the polished wood floor.

Savanna released the whirlwind when she saw us. I waved at her and we met in the middle of the floor.

"We need your assistance," I said. "I see you are working with wind."

Sogbo nodded. "She's wielding my brother's aspect, well."

I tilted my head. "Does Bade ever talk?"

Sogbo rolled his eyes. "Does he ever. If I give him the reins, he won't *stop* talking. He's a real blowhard."

I snickered. "I see what you did there."

Savanna nodded. "Bade handles most of the lectures. The last one he gave took three hours."

I winced. "Ouch. That must've sucked."

"Nope!" Savanna giggled. "It blew!"

I glanced at Holland. "See! They have a sense of humor. I don't know what you were so worried about."

Savanna cocked her head. "What do you need?"

I chuckled. "I was going to ask you to blow me. We need a straight wind strong enough to carry Tommy and me up a tunnel that leads out of Vilokan to Marie Laveau's tomb."

Savanna scratched her head and looked at Sogbo. "We haven't practiced straight winds. Do you think Bade could do it for us?"

"Better," Sogbo said. "It sounds to me like a learning opportunity."

"You can create enough wind to blow Tommy and me at the same time?" I asked.

Sogbo grinned. "Savanna can. She's talented."

Savanna smiled widely. "I really am!"

"We appreciate the help," Holland said. "Pauli isn't around. We don't know where he went. Otherwise we'd ask him to handle this."

Savanna huffed. "I'm your second choice? I'm offended!"

"Trust me," I grinned. "I'd rather not be Pauli's sloppy seconds."

"Or his sloppy thirds, or fourths, or fifths," Holland added.

"Well, lucky for you, this will be my first time! Don't worry, though, I have excellent teachers."

Chapter 11

HOLLAND HAD THE CODE to the security door that led to the emergency Vilokan entrance—in this case, the exit. I made sure to tell her where the farm truck was parked so she could meet us there. Sarah joined us. She'd been watching the monitors and said she'd seen an officer patrolling past one side of the alley. We weren't sure if the police would recognize her. She didn't get out much. Leaving through the door in Pere Antoine alley was too risky. That meant Savanna was going to need to muster enough wind to blow three of us. Holland wasn't a suspect and the harsh winds it would take to force us through the tunnel was more than a mortal could handle blasting up her backside. Tommy, Sarah, and I could handle it.

Sogbo was confident that Savanna could do it. She just had to keep her focus and allow the power to flow at a constant rate. I knew little about wielding the powers of Sogbo and Bade, but channeling any magic at a constant rate can be difficult. Magic is volatile by nature. Most witches weren't very powerful, not because they couldn't channel large amounts of energy, but because they couldn't control it.

If Sogbo was confident, and Savanna was as well, I didn't have any reason to question it. The worst that might happen was that the wind wouldn't be enough and we would go sliding back down the chute on our butts.

I went first. Sarah was in line to go second and Tommy would pull up the rear—while the air blasted up his.

I crawled into the bottom of the channel on all fours. Sogbo directed Savanna, telling her how to access and focus Bade's wind.

Savanna lowered her hands right over my ass. I took the lead and started crawling up as fast as I could. The surface was slick. Holland was right. Without Savanna's help, we'd never make it. Still, I wanted to get a little distance between Savanna's hands and my ass. Taking the full force of her blast in my keister wasn't my idea of a good time.

The wind blew, gently at first, then the force intensified. Before I knew it, there was no reason to even try climbing. I felt like one of those cannisters at the bank drive-through. I covered my head with my hands to prevent goose eggs and concussions. I'd heal, sure, but that didn't mean it wouldn't hurt.

Eventually, I blasted out of the tunnel and crashed into a stone wall in Marie Laveau's tomb. The wind blowing out of the hole was so strong I was afraid it would blow the mausoleum apart. So far, though, the structure remained intact. I pushed open the door to release some of the air pressure. The force of Savanna's power was so strong I had to step outside. I didn't have a mirror, but I was pretty sure I was in for a bad hair night.

A few seconds later, Sarah tumbled out of the chute. Tommy flew out about thirty seconds after.

His eyes were wide, as if he'd just been shell-shocked. I couldn't hold in my laughter. Sarah didn't say much. She looked relieved that it was over.

The wind died down, and I forced the door shut again. I made a mental note to come back and seal the door again later. St. Louis Cemetery No. 1 wasn't open to the public, and there weren't many who knew about the secret entrance to Vilokan, but prudence dictated we keep the mausoleum locked up.

"Well, that was a rush!" I exclaimed.

Tommy shook his head. "I feel violated."

"I feel you," Sarah added.

I chuckled. "We need to go around the block to avoid the cops. It's a short walk to the farm truck. Holland will meet us there."

Since my face was all over the news, I still had to be careful. Even if we didn't run into the cops, if someone recognized me, it could create problems we didn't need.

Tommy and Sarah stood on either side of me, blocking my profile from any passersby. I kept my eyes down, avoiding eye contact with anyone, my blonde hair pulled forward and obscuring as much of my face as possible.

No one screamed or pointed at me. Then again, if they thought I was some kind of mass murderer, the last thing anyone would want to do was let me know they'd noticed me.

We moved at a brisk pace. Fast enough to minimize our time in public, but not so quick that we'd draw unnecessary attention.

When we arrived at the farm truck, Tommy climbed in the bed and laid down. Sarah got in the passenger side. I got in the driver's side.

We waited for Holland. She arrived about five minutes later. She'd made better time than I expected. Getting blown up a chute, as unpleasant as it was, was faster than climbing the stairs out of Vilokan to Pere Antoine alley. Holland had a backpack full of supplies for the summoning ritual. She tossed it in the bed.

"Ouch!" Tommy shouted.

Holland chuckled. "Sorry. Didn't see you there."

Holland hopped in the truck, and Sarah scooted over to the middle.

It wasn't easy to shift gears on the truck with a middle passenger. I made do as I pulled onto the streets and with the farm truck's engine rumbling, we made our way toward Manchac Swamp.

I parked the truck in our usual spot. The side of a rarely traveled gravel road.

There wasn't a clean way to get to the convergence. We'd made the trek through the marsh enough that I knew the best way that avoided most of the muck. Still, my shoes were caked with mud by the time we arrived. Tommy hadn't fared quite as well. He tripped over his own feet once or twice, braced himself, then wiped the sweat from his brow, leaving a brown streak across his forehead.

Tommy didn't realize he'd muddied his face, and I wasn't about to point it out. He'd find out soon enough and wonder why no one told him. Sort of like the time I sat on a chocolate bar and no one bothered to mention that it looked like I'd shat myself until several hours later. Tommy's situation was slightly less embarrassing.

Holland took her backpack off her shoulders and dropped it on the ground. She unzipped it and retrieved a blanket that she spread out over the convergence site.

"A blanket can function as a make-shift altar in a pinch," Holland explained, as she set out several other items she meant to offer the Baron. A flask containing whiskey or rum—I didn't bother asking which. It was all the same to me. I was only sixteen when I was turned, and being a vampire, getting drunk wasn't very easy. I lacked any actual experience or familiarity with alcohol. All I knew was that it all burned on the way down, caused a temporary warmth in my gut, then before I could experience any kind of intoxication my vampirism was already at work to nullify its effects. I'd have to chug an entire bottle, which wasn't enjoyable or pleasant, to get so much as a buzz. It wasn't worth it.

Holland set out several herbs, the same ones she used in our failed attempt to summon Nico.

Nico's phone rang from within my pocket. I checked it. "You won't believe this."

"It's Pauli, isn't it?" Sarah asked.

I nodded and answered the phone.

"Pauli, where the hell did you go? We needed your help."

"Sorry!" Pauli interjected. "I had an appointment. I don't make a habit of stiffing my clients—unless that's what they pay for."

I snorted. "I don't want to know. We're at the convergence in Manchac. We had to sneak out of Vilokan. It wasn't easy."

"I'll be right there!" Pauli hung up without apologizing or making excuses.

Holland huffed. "Don't make me say it again."

I chuckled. "I'll say it for you. Fucking Pauli!"

Not two seconds later, a rainbow flash signaled his impending arrival. He appeared in boa constrictor form in the grass and slithered up my leg. He could still talk as a snake. "Forgot my clothes. I think I'll stay like this."

I nodded as Pauli draped himself over my shoulders. "It's probably for the best."

"What's the plan?" Pauli asked.

"We're going to summon Baron Samedi. We believe someone figured out how to summon Nico and bind him. We're going to find out from the Baron who did it."

Pauli hissed. "Good luck with that. The Baron can be a bitch sometimes."

I chuckled. "You call everyone that."

"Yeah, well, when it comes to the Baron, I mean it."

"We have it handled," Holland said as she unrolled a vinyl replica of Baron Samedi's veve and flattened it over the middle of the rug. The veve looked like a two-tiered altar, a pair of Xs on the right and left. A Christian cross ascended from a third tier, a smaller platform above the altar. Two more Xs were sketched over the horizontal crosspiece. Two small caskets were depicted a couple of inches removed from the cross on either side. To an outsider, the use of Christian imagery in a voodoo veve surely seemed odd. However, most vodouisants understood their faith was a combination of French Catholicism and African religion. "Everyone stay back. If the Baron responds to my summoning, he'll need some space."

Tommy, Sarah, and I stepped back as far as we could. Dry ground was a premium in Manchac Swamp. We couldn't give Holland more than a few paces' worth of space.

Holland started chanting something. For a girl who grew up in Vilokan, she rarely had much of an accent. When she started doing her voodoo, or was visiting with other native Vilokanians, the Creole got thick.

"Baron Samedi!" Holland began. "Vous summon nous. Come to us, Loa of death! First of the Ghede! Mé bind nous to mine will, so long as nous traverse this earthly plane. Mé bind nous to your aspect in me, to the rum, to the veve, the Baron la Croix. These offerings three like a stranded cord tether nous to me. Free nous be to depart if my will conflicts with totchen."

Holland repeated variations of the same petition twice. Each time she spoke louder than the time before. Wind swirled around us, centered on the convergence. Holland started shouting her petition as red energies joined the whirlwind.

The same red energy blasted from Holland's eyes and the veve. The swirling vortex concentrated around Holland and the make-shift altar until a pillar of red energies formed over the veve.

The energies formed into the appearance of Baron Samedi. He didn't have a host. Without a host, a Loa could appear but couldn't wield his own power apart from the mambo or hougan who summoned him. Nico was different. He had a body forged from the power of Kalyptos within him.

Baron Samedi's natural form was haunting. He always wore a suit, black and dingy, reflecting the style of a bygone era. He wore a top hat and held a flask in his hand. That's how he sealed his bargains. Make a deal with the Baron, take a sip from his flask, and the terms of the bargain were sealed and immutable. That is to say, once you made a bargain, you were bound to the terms *unless* the Baron willfully relinquished his claim—which he never did.

Baron Samedi's eyes glowed red—a sign that he wasn't with us in his more benevolent persona. So far as I knew, Annabelle was one of the few mambos who could draw out his better demon. She didn't have the aspect of the Ghede, but her connection to Guinee and the Tree of Life gave her power and influence, a power that the Baron himself craved. More than once, through the years, Baron Samedi had tried to steal Isabelle, the spirit within Annabelle, to bind her to himself. Thankfully, Annabelle prevailed in each encounter. To put it mildly, while Baron Samedi could occasionally aid us and do good—especially in his green aspect—he always had his own agenda. We had to choose our words carefully.

Baron Samedi turned around and examined his surroundings. He fixed his eyes on Holland, then turned to look at the rest of us. He focused on me. "Where is Miss Mulledy?"

I snorted. "Annabelle is in jail."

Baron Samedi's eyes rolled back in his head. He started laughing. "I see that!"

I tilted my head. "You are looking through another vampire's eyes?"

"Of course I am! Any whose souls I still possess I can access. That excludes you and your progeny, of course."

Sarah shook her head. "But not me."

"Precisely," Baron Samedi smirked. "You can do just as I, sweet Sarah. Every vampire has my aspect, though not all of them can access every facet of my power."

"By cycling blood from humans," I added. "We can gain new powers."

"Certainly, but those powers latent in human blood are not the same. Sometimes, the human a vampire bites, if the human has my aspect, grants the vampire access to my abilities."

"That's how I got my ability?" Sarah asked. "I wasn't aware I ever bit a mambo or a hougan."

"But you did!" Baron Samedi grinned widely. "Do you remember the young man whose blood granted you your ability?"

Sarah nodded. "I could never forget. Back when I lived in Exeter, I rarely left my house. The man whose blood gave me this ability came to me."

Baron Samedi nodded. "Rene Grégoire Fontenot."

Holland tilted her head. "He was a hougan. Recruited by Marie Laveau, herself and taught at the academy in the nineteenth century. He wrote a textbook for vodouisants who specialize in the Ghede."

"That was later," Baron Samedi said. "He started as a bokor. I sent him to you, Miss Sarah."

Sarah tilted her head. "He came to me. He offered himself to me. I allowed him to leave. I don't understand. Why would you send him to me?"

"He made a bargain with me years earlier. It was what I demanded."

"What was his bargain for?" Holland asked.

"And you still didn't answer my question," Sarah snapped. "Why did you send him to me?"

"One at a time, ladies."

I cleared my throat. "We need to know who summoned and bound Nico."

Baron Samedi narrowed his eyes. "I said *one* at a time. The bokor made a bargain that I would free him from the thrall of another insidious Loa named Kalfu. You're quite familiar with him, aren't you, Hailey?"

I snorted. When I'd first become a vampire, Kalfu deceived me into working with him in an effort to claim the crossroads, the path through Guinee that the Loa passed through back in the day, allowing them or preventing them from accessing earth of their own accord. "More familiar than I'd like."

"You wanted me to have this ability?" Sarah asked. "For years, all I could do with it was feel the death of vampires worldwide."

"It makes sense, does it not, that the first sensation you'd know once wielding my power is the one most intimate to my nature? I suspect that even now, the death of a vampire speaks to you more acutely than any other vision."

Sarah nodded. "It does."

"You are my conduit, Sarah. Through you and others like you, I have access to the sight of other vampires. This is how I've always worked. If you ever meet the stake and leave the earthly plane, I'll have to replace you with another."

I tilted my head. "You told me before you were willing to grant vampires their souls again precisely because you didn't need to see through them. You said that I'd proven that an ensouled vampire can serve your needs better than one whose soul you possess."

Baron Samedi grinned widely. "I was feeling a little green that day."

I grunted. It wasn't a shock that the red Baron might have a different view of what he'd told me when his green nature prevailed. "Of course you were."

Sarah scratched the back of her head. "Does this mean that I can only sense vampires if you are in possession of their human souls?"

Baron Samedi shook his head. "That's how it should work. It's how it used to work before your power evolved. It's a mystery, I must admit, how your skills have grown apart from my direct involvement. After all, while you are my conduit, I cannot see through your natural eyes despite having your soul. Your sight, to me, is replaced with the sight of every other vampire whose vision is cast into your mind."

"Who summoned and bound Nico?" I asked a second time. "Someone has taken him from us and I suspect is using him in ways he'd never accept."

Baron Samedi shook his head. "Niccolo has a soul. I cannot see through his eyes. As much as I'd love to bargain with you to provide this information, I do not have what you seek. Sarah, however, can see through his eyes in ways I cannot comprehend."

Sarah tilted her head. "Do you only see what visions I consciously call to mind?"

Baron Samedi laughed. "Not at all. I can see whatever I wish through you, Sarah. Anything your abilities allow you to see, I can witness, with or without your consent."

I bit my lip. "So you *can* see through souled vampires, like Nico?"

"That requires her consent. It is why I cannot see through your eyes, Hailey, but Sarah could. It's why she can sense Niccolo. She can provide the answers you seek."

"I don't know how!" Sarah shouted. "I've tried. That power of the demiurge within him creates some kind of interference."

Baron Samedi's eyes widened, and a sly grin split his face. "I can show you. For a price."

"Fuck that," I muttered.

"What's the price?" Sarah asked.

"Sarah!" I interjected. "Don't!"

Baron Samedi laughed. "Let me mount you. Be my host in the world."

"No, no, no!" I screamed.

Sarah narrowed her eyes. "For how long?"

"How about a week?" Baron Samedi proposed.

Holland cleared her throat. "You're bound to me, Baron. If you possess her, I'm still in control."

Baron Samedi tipped the brim of his top hat toward Holland. "Of course, mon petit chou chou."

I clenched my fists. "You only want to possess her so you can access the full breadth of her ability!"

Baron Samedi smirked. "Of course! For the first time, mon amie, I'll be able to see through your eyes."

I narrowed my eyes. "This isn't your call alone, Sarah."

"It's my body." Sarah shrugged. "It will help us find Nico?"

"Of course!" Baron Samedi clapped his hands together. "I will not bury your consciousness. I will not even hold the reins. You will remain in full control of your body unless you choose to take the back seat."

"I don't like this," I huffed. "Remember, when Baron Samedi makes a deal with you, you always end up with the short straw."

"But sometimes, little girl, the short straw is enough. What does it matter if I gain much if it helps you manage this pesky predicament you've found yourself in?"

"What will you gain, exactly, by seeing through my eyes?" I asked.

"It's a gamble," Baron Samedi admitted. "Think of it like a lottery ticket. I might scratch it and find I gain nothing at all."

"What are you trying to find out?" I asked. "I have a soul. Big whoop. You can't see through my eyes."

"It's quite simple," Baron Samedi said. "Of the thousands of vampires who've touched my aspect, you are the only one whose soul I couldn't touch. Color me curious. All I want to find out is how you did it."

"And you can discover that by using Sarah's abilities?" I asked.

Baron Samedi laughed. "Sarah has barely scratched the surface of what she might do. What she stands to gain is also a gamble. Everything I do, while accessing her abilities, she'll be able to do with ease forevermore."

"I won't allow him to harm any of you," Holland added. "The Baron might be a lion, but he's a lion on a leash."

Baron Samedi bowed his head slightly. "For the time being, this is true."

"You don't need a week," Sarah said. "I'll give you twenty-four hours."

A mischievous grin split Baron Samedi's face. "Give me forty-eight and you have a deal."

"Wait," I piped up. "If you make a bargain on these terms, you *must* leave her after forty-eight hours, correct?"

"I am bound to my agreements as much as those who enter into my bargains with me. Two days from now, no matter what occurs, I will be expelled from Sarah's body."

I narrowed my eyes. "If you do this, you must enter Sarah according to your green aspect."

Baron Samedi closed his eyes. He had them shut for nearly three seconds. When he opened them again, they glowed green. "Are you now convinced that I intend no harm?"

Sarah looked at me. I nodded. "Do what you want, Sarah."

"You have a deal." Sarah stepped up to the Baron. He handed her his flask. Sarah tilted it back and took a swig. When she did, the Baron's form disappeared, a green glow radiated from her eyes, then faded.

"It's done," Sarah said. "I can feel him inside of me."

"Where is Nico?" I asked.

Sarah took a deep breath and pressed her eyes shut. She gasped. "I can't believe it."

"You can't believe what?" I asked.

"He's locked himself in a tomb. There's a small altar. Can a Loa summon himself?"

Holland tilted her head. "I've never heard of that."

"I think he's bound himself to himself!"

"Why the hell would he do that?" I asked.

"It has something to do with Kalyptos. He's losing control."

Holland nodded. "Perhaps he thought if he bound himself he could restrain Kalyptos; keep the power under his thrall."

"Is it working?" I asked.

"I can't tell," Sarah said. "Baron Samedi is probing his thoughts and memories. It seems to be working, but I don't think it will for long."

"Why would the demiurge suddenly try to escape him?" Holland asked.

I shook my head. "I don't think it is. Someone else is trying to draw it out of him and use it. It must be Corbin."

"One second," Sarah said, pressing her eyes shut again. "I see a wolf. I see *you* Hailey. They're trying to break into Nico's tomb. It's a large mausoleum. Nico has barricaded the doors. Why doesn't he just fight them off?"

I shook my head. "Maybe he can't."

"Or he won't," Sarah said. "Whatever the case, we have to get to him and stop this."

"Can you tell if it's Corbin inhabiting Connor's wolf body? Is it Bianca impersonating me?"

Sarah nodded. "I'm sorry, Hailey."

"This damn intuition of mine," I huffed. "Sometimes it sucks being right."

Chapter 12

A SURGE OF WARMTH passed through my skull. I wasn't sure if it was Baron Samedi poking around in my head or paranoia. As much as I hated the arrangement, without it we wouldn't have known that Nico was holed up in a mausoleum while Corbin and Bianca were trying to steal the demiurge from him. I didn't have a clue *how* they were trying to do it, but when dealing with the powers of Barbelo, what I knew barely scratched the surface of the abounding mysteries. When dealing with a vampire as ancient and as devious as Corbin, there was no telling what he knew. This wasn't the first time he'd taken me by surprise. It also wasn't the first time he'd escaped death. He was like the corduroy of vampires. As much as I hated him, and wouldn't let him near my lady parts, he kept coming back.

I went through that phase briefly. Never again. It was evil. Corduroy, I mean. Same goes for Corbin.

We'd just come from St. Louis Cemetery No. 1. It was a big place, but Sarah said she'd seen a video camera mounted to the wall. Needless to say, security systems, not to mention electricity, weren't a common feature in mausoleums. It was the mausoleum originally owned by Alberto De Leonne, the original owner of Casa do Diabo—before anyone called it that. It was also where Nico spent two decades staked while his human self grew up, destined to get trapped in Guinee and sent back to the past as the world's first vampire.

If we could get there, I could use Nico's sire bond and compel Corbin to back off. I could even make him stake himself, which was certainly on my agenda—once I cleared my name.

Bianca was the wildcard. I had no control over her. She *hated* me, if for no other reason than I'd infected Corbin with Erzulie's power and made him love me. It was necessary when I did it, but since then, it had created a lot more problems than it originally solved. When a sociopath thinks he's in love, well, have you ever seen *Fatal Attraction?*

First, he wanted to make me his vampire queen. Then, he even took over hell temporarily and tried to have me killed so I could rule hell at his side. He might have been in Connor's wolf-form now, but what he had was hardly puppy love.

I'd have to deal with Bianca the old-fashioned way. With blood magic. I just wished I'd had time to study my grimoires and polish that spell. If Nico had come back to the cabin like he'd promised, the original plan might have worked. I could have studied the spell, learned how to control Bianca and Corbin, and handled them with ease. Even if I had all the purest ingredients for the spell, it would only last a few minutes. That's all I'd need. The cops were everywhere. If I forced her to reveal herself, it might not clear my name. There was no way to prove which one of us they saw on those cameras, but at the very least, it would raise questions about the truth. It would give me enough of a case to establish reasonable doubt.

I suspected that was why they were trying to extract Kalyptos from Nico. Nico hadn't used the power. It was raw and unformed, not like the power that Corbin and Bianca absorbed. They could use that power to do anything. There was no way to know what exactly they planned to do with it, but Corbin's plans were always the same. He wanted power. And he wanted me. What still wasn't clear was why they framed me to begin with. If Bianca's power was what she'd inherited from Nyx, she could have targeted anyone and become someone else's ideal. She targeted Corbin for a reason. If it was just her, I'd assume she did it out of spite. She hated that Corbin thought he loved me. She loved Corbin. She had for centuries. Since Corbin was with her in Connor's wolf shape, though, whatever she was doing, he supported. He was her sire. She couldn't do anything if he didn't want her to do it.

That thought gave me an idea. If I could use Nico's sire status over Corbin to control him, I could make him control her. We'd considered a similar tactic when facing the wraiths. It wasn't a viable option, then. This time was different.

I'd rarely used my sire bond to compel Tommy to do anything. It wasn't my style. Manipulating people or forcing them to obey doesn't really help them grow or mature. I hadn't even used Nico's sire bond but once—when I forced Corbin to leave Lucifer's form and gave the devil back his domain.

The spell to steal a sire's bond was simple, but it wasn't easy to pull off. It involved the use of a proxy sacrifice. It had to be a creature with equal or more mass than the vampire whose sire status you intended to claim. You had to consecrate the sacrifice in your own blood, give it the name of the vampire whose bond you hoped to swipe, and stake it as if it was a vampire. So long as the stake remained intact, the bond remained yours. There were a few other rules. For instance, you had to be on the same plane of existence for any of that to matter. When I took Nico's sire bond, I did it in hell. Corbin was there—he saw me do it, but I pulled it off before he could stop me. I used a hellhound as the proxy sacrifice and left hell before he could unstake the beast. That meant, since the beast and I were no longer on the same plane, it didn't matter. Separated by space and time, unstaking the hellhound couldn't rob me of Nico's sire bond. If I ever went *back* to hell, presuming Corbin unstaked the beast, or the devil did it himself, I'd probably lose the sire bond the second I entered that terrible realm.

If the spell was really so simple to do, why didn't more vampires do it? Why weren't vampires constantly stealing the sire bonds of vampires more powerful than they were? The reason was because outside of me, and Merrick, who was a dead vampire caught in the in-between, something like purgatory, no other vampires knew how it worked. Merrick used the spell to free himself of Nico's influence, then he took his grimoire with him that contained his notes on the spell, and hid it where no vampire would ever find it. In the in-between, in a cave guarded by the Seelie faeries.

Now that we had Pauli, the trip to the cemetery was simpler and a lot faster. We needed a plan.

"Can we all fit inside the mausoleum?" I asked.

Sarah nodded. "It's large enough. It isn't necessary, though. I can see through your eyes. I can hear what you hear. The Baron is awakening all kinds of power within me I couldn't control before."

“She’s right,” Holland added. “You go ahead of us and talk to Nico. Sarah will know when you’re ready for us, and Pauli can come back to take us to corner Corbin and Bianca.”

“Take us there first,” I told Pauli. “We need to talk to Nico so we know exactly the situation we’re walking into. After that, we can go after Corbin and Bianca.”

Pauli’s forked tongue fluttered against my neck. It sent shivers down my spine. “Stop that!”

Pauli giggled. I’d never heard a snake giggle. Then again, most people outside the first few chapters of Genesis had never heard one talk either. “Ready to go?”

I nodded. “Take me to Nico.”

Pauli slithered around my shoulders and wrapped himself around my chest. In a flash of light, I disappeared and found myself standing in Nico’s mausoleum.

He turned to me with wide eyes. “What are you doing here?”

“You didn’t show up at the cabin. Do you realize what lengths we had to go to just to find out what happened to you?”

“It doesn’t matter. You still should have waited. You don’t understand what we’re dealing with here.”

“It’s Corbin and Bianca. They’re trying to steal your demiurge. Just like the time Dr. Evil stole Austin Powers’ mojo.”

“That’s not the same. Dr. Evil went back in time to do that. Corbin and Bianca just escaped hell. If anyone knows about going back in time and coming out of hell, it’s me. That’s sort of the problem. Corbin wasn’t a hotbed of mental health before he went to hell. That much time in hell—even just vampire hell—will warp the mind. That’s why a lot of vampires who have been staked come back and are more unpredictable than vampire neophytes. I’ve encountered more than my share of vampires who’ve been unstaked and weren’t the same bloodsuckers they used to be. Corbin and Bianca are on a whole other level of crazy.”

“Why didn’t vampire hell affect you like that? You spent almost twenty years there, right?”

Nico took a deep breath. “I did. I was prepared for it. I knew what to expect. It took everything I had to hold on to my sanity. Corbin doesn’t have that kind of discipline.”

“Can they get in here?” I asked.

Nico shrugged. “This is the most secure place I know of. I had to make it that way. I couldn’t depend on Mercy and Ramon to stand guard over my staked corpse for twenty years.”

"Is there a way out of here?" I asked.

Nico glanced at Pauli and sighed. "I suppose there is now."

Pauli zapped himself off my shoulders and reappeared curled around Nico's leg.

"Hey there, big guy!" Pauli giggled.

Nico shook his leg. "Get off me!"

"I just need to slither a *little* higher..."

"I don't consent! Ever been bitten by a vamp, Pauli?"

Pauli zapped right off of Nico's thigh and onto my shoulders again. "Sure have. It sucks. No pun intended. You're a party pooper, Nico. Always have been. Who do you think you are to turn down a boa? Did you know I can swallow another snake whole? I don't know what you're packing, but I'm sure I can take it. I can swallow almost as much as my girth."

Nico sighed and shook his head. "You're disgusting."

"Honey, there isn't a hooker in all of New Orleans who could do you better."

Nico shuddered. "You've ruined the Discovery Channel for me forever."

I couldn't help but laugh. I knew Pauli was joking—sort of.

I decided to change the subject. As much as I appreciated Pauli's sense of humor and found his flirtations amusing, he had a knack for interjecting the tensest situations with references to his penis. That wasn't a topic I was eager to stay on. Not that I ever got on his... you know what I mean. "I can sense wards here. It didn't keep Pauli out. Do you really think it will work to keep out Corbin and Bianca?"

Nico nodded. "It's the best I can do. Look, Hailey. This is a great opportunity. We know where they are. So long as I stay here, I can be the bait. Get the attention of the cops. Lure them here. They'll chase you, but they won't be able to catch you. Not with your speed and all your powers. When they get here, and see Bianca in your form, they'll think she's you."

"They'll kill the cops!"

Nico shook his head. "They will try. That's when you show up and protect them. Use my sire bond. Command Corbin to use his sire bond to command Bianca to turn herself in."

I nodded. "Sounds like a plan. I should go back to the convergence in Manchac. I can bring the others."

"You don't want to get them involved. You can do this, Hailey. Choose your words carefully. Remember, the product of a sire bond, the progeny, cannot violate your commands. That doesn't mean they can't do something you don't anticipate to thwart your efforts."

I patted Pauli across his scales. "Alright, Pauli. We know the cops are watching Casa do Diabo. Take us there."

Chapter 13

PAULI TELEPORTED ME TO the front porch of Casa do Diabo. Sure enough, it didn't take long before three officers showed up with their guns drawn.

"Get down on the ground!" one of them shouted.

I grinned. "Make me."

I took off running.

"Damn it!" one cop screamed. "We have wood tipped bullets! Stop or I'll shoot!"

I kept running. I darted back and forth across the street. Before they even had a chance to open fire, there were people between us. They wouldn't shoot. They had no choice but to pursue us—just as I'd hoped.

I had to stop periodically to make sure they stayed on my trail.

"Come and get me!" I shouted before I turned and ran again.

Even with Pauli on my shoulders, slowing me down a little, I could run three or four times faster than any mortal. They didn't stand a chance.

Two more cops approached from straight ahead. I couldn't outrun their radios. It wasn't a problem. I blasted right past them, pushing both of them on their backs, and kept running.

We reached the iron fence surrounding St. Louis Cemetery No. 2. I made sure the cops saw me scale it. I almost cleared it in a single leap. The perks of vampirism are real.

It wouldn't take them long to get through the gates. It bought me enough time to hide.

I spotted myself—really Bianca—along with Corbin in wolf-form just outside Nico's mausoleum. They weren't trying to break through the doors. Maybe they'd tried and gave up. Perhaps they were waiting him out. I wasn't sure if the portions of the demiurge made them invulnerable to sunlight or not. If it didn't, waiting for Nico to come out was a losing effort. Nico could walk in the sun, after all.

Something was off about the whole scenario. Perhaps Corbin and Bianca didn't know that Nico could go out during the day. Even so, there weren't many things a vampire couldn't get into with enough determination. Nico designed the mausoleum, though, specifically to keep powerful vampires out.

I heard sirens in the distance. The cops had called for backup. In just minutes, the whole cemetery would be swarming with the police. There wasn't anywhere I could hide—except inside another mausoleum.

Pauli teleported me into Nicolas Cage's pyramid-shaped tomb. I knew it was empty. Despite the actor's recent role as Renfield the vampire, so far as I knew, Nicolas Cage was still a living, breathing, human.

Why did Nicolas Cage have the tomb? You'd have to ask him. Annabelle believed it was because after Cage purchased the haunted LaLaurie Mansion, he was cursed by the dead serial killer who once inhabited the place and believed being buried near Marie Laveau might free him of his curse upon his death. There was some reason to believe Annabelle's theory. Was he cursed? Check his box office numbers as of late, and you might become a believer.

Not to mention, not that long ago Annabelle and Cain encountered the ghost of Delphine LaLaurie. She'd possessed a few folk and wreaked a lot of havoc in the Vilokan Asylum. Cain wrote about it in his memoir. Check it out sometime if you're curious. So far as I'm aware, Nicolas Cage didn't appear in that tale.

Still, the mausoleum for the actor wasn't especially spacious. I suppose he didn't anticipate the need to do a lot of stretching in the afterlife. Still, it served my purpose.

Pauli teleported in and out a few times to keep an eye on the situation on the ground. We had to time this just right. Let the cops see the *other* me, wait until she started fighting them off, and show up to play the hero.

I'd clear my name, and they'd have no choice but to let Connor and Annabelle walk.

I didn't need Pauli to show up again to know shit was going down. The sound of gunshots, only slightly muffled by the stone and marble around me, made it clear. Short of busting out of the tomb, and earning an enemy out of the *Leaving Las Vegas* star, I didn't have a way out. They didn't usually build exit hatches on mausoleums. A clear ADA violation. Accessibility is important—even for the undead. I blame it on systemic zombiphobia.

A blast of refracted light accompanied Pauli's sudden return. "Be careful! Don't want you to get shot. I'll stay on your shoulders so we can skedaddle if necessary."

I chuckled. "Skedaddle?"

"Retreating is for pussies!"

I chuckled. "Skedaddling is *so much* more manly."

"I was going to say we'd 'high tail' it out of there, but I'm not entirely sure where my body ends and my tail begins. My existence is a paradox. I don't have a tail, but I'm all tail. And I get a lot of tail."

"That's not a paradox," I said. "It's just weird."

"Right now, the cops are chasing Bianca and Corbin around the cemetery. They have them surrounded and are closing in."

"Best get me out there. Once they don't have any place to run, they'll have no choice but to fight. That's when I need to intervene."

"There are too many cops to go out and wait. We need to time this just right. I can keep going back and forth to check, but I can't be in two places at once."

Tell Pauli to stay there. I can see everything.

"Sarah?" I asked.

"Do I look like Sarah? Please."

"No, I think she's talking to me."

It's me! I've always had vampire ESPN. I think now that the Baron is in me, it's like I have ESPN+!

I chuckled. "It's just ESP, Sarah."

Whatever! You can hear me. How cool is that?

"Very cool. Can you tell me exactly when Pauli needs to teleport me out there?"

Sure can. Need any help?

I shook my head. "Not yet. It's too dangerous, especially for Holland. If this doesn't go well, I don't want the cops to arrest or kill you and Tommy, too. I think they have wood-tipped bullets, just like the kind Prince Ladinas and his team in Exeter had."

Sarah sighed. *Ladinas should sue the cops for trademark infringement.*

I chuckled. "Yeah, right. So far as I know, the issue of vampire property rights hasn't come up in the courts. Wouldn't want to press the issue. If Mercy lost her bank accounts, she'd lose her debit card. Then, how could I ever buy anything?"

"Good point!" Pauli interjected. "Not that I really know what you two are talking about."

I chuckled. "Sarah is watching everything go down through Corbin and Bianca. She'll let us know when to move."

"Are you sure her telepathy is on a secure channel?"

I snorted. "I don't know. Sarah, did you hear Pauli? Through me, I mean?"

I did. I think we're fine. This is all a little new, and Baron Samedi is pulling the strings.

I snorted. "Yeah, that's what I'm worried about."

He's been nothing but a gentleman so far!

I chuckled. "Yeah, well, I don't intend to change my clothes for the next forty-eight hours, just in case. Certainly not in front of a mirror."

The Baron will be so disappointed in you. The notes of sarcasm in Sarah's voice were obvious. *That might be the whole reason he did this. Just so he could see you naked.*

More gunshots sounded from outside. "Are you sure it's not time yet? It sounds like things are getting bad out there."

Just so you know, Bianca may or may not look like you. If she targets any of the cops for death, she'll change.

I pressed my lips together. "Well, unless the cops are having secret affairs with each other, she'll be the only non-cop out there."

"Juicy!" Pauli interjected. "Can you imagine? Those tight uniforms. Handcuffs. Night sticks! The things I could do with one of those!"

I shivered. "I'd rather not think about it."

"Keep the pepper spray away, though. You don't want to get that stuff in your urethra."

I cleared my throat. "I'm not going to ask you about the time someone pepper sprayed your junk. I'm not sure I want to know."

"Happens more often than you'd think! It's a real bitch!"

I chuckled. "That doesn't surprise me nearly as much as it should."

"Look, my dick is like the gospel! I have an obligation to share it with anyone who might be open to it."

I rolled my eyes. "Open to it? Let me guess, open *ears* aren't what you have in mind."

"Not usually. But you know, to each his own. A hole is a hole."

I rolled my eyes. "You realize, Pauli, some people would consider that assault. It's no wonder you've been pepper sprayed there."

"Assault with a deadly penis! Guilty as charged!"

I laid there shaking my head as more gunshots sounded through the muffle of the marble tomb. "How many cops are out there, Sarah?"

I can't say for sure. I can only see what Corbin or Bianca see. I'd say at least a dozen. Probably more.

"Please tell me they have body cameras. If I do this, I need evidence. Something more than the word of witnesses. Something that can prove I'm not the homicidal Hailey."

You don't think the cops would testify honestly about it? Sarah asked.

"Usually, I would trust them. Putting something like a shape-shifting vampire on public record, though? They'll be pressured to keep it under wraps."

"They'll just delete the video feeds if that's the case," Pauli said.

I nodded. "Maybe, but all it takes is one cop who refuses to cover up the truth. I have to believe there's at least one good and honest officer in the bunch."

Get ready, Sarah added. *They're surrounding Corbin and Bianca. One row on the east side of Marie Laveau's tomb. Wait for my signal.*

It only took another ten seconds before Sarah shouted in my mind. *Go now!*

"Now, Pauli! One row east of Queen Laveau's tomb!"

Pauli tightened his grip around me and in a flash we disappeared and reappeared right in front of Corbin and Bianca. Only now, Bianca appeared like another woman.

From the look on one of the cop's faces, I knew who she was targeting. "She's coming after you!" I shouted.

I dove in the middle as Bianca shouted. "Sick him, Corbin!"

What was happening? Why was Bianca making Corbin do the dirty work? "No, Corbin!" I screamed. "By the power of your maker, I order you to stand down!"

Corbin didn't listen. Why the hell wasn't he obeying the sire bond?

I dove and grabbed Corbin by his fur. As I did it, I saw Bianca change again—she returned to my form. Was she *targeting* Corbin?

A gunshot went off. The bullet grazed my forearm and blasted right into Corbin's chest.

He fell to the ground and whimpered before he took his usual vampire form again.

"Hailey!" Corbin muttered. "Bianca has the bond!"

"How did she—"

Before Corbin could answer, the wooden bullet in his chest must've shattered, leaving a splinter in his heart. His body went pale—paler than before. I could see it in his eyes as his consciousness left his body. That fucker still thought he loved me.

One cop dove at me and tackled me. He tried to pin me down. I was too strong. I threw him off like he was a rag doll.

Bianca took off running. She was shifting repeatedly as she targeted each of the cops, turning into their wives, their lovers, or the imagined appearance of their ideal fantasy mates. She sank her teeth into some of their necks. Those were the lucky ones. She decapitated at least five of them in only seconds.

"Pauli!" I shouted. "Get as many to safety as you can!"

Pauli disappeared from my shoulders. He wrapped himself around one cop and disappeared before reappearing and taking another one. He couldn't save them all. Bianca was too quick.

When she turned into Connor—his human form—I knew she was coming after me.

I grabbed my wand and aimed it at her. I cast an exsanguination spell at her, but she dodged it. Whatever power she'd absorbed made her fast. Even if I struck her, there was a chance it wouldn't work. I'd trapped the energies of Barbelo in a blood prism before. It was the only thing I could think to do.

Before I could get it off, Bianca flew at me. The force of her tackle loosened my grip on my wand and I dropped it.

"Get off me!" I screamed.

"I've waited for this for too long!" Bianca cackled. She reached into the waistband of her pants and pulled out a wooden stake.

The next thing I knew, Bianca went flying off me.

"Stay away from her!"

"Nico!" I screamed. "Run!"

Nico didn't listen. He went after Bianca. She grabbed him by the head. A bright orange light blasted out of Nico's eyes and flowed right into Bianca's waiting mouth. Nico fell to his knees.

Bianca ran past me and scooped up Corbin's staked corpse. Then the two of them disappeared in a flash of light.

I ran over to Nico. "Are you alright?"

Nico huffed. "I'm sorry. I had to save you, but she got my power."

"All of it?" I asked.

Nico sighed. "The power of Kalyptos. I'm still a Loa and a vampire. She can't take that from me."

"How the hell did she do that?" I asked.

"I don't know. How did she steal my sire bond?"

Come back to the convergence, Sarah said. *The answer is here. So are the cops that Pauli saved.*

"Send him back to pick us up," I said.

I helped Nico to his feet. I'd never seen him so weak. Extracting Kalyptos from his body must've taken a toll.

"I'm going to need blood."

I helped Nico over to one of the headless bodies. "There should still be enough soul in the blood."

Nico was about to sink his teeth into the man's neck when he realized his entire head and neck were gone. He grabbed the dead man's wrist instead and drank.

Chapter 14

Corbin wasn't dead. If the bullets the cops had were like those that Prince Ladinas and company used in Exeter, they splintered on contact. Removing the wood from the heart was possible. It just took more effort than yanking out a stake. What baffled me the most was that it was Bianca, not Corbin, who was pulling the strings.

Had she gone to the in-between and found Merrick? Did she learn the sire-bond spell from him? More likely was that Corbin *saw* me do it when I took Nico's sire bond in hell. He was there. Did Corbin really want Bianca to have that information?

I thought he loved me!

Maybe he thought he did. He certainly didn't trust me. Corbin was no dummy. He knew Bianca was in love with him. I didn't give two hoots about him. Who *he* loved was irrelevant. This wasn't about love. It was about self-preservation, and Bianca was a better bet even if she did send him to a temporary death just moments earlier. If anything, it was a distraction. If she didn't care about Corbin and she was content to let him languish in vampire hell, she could have left his body there and allowed us to deal with it. I would have burned out his heart and that would be that.

What Corbin *might* have underestimated was Bianca's disdain for *me.* Was it Corbin's plan to frame me for murder, or did Bianca do that on her own once she had Corbin in her thrall? Corbin's last words to me suggested that something hadn't gone according to plan. He wasn't my ally—not in the least. But he also wasn't the primary villain in this scenario.

The cops left in the cemetery were in a state of shock. Several officers were murdered by a shape-shifting vampire in front of them. Some of the police on the scene knew about vampires. That's why they had wooden bullets. That didn't mean all of them understood the whole situation. If they didn't know about vampires already, or the supernatural, they'd not only seen their colleagues killed in front of them, they'd seen a reality that shook them to the core.

Waiting around to figure out how they'd respond to all that happened wasn't wise. This wasn't the first time I'd encountered people who were confronted with the supernatural in a horrific way. Sometimes they retreated in shock. At other times, they lashed out violently—a desperate effort to hold on to the fictitious world they used to live in.

Debriefing the officers at the scene wasn't my job. The police chief knew the truth. If he hadn't been upfront with the officers he charged to go after me, that was on him. He'd have to deal with them later. I had to get back to the convergence.

Pauli knew what to do. Nico wrapped his arms around me. Pauli enveloped both of us. In a flash, my feet were back on the soft ground of the Manchac marshlands.

There were police there, too, who were just as rattled as those at the cemetery. The difference was that they'd been removed from the scene. The bloodied bodies of their fallen brothers and sisters weren't lying in front of them. They'd also been teleported by a rainbow-colored snake in an instant. At the very least, they were more likely to hear us out.

Holland and Sarah were already talking to them, doing their best to explain everything they'd seen. Tommy was standing idly by, like a neophyte should.

When they saw me, Sarah came over and took me by the arm. "There's something you need to see."

I looked around. "Shouldn't I talk to the cops?"

"Holland is handling it for now. This is more pressing."

Sarah pointed across the water to another patch of ground. "See that dark mass behind the tree?"

I rubbed my eyes. "Sort of. It's hard to make out."

"Come with me."

I waded through the knee-deep water beside Sarah. My feet sank a good eight to twelve inches into the mud with each step. The suction against my feet almost made me lose my shoes. We climbed back on dry ground and I got a better look at what Sarah meant to show me. The creature was large, more than twice my size. It had dark fur. It wasn't a werewolf—but someone who didn't know better could have mistaken it for one. It also had a wooden stake in its chest.

"That's the hellhound I killed when I claimed Nico's sire bond in hell."

Nico wasn't far behind us. He saw what I saw. "They must've brought it back with them when the convergence opened and spat out the wraiths."

"How could they do that?" I asked.

Nico scratched his head. "Corbin wasn't a wraith. He was in vampire hell. He must've pulled it through with him and hid it here. Only after the demiurge split into separate energies and he absorbed a part of it was he able to use it to assume a body.

I sighed. "A body like Connor's. Bianca must've done the same."

"I can't say for sure," Sarah added. "Baron Samedi isn't giving me access to past memories, only what's happening at the moment. What if Corbin brought it back with him, knowing that he'd be vulnerable to Nico's sire bond?"

I nodded. "He unstaked it. I must've lost Nico's sire bond, but didn't even realize it. If Bianca was with him, and got him to explain what was happening, all she'd need to do is reconsecrate the hellhound, name it, and stake it again."

Nico bent over and grabbed the wooden stake. "If that's the case, all we have to do is remove the stake from the beast. The bond should return to me by natural right."

I tilted my head. "Why would they leave it here for us to find?"

"They probably dragged it over here hoping we wouldn't. This hellhound is huge. Even for two vampires, it wouldn't be easy to move."

"They could have covered it in brush or something. We don't know what will happen if we pull out the stake. This isn't an earthbound creature. It might revive."

"If that's the case," Nico said, "Corbin and Bianca likely faced that problem themselves. If they unstaked it, they must've staked it again quickly. It takes a moment for a vampire to completely revive after a stake is removed. He's usually disoriented for a few minutes."

I rubbed my brow. "It's still odd that it's here. There must be a reason. I have a theory I'd like to test."

"What is your theory?" Nico asked.

"Can you two help me move it? Let's see what happens as we move the hellhound further from the convergence."

All three of us grabbed onto the beast's limbs and pulled it. We didn't get more than a few feet and my grip passed straight through the hellhound's paws as if it wasn't there at all.

"That's it," I said. "The hellhound's proximity to the convergence allows it to maintain its form. They must've discovered the same thing. They couldn't toss it in the water. Alligators would be more likely to tear it apart, or pull it away. All Corbin knew about how Merrick's spell worked was what he saw me do in hell. If he'd let the beast return to hell by pulling it away from the convergence, we couldn't do anything about it short of going to hell to reclaim your sire bond. He must've thought the best course of action was to leave it here."

"Alright," Nico said. "All I'd have to do is remove the stake, consecrate the thing in blood, give it my name, and stake it again."

I grabbed Nico's hand. "I have a better idea. What is Corbin's surname?"

Nico nodded. "Corbin Cel Tradat. I think I know where you're going with this. Are you sure it's wise to claim Corbin's sire bond over Bianca? Corbin has always been more dangerous than Bianca."

I sighed. "Corbin still thinks he loves me. It's a warped, demented love, no doubt. But if we claim his bond over Bianca and if by removing the stake, you regain your sire bond, we could control both of them. I'll use Corbin's bond against Bianca. You can use your natural bond over Corbin."

Nico grinned widely. "That's brilliant. It *might* work."

"It might?" I asked. "Do you have any doubt?"

Nico sighed. "Bianca took the power of Kalyptos from me. She's wielding some kind of magic that we aren't accounting for, and with the raw power of Kalyptos, she could use it to do almost anything. When *anything* is on the table, there's no such thing as a foolproof plan."

"I didn't feel a thing when they took your sire bond away from me. At the very least, they won't see this coming. It might not guarantee we can beat them, but it gives us a damn good shot. We'll have the element of surprise on our side."

"I say we do it," Sarah said. "Hailey's right. If Bianca really stole Kalyptos from you, that's the case whether or not we do this. At least this way we have *something.*"

I nodded. "Exactly. Besides, I've done this before. No offense, Nico. I have more experience."

Nico chuckled. "When it comes to spells of any sort, Hailey, I'd never question your experience over mine."

"We'd better do this fast," I said. "We're running out of moonlight."

"Before the sun rises, we should talk to the cops. Holland and I were trying to convince them to release Annabelle and Connor. Hearing you explain what happened might help. These men are willing to help, I think. But they will be taking a risk undermining their chief if they let them go."

"I hate to admit it," Nico said. "Annabelle could be of assistance, especially since we can't say for certain what Bianca plans to do with Kalyptos."

I looked back across the waters. Even through the darkness, the look of annoyance on Holland's face was evident. Still, she was demonstrating uncharacteristic patience as she talked with the policemen that Pauli saved. Pauli, meanwhile, was slithering around Tommy's thigh. He was probably propositioning my progeny, which made me laugh. The wide-eyed look on Tommy's face told me all I needed to know.

I knelt down. Nico and Sarah helped me roll the hellhound on its back. I bit my own wrist. My blood was a part of this. I grabbed the stake with my right hand and yanked it out of the beast's chest. The hellhound roared. The fire of hell on its breath felt like I'd just reached into an oven set at four-hundred-and-fifty Fahrenheit.

"Corbin Cel Tradat!" I screamed as I plunged the stake back into the hellhound's heart.

The monster stopped roaring and fell back into a slumber.

"Did it work?" Sarah asked.

I shrugged. "We won't know until I try to use Corbin's sire bond on Bianca."

"I cannot say for certain if I've recovered my sire bond, either," Nico added. "I'm different than I was before. Still, I remain the vampire I was. It should work."

Sarah was about to wade back into the water. I grabbed her arm. "I don't know why I didn't think of this before."

I cupped my hands around my mouth. "Hey, Pauli! How about a lift across the water?"

"Bitch, seriously? I'm trying to get a little snake-on-snake action here!"

"He can't have my snake!" Tommy shouted back. "This thing is a freak!"

Pauli slithered his way up Tommy's body and flicked his snake tongue in my progeny's ear. It took all my effort to stifle my instinct to laugh.

"You realize, Tommy, he's just trying to get a rise out of you."

"Yeah!" Tommy shouted. "In more ways than one!"

Nico shook his head. "Pauli. If he wasn't so damn useful, I'd consign him to a herpetarium."

In a flash of light, Pauli disappeared off of Tommy and onto Nico. "Honey, the herps have never stopped Pauli!"

"I didn't say herpes!" Nico huffed. "I said herpetarium."

"Sounds like a magical place!" Pauli giggled. "Maybe I'll give you mine!"

Nico grunted. "Vampires can't get STDs. We are immune."

Pauli tilted his giant boa head. "Well, where's the fun in that?"

I rolled my eyes. "There's nothing fun about herpes, Pauli."

"Like you'd know! You're immune. Don't knock the love bumps. They might hurt, but they add *texture* to the experience."

Nico shuddered. "Gross."

I shook my head. "Just take us back across the water, Pauli."

Chapter 15

After Pauli teleported us back to the ground around the convergence Sarah introduced me to one of the police officers.

He extended his hand. "I'm Lieutenant Martin Cavanaugh."

I shook his hand. "Hailey Bradbury. But you probably knew that already."

Cavanaugh smirked. "You realize your name is still a missing persons cold case?"

I nodded. "Undoubtedly on account of my parents. They know the truth now. Clearly, I'm not missing."

"You became a vampire..."

"Does that make you uncomfortable?"

Cavanaugh scratched his forehead as he laughed. "I only learned that vampires exist when this case came up. I thought it was a joke. When I learned it wasn't, I thought you were a mass-murderer. My chief still believes that's true."

"But you don't?" I asked.

"I watched someone who looks like you change her face in front of me and proceed to murder my partner. I'd say that this case isn't as cut and dry as the security footage suggested."

"You realize," Holland added. "If it wasn't for Hailey, this city would have been overrun by evil vampires or other monsters years ago."

"Apologies," Cavanaugh said. "This is all new to me. I'm still trying to put all the pieces together and it still feels more like I'm living in the middle of a *Supernatural* episode than reality."

"My name is Niccolo Freeman," Nico said, extending his hand. Cavanaugh hesitated a moment before shaking it.

"Your hands are cold," Cavanaugh said. "Unnaturally cold."

"I'm the first of our kind," Nico said.

"I've seen your name in our files," Cavanaugh said. "How is this possible? You can't be older than thirty."

Nico chuckled. "It's a long story. In short, during a battle against an evil demigod, I was caught in another realm and turned into a vampire. When I came back to earth, it was in the distant past. I've existed for centuries."

Cavanaugh shook his head. "I'm sorry. This is all a lot to take in."

"I understand," I said. "When I was sixteen and I became a vampire, it rattled my world. It takes time to wrap your mind around this kind of thing. The fact is that you've seen the real murderers. You know it isn't me. The evidence literally stared you in the face an hour ago. As the police, your job is to serve and protect, is it not?"

"Of course it is."

"The best way to do that is to allow us, along with my friends that you have in custody, to fight against the actual killers. We can stop them and, frankly, if you were on our side, it would help."

"Because of our bullets."

I nodded. "And because you're detaining people who could make a difference."

Cavanaugh narrowed his eyes. "If I free these people, I'm taking a personal and professional risk. Can you guarantee you'll be able to stop these killers?"

"Honestly, no. I can tell you I've beaten both of them before—with the help of my friends. I can also promise I'll do everything I can to stop them again. Even if it kills me."

Cavanaugh turned to his fellow officers who, until this point, had largely stayed silent, appearing overwhelmed by all that was happening, but were listening to our conversation. "Do you agree? I can't do this alone. I need your support."

"We have all the evidence we need on our body cameras to justify our actions," a female officer responded. "I say we help this girl. She's not the perp. If she can help us stop the actual killers and end this nightmare before anyone else dies, I say we do whatever we can to support her."

I smiled and nodded at the woman. She nodded back. "This will not be easy. I have to warn you, there's a new power these vampires wield that's unpredictable, to say the least. There's no telling what they might do once we come after them."

Cavanaugh nodded his head resolutely. "All the more reason we have to stop them."

"We can locate them," Sarah said. "We don't have a lot of time to act. How soon can you free our friends?"

"It might take a little while," Cavanaugh sighed. "After the cemetery happened, the department will be in a state of chaos. Give us a couple hours. Presuming this snake-guy who brought us here can take us back to our squad cars."

"Sure can!" Pauli piped up, zapping himself onto Cavanaugh's shoulders. The officer shivered on contact.

"What the—"

"That's Pauli," I said. "Don't let him get to you. He's a good guy, even if he gets easily distracted by men in uniform."

"I'm more interested in men *out* of their uniforms!" Pauli piped up. "But you have to unwrap the candy before you get to taste the sweetness."

Cavanaugh gulped. "I'm not sure if I'm more disturbed that this snake is talking right now, or by what he's saying."

Nico sighed and shook his head. "Welcome to our world."

"Welcome to Pauli's world!" Pauli slithered around until he was staring Cavanaugh straight in the face. "Where all of my dreams come true, and you get to go along for the ride!"

"Just take them back to their squad cars," I said, laughing a little. "When you've done that, meet us back here. We need to track down Corbin and Bianca."

"Already on it," Sarah said, her eyes clenched shut as she focused on whatever vision her power, with Baron Samedi's aid, revealed. "I'm trying to figure out what Bianca is doing with the power she stole from Nico. So far, I'm not seeing anything."

"If they're smart," Nico added, "they'll wait until they see what our next move is. If you have an ace up your sleeve, you don't play it until you're dealt a hand that gives you a good chance at winning the pot."

I laughed and shook my head. "We're going into this with a plan that we can *expect* will be a lot more complicated once we face them. Just once, I'd like to see one of our strategies pan out exactly the way we planned."

"Has Bianca restored Corbin yet?" I asked.

Sarah shook her head. "Not yet, but I think she's planning to do it soon. I see a scalpel, a bucket full of water, and a lot of rags. I think she's going to try to dig the splinters out of his heart."

"Do you have their location?" I asked.

"I think so," Sarah said. "They haven't gone far. I think they're in an abandoned apartment just a couple of blocks away from the cemetery."

"Hurry," I told Pauli. "If we're going to finish this before sunrise, we need you to drop off the officers and get back so we can stop Bianca. Ideally *before* she unstakes... or unsplinters... Corbin."

Chapter 16

CORBIN AND BIANCA DIDN'T have their own apartment. Vampires had a long history of kleptoparasitism. Are you impressed? I learned that word on Animal Planet. Like the Blue Jay, which doesn't bother building nests of its own but steals the nests of robins and sparrows, vampires often formed their own nests out of other people's homes. People they fed from and either kept on hand and fed as a constant blood supply, or attempted to turn them. By becoming their sire, they could basically claim their home without raising suspicions. It was risky, of course, because turning a new vampire wasn't a simple process. Not every vampire could do it and, more often than not, it required either a lot of extra blood on hand and some medical expertise, or a bit of magic.

In a lot of movies and films, the vampire fed someone they drained with their own blood to effect the change. Like most myths, that had its root in reality. Sometimes a vampire's blood could sustain someone's life long enough for them to complete the transformation. It wasn't a guarantee, though. More often than not, it didn't work. If someone was AB positive, they had a better chance of completing the transformation that way. Universal recipients were less likely to reject the vampire's blood. Also, ingesting the vampire's blood wasn't the proper method. If you drank blood, it didn't enter your bloodstream. Most people vomit. It requires a transfusion.

Corbin and Bianca had been at this game a long time. It had been a long time since they'd had to secure shelter or forge a nest, but I suppose for older vamps, it was like riding a bike.

From what Sarah described, the apartment that Corbin and Bianca retreated to resembled a senior living facility. Not a nursing home. The kind of place where old folks still live independently but have help nearby if required. How'd she know? She spotted an emergency call button next to the bed. There were also a lot of doilies, family photographs, and throw-pillows decorated by needlepoint. Nothing that reflected Corbin's old world tastes. Maybe that was the point. Of all the places for ancient vampires to hide around the French Quarter, we'd never suspect they'd be holing up in a retirement center.

Sarah also saw a sign when Bianca entered the place, carrying Corbin in her arms: The Carlyle.

At that time of the night, it wasn't surprising that Sarah didn't see anyone else. Older folks aren't exactly known for keeping late hours. Perhaps that explained it. Bianca needed a place where she and Corbin could come and go at night with minimal interference. What was strange was that whoever that apartment belonged to wasn't around. What was even stranger is that after Sarah saw Bianca cutting into Corbin's chest with a scalpel, her vision went blank.

Sarah didn't know why. She said Baron Samedi within her was equally confused by his sudden inability to access Bianca's sight. All we could figure was that Kalyptos had something to do with it. When Nico became a Loa, a portion of the demiurge was used to forge his new nature. There was more left over he didn't need, raw and unformed power that Bianca was using—somehow, someway, to do something indeterminably nasty.

We decided to split up. If Annabelle and Connor were released, someone needed to pick them up and update them on everything. Pauli was going to be a busy boa. With his help, we could get backup at the Carlyle if we needed it fairly quickly. Pauli took Holland and Tommy to pick up Annabelle. If we needed her, she could also go back to Vilokan to gather reinforcements—Sogbo and Bade with Savanna, or Ellie and anyone else whose skills might help.

If our sire bond spell worked, though, we wouldn't need it. Nico was Corbin's natural sire, and I'd taken Corbin's sire bond and could control Bianca. If all went according to plan, we'd enter the retirement facility, bind both Corbin and Bianca, and whatever Bianca was doing with the demiurge would be inconsequential. No matter what she'd done, if I could control her, she wouldn't be able to use it.

After Pauli returned from dropping off Holland and Tommy somewhere within walking distance of the police station, he took Nico, Sarah, and me to the sidewalk outside the retirement center.

It was a relatively small brick-faced facility with well manicured floral bushes surrounding the circle drive that curved around the covered entrance.

We stepped through the front doors. The desk where I assumed visitors were supposed to sign in was vacant. There wasn't anyone in the foyer. It was almost five o'clock in the morning. One would think that the doors would either be locked or there'd be *someone* manning the front desk.

"Picking anything up?" Nico asked Sarah.

Sarah took a deep breath. She rested her hand on Nico's shoulder. "Baron Samedi suggests channeling our energies together. He can't pick up anything. Maybe you can give us a boost?"

Nico shrugged. "I'm not sure what to do."

Sarah didn't respond. She closed her eyes and grimaced. "It's no use. They're blocking us, somehow."

We didn't know our way around the facility and weren't entirely sure which apartment Bianca and Corbin were using. Without Sarah's abilities, we didn't have many options. Even if we knocked on doors, waking up and irking a lot of grumpy old people, would Bianca really *answer* the door for us? Probably not.

"Can the sire bond work through walls?" I asked.

Nico nodded. "So long as they can hear us. Vampires aren't like humans, whose senses dull as they get older. Our sense of hearing improves with age. If we speak clearly and forcefully, they'll hear us. They might even hear us now. We should act before they have a chance to take us off guard."

We moved through the foyer into a common area. Several game tables and couches were arranged into miniature gathering spaces within the expansive room.

"Bianca!" I shouted. "Come out and don't you dare try to attack us."

"Corbin, my son," Nico added. "I demand you join us and refrain from attacking anyone unless I allow it."

We stood in silence for a few minutes. Several doors opened and closed from a distant hallway. A crowd of people with glazed-over eyes and blank stares entered the room. They parted like the red sea for Moses as Bianca moved through the crowd, Corbin a few paces behind her, and an old woman with red vampire eyes right beside Corbin.

"What is going on here?" I asked.

Bianca laughed. "I've changed! I'm like you now, Nico."

"What are you talking about?" Nico asked.

Bianca smiled widely and snapped her fingers. The people who'd gathered in the room fell to their knees and bowed toward Bianca.

Bianca gestured toward the old vampire next to her. "I turned the host of Erzulie. As her sire, I commanded her to use the power of the demiurge to make me like her."

I gulped. "You're a Loa, now?"

"Just like Erzulie! With a few unique powers, of course."

Corbin knelt down in front of Bianca and kissed her boots.

"Look at that! He loves me now!"

I huffed. "You did this to force Corbin to love you?"

Bianca rolled her eyes. "I'm not that desperate, child. When you can compel people to love you, to worship you, there's nothing you can't accomplish."

Bianca snapped her fingers. A pulse of pink energy blasted from her eyes and settled on Nico and Sarah. They fell to their knees and bowed down with the rest.

"Stop this!" I demanded. "Release them!"

Bianca laughed. "I'm more than a vampire now. I must hand it to you, claiming Corbin's sire bond was a clever move. It would have worked if I had remained as I was."

"I'm not worshiping you!"

"Of course you won't. You already hold the aspect of Erzulie. I control Erzulie, herself, through a sire bond. Sadly, I can't control you. As one who can wield Erzulie's aspect, you're immune to the power. I suppose, though, that my worshippers, even Niccolo here, would love to pay homage to their goddess. You'd make a fine sacrifice!"

I took a couple of steps back as the people rose and circled around me. Sarah was leading the group. She looked me in the eye and smirked.

She can't control me. The Baron is protecting me. I need to give him control.

I gulped and nodded.

He is going to take Bianca to the crossroads. It's the only place where we can fight her fairly. Get to Annabelle. She can get you there. We will need your help! When the Baron takes me over, get out of here. Whatever you need to do. Even if the Baron succeeds, the power of Erzulie will still have a hold on the rest. Including Nico.

A list of questions that I couldn't ask scrolled through my mind. Why was Nico still vulnerable? I could take a guess. He was a vampire and a Loa, but he didn't know how to wield any of his Loa abilities. Or, perhaps, he was also pretending. It wasn't likely. Bianca knew about Nico's true nature. She didn't realize that Baron Samedi inhabited Sarah. Was she sure we could trust Baron Samedi if he took full control of Sarah's body? What other option was there? I didn't even know that Baron Samedi could take someone straight to the crossroads. As a Loa of death, I suppose, it made sense that accessing other realms with or without a convergence was within the scope of his power. Then there was Erzulie, herself. What commands had Bianca already issued her via the sire bond? Erzulie was immune to the effects of her own power, just as I was. I knew that the influence of a sire bond remained even if the sire left earth, even if they were staked and dead. Whatever commands were issued remained in force, written into the vampire's blood. That was why Corbin and Mercy never killed one another—Nico had forbidden each of them from harming the other directly.

Perhaps the biggest question was how the hell was I going to escape these people, especially Nico, if they thought they were in love with Bianca and worshipped her as a goddess?

My only chance was to take advantage of the wake of confusion that would spread in the moments after Sarah and the Baron seized Bianca. *If* they succeeded and pulled it off without getting eviscerated by the crowd of the elderly enthralled.

A blast of green energy encircled Sarah's entire frame. Baron Samedi was in control. The green energy turned red as Sarah' s body collided with Bianca's. Which Baron were we dealing with? Whatever the case, he was doing what Sarah said he would.

"Get off me!" Bianca shouted.

Corbin sprang to his feet and tried to pull Sarah off Bianca, but the blast of the Ghede's energy enveloped him, too. In a blinding red flash, they disappeared.

Ear-piercing screams sounded from the group. Nico grabbed me by the wrist. "What did you do to my love?"

I pulled my wand from my pocket with my free hand. He'd probably make me pay for it later, but I didn't have a choice. He was too strong, and Bianca's love spell still warped his mind. I blasted Nico with a partial exsanguination spell. It gave me a brief advantage over him in terms of strength. Enough that I wrested my wrist out of his grip.

Run, Hailey, Run!

Sarah's voice still echoed through the ether—somehow—and I didn't question it. I made like Forrest Gump and ran as fast as I could. I hit the doors of the retirement center and hurried across the street.

The old folks and Nico pursued me as blue and red lights flashed across my face. With a squeal of his tires, Lieutenant Cavanaugh's squad car stopped between us. "Go!" the officer shouted. "I'll hold them off!"

Fists and aluminum canes beat against the cop's car. Poor Cavanaugh didn't have a clue why a geriatric mob was assaulting his car, but all things considered, it was the least strange thing he'd seen all night.

Cavanaugh bought me just enough time to put some distance between myself and the crowd. I heard Cavanaugh's engine roar as he pulled away. I was relieved that he had gotten out of there, but I didn't turn back. Like the iconic Tom Hanks character, I just kept running. I didn't run cross-country. I only had an hour or so before sunrise. I ran straight to Vilokan. If Annabelle and Connor were free, that's where they'd be. Presuming, of course, that Pauli got them back safe and sound.

Sarah, possessed by the Baron, was facing off with Bianca and Corbin at the crossroads. Annabelle's familiar spirit, Isabelle, was one of the keepers of the crossroads. She could take us there and, hopefully, we could stop them.

Everything had come full-circle for me. It was under the influence of a nasty Loa, Kalfu, who had aspirations of claiming the crossroads that I first experienced the place. Kalfu had intended to make me his second. The crossroads had always been guarded by a pair. It was Legba and Kalfu, before. Kalfu tried to replace Legba with someone he *thought* he could control and dominate—me. I wasn't half the witch or a fraction of the vampire then that I am now. Annabelle defeated him and freed me from his thrall. She released Isabelle, and the spirit of another vodouisant named Mikah, to claim the crossroads. They'd governed it ever since. It wasn't a typical gateway or convergence. It was a unique path that the Loa could use to cross between realms.

With Isabelle on earth with Annabelle, it left the crossroads vulnerable. Could Baron Samedi defeat Bianca? Probably. He was a lot older and more powerful. Then again, it was the Baron's red power that took over at the last minute.

My stomach turned in knots as I made my way through the doorway on the side of the St. Louis Cathedral and descended into Vilokan. Bianca and Corbin were still vampires. Bianca was a Loa, like Baron

Samedi and Erzulie. She was new, sure, but she'd made herself a Loa by compelling Erzulie to do the same thing for her that Baron Samedi did for Nico before.

Bianca and Corbin were *still* vampires. What control did the Baron maintain over them since he still held their souls?

I pieced it all together as I flew down the stairs and made my way back to Annabelle's office. The Green Baron, who initially took control of Sarah, was the one who'd given her the initial plan. Perhaps his intentions were sound—send Bianca to the crossroads so we could go there and defeat her. Once the red Baron took over, though, I suspected the worst. If two vampires defeated Mikah and Isabelle—and Isabelle was with Annabelle on earth at present—the Baron could have influence over the crossroads. That meant he could send any Loa he wished to earth. He could also recall them at will.

Annabelle could force the Baron back into his green essence. She'd done it before. The question was, could we get there in time to save the crossroads? How long could Mikah hold them off, especially if he was facing Baron Samedi, Bianca in goddess form, and Corbin all at once? He didn't stand a chance. Not without our help.

Chapter 17

NO SOONER DID THE elevator doors part and Connor had his arms wrapped around me. It was good to have him in my arms, but with the impending crisis at hand, I resisted the urge to bask in the warmth of his embrace.

"We have a problem," I blurted out as I marched into the room. Annabelle looked at me with wide eyes. I continued to explain. "Bianca stole Nico's power. She turned Erzulie's host into a vampire and used her to turn herself into a love goddess. She forced Corbin and a whole slew of old people to worship her. They think they're in love. But that's not the worst part—"

"Bianca and Corbin are at the crossroads," Annabelle said. "Isabelle already knows. She sensed it the moment it happened."

I exhaled. "Okay, then, no need to explain. We have to go there. Can she take us?"

"Beli!" Annabelle shouted, summoning her soul-blade to her hand. "We were waiting for you."

I looked around the room. Everyone was there. Holland, Tommy, Ellie, and Savanna. Pauli was draped over Annabelle's shoulders.

"What about Sarah?" Tommy asked.

"She allowed Baron Samedi to take her over. He turned red just after he did."

"Damn it," Holland muttered. "I should have been there. If he's still in Sarah, though, I should be able to restrain him."

I nodded. "I don't think it's just Bianca and Corbin we have to deal with. I think Baron Samedi is connected to all of this. He wants to make Bianca the new prime guardian of the crossroads and Corbin her second."

Holland stared at me with wide eyes. "You've said enough. Remember, Baron Samedi can see and hear what you see and hear, now."

I grunted. "I know, that bargain we agreed to was a mistake."

"Technically, Sarah agreed to it," Holland said.

"Yeah, well, I could have stopped her. I consented to allow her to make the bargain. I should have known better."

"What's done is done," Annabelle said. "We don't have time to nurse our regrets. The longer we wait, the more likely it is that they'll overpower Mikah and take control. It's a lot harder to usurp a lord of the crossroads than it is to defend one."

"Let's do this," I said. "We may need each and every one of you to help. Remember, we're not just dealing with two ancient vampires and a couple of demigods. We're dealing with vampire-gods wielding the power of Kalyptos."

"They've already purposed that power," Annabelle said. "Let's hope they don't have any left."

Annabelle's eyes and blade glowed green as she cut a portal in the room. Pauli resumed his human form and cast a rainbow into the portal.

"Pauli will stay here and hold the portal open," Annabelle said. "It's the only way we can be sure we all get back"

I tilted my head. "What about Nico?"

"What about him?" Annabelle asked.

No sooner did I say it and the elevator dinged. Annabelle ran to her desk and pressed a button to hold the doors closed. It didn't matter. Nico tore through the doors like paper. He pushed his way past me and didn't say a word. He dove right into Annabelle's portal.

"Fucking Nico!" Annabelle screamed. "Is he going to help us or fight against us?"

"He's under Bianca's power. He thinks he's in love with her."

"I'll deal with that," Ellie said. "I might counteract the spell to a point."

"Erzulie is still out there somewhere as well."

"If she doesn't come bursting into my office," Annabelle said, "we can deal with her later."

I nodded. "Right. I can take Bianca's sire bond and free her from her influence. But we have to stop Bianca and the others first."

"Let me get this right," Tommy piped up. "It's us against the original vampire who also happens to be a Ghede Loa, Baron Samedi in his darker aspect, Corbin who has been nearly impossible to get rid of for months, and Bianca, who is also a demigod, now?"

I shrugged. "We have the Voodoo Queen, three more powerful mambos, and both of us."

"Not to mention Isabelle and Mikah," Annabelle added. "We have the advantage numbers wise."

"Sure," Tommy said. "But none of us are wielding a demiurge. We aren't demigods."

I chuckled. "Welcome to the team. This is what we do."

"No time to waste," Annabelle said. "Keep the portal open, Pauli."

"Good luck, bitches!" Pauli piped up.

"I'm not a bitch," Tommy huffed.

"Bitch, please!"

Tommy shook his head. I grabbed him by the arm and pulled him into the portal. Annabelle, Ellie, Holland, and Savanna followed close behind.

The crossroads appeared exactly like you'd think. It looked like two dirt roads intersecting in the middle of nowhere, with dark, impenetrable forests surrounding us on all sides.

Mikah had the aspect of Ogoun. He was strong. Even so, he was struggling to hold off Corbin, who had him pinned to the ground.

Isabelle separated from Annabelle and charged Corbin, knocking him back into the dirt.

With my wand in my hand, I blasted Bianca with an exsanguination spell. She deflected it with ease. Whatever power she had now was hard to penetrate.

Nico ran towards me, his eyes wide with fury. He was standing there almost frozen, as if Sarah was fighting off his influence. Baron Samedi was still in Sarah's body. Ellie clapped her hands together and released a concussive blast of pink energies, striking Nico in the chest.

Annabelle went after Sarah. She was the only one of us who really knew how to bring out the best of the Baron. Holland joined her. She was the one who summoned Baron Samedi to begin with and bound him to her will. I had to hope that together they'd restrain him.

"What do I do?" Tommy asked.

"Help Mikah!" I shouted as I got back on my feet.

I grabbed Savanna by the arm. "Before, the storm power you used silenced the power of the demiurge. I don't know if it will work here, but if you can suppress the power of Kalyptos, it may give us a chance against Bianca."

"Got it!" Savanna raised her arms and formed a dark storm cloud overhead. Every hair on my arms rose as the electric charge filled the air.

"No!" Bianca shouted. She charged after Savanna. I blasted her again with an exsanguination spell.

This time it worked. Her blood blasted out of her body, but it didn't stop her. Did it turn her feral? Maybe—what could be worse than a feral demigod? Once the storm faded, I'd lose my chance.

"Bianca!" I screamed. "Release her!"

Bianca dropped Savanna, the mambo's blood dripping from her chin. Savanna kept the storm brewing as lightning crashed all around us. With the storm in the air, using Corbin's sire bond against her worked.

"Release Nico from your influence! Remove the love spell from him!" I screamed.

Bianca waved her hand through the air. Ellie had already restrained him. Before I could direct her again, I saw Corbin flying toward me, a wooden stake in his hand.

"Stop!" Nico screamed. Corbins' eyes widened in horror. I raised my wand, and it struck him right in the chest—just like a stake—as his stake tore through my flesh and struck my heart.

Everything went black. The next thing I knew I was standing in darkness—Corbin's red eyes and wide smile greeting me. We were in vampire hell. Together.

Chapter 18

"WE HAVE LITTLE TIME," Corbin said. "One of us is going to revive. Whichever side prevails. The other one of us will remain here."

"We're going to win." I took two steps back avoiding Corbin's attempt to take my hands.

Corbin shook his head. "You can't manipulate Bianca from here. Do you really think that Annabelle and that other mambo can keep Baron Samedi's darker nature suppressed forever?"

I nodded. "You don't know my friends the way I do."

Corbin sighed. "In that case, it's time you released me."

"Released you?"

"From your love spell."

"I don't know how to do that!"

"Sure you do," Corbin said. "As I stand here, in front of you, I still love you Hailey. I can't help it. So I'm going to tell you what you need to know. After that, release me so I can rest here at peace. It's the power of your spell that's brought me back to you time and time again, but you won't love me back. You never will."

I shrugged. "Yeah, sorry. I have a strict rule against dating sociopaths. Call me old-fashioned."

"I didn't want to date you. I wanted to court you and marry you. I wanted to rule the world, hell, and every dimension with you at my side. It seems even if I offer you the world, it won't be enough."

I rolled my eyes. "You don't get it, do you? I don't want to rule. I'm content with the power I have. All I want is to keep the world safe from people who might do others harm. That means I have to keep the world safe from you."

Corbin rubbed his eyes. "I understand. I know I'm going to regret this the moment you release me. Still, you have to know something about Bianca and what she's become."

"What do you mean? She's like Erzulie Junior, right?"

"She was using Erzulie as her sire. That's why she had that power. You might have commanded her to release Nico, but Erzulie's influence over him remains. Bianca played along to let you think it was safe."

"I don't understand. Nico tried to stop you before you staked me."

"The mambo who also wields Erzulie's power suppressed its influence over him for a moment. When she stops channeling her power, Nico will do whatever he can to defend Bianca."

"Isn't Bianca feral? I blasted her with an exsanguination spell."

Corbin shook his head. "Vampirism is still very much a part of her. She also drank a bit of that Sogbo mambo's blood. That's why you were able to use my sire bond once the electricity in the air nullified the effects of Kalyptos. She's also something more."

"Right. She made herself a demigod."

"In a way. She also changed her vampirism, she reordered it. She's also turned a half dozen more of the people at the Carlyle to be like her. Bianca intends to turn all the residents. She's not just a vampire, now. She's the next evolution of vampires. When she bites someone, she doesn't just siphon someone's soul. She unmakes the soul, reforges it into its original form."

"What does that mean?" I asked.

"The power that *made* souls to begin with. Every vampire she makes will have the power of the demiurge, and they'll be able to get more of that power every time they feed. Bianca doesn't just want to rule the crossroads. She wants to remake the world, using her new breed of vampires to do it. She also loves me. Not because of her magic, but because she always has. Like I desired with you before, she wants nothing more than for me to rule at her side in her new creation."

"We can stop her! We were winning the fight!"

Corbin sighed. "Perhaps you were. But Bianca also bit the mambo who cast the storm. You might have exsanguinated some of the blood from her body, but she has fresh blood. She'll recover quickly."

"I have to get back there!"

Corbin nodded. "Exsanguinate her again. That won't be enough. There's only one thing more dangerous than a powerful ancient vampire. That's a youngling with all the power in the world to do whatever they wish. Bianca's new progeny, the new kind of vampire, who now roams the streets of New Orleans."

I gulped. "So what do I do?"

"You won't be able to claim her sire bond over her neophytes. She's not like you. You can't harness that kind of bond. My bond over her still has sway. You can't let Bianca win. You can't kill her, either. She's the only one who can call off her progeny."

I sighed. "Well, fuck me!"

"Can I?" Corbin asked.

"No. Nice try."

"Come on, Hailey. Just once for old time's sake. What happens in vampire hell, stays in vampire hell."

I chuckled. "Sorry, Corbin. Thank you for telling me this."

Corbin bowed his head. "As I said, it's only because of the spell you cast on me in that church months ago that I'm willing to tell you. Maybe this love isn't real. It sure feels that way. Remember what you promised. You will release me from the power before you leave."

I narrowed my eyes. "I'll try. That's sort of the problem, though. Any kind of magic I release here will attract wraiths like flies to shit. I don't know if I can do it. Even if I do, though, there will be hundreds of wraiths swarming on me before I can even finish the spell."

Corbin nodded. "Allow me to deal with the wraiths. I'll hold them off. Unless, of course, your side fails and I'm the one who returns to the crossroads. If your side loses, the wraiths will consume your magic and your mind until you're one of them."

I chuckled. "That will never happen. I have faith in my friends. Still, I could just leave you here. I could wait this out and avoid attracting the wraiths altogether."

Corbin shook his head. "I told you, already. I won't rest until we're either together or you remove the spell from me. I will come for you again, somehow, someway, if you don't do this."

"Why would you tell me that?" I asked. "Isn't that what you want?"

"My feelings for you don't erase the heartbreak I feel every time you reject me. Still, I cannot help but pursue you. I'm telling you this now, so we can both be free. I can finally die, even if it means I exist here as a wraith, and you can go back to earth without worrying about my eventual return."

I shook my head. "You could really use a session or two with Dr. Cain. Maybe Dr. Freud. They specialize in the magically and mentally deranged."

Corbin chuckled. "They could try. It probably wouldn't work. I know my nature. I've been a vampire for far too long. I'm too set in my ways to benefit from a couple of supernatural psychotherapists."

I nodded. "It might surprise you what they can do. Still, I never thought we'd agree on something, but your insanity is a topic upon which we share common ground."

Corbin smirked. "Even now, you have jokes."

I snorted. "Those same therapists would probably say I use humor to deflect when I'm in a tense situation. They might be right, but so far, it's worked pretty well."

"We may not have much time, Hailey. It's your choice. Free me, or don't. You'll have to live or die with the consequences either way."

I took a deep breath. Corbin was right. If I didn't free him, in a few weeks, months, or maybe years, he'd come back. He'd find a way. He did it before, he'd do it again. Though, if this didn't work, and the wraiths descended upon me and warped my mind, I might not be the same person even if I got unstaked. Could Corbin defend me? Would he even try to defend me if it worked, and I released him from the spell? Why would he defend me if he no longer loved me? If Corbin's side won, if Bianca beat my friends and the red Baron regained control over Sarah, and Bianca reclaimed her influence over Nico, we'd all be screwed. Corbin would be back with her, too, and no longer conflicted by his imagined love for me. This wasn't a straightforward decision, but my gut told me it was the right thing to do. Was Mercy right about my gut? Was it a special vampiric ability that guided me by intuition? Whatever happened to me was bound to happen. What it really boiled down to was whether I had enough faith that my friends would prevail.

I'd never doubted them before. I wasn't about to question their resolve when I had a chance to finally stop Corbin once and for all.

The only way I knew how to tap into Erzulie's power was to think about Connor. He was the man I genuinely loved. If I could draw on that power, and focus it, perhaps I could pull the spell out of Corbin and free him.

As I focused my mind, a pink glow emitted from my eyes. Shrieks filled the air. The wraiths had already sensed the power I was wielding and were coming for me.

Corbin took off and grabbed them one by one as they approached and tossed them aside. I focused my power while Corbin fought to defend me. It was a lot like how I focused my blood magic. The power of Erzulie that I released was like an extension of me. All I had to do was make it move.

I narrowed my eyes until I saw it. A single ball of my power, Erzulie's power, in the middle of Corbin's chest. I drew it out of him and pulled it into my body. It joined the rest of my power.

Corbin didn't stop fighting the wraiths. I thought he would. He turned to me and smiled. Did he actually love me for real? Had Erzulie's power initiated it, but now it was a part of him that only he could release?

I'd never know. That was the only thing I could imagine that kept him fighting. For a moment, I felt bad for him. There was nothing I could do to make him fall out of love with me. Time would have to heal that wound and, perhaps, with the spell gone, he'd have that chance.

The last thing I saw was Corbin grabbing a wraith and tossing it back into the darkness. My vision went black again and when I opened my eyes, I was back at the crossroads.

Tommy was hunched over me with a bloodied stake. Connor ran over and licked my face. He was in wolf form. He must've been fighting that way.

Annabelle had Bianca by the throat. Isabelle had rejoined her and her blade was back in her hand.

"Stop!" I shouted. "We can't kill her!"

"What?" Annabelle asked.

"Not yet. We need her. I'll explain fully later, but she's created a new kind of vampire and without her, they'll spread with more power than we could ever imagine."

Annabelle lowered Bianca to the ground. I looked around. Mikah had regained his hold on the crossroads. Ellie still had her magic enveloped around Nico.

"Don't let go of him," I said. "She didn't actually release Nico before. Only Erzulie can do that."

Ellie nodded. "I assumed as much."

Bianca laughed. "Clever. How'd you figure it out?"

I shrugged. "Corbin told me. He sold you out."

"That damn spell!" Bianca screamed. "Erzulie made him a liar when it comes to you!"

"You won't hurt any of us," I told Bianca. "You're going to gather all your progeny and end this once and for all."

Bianca huffed. "We'll see how long you can hold me."

A bolt of lightning struck Bianca from above. I turned to Savanna, who looked back at me and shrugged. "I can do this all day."

"You'll have to keep her charged with electricity until this is over. Can you do that?"

Savanna winced. "Getting through the portal together might be tricky."

"I'll go through first," Annabelle said. "I'll make sure Sogbo is there and can keep her in a storm cloud after she goes through."

"That will work!" Savanna exclaimed. "Once I get through, I can take over again."

Bianca shook her head. "Damn you, bitches!"

I stepped over to Mikah. "Can you deal with Corbin's body? We don't want anyone to find him and unstake him."

Mikah nodded. "I'll bury him. No one will be able to reach him without my consent."

Chapter 19

SAVANNA PASSED BIANCA LIKE a hot potato through Annabelle's portal and Sogbo caught her in his storm cloud on the other side. Savanna cast another cloud over Bianca when she got through. I couldn't help but laugh. With the cloud all around her she looked like Pig-Pen from *Peanuts.*

Bianca didn't find it so amusing. When I laughed, she flipped me off—which only made me laugh more.

"You're laughing now. I *will* get the last laugh."

I didn't challenge her. The truth was, I knew I could only do so much with a sire bond. I had to stay on my game. If I gave her any loophole at all to act, she could do something I didn't anticipate and wreak unexpected havoc.

Holland and Annabelle stayed in her office to babysit Sarah. Sarah didn't usually need supervision, but until the forty-eight hours expired, they had to keep Baron Samedi suppressed and his green aspect in control. If they didn't, I wasn't entirely sure what might happen. Baron Samedi could see through me. Could he do more than that? Could he use the connection to manipulate me somehow? Probably not, but we couldn't risk it. There was too much at stake, and if I lost focus for even a moment, I couldn't control Bianca.

Nico and Ellie were equally occupied suppressing the love spell that Bianca commanded Erzulie to afflict him with. They stayed with Annabelle, Holland, and Sarah.

That meant Tommy, Connor, Pauli, Savanna, and I were all that remained to deal with Bianca and her super-vampire offspring.

All that begged the question: how were we going to deal with them? These were innocent people, elderly men and women who'd been turned against their will. I couldn't compel Bianca to order them to simply use up whatever power from the demiurge they'd absorbed. The next time any of them fed, they'd have pure energy, forged from human souls, to use however they wished.

We had two choices: stake them all and burn out their hearts, or commit them to the Vilokan Asylum while we worked on a way to turn them back into normal vampires. Then we'd have to help them tame their natural thirst and help them become responsible vampires.

The second option was preferable on the surface, but there were a few problems with that. First, older folks, when turned into vampires, tended to be more difficult to manage. The human body is the template for what kind of vampire someone will become. Vampirism healed a lot of human infirmities. Any aches and pains or physical limitations these people experienced as humans quickly healed after they became vampires. Brain plasticity, however, was a problem.

Cain worked on that issue while he was still in charge of the Vilokan Asylum. It came up when Devin—Nicky's husband—brought his mother to the asylum after she'd become a vampire. Aging brains could change, they could adapt sometimes more easily than younger brains, but those changes were more volatile. Any changes made tended to be short-lived and their minds—and consequently their behaviors and habits—quickly bounced back to their original state. That meant helping a vampire turned in old age to tame their bloodlust could lead to quick initial progress, then, quickly, they'd behave like blood-thirsty younglings again.

The bottom line? These vampires could adapt to life at the asylum, but without constant reinforcement of responsible feeding behaviors, they were unlikely to maintain that progress. That meant they'd have to stay in the Vilokan Asylum indefinitely, or at the very least, spend eternity in daily group therapy sessions. Impossible? Probably not. There were addicts and alcoholics who spent decades attending meetings and had success living according to the twelve steps. It was possible, but we were talking about a potential eternity where these folks would have to stay close and connected.

This was the sort of decision I'd usually turn over to Mercy. Annabelle didn't get it. She was as understanding as a non-vampire could be, but she didn't know what it felt like to crave someone's blood, to see every human who walked by as if they were a steak with legs.

The long-term solution wasn't unthinkable. I'd have to monitor them if or when they ever left the Vilokan Asylum and make sure they stuck to their recovery program—if you could call it that. The more pressing issue was how to convert these super-vampires into normal ones.

That meant using Bianca to harness the power they siphoned when they fed and to use it to reform their own nature. Theoretically, we could make them human again—if that's what they wanted. They'd die, probably sooner rather than later. Their aches and pains would return. They'd go back to the Carlyle and resume their autumn years as before.

What if they didn't want to change back? Most young vampires—even if they were old humans—saw and appreciated the immediate benefits of their transformations.

I decided to give them the choice. I was determined to do whatever I could to help them adapt to their vampirism if that was their choice, and to ensure they stuck to whatever long-term therapy Dr. Freud believed was necessary. We'd use Bianca to gather them together, to harness the power they had, and to use it to reform themselves into what they wanted to be—human or vampire. Then, just in case we needed her sire-bond, I'd force Bianca to do the same thing. She'd become a regular vampire again. I'd do the spell to claim her sire bond, then we'd stake her and send her to her beloved in vampire hell.

With all that was going on, I had to make the call. I was an orphan vampire, myself. I didn't have the benefit of a sire to guide me. I was adopted by both Annabelle and Mercy. I turned out alright—relatively speaking.

I could give these new vampires more. Presuming vampirism was the choice they made. I could be a sire to them. I couldn't ask anyone else to do it. I knew the spell. Sarah had too much going on in her head most of the time to handle it. Tommy was too young, himself.

All those plans would be for naught if Bianca weaseled her way out of my commands.

Pauli teleported us back into Pere Antoine alley. He remained in boa constrictor form on my shoulders. Bianca glanced at Tommy and Connor, then back at me. "Looks like I'm stuck with the B-team."

I chuckled. "Keep telling yourself that. I'm very much a first-stringer."

"You're an eight-year-old vampire. I'm centuries old. Do you really think your fragile constitution can maintain a sire bond that belongs to a vampire as old as Corbin?"

I smirked. "You've underestimated me before. Corbin did, too. How did that turn out?"

Bianca shrugged. "The jury is still out."

"Maybe, but the verdict is predictable. Here's what's going to happen. You're going to do nothing at all that I don't tell you to do."

Bianca bowed her head slightly. "Yes, madam."

"I didn't tell you to say that."

Bianca smirked. "You really don't know how this works, do you?"

I rolled my eyes. "Enlighten me."

"You'll have to be more specific than that," Bianca said. "I've lived a long time and learned a lot. I could teach you many enlightening things."

I snorted. "You know what I meant. Tell me how this sire bond works."

"Your 'commands' have to be connected to a specific action you wish me to do or not to do. Blanket orders to do nothing at all are weak. The more specific the command, the greater the compulsion to 'behave.'"

I pressed my lips together. "Follow me."

I started walking down the alley. Bianca got down on all fours and started crawling slowly behind me.

"What the hell are you doing?"

"You told me to follow you. You didn't say *how.*"

"You know what I meant!" I grabbed my wand and pointed it at Bianca. "I could exsanguinate you again."

"Perhaps, but if you think I'm difficult to manage now, how do you think I'd behave if I was feral? I can't do anything you tell me to do if I don't remember how to do it. If I was feral, I certainly couldn't locate my new creations."

I rolled my eyes. "Your *new* creations? That's some kind of hubris."

"I am a goddess now, you know."

"A *demi*goddess. There's a difference."

Bianca shrugged. "Semantics."

"Whatever. *Walk* beside me. Take me to each of your progeny."

"I don't know where they are!"

"I thought you were a goddess. Surely you can find them."

A wide grin split Bianca's face. "We don't have to find them. They've already found us."

Connor cleared his throat. "I think she's right."

I followed Connor's eyes toward the far end of the alley. Three grey-haired, red-eyed super vampires were making their way down the alley toward us.

I turned around. Three more approached from the opposite direction.

Then they ran so fast I couldn't react. Before I knew it, one group of three seized Tommy. The other three grabbed Connor.

"If Hailey issues one more command, if she tells me to do anything at all, kill those boys!"

"Yes, goddess!" the six super vampires said in concert.

I narrowed my eyes and stared at Bianca. "Tell them—"

"Wait just a second," Bianca interrupted me. "That sounds like a command. Choose your words carefully or your boyfriend and your progeny are dead."

I clenched my teeth. "What do you want, Bianca?"

"Let us go," Bianca said. "We'll take the boys with us for safe measure. If you follow us, they die. If you do not return to the crossroads and bring Corbin's body to me, they die. It's really very simple."

I stood there, staring at Bianca. I was speechless—afraid to speak lest Bianca's progeny fulfill her prior command.

"If you kill Tommy and Connor, you lose your leverage. I won't have any reason to retrieve your precious Corbin."

Bianca shrugged. "Are you really willing to gamble their lives on that assumption?"

"You love Corbin. You wouldn't risk it."

"You're right. I love Corbin, but you know, I'm both an ancient and a modern woman. I adapt. If given the choice, do you think I'd really choose Corbin over myself?"

I glanced at Pauli. He could get to Connor or Tommy, but not both of them. If he took one of them away, Bianca's progenies would kill the other.

I took a deep breath. "Alright, I'll do it. But only if you release Tommy and Connor the moment Corbin returns."

"I'll release them once I have Corbin's staked body. I am the one who will bring him back, understood?"

I nodded. "Yeah, I got it."

"Good!" Bianca laughed. "A pleasure doing business with you, little girl."

"Where do I meet you when I get back?"

"You'll find us at the Carlyle."

I grunted. “It’s almost morning. I don’t have much time.”

“You’d best hurry, then. If the sun rises, your snake can bring you to us. I can assure you, all the curtains at the Carlyle will be drawn shut.”

Chapter 20

PAULI TELEPORTED ME BACK to Annabelle's office.

"I need another portal to the crossroads."

"Why?" Annabelle asked.

"Because if I don't bring back Corbin, Tommy and Connor are dead!"

"What happened?"

"The bitch outsmarted me, that's what happened. She used her super-vampires to take them and commanded them to kill Tommy and Connor if I issued her a single command."

"Damn," Annabelle said. "Are you sure this is the best course of action?"

"Erzulie wasn't among the progeny who took Tommy and Connor. If Pauli can get Erzulie, she can release Nico. He can help ensure that Corbin stays in line."

"That might work," Nico said. "But it's still risky. If Bianca has Tommy and Connor, won't she be equally pissed if we abduct Erzulie?"

I scratched the back of my head. "That's a good point. Ellie, do you think you can maintain this? Make sure Nico doesn't suddenly get horny for Bianca while he's influencing Corbin?"

Ellie nodded. "I've got it handled. Easy peasy. Just like taming a lion."

Nico tilted his head. "Taming lions is easy?"

"With magic, sure!" Ellie piped up. "You think love magic only works on humans? Any mammal is open to Erzulie's influence."

Pauli snorted. "Speciesist. What's wrong with reptiles? You think we're not capable of love?"

I tilted my head. "Have you ever been in love?"

"No, but that doesn't mean I can't love!" Pauli whined. "I just don't love people for who they are. I love them for what they're packing!"

I sighed. "Speaking of love. Corbin still loves me. I released him from Erzulie's spell, but he still fought off the wraiths until Tommy unstaked me. I don't trust him one bit, but we don't have a choice."

"I will keep Corbin under control," Nico said.

Sarah rubbed her brow. "I want to help."

I shook my head. "Are you sure that's wise? The Baron is unpredictable."

"We've got it handled," Holland said. "For now, anyway."

"We can cast out Baron Samedi," Annabelle said. "The problem is that Sarah agreed to the bargain. If she breaks the bargain and we exorcise him early, there could be consequences."

"Consequences be damned," Sarah huffed. "If he manipulates me again, if his red aspect gains power, kick his Ghede ass out of me."

Annabelle nodded. "If that's what you want."

Sarah sighed. "We can't let Bianca's progeny reproduce. This new kind of vampire could destroy all of us. I will deal with whatever the Baron requires of me. Besides, he needs me. What can he really do?"

Annabelle tilted her head. "If you attempt to violate the agreement, and I can't cast him out, he might not leave when the time expires."

"But you *can* cast him out, right?" I asked.

Annabelle nodded. "I believe I can. With Isabelle's power in me again, we should be able to do it. So long as Mikah and Isabelle remain in control of the crossroads, he won't be able to come back if he isn't summoned. Still, there's a strange connection he has to Sarah's mind. He may be able to use that connection as a kind of gateway, or even find his way through a convergence, bypassing the crossroads entirely."

"It doesn't matter," Sarah said. "You need to be out there, Annabelle. So long as you're here trying to keep the Baron under control with Holland, you can't fight."

"There may be another option," Holland said. "The Baron may release Sarah from her deal if he's offered something he values more in exchange."

I sighed. "Like *my* soul."

Holland shrugged. "That would probably do it."

I grunted. "Fine. He can have it."

"Hailey!" Annabelle snapped. "You don't want to do that! We aren't that desperate. I can keep the Baron in his green essence."

I didn't want to reveal my plan—especially since the Baron was likely listening in on our entire conversation. I simply nodded. "The bargain was with the red Baron, correct?"

Holland nodded. "He'd have to be in his red nature to nullify his bargain with Sarah."

I turned to Annabelle. "You sent us to the crossroads before and Pauli held open the portal."

"Right," Annabelle said. "It was the easiest way to ensure that we kept the time we spent in the crossroads in sync with time as it passed on earth."

"What if you came with us and used Beli to bring us back? Couldn't the spirit-dragon in your soul-blade return us to earth, say, five minutes from now?"

Annabelle nodded. "I can't summon Beli as a dragon at the crossroads. We'd have to follow the path in the crossroads back to Guinee. From there, I could call Beli and he'd bring us back."

"How does the Baron reckon time?" I asked.

"Like any Loa would," Holland said. "If you're thinking you'd just send Sarah to the future after the forty-eight hours passed, it wouldn't work. The bargain was for two days within Sarah. It has to be a two-day period relative to her personal timeline, two days as she experiences it."

I nodded. "We go to Guinee, we spend two days until the deal expires, then Beli sends us back to earth just after we left."

Nico grunted. "If Baron Samedi leaves Sarah in Guinee, he'll be in his realm. He'll try to stop us. Take it from someone who was caught in Guinee with the Baron before. He won't let anyone go if we don't give him something in return."

I nodded. "Exactly. If there's anything he wants more than Bianca's success, or his connection to Sarah, it's my soul."

"I'm coming with you," Nico said. "Bianca isn't there. Her spell won't affect me in Guinee. Besides, it will give Ellie a break."

I chuckled. "A brief break if Beli brings us back here just moments after we leave."

"Not if I go with you as well," Ellie added.

"Well hell," Savanna said. "I wouldn't mind seeing Guinee in person. We've learned about it in class. Nothing is better for one's education than a field trip!"

"I will not sit here on my thumbs," Holland said. "I am the one who bound Baron Samedi when we summoned him. So long as he remains in Sarah, I still have a semblance of control."

I chuckled. "Looks like we have the whole team back together again, minus Connor and Tommy."

Chapter 21

ANNABELLE SUMMONED BELI AND cut another portal back to the crossroads. We had a lot to do. First, we had to recover Corbin. Bianca wanted him staked when we delivered him so she could be the one to revive him. That didn't mean we couldn't unstake Corbin then stake him again before we handed him over.

We arrived at the crossroads. Mikah sighed when he saw us. "What now?"

"We need Corbin's body back," Annabelle said.

"I just finished burying him!"

My eyes darted back and forth. I shrugged. "Sorry, dude."

Mikah grumbled a bit, but he was strong. It took him less than five minutes to uncover Corbin's dirt-covered body. I pulled the former self-proclaimed vampire king out of his temporary grave and removed his stake.

Corbin gasped as his eyes shot open.

"Rise and shine, valentine."

Corbin looked at me with wide eyes. "I'm your valentine?"

"It's just a saying, buddy. Don't make too much of it."

"And here I was hoping you'd give me candy hearts that say 'be mine.'"

I chuckled. "I'd give you candy hearts, but they'd say 'bite me.'"

"Not a good thing to tell a vampire."

I chuckled. "Good point! I thought I removed Erzulie's spell from you."

"You did." Corbin stood and dusted himself off. "Some feelings die hard."

Annabelle chuckled. "Move on, buddy. Hailey isn't interested."

Corbin nodded. "I know that. Why did you bring me back?"

I took a deep breath and explained everything that had happened with Bianca. Surprisingly, even without Nico saying a thing, Corbin agreed to help—with one condition.

"I want to resume my life on earth," Corbin said. "No more attempts to take over the world."

I tilted my head. "Is that a promise?"

Corbin nodded and crossed his finger over his chest. "Stake my heart, hope to die."

Nico cleared his throat. "If you start your old shit again, I'll end you myself."

Corbin bowed his head slightly. "Understood. After spending a little time in actual hell, then vampire hell, I've decided that it's a shitty way to spend eternity."

I chuckled. "You think?"

"I will help you stop Bianca. What she intends to do is an abomination. After that, I'll return to Romania. You won't hear from me again. Unless you have a change of heart, of course."

"What will you do when you return to the old world?" I asked.

Corbin sighed. "I'll return to my chambers. I have a network, an underground community of vampires. I'll resume control and ensure that my offspring in Vampireland behave."

I chuckled. "You seriously call it Vampireland?"

Corbin snickered. "It wasn't what I used to call it. It's a long story. The former nightwalker, Alice, called it that when she first visited us and set up the original meeting between myself and the Vampire Council."

Nico laughed. "Alice in Vampireland?"

"Has a ring to it, don't you think?" Corbin grinned.

I laughed. "Vampireland. The deadliest place on earth."

"Whatever happened to Alice?" I asked. "I was there when Mercy first sent her to you in Romania."

Corbin shrugged. "I can't say."

"She's back in Exeter," Sarah added. "She's helping Mercy. I'm not sure how long that will last, though. From what I understand, Alice is in love with Prince Ladinas, and he's torn between Alice and Mercy. He loves both of them."

Holland shuddered. "Vampire love triangles. Gag me with a foot."

"Which way to Guinee?" I asked.

Mikah pointed down one of the paths of the crossroads. "That road will lead you into the garden groves."

We followed the dirt-packed road until the ground beneath us turned into luscious green grass and a bright light appeared overhead. I turned back and didn't see the path back to the crossroads. Instead, we were surrounded by fields of green, bubbling springs of pure water, and trees that stretched toward the heavenly skies.

Nico and Corbin stood side-by-side as we strolled through the garden groves. I imagined they had a lot to talk about. Nico was Corbin's sire, after all. I gave them their space.

We had to wait a while for Sarah's bargain with Baron Samedi to expire. It gave us a much needed respite from the fight. Not to mention, bathing in light wasn't an experience I had the opportunity to enjoy very often. The light in Guinee didn't burn vampires—not like the earth's sun. It was warm, comforting, and invigorating.

The time passed quickly. You'd think with nothing to do in paradise, time would creep along slowly. It didn't. Before I realized it, Sarah gasped. Annabelle ran to her and took her hands as Baron Samedi stepped out of her body.

He wasn't red *or* green. One eye matched each of his aspects.

"I don't understand," Annabelle said. "You should be green!"

"I am!" Baron Samedi laughed. "And I'm not."

Nico approached the Baron. "You must let us leave."

"I can't stop you," Baron Samedi said. "However, I now have a connection to Sarah and Hailey that cannot be purged. Now that I've tasted Sarah's essence, I will always have influence over them."

"That wasn't a part of the deal!" Sarah snapped.

"Whatever isn't delineated in a bargain, dear girl, is fair game."

"I can deal with that," I said. "I'd like to propose another bargain."

Baron Samedi clapped his bony hands together. "Goodie! I love bargains!"

"I want Bianca's soul."

Baron Samedi tilted his head. "Interesting. What do you intend to do with it?"

"I'm a Blood Witch. Having her soul is like wielding the power in her blood. It will give me control over her progeny, will it not, just like if I claimed her sire bond?"

"More than that!" Baron Samedi laughed. "Her soul comes with every power she's ever gained since she became a vampire. That includes the power of the demiurge, the ability to change shape."

I nodded. "I'll be able to take the form she desires the most."

"That's my form!" Corbin piped up.

I smiled. "Exactly. We're not going to stake you again, Corbin. When we leave, you're going to stake me. Nico will stay with you to ensure you behave. When Bianca unstakes me, and releases Tommy and Connor, I'll stake her *and* claim control over her progeny."

Annabelle laughed. "That's brilliant, but Baron Samedi is going to want something in return."

"Right you are, Miss Mulledy! Tell me, Hailey, what do you offer in exchange?"

I gulped. "My soul."

"Hailey!" Annabelle huffed. "You don't have to do that!"

I shook my head. "It's the best way to beat Bianca. I have to do this."

Annabelle sighed. "Won't Bianca expect you to deliver Corbin?"

I nodded. "Tell her that the Baron kept me in Guinee. He'll have my soul. In a sense, you'll be telling her the truth. She'll be thrilled that I'm out of the picture. Don't deliver my body to her until she releases Tommy and Connor. I'll take it from there."

Baron Samedi laughed and pulled out his flask. He took a sip and handed it to me. "Shall we seal our agreement with a drink?"

I took the flask and drank. I handed the flask back to Baron Samedi. He placed his hand on my chest. Then he reached into a small satchel and retrieved a box of cigarettes. He handed me one of them. "Smoke this, and you'll consume Bianca's soul."

I placed the cigarette to my lips and inhaled. A surge of energy coursed through my body, like when I fed and cycled someone's soul. I focused my mind, my rage, and killer-instinct on Bianca, whose soul now coursed through my body.

Then my body changed. My flesh expanded. My hair turned dark. Corbin stepped up to me. "You've never been more beautiful."

I chuckled. "You're an arrogant ass."

Corbin laughed. "I'm kidding, Hailey. I love you just the way you were."

I rolled my eyes. "Well, you're going to have to stake me. Might be a little awkward since I look like you now."

"Beli!" Annabelle shouted. When she was in Guinee, her soul-blade manifested not as a dagger, but as a dragon. The beast roared as he appeared in mid-flight over our heads and crashed down at our feet.

"Everyone climb aboard," Annabelle said. "Let's go home and end this."

Chapter 22

CORBIN USED THE SAME stake that had been in his heart before to stake my heart. Annabelle held me in her arms as Corbin plunged his stake into my chest. It sent me to vampire hell—temporarily.

The plan was for Pauli to teleport Annabelle and me both to the Carlyle. I wouldn't know how things played out until I woke up. Ideally, if the ruse worked, by the time I came back to earth, Tommy and Connor would be safe and I'd be in Bianca's waiting arms. They had to change my clothes. Shapeshifting doesn't come with a wardrobe change. I instructed them to make sure I had my wand on me in case I needed it when I fought Bianca. I might not have access to the stake, especially since Bianca was the one who'd pull it out. In a pinch, my wand could stake a vampire just as well.

I didn't dare channel any magic as I wandered through vampire hell. I hated the place. Without a soul of my own, going to hell was even more uncomfortable. The temptation to let go, to forget who I was, to become a wraith, was more forceful than I expected. It was a wonder that so many vampires held on in hell as long as they did. Nico had done it for twenty years! I couldn't imagine lasting that long in vampire hell without losing myself.

Thankfully, it didn't take very long.

My eyes shot open and the first thing I saw was Bianca looking back at me lovingly. She pressed her lips to mine.

I had to play the role. I was no Katy Perry. I'd just kissed a girl, and I didn't like it.

When Bianca pulled back, I looked at her with wide eyes. "You saved me from hell!"

Bianca stroked her fingers through my hair. "I did, my love! Are you free from the witch's spell?"

I nodded. "I am. I love you! I always have!"

My stomach turned in revulsion, but I had to stick to the script. If this was going to work, I had to play on Bianca's emotions.

"I've done it, my love! I've turned everyone here! We have an army of new vampires, better vampires! Soon, with a simple feed, I'll have the power to change you so you'll be like us. We will remake the world, it will become our vampire paradise. You and I will be the god and goddess of our new earth!"

"I can't wait!" I exclaimed, feigning excitement. "Kiss me again!"

I couldn't believe I said it, but I needed to keep her distracted as I reached into Corbin's boot and pulled out my wand. Bianca pressed her lips to mine. She forced her tongue into my mouth—and I forced my wand through her back into her heart.

"Corbin!" Bianca cried as the life faded from her eyes. "What... I don't understand..."

My body shifted back into my natural form the moment I staked Bianca. She gasped as her consciousness left her body.

"Not bad for an eight-year-old neophyte, huh, bitch?"

I don't know if she heard me before she went to vampire hell—but it felt good saying it. With my hand still fixed on my wand, I channeled a basic fire spell from my wand into Bianca's heart. I didn't use nature magic often, but it was elementary stuff. The sort of thing I'd learned from Moll and incanted into my wand long before I became a vampire.

With Bianca's heart consumed by flames, her body turned to dust in my arms.

I stood up and looked at the crowd of elderly super-vampires who surrounded me. "I'm your sire now," I declared. "I'm going to give each of you a choice. You can continue as vampires. We'll use your power to turn you into normal vampires, or you can become human again."

The people all looked at me with wide eyes but didn't speak. They were in shock. Becoming a vampire doesn't mean that the reality of vampires and the supernatural world isn't jarring. It would take some time for these super-vampires to come to grips with what they were and make their choice. My only regret was that Bianca had turned every resident in the Carlyle before we delivered Corbin's body—my body—to her and ended this.

The doors of the facility swung open. Annabelle stepped through with Connor and Tommy. They ran up to me. Connor kissed me on the lips.

He furrowed his brow. "Why do you taste like apple-blossoms?"

I laughed as I shook my head. "Bianca's lip gloss. Disgusting, right?"

"A vampire uses apple-blossom lip gloss?" Tommy laughed. "How gross is that?"

I shrugged. "I guess they don't make an O-negative flavored lip gloss. Not a bad idea, though."

"How many of these people are vampires?" Annabelle asked.

"All of them. Bianca turned all of them. Should we bring them to the Vilokan Asylum?"

Annabelle shook her head. "Let me make a call or two. We don't have the space in the Vilokan Asylum for all these people. Freud is also booked up."

"We need his help! These fledglings are going to need to tame their blood thirst, and I don't think I can help all of them alone."

"I didn't say you'd be alone," Annabelle said. "I'm calling Dr. Cain. He contacted me last week and said he'd be in town for a visit. I'm going to see if I can convince him to stay for a while."

"Cain and Rutherford? With their baby?" I asked.

Annabelle nodded. "Absolutely. I also need to see what I can do about purchasing this facility. It shouldn't be a problem. It's owned by the same people who operate the funeral home. They are already aware of the realities that lurk in the shadows of New Orleans. When I explain the situation, they'll give me a good price."

Chapter 23

THE SUN WAS RISING, and I didn't have a place to go. It was for the best. I needed to keep these elderly younglings inside and under the thrall of my sire bond. It wasn't Bianca's sire bond anymore. I'd cycled her power. It really was mine. For all intents and purposes, I was their natural sire.

Thankfully, Annabelle sent Jessie, a junior psychiatrist at the Vilokan Asylum, to help during the day.

Connor and Tommy stayed with me. We did our best to provide for the new vampires. They needed to feed. They also couldn't feed until we had a plan in place to help them make their choice and to use their power to become human or vampire.

Cain and Rutherford arrived in the early afternoon. Annabelle arranged for a local blood drive to set up camp just outside the Carlyle. Annabelle had a lot of connections. The people didn't know they were giving blood to vampires, of course, but they were saving lives. More lives than they realized.

We had a simple plan. Pauli brought Nico, Sarah, and the other mambos to the Carlyle to help manage the situation. Meanwhile, I joined Cain in a small room. He counseled each of the super-vampires, presented them with their choice, and a bag of freshly drawn blood. There was a lot to consider. If they became human, while some of their ailments and frailties might have healed when they were vampires, they'd quickly age again and most of their problems would return. Conversely, if they chose to remain vampires, they had to know the risks and limitations of an eternity in the shadows, craving blood. They needed to understand that they wouldn't get any younger. They'd maintain their appearance, perhaps with a little more allure than they had before, but they'd be strong. They'd also have to remain vigilant and stay at the Carlyle for group therapy sessions so they could maintain control over their cravings.

I clarified that the consequence of failing to abide by the plan meant a stake to the heart. It was a big choice and, under most circumstances, they'd have more time to decide. Given their cravings, though, time was a luxury they didn't have.

Annabelle made arrangements to relocate any who decided to become human again to another nearby retirement community.

Altogether, there were about fifty residents at the Carlyle, some of them married couples who'd become super vampires. A little more than half of them chose vampirism—more than I'd anticipated. Twenty-eight younglings, under my thrall, to tame and mentor. I was going to be a busy girl for a while. Thankfully, Cain agreed to stay in town until we had the situation under control.

The process was simple. After we had our discussions with the super vampires, they made their choice. They fed from freshly donated blood and I used my sire bond to compel them to use the power of the soul, the energy they deconstructed into the power of the demiurge, to change their bodies to the form they chose.

Annabelle took those who chose humanity and handed them off to Ellie, who took them on a bus that was chartered to take them to their new home. The rest remained at the Carlyle.

We had a lot of empty rooms since so many of the former residents moved out to resume the autumn years of their human lives. When we'd finished, Connor came and got me.

"We have something we'd like to show you."

"What do you mean?" I asked.

Connor laughed. "It's a surprise."

I rolled my eyes. "I think I've had my fill of surprises for the next century or so."

"I think you'll like this one." Connor interlaced his fingers with mine and led me into one of the abandoned rooms.

Holland and Annabelle were there. There was an altar set up on what used to be someone's dinner table. I recognized the veve—it was Baron Samedi's.

"What is going on here?"

"Come on out," Annabelle said.

I followed Annabelle's eyes and saw Baron Samedi, his eyes glowing green, step out of the bathroom. "I have something for you."

I gulped. "You do?"

Baron Samedi reached into his satchel. "I told you before, when I was in my right mind, I have no desire to retain souls. My lesser half doesn't agree, but I'm inclined to return yours to you."

"Seriously? We made a bargain!"

Baron Samedi shrugged. "Your bargain with my red aspect was to give up your soul. The terms of the agreement dictated nothing about retaining your soul indefinitely. If you'd like it, it's yours."

Baron Samedi handed me a cigarette. "You know what to do."

I pursed my lips. "This won't overwrite Bianca's soul, will it? I'll still have her sire bond, right?"

"You cycled it," Baron Samedi said. "Truth be told, what was hers is also bound to your soul just as well. You will lose none of your new abilities. There are a few, in fact, I suspect you've yet to experience. I'm sure Bianca's sire can fill you in on those details."

"Where is Corbin?" I asked.

"He's still in Vilokan," Annabelle said. "I told him he could return to Romania after Dr. Freud cleared him."

I chuckled. "That might take a while."

Annabelle smirked. "Indeed."

"Are you going to smoke your soul or not?" Baron Samedi asked. "I'd very much like to return to Guinee."

I placed the cigarette to my lips and inhaled. A surge of energy washed over my body. I licked my lips after the cigarette burned out between my fingers. "Refreshing!"

Baron Samedi grinned. "Might I offer a piece of advice?"

I nodded. "Certainly."

"Don't enter any subsequent bargains involving your soul with the *other* me. Now that you've recovered your soul, if he gets it a second time, expect him to account for that in the future."

"Thanks for the tip. I don't intend to bargain away my soul again anytime soon. I might need it. I have a lot on my plate."

"You have many new vampires," Baron Samedi said. "I'm sure you will do well."

I chuckled. "I feel like Miss Flanagan in *Annie*. Only I'm not surrounded by little girls. Old people, everywhere!"

"May I have my leave?" Baron Samedi asked.

"Very well," Holland said. "You're free to go."

Baron Samedi disappeared in a flash of green light—presumably back through the crossroads and back to Guinee.

"Did you like your surprise?" Connor asked.

I kissed Connor softly on the lips. "Very much. Thank you, everyone. I didn't expect this."

"It was the right thing to do," Annabelle said. "We still need you, Hailey. I know you'll have your hands full here at the Carlyle. But we still have a city riddled with convergences. We need our guardian."

"About that," Nico's voice echoed from behind me. I turned and saw him holding Sarah's hand. "I've decided to stay."

"The demiurge is gone," I said. "You could leave if you wished."

Nico looked at Sarah and smiled. "I have a reason to stay. We're going to give this a chance."

I clapped my hands and giggled. "Yay! Young love!"

Nico laughed. "It may be the only thing about me that's young."

"This wasn't on account of Erzulie's magic, was it? I imagined once I killed Bianca, the spell she'd cast on you lost its hold."

Nico nodded. "It did. We've also spoken to Erzulie. She's back in Vilokan. She assured me, though, that her power no longer had a hold on me."

"We aren't in love," Sarah said. "Not yet. But you have to start somewhere! And now Nico has a bed he can use back at Casa do Diabo."

I grinned. "I'm sure you'll both *use* your bed well."

"About that," Connor said. "Will you be coming back home?"

I shook my head. "Not right away. I need to be here for my new younglings."

"I'll keep your bed warm," Connor said. "Unless you'd like me to join you here."

I chuckled. "Are you asking if you can move in with me?"

"I never officially moved into Casa do Diabo. Maybe it's time we take the next step."

"Eeek!" Sarah exclaimed. "There *is* young love in the air!"

"Connor and I have been together for a while now!"

"Sure," Connor said. "But we're immortals. The way I see it, we get to enjoy the young love phase of our relationship a while longer. Why rush things when you have forever?"

The End (for now)

Continue with Mercy's Story in BLOODY QUEEN

Also By Theophilus Monroe

Gates of Eden Universe

The Druid Legacy
Druid's Dance
Bard's Tale
Ovate's Call
Rise of the Morrigan

The Fomorian Wyrmriders
Wyrmrider Ascending
Wyrmrider Vengeance
Wyrmrider Justice
Wyrmrider Academy (Exclusive to Omnibus Edition)

The Voodoo Legacy
Voodoo Academy
Grim Tidings
Death Rites
Watery Graves
Voodoo Queen

The Legacy of a Vampire Witch
Bloody Hell
Bloody Mad

Bloody Wicked
Bloody Devils
Bloody Gods

The Legend of Nyx
Scared Shiftless
Bat Shift Crazy
No Shift, Sherlock
Shift for Brains
Shift Happens
Shift on a Shingle

The Vilokan Asylum of the Magically and Mentally Deranged
The Curse of Cain
The Mark of Cain
Cain and the Cauldron
Cain's Cobras
Crazy Cain
The Wrath of Cain

The Blood Witch Saga
Voodoo and Vampires
Witches and Wolves
Devils and Dragons
Ghouls and Grimoires
Faeries and Fangs
Monsters and Mambos
Wraiths and Warlocks
Shifters and Shenanigans

The Fury of a Vampire Witch
Bloody Queen
Bloody Underground
Bloody Retribution
Bloody Bastards
Bloody Brilliance
Bloody Merry
More to come!

The Druid Detective Agency
Merlin's Mantle

Roundtable Nights
Grail of Power
More to come!

Other Theophilus Monroe Series

Nanoverse

The Elven Prophecy

Chronicles of Zoey Grimm

The Daywalker Chronicles

Go Ask Your Mother
The Hedge Witch Diaries

AS T.R. MAGNUS

Kataklysm
Blightmage
Ember
Radiant
Dreadlord
Deluge

ND - #0189 - 130824 - C0 - 229/152/29 - PB - 9781804679968 - Gloss Lamination